Jack London's
Tales of Cannibals and Headhunters

Jack London's TALES OF CANNIBALS AND HEADHUNTERS

Nine South Seas Stories by America's Master of Adventure

EDITED AND ANNOTATED BY
GARY RIEDL
AND
THOMAS R. TIETZE

With the Original Magazine Illustrations, Maps, and Photographs by JACK and CHARMIAN LONDON

University of New Mexico Press
ALBUQUERQUE

PRINTED IN THE UNITED STATES OF AMERICA

YEAR 10 09 08 07 06
PRINTING 1 2 3 4 5

Library of Congress Cataloging-in-Publication Data

London, Jack, 1876–1916.
Jack London's tales of cannibals and headhunters : nine South Seas stories by America's master of adventure / edited and annotated by Gary Riedl and Thomas R. Tietze ; with the original magazine illustrations, maps, and photographs by Jack and Charmian London.
p. cm.
Includes bibliographical references.
ISBN-13: 978-0-8263-3791-7 (pbk. : alk. paper)
ISBN-10: 0-8263-3791-0 (pbk. : alk. paper)
1. Oceania—Fiction. 2. Adventure stories, American. I. Title: Tales of cannibals and headhunters. II. Riedl, Gary, 1945– III. Tietze, Thomas R. IV. Title.
PS3523.O46A6 2006
813'.52—dc22

2005028716

Book design and composition by Damien Shay
Body type is Utopia 10/13
Display is Headhunter and CaslonAntique

The editors wish to dedicate
their work on this volume to

Lawrence I. Berkove

Sara S. Hodson

and

Jeanne Campbell Reesman

Contents

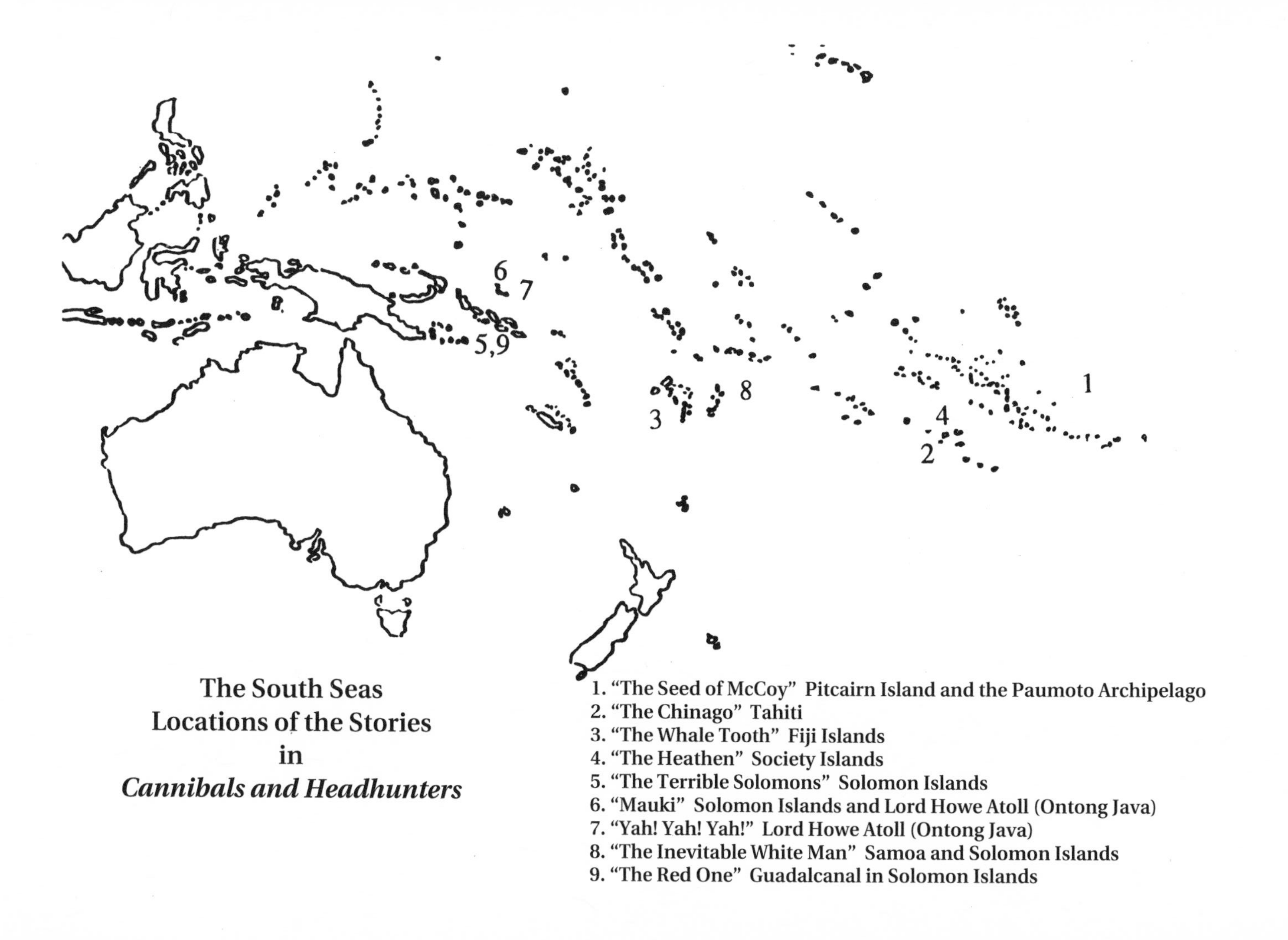

The South Seas
Locations of the Stories
in
Cannibals and Headhunters

1. "The Seed of McCoy" Pitcairn Island and the Paumoto Archipelago
2. "The Chinago" Tahiti
3. "The Whale Tooth" Fiji Islands
4. "The Heathen" Society Islands
5. "The Terrible Solomons" Solomon Islands
6. "Mauki" Solomon Islands and Lord Howe Atoll (Ontong Java)
7. "Yah! Yah! Yah!" Lord Howe Atoll (Ontong Java)
8. "The Inevitable White Man" Samoa and Solomon Islands
9. "The Red One" Guadalcanal in Solomon Islands

Acknowledgments

Staff of the Henry E. Huntington Library, San Marino, California

San Francisco Maritime Museum

Sonoma State University, Jean and Charles Schulz
Information Center

Members of the Jack London Foundation

Members of the Jack London Society

Members of the 1990 and 1994 NEH Summer Seminars
for Teachers, "Jack London: The Major Works"

Don Anderson

Gail Berkove
(who has helped us understand Larry)

Ron and Sue Billings

Lincoln Bramwell

Glenn Burch

Donna Campbell

Tim and Lauri Carlson

Shannon Cotrell

Jesse Crisler

Acknowledgments

Ross Downing

Daniel Dyer

Roger and Kinny Eberhart

Philip and Marion Fraser

Herbert Ford

David Haley

Larry Hammerlin

Maya Allen-Gallegos

Greg Hayes

Waring Jones

Tiffany Joseph

Winnie Kingman

Richard Kopley

Earle Labor

Jim and Connie Lewis

Joseph McCullough

Joseph McElrath

Susan Nuernberg

Raleigh Patterson

Frances Purifoy

Debra Rawlings

Marty Roth

Gary Scharnhorst

Bob and Mari Schestak

Damien Shay

Milo Shepard

R. Dixon Smith

Paulina Smith

Clarice Stasz

Steve and Jean Stilwell

Deb Swan

Marc and Mary Terrass

Bill Vieth

Karen Wieder

James Williams

Luther Wilson

Geoffrey Wong

Karen Ylinen

Our friends on the staff of Wayzata High School
(You know who you are.)

Students of Wayzata High School, the teaching of
whom substantially delayed this work.

Corinne, Kathryn, Renneca, John, and Hugh. Special thanks are
due to Sam Tietze, who prepared the maps and illustrations.

And, as always and inevitably, Mrs. Jewell.

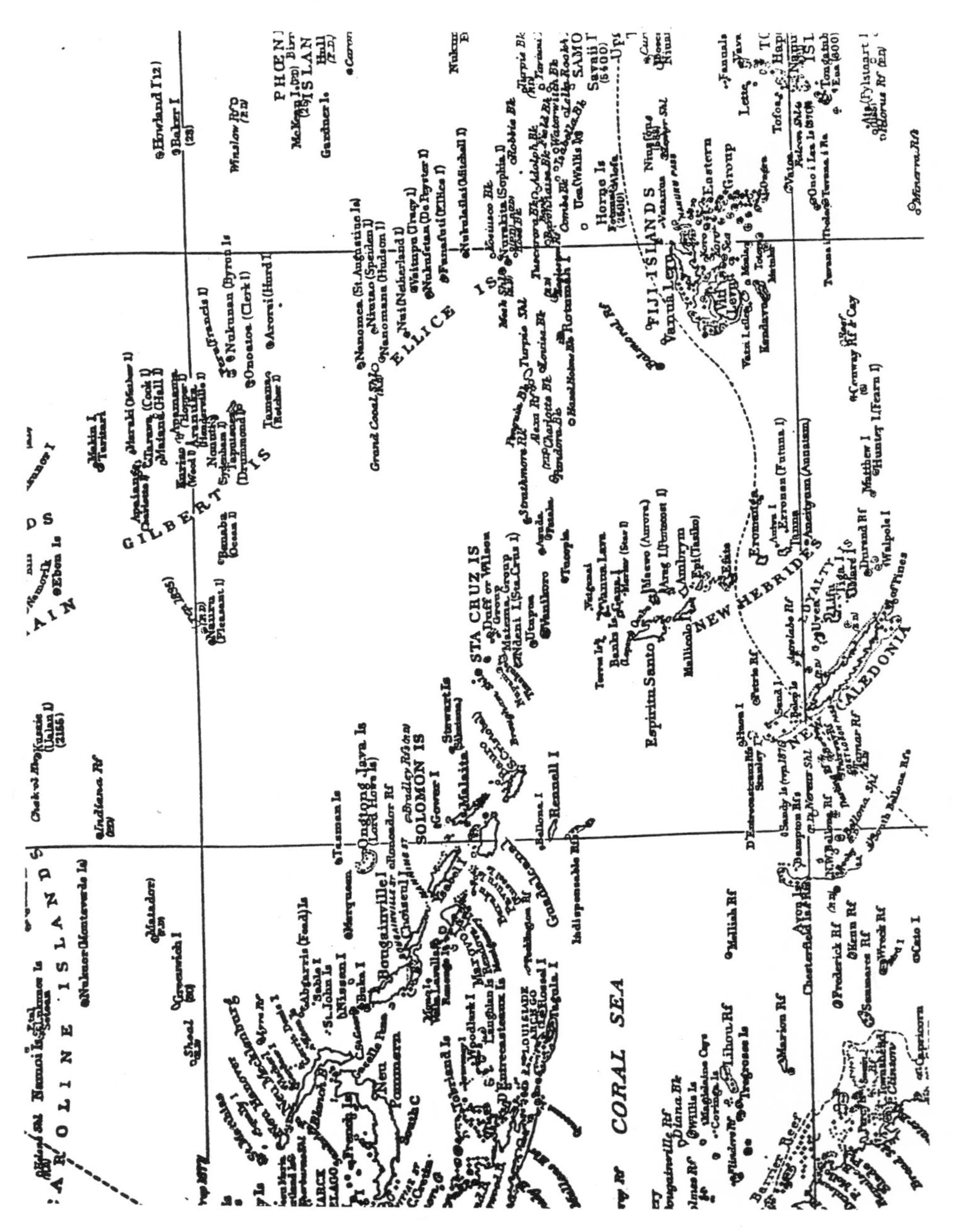

Portion of one of the maps owned by Charmian London. Most of the Londons' charts of the Pacific were taken by the U.S. Navy during WWII to aid in the Pacific campaign. (Courtesy of the Jack London State Historic Park)

Introduction

Jack London glanced toward the island and saw the headhunters gathering on the shore. He was stranded on the reef at Maluu, in Malaita, purportedly the most savage and dangerous of the South Seas cannibal isles. In the summer of 1908, the world-famous author of *The Call of the Wild* and his wife Charmian were engaged in a planned round-the-world voyage on their yacht, the *Snark*. Having temporarily left their boat at Ghavutu in the Florida Islands just north of Guadalcanal, London was gathering local color to enrich his fiction by taking a jaunt through the Solomon Islands on the vessel *Minota*. The rough-and-ready skipper, Captain Jansen, had won the job only a few months before, when Mackenzie, the previous captain, had been murdered and beheaded at Langa Langa by a party of Malaitan headhunters. Jack noticed with grim interest that hatchet marks on the ship's cabin door were still fresh.

But suddenly real life was becoming as red and raw as any story he'd ever imagined. Jansen had just gathered two labor recruits for the local copra plantations. The process was often less like recruiting than it was like kidnapping, and the luckless victims were transported into virtual slavery on distant islands. The Malaitans, familiar with white treachery, particularly resented this traffic in human beings, a trade known locally as blackbirding. Important parts of the process involved threats with guns, sometimes demonstrations with dynamite, and always a quick getaway. But this time, Jansen's plans for a rapid departure hit a snag. He had barely loaded the natives on board before he ran the ship aground on a hidden reef.

Stranded in the shallow water, Jansen, London, and the native crew desperately tried everything they could think of, but the ship wouldn't budge from the reef. In a very short time, the tremendous waves pounding on the teak-and-cedar craft were bound to break her up. On the nearby beach, the naked warriors clearly began to take a keen interest in the plight of the strangers. Generations before, white traders had made tobacco addicts of the Solomon islanders, and the natives knew the *Minota* had cases of it in her hold. Charmian London, who had heard all the usual tales of local cannibal practices, also suspected from their expressions that they were after "rounder prizes" than tobacco.[1]

Things began to look worse as the tide started to go out, stranding the *Minota* even more thoroughly, and Jack noticed several hundred headhunters gradually slipping into their canoes, slowly but deliberately paddling toward the ship. As he sized up the danger of their situation, London bribed a rather sullen islander with a fortune of tobacco—half a case—to help them. The native paddled off in a canoe to find the *Eugenie*, which Jansen had told them was nearby. A short time later, the messenger found the other ship and handed young Captain Keller a note hastily scribbled by Jack. The blond-haired and handsome youth acted at once. In the nick of time, Captain Keller appeared on the scene and rescued the author and his party on August 20, 1908.

In a letter written in the fall of 1916, near the end of his life, London recalled the panic and exhilaration of the incident:

> I was wrecked on the outer reef of Malu . . . with fifteen hundred naked bushmen head-hunters on the beach armed with horse-pistols, Snider rifles,[2] tomahawks, spears, war-clubs, and bows and arrows, and with scores of war-canoes, filled with saltwater head-hunters and man-eaters holding their place on the fringe of the breaking surf along side of us, only four whites of us including my wife on board—when Captain Keller burst through the rain-squalls to windward, in a whale-boat . . . rushing to our rescue, bare-footed and bare-legged, clad in loin-cloth and sixpenny undershirt, a brace of guns strapped about his middle. . . .[3]

Such was the steaming, tropical setting, packed with danger and thrills, fears and horrors, beauty and high adventure, that forms the background of the collection of stories you now hold in your hands. But, entertaining as they are, these are not merely the stuff of pulp fiction or boys' adventures, for they yield a great deal more under close examination than has hitherto been believed.

These unjustly neglected short stories, which Jack London wrote between 1908 and 1916, give evidence of a master at the top of his form. Consider, among many other strengths, their flashes of insight into the nature of colonialism; their brilliant portrayal of fully developed characters; their detailed and vigorous depiction of the natural setting; their geographical and anthropological accuracy; their philosophical challenges to the majority of his readers' core beliefs about the question of race; and their conscious experimentations with narrative voice, with point-of-view, and with ideas that a generation later would become classified under the heading of existentialism. Finally, perhaps the most important reason for collecting these nine stories is a formal, underlying principle that makes the text a unified whole: London delves here into an emotional examination of the profound social issues that confronted the Pacific region. The stories move from the depiction of a tentative hope for the brotherhood of man and the redemptive qualities of selflessness to the expression of persistent, darker themes of depravity, disgust, and decay that run through the last stories with increasing urgency.

I

The islands of the South Pacific were, to the western world, the last mystery of global exploration. Though no European knew they were there until the sixteenth century, islands and atolls dotted the surface of the Pacific, and a great many of them were inhabited. Here had been demonstrated the intrepid human spirit of epic exploration of the unknown, carried out perhaps seven centuries before the siege of Troy. Here were enacted in microcosm the same political challenges, erotic obsessions, and dark visions of divinity that had also tormented the lives of Europeans. Here, too, were played out for centuries the sanguinary conflicts of racial warfare that often seem to be a reflexive human response to Otherness, here made more horrific by the warriors' widely reported drive to eat the bodies of their enemies and, in ways that varied from culture to culture, to preserve as trophies their opponents' heads.

Papuan hunters probably migrated from New Guinea during the last Ice Age, some 12,000 years ago, perhaps literally walking to the Solomon region. With the subsequent warming of the planet and rising of the sea level, their short, dark-skinned descendants became islanders, and centuries later the place would be called by Europeans "black islands"—Melanesia. As well, these adventurers tended to be curious enough—and daring enough—to want to spread out across the unknown seas, indulging in heroic canoe journeys, long before any reliable systems of navigation had been discovered. Somehow, they managed to settle throughout the Solomons and the New Hebrides, and got all the way to Fiji, an archipelago of some three hundred islands in the virtual center of the South Seas.

The process took centuries to accomplish, and Melanesian hold on Fiji was still newly established when the black explorers met a new challenge. Light-skinned medieval Polynesians, after having spent more than a thousand years colonizing the islands to the east of their Samoan homeland, had decided to canoe toward the west, aggressively establishing settlements wherever possible on all but the most marginally fertile islands.

Though scarcely any more precise than that of the Melanesians, Polynesian navigational *élan* was impressive: they believed they could gauge their distance from land by dipping one of the crew over the bow of the canoe into the sea. The immersed individual could then sense through his testicles the vibrations borne by the waves resounding off the shore. The elders, too, had a system known as *kavenga*, which allowed the voyagers to consult patterns in the stars.[4]

In Fiji, the two cultures, black and bronze, met in mutual horror of each other. Even today, remains of impressively fortified villages in the islands provide evidence of the centuries-long struggle for dominion that ensued between Melanesian and Polynesian warriors during subsequent generations. Violence and bloodshed became a way of life in Fiji, and cannibalism and headhunting purportedly became their grimly formal and ecstatically ritualized expression.

After a battle came the celebration. Warriors reenacted their achievements and enlarged on their prowess, hurling insults at their vanquished opponents, whose butchered bodies were readied for the fires. In some cases, it is believed that, as the frenzied ceremonies proceeded, some victims were left alive in order to assure the freshness of the meat. In other Pacific regions, traditions demanded that the major bones be broken and the victims tenderized through a day's soaking in water. For the most effective eating of their grisly repast, the Fijians designed a special tool keenly sought today by curio collectors—a four-pronged fork that gave participants access to the choicest pieces of flesh. These were usually offered first to the chief, who accepted them with formal acknowledgment. The feast was followed by more boasting and self-congratulatory rhetoric as the excitement began to take a sexual turn. One horrified white castaway, whose name history has forgotten, left behind a short account of his experience in 1809: "That night was spent in eating and drinking and obscenity. The blood drank [*sic*] and the flesh eating seemed to have a maddening effect on the warriors. I had often seen men killed and eaten, but I never heard or saw such a night as that. Next morning many of the poor women were unable to move from the continuous connections of the maddened warriors."[5]

This was the world discovered by the first curious probes of European exploration when, in 1567, Alvaro de Mendana sailed from Peru into the South Pacific. Puffed with the divine ambition of the Renaissance, Mendana longed to learn about the Unknown, a motivation that was coupled with his hope to claim new land for Spain and new souls for the Church. Also, he had heard legends of a land filled with gold, *Terra Australis Incognita*. By maintaining a course of due west, Mendana somehow missed most of the islands between Peru and the Solomons. When he at last spotted a large landmass, he called it Santa Ysabel. He was delighted with the prospect of exploring these new finds and giving them names. Guadalcanal (sometimes spelled "Guadalcanar"), for example, is a corruption of Wadi al-Kanar, the name of the hometown of one of his Arab officers. Perhaps Mendana named the entire group *Yslas su Llamen de Salomon* in the hope that the suggestion of the biblical King Solomon's unlimited wealth would make financial supporters eager to fund future ventures.

These early efforts struck the template for future relationships between Europeans and the islanders, for the expedition was plagued with relentless violence. Convinced of their racial superiority, the Spaniards preferred to take what they wanted from the population, incorrectly assuming that the natives could not tell they were being cheated. Mistreatment of natives far surpassed mere dishonesty, however. The Spanish soldiers assigned to Mendana's expeditions were cruel, sadistic, and often casually murderous, sometimes killing islanders for sport. Mendana left under a cloud, frustrated by the continual, often fatal, tensions between the blacks and the whites, which he himself had unthinkingly created.[6]

On his return to Peru, instead of awakening European interest in the region, Mendana's reports tended to dampen investor enthusiasm. In fact, it took him nearly three decades to raise funds to return to the area. A happy accident during his second voyage in 1595 resulted in his discovery of the Marquesas Islands, but his primary scheme demanded that he not linger unnecessarily in the pleasures of exploration, so he soon continued westward. An ambitious and daring expedition, this second voyage was undertaken with a fleet of four ships, filled with nearly three hundred men and women, including Mendana's wife. Their hope was nothing less than to convert the natives and colonize the land of the Solomon Islands. Ironically, this time Mendana couldn't find the Solomon Islands at all; in his excitement over their original discovery, he had made a mistake in plotting the location.[7]

He finally lighted on Nendo, an island in the easternmost region of the Solomon group, just a few miles from the islands he sought. The explorer renamed the place Santa Cruz, and he eagerly began his scheme to forge a community. However, it took the settlers a mere ten weeks to confirm that they were not up to the challenge presented by these rugged islands and their fierce inhabitants. With Mendana laid up with fever, the vicious excesses of some of the Spanish soldiers worsened. Ultimately, the enfeebled Mendana was coerced into agreeing to execute the military commander of the expedition in order to restore discipline and end the wanton cruelty to the natives. It did not work. A party of soldiers murdered Malope, the main chief of the area, even though he had been willingly cooperating with the expedition. Mendana never rallied from his fever, and he finally died there at the age of fifty-four, having lived only to see his fabulous islands lost and his ambitious colonial adventure dissolved in misery and futility.

Though European sailors occasionally spotted the legendary Solomon Islands, they were not formally rediscovered until 1767—and then only by accident. Captain Cartaret, an Englishman, found Santa Cruz and later sighted Malaita, though he had trouble believing that these almost mythical places really existed.

Meanwhile, the most famous of all sea-borne explorers, Captain James Cook, charted much of the Pacific in his appropriately named vessels, *Resolution* and *Adventure*. From 1768 until his murder at the hands of Hawaiian islanders in 1779, Cook sailed into unknown seas. His daring explorations, for good or ill, were largely responsible for creating an interest in discovering and exploiting the resources of Oceania. In 1788, one of the greatest experiments in penal history—shipping and virtually marooning boatloads of English convicts in Australia—began with the voyage of a prison ship commanded by Captain Shortland. On his way back, after dropping off his cargo of felons, Shortland confirmed Cartaret's discovery.[8]

In sharp contrast to the indifference experienced by Mendana almost two centuries earlier, word of the find spread rapidly, leading to a number of British and French exploratory projects in the area. By the early nineteenth century, something else contributed to European awareness of the Pacific region. During the great age of the whaling industry, ships often anchored in Solomon Island lagoons, where crewmembers would take their ease for short periods. These adventurers were so rough and tumble (or so unimaginative) that they showed no fear of the headhunters often dwelling in the interior of many of the islands. Sometimes marooned recalcitrants and deserters from whaling vessels became island inhabitants themselves—the first beachcombers.[9] In some cases, these men took wives, raised families, and for a number of years threw themselves fully into native life.

More wild and ruthless were the sandalwood traders.[10] By the mid-nineteenth century, enterprising white men had learned of four related facts: the Solomon Islands enjoyed a relatively large population of pigs; Chinese merchants desired sandalwood for incense and soap and as liners for small boxes; the people of the New Hebrides desired pork, but had few pigs; and the islands of the New Hebrides were full of sandalwood, a virtual weed that choked more desirable plants. In a more sensible world, an obvious cycle of simple trade would evolve, resulting in benefits to all parties. Instead, only massacre and villainy followed the sandalwood men wherever they went. Some of it was even internecine: so fierce was the competition among the traders that, once they had stuffed their ships to the gunwales with the fragrant wood, it was typical of them on their departure to shoot randomly into the villages that lined the island beaches. The purpose of such criminality was purely commercial. They wanted the islanders to hate the sight of any white men, so that any competitors in the trade following in their wake would be attacked and perhaps killed by the angry islanders. Apparently sublimely confident of their superiority, or merely heedless of the probability that they themselves would also suffer consequences should they return for another load, the sandalwooders also traded such weapons as Snider rifles and steel-headed tomahawks for wood.

Ostensibly on a more businesslike level were the copra producers, including Lever's Pacific Plantation, Ltd. (later Lever Brothers), Burns Philp South Seas Company, W. R. Carpenter, the Samoan Reparations Estates, and smaller concerns that established themselves throughout the Pacific, some building impressive facilities in the region. The enterprising could grow coconut trees on plantations or else gather nuts from the beaches of nearby islands, dry the meat, and render it into an oil that would be used primarily in the United States and Britain to make soap, margarine, cooking oils, and cosmetics. The demand for copra always exceeded the supply and thus encouraged the growth of the industry throughout the South Seas.

But even in this apparently benign business, the white intruders managed to bring misery to the islands, for a fundamental axiom of plantation life was that white people could not do manual work in the tropical climate. The prevailing impression in Australia was that white-skinned people would be killed by exposure to the intense sun, so plantation owners were convinced that they required black-skinned workers. Fortified by this racist logic, they conceived that labor must be drawn from other races. First it was indentured Indians, then Chinese, and finally black islanders from Melanesia who were, as the euphemism went, "recruited" by blackbirding. Since it was believed that white farmers, particularly women and children, could not work effectively under the tropical sun, it would make sound practical sense to recruit Pacific islanders to provide the labor force on cotton plantations. In their correspondence—and probably in their hearts as well—these Australian and British entrepreneurs were clear about the distinction between the recruiting of laborers and the capturing of slaves, especially because Britain had, in the 1830s, taken the moral high ground by emancipating all the slaves in the Empire, and consequently her government's officers would inspect very closely the methodology of the labor recruiting project. The concept of islander labor carried with it as well a humanitarian intention (however misguided) to raise the standard of living for these laborers by exposing them to the advantages of middle-class customs and values.

Meanwhile, the urgency of the Australian cotton venture was intensified by the outbreak of the American Civil War, which helped potential investors to see the opportunity presented in the opening up of another source to supply the world's market, now that cotton from the American South would be unavailable for the foreseeable future. In the spring of 1863, agricultural visionary Robert Towns had gained permission to outfit his first recruiting vessel, the *Don Juan*, under the command of Captain Grueber, and by late summer the first Kanakas (islanders) arrived in Brisbane, having signed an indenture for a period that could vary between one and five years. Though Grueber's voyage went without misadventure, it turned out to be the beginning of a cycle of bloodshed and iniquity that would characterize cultural interactions in the South Seas for more than three-fourths of a century.[11]

Indeed, it can be argued that the darkest side to the colonial enterprise was labor recruiting. Blackbirding was carried out by small bands of generally ruthless rascals in small vessels, cruising the coastal shores throughout the South Pacific and seeking recruits. Over the decades, tens of thousands of Solomon Islanders were gathered: sometimes kidnapped, sometimes sold by their own kin, sometimes terrorized into "volunteering" to work on the cane or copra plantations. The dangerous practice of sailing around the South Pacific kidnapping natives promised a lot of fast money and excitement, provided its practitioners were not hacked to death by resentful islanders or flung into jail by the British inspectors. Blackbirding could be forceful, violent, and coercive; and it was not unusual for a chief to sell the recruiters members of his own tribe or slaves captured in intertribal fighting. However the recruits were obtained, blackbirders then would sell their labor contracts to a plantation. The recruits would typically serve an indenture for a sum of six pounds per year. Work on plantations was physically demanding: typical tasks included clearing land, planting crops, harvesting and drying copra, and building roads. These arduous and onerous tasks were nothing like the normal daily drill for any of the natives, for their culture had never taught them the spartan European virtues of providing service through backbreaking work for foreign bosses.

Furthermore, with the clearing of land came exposure to blackwater fever and malaria, fearful diseases that in one year could fell an estimated 10 percent of the workmen. These diseases remain serious threats to people living in the area. As recently as the early 1990s, the World Health Organization cited the Solomon Islands as one of the world's most dangerous environments for malarial infection.[12] The most serious form of the illness, *Falciparum*, or cerebral malaria, accounts for two out of three cases in the Solomons. Most islanders are likely to fall into malarial fevers once a month; men who have not had an attack in four years count themselves very lucky; and nursing mothers pass the disease on to their babies. By the late 1990s, insecticide spraying brought the danger down, but, in Jack London's time, anybody who spent time on Guadalcanal was likely to become infected.

Creating a further strain on morale, European owners of plantations found it very difficult to hire white management because of low pay, extreme isolation, and primitive living conditions; in some cases only the dregs of society were available. Degraded sadists and sodden alcoholics were sometimes hired without any inquiry into their sordid pasts. Such overseers, not paid well themselves and removed from their employers' supervision, had little incentive to treat the laborers well. On some isolated plantations, beatings and sometimes murder could be concealed easily. In his essay on London's novel *Adventure*, Lawrence Phillips cites Amie Cesaire's assertion that "colonisation works to *decivilize* the coloniser, to *brutalise* him in the true sense of the word, to degrade him, to awaken him to buried instincts to covetousness, violence, race hatred, and moral relativism."[13] One of London's literary heroes, Joseph Conrad, made this danger the center of his story

Heart of Darkness, in which the commercial agent Kurtz descends into savagery after a prolonged involvement with colonialism. And, of course, this is, on one level at least, London's very theme in several of the stories in this collection.[14]

That the colonialist experience is still capable of twisting civilized moral values was demonstrated as recently as 1988, in New Caledonia. As part of a move to quash the New Caledonian independence movement in 1984, seven French planters ambushed and killed ten unarmed aboriginals. Though evidence indicated that they were apparently guilty, the Frenchmen were acquitted in a 1988 trial that raised international concern. In retaliation, a group of Kanaks kidnapped sixteen French policemen and held them hostage in a cave. Three hundred elite French troops stormed the cave, massacring nineteen Kanaks and summarily executing six others who had surrendered. Their bodies were so bullet ridden that none could be positively identified. The French soldiers responsible for this action have never been charged.[15]

Such was the prevailing attitude of white labor recruiters toward the Pacific islanders at the beginning of the twentieth century that it is little wonder that laborers often deserted into the bush or, once they had finished their indenture, were loath to sign for a second term. And once they had been repatriated, they did not encourage other members of their tribes to sign indentures.[16] The Kwaio natives of the interior of Malaita offer a prime example of the kind of racial tension that the economic system fostered. They were particularly hesitant and often resisted the efforts of the blackbirders violently. Deserved or not, so savage was the reputation of the natives on Malaita that it was not until years after the Londons' visit to the area that a white settlement was effected.[17]

Even twenty years after the period London describes in his stories, Malaita was far from stable, as evidenced by the Kwaio Rebellion of October 1927. The District Officer in charge of the administration of justice on the island was William Bell, an extremely able man by all accounts, with a reputation for dealing firmly but fairly with natives. Though admired and honored by the islanders for his calm authority, by the 1920s the Englishman had become strangely subject to fits of anger and even brutality, occasionally even striking the Malaitans under his authority. Bell's superiors, concerned about the number of injuries caused by the careless handling of the many Snider rifles in the possession of the Malaitans, ordered Bell to confiscate all of these guns during a public meeting.

Though Bell felt that this was a bad idea, he knew he had to proceed. Bell was well aware of the bitterness with which the warriors chafed under foreign bullying. Particularly offensive to them was the idea of parting with their guns. Some of those weapons, habitually unmaintained and rusted from the moist tropical environment, were occasionally more dangerous to the person firing them than to any target aimed at, but some of them functioned well enough to kill enemies. Whether the guns worked or not, the men had used their Sniders as emblems of their masculinity and self-reliance since the last quarter of the nineteenth century, and "top gun" status was accorded island *ramos*—paid killers—who had managed to hoard the precious ammunition. It occurred to Bell that he might conveniently carry out his orders by confiscating their Sniders at the same time that he collected the annual three-shillings-a-head tax. This tax itself reveals some of the cynicism the colonial whites felt toward the blacks who were under their control. Each of the Kwaio families was ordered to pay a tax of three shillings per male member of the family, ostensibly to help maintain the government services, including the safety provided by a police force and justice assured by Bell's trial process. However, as the government knew, the only way a Kwaio could possibly obtain European money was by enlisting with the recruiters for the plantations. Through his intelligence officers, Bell knew that resistance to the tax was threatening to take the form of open rebellion, but his confidence seemed to know no bounds, and he went ahead with his plans anyway, reluctant to back down before the blacks.

He set up a temporary meeting place in a pleasant-looking valley called Gwee'abe and began to collect the tax and the rifles. While Bell was somehow distracted during the process, an island strongman named Basiana crept up behind him, raised his old Snider over his head like a club, and with a single stroke crushed Bell's skull. At once, the Kwaios turned on the other government representatives and, in a wild rush, massacred all fourteen of them. Because of the small number of white people in all the Solomons—rarely more than six hundred souls—native violence and rebellion were constant dangers.[18]

And then there were the missionaries. Even the first exploratory expeditions mounted by the Spaniards in the sixteenth century had as one of their prime goals the conversion of the pagan people of the Pacific to Christianity. However, such were the perceived evils of Roman Catholicism that many Protestants sincerely considered orthodoxy only a little less wicked than headhunting itself. And so, simultaneous with the swollen cupidity that brought traders and profiteers to the South Seas, Protestants from America and England set out as early as the 1790s to bring a non-Catholic view of salvation to the heathen islanders.

It is tempting to sneer at the middle-class pomposity and narrow-minded certitude that motivated flocks of Protestants to uproot themselves from the security of a normal life at home to cross dangerous seas and settle treacherous islands, but to do so is to miss the genuine heroism of the venture. Pacific missionaries often represented the minority splinter sects that bristled from the core of Protestantism: Boston Calvinists, Seventh-Day Adventists, and Pentecostal enthusiasts shouldered each other for dominion from island to island. There was no urge to ecumenism. Each group sought to convince the respective islanders that it taught the Only True Religion, and this claim tended to be taken at face value by their phlegmatic congregations. Even today, travelers to the Solomons are advised to avoid flippancy on the topic of religion; islanders tolerate differences of opinion, but not indifference of attitude.

Often, along with their teachings, the missionaries, like the explorers and traders before them, brought diseases common in the Western world, against which the islanders had no immunity. Even without the notion of germs or viruses, the natives were able to note the conjunction between the arrival of churchmen and the outbreak of new and fatal sicknesses. Ultimately, health-conscious tribesmen frequently massacred many missionary families. The natives had been terrified of "white" diseases since the early days of the sandalwood traders, who would sometimes purposely spread deadly diseases as revenge against uncooperative islanders. Whether the white men came to exploit the people or resources or to save their immortal souls, tragedy seemed inevitably to result from the meeting of the races.[19]

By the time Jack London sailed his yacht, the *Snark*, out of San Francisco Bay in the spring of 1907, the Pacific region had been in racial turmoil for three hundred years.

II

The voyage of the *Snark* grew ineluctably out of the character of Jack London. That boat, he determined, was to be an expression of his own will—its construction and later journeys a physical representation of the idea the thirty-one-year-old author expressed with the words "I like. I am so made." Because he planned a round-the-world trip, London was adamant about overseeing the *Snark's* construction personally, designing her every detail, selecting only the best materials available, securing the most modern, efficient engines. London's itinerary seems ambitious even today. The fifty-seven-foot ketch was to sail from San Francisco to the South Seas, the canals of China, the Nile, the Thames, the Seine, the Atlantic, the Great Lakes, the Mississippi, and the Gulf of Mexico before returning home via Cape Horn. But no one could have foreseen the circumstances that would intervene in their plans—not the least of them the San Francisco earthquake of 1906, which happened the very day the keel was being laid. The great fire that followed kept all shipbuilding on a considerably lower priority and caused all materials and supplies to be three times more expensive than before.

Finally, the *Snark* weighed anchor on April 23, 1907, with its first destination being Hawaii. From the beginning, however, there were troubles with the *Snark*; contractors had cheated London relentlessly, resulting in unreliable engines, substandard fittings, and a leaking hull. To make matters worse, he was sailing with an untested and sometimes incompetent crew. The most reliable of the crew—indeed, the only one of the group to last the whole voyage—was a tall, strapping, twenty-two-year-old Midwesterner named Martin Johnson, who had signed on as cook, though his claimed expertise in that regard was less valuable than his determined resolution to tinker with the *Snark*'s problematical engines. After the cruise, Johnson began a career of adventurous independent filmmaking and photography. For three decades, traveling with his wife, Osa, he took thousands of feet of motion pictures and thousands of still photos of wild animals and indigenous people in exotic locales. For a generation of audiences, Martin and Osa Johnson's exhibition of photographs and films often provided Americans with the only information they would ever be likely to receive about life in the remote corners of the world.

Though it took nearly a month—delayed long enough to have generated rumors that they had been lost at sea—the London party eventually arrived in Hawaii on May 20. There the *Snark* was refitted and repaired, while Jack and Charmian enjoyed the pleasures of the island paradise, riding, surfing, dining and dancing, touring plantations, getting sunburned, and generally behaving like the tourists they were. And typically for Jack, almost everything they did occasioned or suggested a story. For example, one evening they attended a military dance that inspired "The House of Pride."[20] From shipmate Bert Stolz, Jack may have learned the story behind London's "Koolau the Leper." Stolz was the son of the law enforcement agent shot by the real-life Koolau.[21] Later Jack visited the leper colony on Molokai. Jack and Charmian also stayed as guests at the 50,000-acre Haleakala Ranch, and rode into the huge volcanic crater known as the House of the Sun. Jack even got involved in a saloon brawl, which he improbably attributed to drinking "a couple of cocktails" on an empty stomach, but which Charmian understood to be a need to blow off steam after all the delays they had endured.

From there they sailed to the Marquesas where they visited the Typee Valley, which had fired Jack's imagination when he had first read Melville's novel. Jack was disappointed with what he found—islanders very different from those Melville had described, sick and debilitated from contact with white men's diseases.

The *Snark's* touchy engines caused more problems as they continued on to Tahiti. On arrival Jack was dismayed to learn of a negative article about him written by no less than President Teddy Roosevelt, who called Jack a "nature faker" for suggesting in his fiction that animals could think. About the same time, London was disappointed to learn that the *Snark*'s Captain Warren had been inflating the repair bills for the *Snark* and pocketing the money for himself. He was fired. On Bora Bora, Jack and Charmian became friends with a native couple, a warm association that inspired Jack's story "The Heathen." In Samoa, the Londons visited the grave of Robert Louis Stevenson, one of Jack's favorite authors.

Here also, Jack lectured on socialism in the Central Hotel in Apia and participated in the local tradition of stone fishing. And finally on to the Solomons, where they visited a large copra plantation, photographed cannibals, tried hashish, and went on their blackbirding expedition with Captain Jansen. Here they also met Harold Markham, who may have been an inspiration for London's intrepid character Captain David Grief.

Jack and Charmian had the time of their lives, experiencing excitement and danger all along the way, as Jack's *The Cruise of the Snark* (1911) and Charmian's *The Log of the Snark* (1915) attest. Charmian was the best of shipmates. Unmistakably feminine and deeply in love with Jack, she yet was far from the stereotype of the delicately reserved and sheltered Edwardian woman. She thrilled at the thought of real adventure and eagerly took part in every aspect of the voyage, including putting herself in danger of bodily harm from the perils of remote seas, exotic diseases, and threats from islanders widely reputed to be savages. Every day of the voyage Jack kept to his customary writing stint of one thousand words. Charmian meanwhile gamely kept up with typing the manuscripts of his novel *Martin Eden*, along with a series of short stories, nine of which are included in the present volume.

Troubles, though, still arose. Occasionally the Londons became lost, battled through severe storms, and once almost died of thirst. These experiences, as he wrote in his boyish scrawl day after day, vitalized London's Pacific fiction. However, some of their trials were far from glamorous. In his chapter on the Solomon Islands in *The Cruise of the Snark*, Jack detailed the enervating effects of malaria as well as the virulent infections that resulted whenever one of them got even the slightest open wound, forming massive "Solomon sores."[22] Beyond even these, Jack became afflicted with a variety of exotic ailments, including bowel inflammations and a frightening one that caused the skin of Jack's hands to peel off in large patches.[23]

By late October of 1908 almost all the crew of the *Snark* were suffering from various ailments. Most common were Solomon sores, infections that refused to heal in the hot and damp climate of the islands. Jack suffered most. His teeth gave him almost constant problems, and he took every opportunity to visit dentists. He was also concerned, mistakenly as it turned out, that his worsening skin condition and deformed fingernails and toenails might be early symptoms of leprosy. Finally Jack decided their journey would have to be interrupted so that he could seek medical attention in Sydney.

It was here that Jack was first prescribed opium for his postoperative pain, and in the years that followed he turned increasingly to the narcotic for relief as his physical conditions worsened. Ironically, an arsenic compound he was using as a medicine for his skin condition probably exacerbated Jack's kidney problems.[24]

After several months recuperating in Sydney and with a side-trip to Tasmania, Jack and Charmian reluctantly and sadly decided that their dream of a world cruise would have to be deferred. On April 8, 1909, they boarded the *Tymeric* for Guayaquil, Ecuador, where they arrived on May 19. Jack felt stronger as the days passed, and they crossed the Andes to Quito to do some sightseeing before returning to Guayaquil and catching the S.S. *Erica* to Panama. From there, they steamed to New Orleans aboard the S.S. *Turrialba*. On October 21, 1910, Jack and Charmian finally reached Oakland and soon returned to their beloved Beauty Ranch in Glen Ellen.

The *Snark* was sold in the South Seas for a fraction of its original cost. The new owners turned it into a blackbirding ship, an ironic finale for such a game vessel. In her memoir, *I Married Adventure*, Osa Johnson recalled seeing the ship in the summer of 1917:

> [Our] ship stopped at the little port of Api [Epi, in present-day Vanuatu] to leave mail and supplies and to take on copra. Leaning on the rail we were watching the activity in the harbor when Martin straightened suddenly. His face was drawn and tense. I followed the direction of his gaze, but all I saw was a small, dirty recruiting ship.... The paint had once been white under all that filth, and her lines were beautiful. Suddenly my breath caught in my throat.
>
> "Not the *Snark* !" I said.
>
> She was a pitiable sight. They could not alter her trim lines; but her metal, her paint, her rigging had been shamefully neglected and ill-treated. Frowzy and unbelievably dirty she reminded me somehow of an

> aristocrat fallen upon evil days. I looked up at Martin. He shook his head.
>
> "I'm glad Jack and Charmian never saw her that way," he said, swallowing hard.[25]

Only the hatch cover remains today.[26]

Back home in the warm and inviting atmosphere of Sonoma Valley, Jack's health steadily improved, and within a few months he seemed to be completely recovered.[27] Jack now threw himself into enlarging and improving his ranch, determined to implement all the new agricultural techniques of the day. He also began putting into reality another dream, Wolf House, a huge lodge to be situated on the side of Sonoma Mountain looking out on the beautiful Valley of the Moon. The house was built out of rough-hewn redwood logs and uncut volcanic boulders quarried from the area. At the same time that he tackled this monumental project, Jack also kept up a steady stream of correspondence, entertained a seemingly endless list of visitors, and, of course, continued to write.

London indeed had many successes and much happiness in his last few years, but failures and personal sadness also marked this final period of his life. Jack was saddened when one of his prize horses died. The bitter divorce in 1904 from his first wife, Bess, continued to cause estrangement from his daughters Joan and Becky. Wolf House was destroyed by fire shortly before the Londons were to move in. Jack and Charmian's infant daughter, Joy, died two days after her birth. The author was involved in legal tangles over the ranch and movie rights to his books. These emotional strains inevitably affected his worsening physical condition, one that he did little to ameliorate since he continued to eat unwisely, smoke incessantly, drink intemperately, and generally drive himself to physical exhaustion. The progress of his kidney disease and the pain-killing drugs he was taking for its symptoms both continued to take their toll. Jack London died at Beauty Ranch on November 22, 1916. Charmian continued to live on the ranch. She built the massive residence she called "The House of Happy Walls," corresponded with friends, wrote books, and lovingly kept her husband's memory alive. She outlived Jack by nearly forty years and died on January 13, 1955, designating that her home become a museum to commemorate their lives. She never remarried.

During the last two years of his life, Jack and Charmian spent a great deal of their time in Hawaii and developed a deep affection for the islands, as Charmian testified in her book *Our Hawaii*. Perhaps here they came close to the paradise they had sought during the voyage of the *Snark*. In any case, just as he had done during his trip to the Klondike, Jack had acquired during the *Snark* voyage a wealth of material for his writing, and the Pacific occupied London's imagination in ways that were at least as complex as his better-known fascination with the frozen Northland.[28] Indeed, from the idyllic languor of "The Water Baby" to the monstrous agonies of "The Red One," Jack's later fiction continued to bring him back to the South Seas.

III

The nine stories in this volume are arranged in the order Jack London wrote them, as determined by James Williams in his article "Jack London's Works by Date of Composition." As Jeanne Campbell Reesman has pointed out, the stories give evidence of the author's interest in literary experimentation. In her book *Jack London: A Study of the Short Fiction*, she explains: "London's entire life was a sort of experiment, and he could not resist the challenge of seeing life from as many vantage points as possible, from within ethnic communities scattered across the Pacific Ocean, from feminine as well as masculine points of view, from the minds of both the ruling class and the ghetto."[29] The settings of these stories tend to grow out of the cruise of the *Snark*, generally reflecting the east-to-west movement of the voyage: "The Seed of McCoy" is set in the Tuamoto Archipelago; "The Chinago," in Tahiti; "The Heathen," in Bora Bora; "The Whale Tooth," in Fiji; and the rest, in the Solomon Islands.

"The Seed of McCoy," written first and set easternmost, contains London's positive vision of redemption made possible by sacrifice. "The Red One," written last and set far to the west, represents the author's ever-deepening sense of alienation and perhaps a kind of racial guilt that underlies his final characterization of white men in the Pacific. Though these features were present from the earliest works in this collection, they became more intensified in the years between 1908 and London's death in 1916.

The tales collected in this volume have been little read and rarely discussed in print or classrooms, in part because there is a kind of "common knowledge" that they defend racist assumptions. The charge, however, is fraught with irony, since it seems to have been hard for London in his own day to sell these stories to the popular media for the very opposite reasons. Editors at the turn of the twentieth century often were not interested in fiction that depicted the brutal details of white colonialism—stories in which the magazine-reading public's widely accepted assumption of white supremacy would be exposed to uncomfortable scrutiny.

It is the business of the writer to awaken in the reader some emotion, generated by the reader's involvement with the text. Certainly, some writers can evoke sympathy, laughter, anxiety, and other similar emotional responses, as long as the reader willingly enters into the transaction. The reader may also enter into an intellectual exchange and perhaps alter an opinion through the reading of a convincing argument. Jack London wrote more than his share of literature in which he voiced his own position and opinions, particularly in his volatile socialist writings. On the other hand, he also often wrote with his emotions concealed, as a good Naturalist author ought to do. Naturalism, in its purest form as a literary school, imposed the discipline of writing with a scientifically detached descriptive attitude, even though the writer personally might be outraged about the situation he so objectively describes. Also significant in Naturalistic fiction is a moral dimension, one in which social injustices will be explored, resulting in a sense of disturbance or even outrage in readers. Naturalist writers, perhaps even more than others, demand that their readers do their own thinking and come to their own conclusions. It is important to understand that a description of a racist scene is not necessarily an endorsement of racism, any more than Swift's "Modest Proposal" is really a document advocating British exploitation of Ireland. In any case, as Engels pointed out, the writer "does not have to serve the reader on a platter the future historical resolution of the social conflicts he describes."[30]

Recently these issues have become more interesting and challenging. In the years since the Second World War, many philosophers and literary theorists have pointed out that the act of reading itself is fraught with more complexities than common sense might suggest. These critics argue that it is unduly simplistic to assume that emotions awakened in the reader are related closely to the intentions of the writer. They go on to claim that no one can guarantee closure—absolute identification—between the writer's originating idea and the reader's response. Some of them say that such interpretive closure, however obvious it might seem to common sense, is actually an indemonstrable and probably unnecessary notion. Texts are public while originating ideas and authorial intentions are private. No one can know with any level of certainty what Jack London, the author, really thought or intended. As we, the editors, have approached these stories, one belief has emerged: if London had as his originating idea the intention of depicting racism as unambiguously just and ethical, it seems to us that he did a bad job of it. London scholar Lawrence Phillips seems to agree, suggesting that London's Pacific fiction "fails miserably as an exemplar to underpin an argument for racial hierarchy and superiority."[31] This belief has convinced the editors that it is time to approach these texts from other perspectives.

Apart from the critical response to the South Seas stories, it is rare for London to be charged with an inability to deal subtly with his material. Thus London's socialist stories may be analyzed with due attention to their unexpressed (but nonetheless obvious) politically subversive implications. London's "The Apostate," for example, grimly details the life of a child of a white, working-class, urban single parent, but no one would read the story as an endorsement of the injustices growing out of the uncaring economic system described in the tale. In London's Pacific fiction, however, his straightforward depiction of racism and its attendant brutalities seems, in our contemporary political climate, somehow supportive of "the inevitable white man" and of the colonialist system that exploited the human and natural resources of the South Seas. A careful reading, however, will reveal that these stories cannot be read so superficially. Indeed, we have difficulty in understanding how any reader can interpret these texts as representing or encoding a racist intention at all.

Nevertheless, though the critical literature centering on London's Pacific fiction is sparse, and most of the stories have not been widely read, some people continue to assume that London's work expresses a racist thesis. Those who do not like what they perceive to be the political agenda of the stories included here might support their condemnation of London by arguing that his representations of ethnicity are distorted, and that such distortions cannot be excused by urging that similar representations were widespread at the time. If racism is objectively wrong today, then it was wrong in the past as well. Racists had to have made the decision to be racists—and they are therefore culpable for their choice, without recourse to anthropological or sociological analyses of the "causes" of prejudice, just as a thief must do his stretch, even though he had been born into and raised by a family of thieves.

But this rather simplistic argument fails to account for the complexity of London's fiction. As one consequence of modern considerations of the proper and ethical relations that ought to exist within a racially diverse world population, readers of our day may tend to be uncomfortable with London's depiction of islander characters, perhaps because in some way he ought to have described them as behaving like noble, urbane Western sophisticates. It could be argued that this embarrassment itself betrays a racist reluctance to believe that these indigenous peoples often looked, acted, and intentionally decorated themselves in ways they hoped would enhance their formidable ferocity. It is no surprise that the most objective anthropologists of the period—with the possible exception of Franz Boas—would have labeled these people as "savages." Boas, writing in 1928, argues that

> the way in which the personality reacts to cultures is a matter that should concern us deeply and that makes the studies of foreign cultures a fruitful and useful field of research. We are accustomed to consider all those actions that are part and parcel of our own culture, standards that we follow automatically, as common to all mankind. They are deeply ingrained in our behavior. We are molded in their forms so that we cannot think but that they must be valid everywhere. Courtesy, modesty, good manners, conformity to definite ethical standards are universal, but what constitutes courtesy, modesty, good manners, and ethical standards is not universal. It is instructive to know that standards differ in the most unexpected ways.[32]

Instead of acknowledging universal ideals being filtered through differing behaviors, today there somehow exists a need to deny the behaviors or appearances, patronizingly refashioning naked headhunters into freethinking noblemen who were merely misunderstood by the white explorers who saw them. Fear of the cultural Other is indeed betrayed by early European accounts of islander appearance and behavior. Perhaps it would make reports of the clash of these different worlds less embarrassing for today's readers, if only islander customs had been reported with anthropological objectivity.[33]

Furthermore, there are complicated moral issues in these stories to confront. Blacks as well as whites commit criminal acts, and one of the underlying features of Pacific life rarely far from London's mind is cannibalism. Despite modern reluctance to confront this controversial topic, even the most broad-minded among us would agree that consuming human flesh is not acceptable as an "alternative life style." It may be tempting to excuse hideous tortures and murderous activities by discovering their "causes" in culture and tradition. The danger of providing such a rationale for cannibalism is that it exhibits the same kind of moral relativism considered inappropriate when used as an explanation of the white racism of the period. To say that only white people ought to be held to an objective ethical standard is itself a racist statement.

So marked has this discomfort become that some representatives of contemporary anthropology have actually argued that the practice of ritual cannibalism never, in fact, occurred. These critics, most notably the controversial anthropologist William Arens—whose interest in this argument has unwillingly earned him the nickname "Mr. Cannibalism"—have criticized the limited and sometimes dubious reliability of the evidence, concluding that the allegations arise from white racist fears of alterity, supplemented by testimony provided by islander informants whose waggish sense of humor may have prompted them to tell the wide-eyed white inquirers what they wanted to hear. Other scientists, however, who have studied aboriginal cultures in Australia and New Guinea, argue that the evidence for the pervasiveness of cannibalism is too strong to brush aside. Pacific expert Laurence R. Goldman concludes that the "articulation of regional patterns based on linguistic and historical associations between cultures . . . compel us to appreciate that the case for past cannibalism in parts of Papua New Guinea is no longer an issue for the majority of Melanesian scholars."[34]

Moreover, another indication of the persistence of the practice comes from medical science. Recent research has shown that *kuru,* a debilitating and fatal neurological condition observed in isolated populations in New Guinea, is caused only by eating human brains infected with this prion agent. The disease was first recognized in the early 1900s and achieved epidemic proportions in the 1960s, when over a thousand people died.[35]

Because the question has not been studied with the same depth as in New Guinea, the practice of cannibalism in the Solomon Islands has not been verified. Whether the natives of the Solomons were cannibals or not, however, certainly Jack London had every reason to believe that they were. As an author though, he seems not to have been interested in placing blame for the excesses of violence or lack of morality on either side. It was in the interests of the Naturalist writer to maintain at least the emotive pose of objectivity. Though London does not use his authorial voice to mitigate or excuse the behavior of the natives, the careful reader will also notice that he refrains from doing likewise for his white characters. London's stance in these tales is consistently evenhanded, showing us the islanders as he found them and pulling no punches, in the same way that he describes the crimes of the white invaders. If there are few heroes in these tales, all of them happen to be islanders. Indeed, readers of London's day who sought a sanitized version of the colonial scene might well have been shocked by the way the author refused to offer them heroic white characters, often choosing to show instead the point of view of people of color.

London, however, certainly was capable of taking the other perspective, as he did in his South Seas novel *Adventure,* written during the same period as the majority of the stories in this collection. Long regarded by London's readers as a failure, *Adventure* tells the tale of a small group of white plantation managers who base their authority over a blackbirded work force on their unquestioned conviction of their own racial superiority. Owing to its apparently complete disregard for modern standards of political correctness—or even basic humanity—the novel seems shocking and insensitive today. Clarice Stasz notes that *Adventure* is a departure from the evenhandedness with which London examines racial conflict in his short fiction, pointing out its failure to use "comic rhetoric in ways that foster the effectiveness of related works." Stasz further argues that missing in the novel but present in the short fiction is the successful depiction of "the ever-present threat of violence and disease, the corruption of the Whites, the concept of survival despite crude aggression."[36]

However gifted and insightful London was as a writer, still his understanding was limited by his own cultural background. But even to take the effort to describe the world through the eyes of nonwhite characters shows that London was (to use a self-congratulatory and chronocentric phrase) ahead of his time.[37]

It is, of course, obviously—almost necessarily—true that the response of the white visitors at the turn of the twentieth century was without question biased and riddled with racism. After all, they had come in the first place, both entrepreneur and missionary, with the conviction of their own cultural and spiritual superiority. Both sought for different reasons to exploit or sublimate the cultures of the people they found. Both, consciously or unconsciously, often succeeded in exploiting and even eradicating the islands' people as well.

Many readers coming to these wild, hell-bent-for-leather stories for the first time might not be aware that London's anthropological and geographic details accurately depict the people, places, and customs of the region. Some of these details came from the Londons' own experiences; others, from grisly accounts given them by eyewitnesses such as the missionary at Maluu, J. St. George Caulfeild.[38]

Trophies of the old days are still visible on the islands today, as on the hill of the appropriately named Skull Island, in the Solomons' Western Province, where human heads have been saved and stacked in a grisly tabernacle. For ten Solomon dollars you can hire a guide to visit it today. Some senior islanders, who obviously enjoy a good story, still recall with chuckling gusto the peculiar pleasures of man eating. In a recently filmed interview, Enos, a Vanuatu chief, with an unconscious dereliction of the past tense, explained the allure: "If you are champion—a strong man—then we will eat you because we will be strong like you. And we will use all your bones to make arrow to kill other people. Very sweet—better than all other meat. That's what they say. . . . Cannibalism is finished about 1939. They eat some white man."[39]

Enos's testimony, however, presents some intriguing challenges. First, though cannibalism may have declined in the region, colonial officials were still making arrests in Papua of groups caught in the act of carrying human meat away from a tribal raid as recently as the 1970s. Second, Enos's psychoanalytic thesis in explaining cannibalism—the literal incorporation of the object of desire—is tainted by the failure of any modern anthropologist to find evidence of this belief in the cultures of practicing cannibals. A witty Papuan informant blandly responded, when told that a man might gain the strengths of another man by eating him, "If you eat a bird, can you fly?" The actual motivation for cannibalism appears instead to have been the victor's expression of ultimate contempt for the defeated enemy.

Serious and thorough anthropological research indicates that even the most urgent contemporary desire for political correctness cannot gloss over the historical evidence of human sacrifice, cannibalism, and head-hunting throughout the Pacific, lasting for decades past the time of London's fiction. But it is also true that white South Seas veterans often embellished the horrors of the island customs for newcomers. London actually made use of this practice in his short story "The Terrible Solomons." Moreover, because he never witnessed a cannibal feast himself, it is certain that all Jack's knowledge of cannibal activities was drawn from these sometimes mendacious old hands, supplemented by his reading of the experiences of other white visitors.

Jack and Charmian may also have heard other accounts of islander savagery that might have stemmed from misinterpretation. It is likely, for example, that white men seeing a collection of skulls in the interior of Malaita would not take the time to inquire about whose heads they were. Sensibly cautious white visitors would probably assume that these were the preserved heads of enemies—even though such collections were actually shrines and those of valued family members who had died—usually of natural causes.[40] But if the stories circulating about the headhunters of the Solomon Islands were sometimes exaggerated for effect, it seems to have been a widespread and quite sincere feeling that one's life was constantly in danger in the region, whether islander or white visitor.

London's stories set in the South Seas show the author's interest in questions of race, culture, justice, and heroism. Though obviously refusing to ignore the violence committed by both sides, London accurately and consistently showed the islanders as individuals who had to deal, in one way or another, with white intrusions—of capitalist brutality, of inhumane legal systems, of foreign diseases, and of racist social practices. Ambivalent about the character of the white intruders, and sympathetic to the plight of islanders caught up in the grinding mill of European economic and religious expansion, London takes a stance in these stories that allows him to elicit from the reader a deep sense of uncertainty about the morality of the South Seas adventure itself.

Through what surely are the inexplicable vagaries of public taste, these stories have been overshadowed by the popularity of London's Northland fiction, and many are hardly available to readers today. Few of them have received any scholarly attention whatever—and, when these stories have been discussed, they usually have been dismissed, occasionally with some asperity, often because of an apparently hasty and superficial reading of what are actually layered and densely ambiguous texts.[41]

London's Pacific fiction reflects the political turmoil, economic piracy, physical violence, religious idealism, and racial antagonism of a remote and romantic location, where white men sought to wrest a fortune from a people for whom they often had little more than contempt. Jack London was there, and these stories emerging from his Pacific adventure demonstrate as clearly as any of his works his characteristic ability to tell riveting stories that are driven by social and philosophical themes.

Once apparently confident of the possible redemption of the colonialist enterprise, London ended by writing stories chronicling white penetration into the Solomon Islands that can scarcely be read without a wince. Like his literary hero Joseph Conrad, London became increasingly absorbed by the "fascination of the abomination." In the weird and problematic motivations, the wild potential for moral corruption, the inhuman savagery of which both sides in the venal project were capable, and the stench and rot and meaninglessness at the core of this racial interaction, London found his own heart of darkness.

Notes

1. Charmian London, *The Log of the Snark* (New York: Macmillan, 1915), 413.
2. The Snider rifle was created in mid-nineteenth-century America to modify muzzle-loading Enfield rifles into more effective breech-loading

weapons. By the end of the century, the composite gun and its immediate descendants were obsolete, and so began the concerted effort of American and European colonists to distribute Snider rifles throughout the world, particularly in Turkey and the South Pacific region. It is difficult to overemphasize the importance of these weapons to the islanders. As years went by, Snider rifles assumed a symbolic function as emblems of status and masculinity, even though bullets were scarce and the guns were rarely fired. (For everything you've ever wanted to know about the Snider rifle, see Charles J. Purdon, *The Snider-Enfield Rifle* [Alexandria Bay, NY: Museum Restoration Service, 1990] and Roger M. Keesing and Peter Corris, *Lightning Meets the West Wind: The Malaita Massacre* [Melbourne: Oxford University Press, 1980].)

3. Earle Labor, Robert C. Leitz III, and I. Milo Shepard, eds., *The Letters of Jack London*, vol. 3 (Stanford, CA: Stanford University Press, 1988), 1599.
4. Mark Honan and David Harcombe, *Solomon Islands*, 3rd ed. (Hong Kong: Lonely Planet, 1997), 14.
5. Cited in John Fowler, "Fiji: The Warrior Archipelago," http://www.tribalsite.com/articles/fiji.htm.
6. Frank Sherry, *Pacific Passions: The European Struggle for Power in the Great Ocean in the Age of Exploration* (New York: William Morrow, 1994), 102–18.
7. Alan Reid, *Discovery and Exploration* (London: Gentry Books, 1980), 234–35.
8. David Harcombe, *Solomon Islands*, 1st ed. (Singapore: Lonely Planet, 1988), 11.
9. Caroline Ralston, *Grass Huts and Warehouses: Pacific Beach Communities of the Nineteenth Century* (Honolulu: University Press of Hawaii, 1978), 20–43.
10. For a detailed study of the sandalwood traders, see Dorothy Shineberg, *They Came for Sandalwood: A Study of the Sandalwood Trade in the South-West Pacific, 1830–1865* (Carlton, Victoria, Australia: University of Melbourne Press, 1967). See also Douglas L. Oliver, *The Pacific Islands* (Cambridge, MA: Harvard University Press, 1958), 176–79.
11. See Edward Wybergh Docker, *The Blackbirders* (Sydney: Angus and Robertson, 1970).
12. Harcombe, *Solomon Islands*, 1st ed., 45, and Mark Honan and David Harcombe, *Solomon Islands*, 3rd ed. (Hong Kong: Lonely Planet, 1997), 60–61.
13. See Lawrence Phillips, "The Indignity of Labor: Jack London's *Adventure* and Plantation Labor in the Solomon Islands," *Jack London Journal* 6 (1999): 182–83.
14. See particularly "The Chinago," "The Terrible Solomons," "Mauki," "Yah! Yah! Yah!," "The Inevitable White Man," and "The Red One." It is also a prevailing theme in London's collection *A Son of the Sun*, eight stories centering on the character Captain David Grief.
15. David Stanley, *South Pacific Handbook* (Chico, CA: Moon Publications, 1996), 668–70.
16. For a divergent view of the islanders' attitudes toward indenture, see Philip Cass, "The Infallible Engine: Indigenous Perceptions of Europeans in German New Guinea through the Missionary Press," paper presented to the Media History Conference, University of Westminster, London, July 1998. http://cci.wmin.ac.uk/hist98/cass.html
17. Harcombe, *Solomon Islands*, 174.

18. For the complete story behind the murder of William Bell, see Roger M. Keesing and Peter Corris, *Lightning Meets the West Wind: The Malaita Massacre* (Melbourne: Oxford University Press, 1980).
19. C. Hartley Grattan, *The Southwest Pacific to 1900* (Ann Arbor: University of Michigan Press, 1963), 179–207, and Douglas L. Oliver, *The Pacific Islands* (Cambridge, MA: Harvard University Press, 1958), 126–34.
20. See Gary Riedl and Thomas R. Tietze, "Fathers and Sons in Jack London's 'The House of Pride,'" in *Jack London: One Hundred Years a Writer*, ed. Sara S. Hodson and Jeanne C. Reesman (Los Angeles: Henry Huntington Library Press, 2002), 44–59.
21. James Slagel, "Political Leprosy: Jack London, the 'Kama'aina' and Koolau the Hawaiian," in *Rereading Jack London* , ed. Leonard Cassuto and Jeanne Campbell Reesman (Stanford, CA: Stanford University Press, 1996), 172.
22. Of treatment for these sores, London said, ". . . when corrosive sublimate is slow in taking hold, alternate dressings of peroxide of hydrogen are just the thing. There are white men in the Solomons who stake all upon boric acid, and others who are prejudiced in favour of lysol. I also have the weakness of a panacea. It is California. I defy any man to get a Solomon Island sore in California." Jack London, *The Cruise of the Snark* (New York: Macmillan, 1911), 255–56.
23. See London, *Cruise of the Snark*, chap.15.
24. Clarice Stasz, *American Dreamers: Charmian and Jack London* (New York: St. Martin's, 1988), 186–88.
25. Osa Johnson, *I Married Adventure: The Lives and Adventures of Martin and Osa Johnson* (Philadelphia: Lippincott, 1940), 128.
26. According to Toby Watson, author of *Jack London's Snark: San Francisco*, the *Snark's* hatch cover washed ashore in the New Hebrides (now Vanuatu) after the vessel was destroyed in 1917. The owners of a coconut plantation rescued it, but from there its location remains a mystery, since the plantation owners have died, and their children have moved to New Zealand, taking the remains of the hatch with them. Mrs. Watson further states that Reece Discombe, who lives in Vanuatu, made for some years an extended attempt to find the family members but to no avail. Recently, however, Mrs. Watson has discovered a 1932 photograph of the *Snark* at anchor near Noumea, New Caledonia, and she is examining several hypotheses, including the possibility that the vessel remained afloat much longer than has hitherto been supposed. (See *Jack London Foundation Newsletter* 13, no. 3 [July 1, 2001]: 9–10.)
27. Russ Kingman, *A Pictorial Life of Jack London* (New York: Crown, 1979), 212.
28. It is interesting to note in this regard that Jack wrote his most famous short story "To Build a Fire" (the second version) while he was in Hawaii.
29. Jeanne Campbell Reesman, *Jack London: A Study of the Short Fiction* (New York: Twayne, 1999), xv.
30. Frederick Engels, "Letter to Minna Kautsky," in *Marx and Engels on Literature and Art* (Moscow: Progress Publishers, 1976), 88.
31. Lawrence Phillips, "The Indignity of Labor: Jack London's *Adventure* and Plantation Labor in the Solomon Islands." *Jack London Journal* 6 (1999): 186.
32. Franz Boas, "Foreword" in Margaret Mead, *Coming of Age in Samoa* (New York: Dell, 1961; repr. of 1928 ed.), 9–10.
33. Even this, however, may be an unrealistic expectation, for anthropology itself has, as an allegedly scientific discipline, received its share of

criticism in the postcolonial world. Cultural anthropologist Steven Caton outlines the results of this contemporary soul-searching:

> [This] critical reading suggests that the practices of modern anthropological fieldwork are not that far removed from the work of nineteenth-century missionaries, explorers, travelers, and colonial agents . . . with the result that the too convenient *cordon sanitaire* that has been thrown up by anthropologists between themselves and these other, now perhaps discredited, practitioners has crumbled. The effect has been salutary, prompting a more honest, searching appraisal of their own discipline as having been and continuing to be racist and colonialist. Or consider the way in which the writing of ethnographies has become complicated, as the boundaries between science and art, fact and fiction, objective and subjective have been blurred, thus heightening our awareness of what Clifford Geertz over two decades ago called the *fictio* of ethnographic writing—its intricate constructedness. Finally, the concept of culture as a static, bounded, and holistic object of study—long the theoretical foundation of the discipline—is all but moribund in the wake of criticisms that have stressed its processual nature, porousness, hybridity, discursiveness, and fragmentariness.

(See Steven C. Caton, *Lawrence of Arabia: A Film's Anthropology* [Berkeley: University of California Press, 1999], 144.)

34. Laurence R. Goldman, ed., *The Anthropology of Cannibalism* (Westport, CT, 1999), 19. The articles in this fascinating collection examine the political implications of certain anthropological findings related to Melanesian cannibal practices. Today, as Melanesian populations struggle to gain rights in a postcolonialist environment, their progress is frequently stalled by the demonizing tactics of racist opponents who exploit claims about the aboriginal "savage" past; this results in lively and occasionally borderline unprofessional debates whenever evidence of cannibalism or headhunting is secured. This is the single most illuminating text to help determine how accurate London was in his depiction of this aspect of Melanesian life.
35. James R. Bindon, "Kuru: The Dynamics of a Prion Disease," http://www.as.ua.edu/ant/bindon/ant570/Papers/McGrath/McGrath.htm
36. Clarice Stasz, "Sarcasm, Irony, and Social Darwinism in Jack London's *Adventure*." *Thalia* 12 (1992): 84.
37. Indeed, modern anthropology and current studies on colonialism and orientalism demand that we turn away from the consideration of the European perception of the islanders and shift our attention to the ways in which the indigenous people viewed the Western presence. For example, Philip Cass, a scholar of the missionary presence in the Pacific, insists that the modern, "fatal impact" view in which the

unfortunate natives were defenseless victims of Europeans and their technology is necessarily skewed because it is presented through white eyes. A more accurate picture is revealed by a study of early missionary papers that were written by newly literate islanders in their own languages or sometimes *Tok Pisin*, another term for pidgin. "Island centered history," Cass argues, "shows the Islanders to have been active participants in the process of colonization, quite willing to sign on as boats' crew with sandalwood traders and beche de mer hunters, willingly signing on for a second or third indenture on plantations in order to bring back trade goods (including, in the early days, guns) to their villages and to work as domestic servants when it suited them." See Philip Cass, "The Infallible Engine: Indigenous Perceptions of Europeans in German New Guinea Through the Missionary Press" (Paper presented to the Media History Conference, University of Westminster, London, July 1998), http://cci.wmin.ac.uk/hist98/cass.html.

38. For example, Charmian London reported a discussion with Captain Jansen of the *Minota* and Caulfeild

> Jack and I absorbed many significant items of Solomon life. Jansen mentioned to Caulfeild the murder of a planter in the Group:
>
> "Which murder do you mean?" mildly inquired the gentle disciple of peace. "Oh, man, that was a month ago. I thought maybe you were referring to . . . or . . ." And then would follow the curdling details of one or more outrages that had been committed in the interim.
>
> "They're careless—they get careless, and let the beggars get behind them," Jansen would complain. "Mackenzie, poor chap, had no manner of business to be alone on this boat that day, or any day. A Mary did the trick, I understand—a nice harmless female woman peaceably aboard with three or four men. Mackenzie'd no business to be fooled."
>
> Caulfeild told with a shudder how a chief on one of the islands had stalked into a mission dining-room and tossed a white trader's freshly severed head down the long table—a head that had once talked and eaten at that very board. And there were sanguinary tales of the reeking bush, such as what happened at one place on Malaita, where two hundred men were cut up by their enemies, and the women forced to carry the decapitated heads down to the beach, where they were themselves beheaded. Jansen had already recounted to us how, five months previous, thirteen boys ran away in a stolen whaleboat from Ysabel plantation, and during their voyage to Malaita killed a Guadalcanal boy, and one other, who were with them, and kept the heads under the sternsheets. [London includes a variation on this incident in his story "Mauki."]

> Jansen, who had followed in the *Minota,* recovered the boat, and saw the butchery mess, which, he assured us, was very "loud" by that time.... It is nothing to find an arm or a leg, fresh or otherwise, hanging in a tree—ghastly warning or signal of one tribe or faction to another.

(See Charmian London, *Log of the Snark,* 405.)

39. *The Pacific Islands Experience,* videotape (San Ramon, CA: International Video Network, 1990).
40. See Roger M. Keesing, *Kwaio Religion: The Living and the Dead in a Solomon Island Society* (New York: Columbia University Press, 1982), esp. chap. 10.
41. See, for example, James I. McClintock, *Jack London's Strong Truths: A Study of His Short Stories* (East Lansing, MI: Michigan State University Press, 1997). McClintock scornfully dismisses some of these stories as "perverse sensationalism of the stag-magazine variety" (135).

An Introduction to "The Seed of McCoy"

Early in 1908, the *Snark* was docked in Papeete, Tahiti, having multiple breakdowns repaired by corrupt machinists. During the several months the repairs required, the Londons had a number of adventures, including a chance meeting with "dear old man McCoy,"[1] who probably provided the author with the inspiration for this story. When the Londons arrived in Tahiti during the cruise of the *Snark*, the story of the near-immolation of the cargo vessel *Pyrenees* in 1900 was still recent news. London, however, saw more in the event than the simple facts suggested, and the story that emerged in London's imagination began on February 25 and took shape on paper between March 12 and April 24, 1908.[2] "The Seed of McCoy" provides us with an opportunity to watch the author's mind at work, manipulating the basic historical materials and transforming them in order to create an epic sea story of intricate complexity. "The Seed of McCoy" demonstrates the author's creative reinvention of an actual person, one of the descendants of the mutinous crew of the *Bounty*, into a mythic hero who becomes an agent of redemption. The story grows from a South Pacific "local color" incident to become a mythic quest for deliverance. In the process, the events gain a spiritual perspective in which some sort of Destiny works its way through human history.

The 1787–1790 voyage of His Majesty's Ship *Bounty* has become one of the most familiar tales of adventure in the history of European exploration of the South Seas. Popular literature and the movies have immortalized the classic personal conflict between Captain Bligh's tyranny and the barely controlled volatility of the beleaguered English crew, mediated through the mixed sympathies of First Mate Fletcher Christian.

The purpose of the adventure is probably less well known and much more sinister. Any discussion of the thinking behind the voyage identifies the enterprise in a single stroke as a kind of emblem of European involvement in the South Pacific. It established a cycle of exploitation and slavery, which spun through all the subsequent history of white intrusions into the island world. In the late 1700s, British commercial investors needed a cheap way to feed the African slaves laboring on their Caribbean cane plantations. Hearing that Captain Cook had found Pacific islanders eating the breadfruit plant, it occurred to them that samples ought to be obtained as soon as possible for transplantation. To supply this need, the *Bounty* was commissioned and a crew selected. Lieutenant William Bligh, who had sailed with Captain Cook, was a logical choice for command.

The *Bounty* reached Tahiti in October 1788, and there the exhausted and abused crew members found a way of life so dramatically different from their own that it only added another layer of suffering to their plight. Recall Dr. Johnson's comments in 1759: "No man will be a sailor who has contrivance enough to get himself into a jail; for being in a ship is being in a jail, with the chance of being drowned.... A man in a jail has more room, better food, and commonly better company."[3] The inflexible repression that characterized the management of the long sea voyage of the *Bounty* contrasted poignantly with the freedom, sensuality, and open cheerfulness of island life. Through the acuteness of vision supplied by hindsight, the mutiny that erupted during the return voyage on April 28, 1789, seems an inevitability. What happened afterward was even more dramatic.

Set adrift in a twenty-three-foot-long open boat with eighteen loyal men, Captain Bligh achieved the most heroic feat ever accomplished in such circumstances, sailing with meager rations of food and water from the Society Islands region to Timor in Indonesia, a distance of some 3,600 miles. The mutineers, on the other hand, experienced not the anticipated return to paradise, but instead a rapid descent into hell. Fletcher Christian, erstwhile officer of the *Bounty*, preserved his command of the crew and ordered a return to Tahiti, where the men sought wives, families, and easy living. The idyll was short-lived, however. Christian, increasingly obsessed with guilt at having broken the most fundamental law of life at sea and tortured as well by the fear of being caught, began to take out his anxieties on his fellows as well as on the Tahitians who had offered him a home.

Christian ultimately convinced eight of the mutineers—one of them twenty-six-year-old, able-bodied seaman William McCoy—to come along with him to search for some remote desert island where they could settle and live without fear. Accompanied by eighteen Tahitians, he had just enough manpower to work the *Bounty* out to sea, where they finally selected remote and unwelcoming Pitcairn Island as suitable for their needs. In 1790, they crashed the ship on the rocky coast and set her afire, thus at once eliminating the possibility of escape, assuring an urgent commitment to their new life, and destroying any evidence that might have been spotted by a passing vessel.

Again, the hopeful mutineers found only a fallen Eden. Eking out an existence on the mountainous, isolated island inevitably brought out the worst in nearly everyone. Quarrels over food, property rights, and particularly sexual access to the minority of women fueled resentment that finally boiled over into armed rebellion—Tahitian wives against Tahitian husbands, Tahitian wives against their white husbands, whites against natives, whites against whites—all resulting in bloodshed and death. In 1794, during a revolt fraught with shifting allegiances and treachery, Christian was killed by a Tahitian man whose wife Christian had forcibly seized earlier. All but four of the other mutineers were also killed over the course of a few days, along with several of the Tahitian men.

A later casualty was the heavily bearded, prodigiously tattooed William McCoy, a sullen loner who had had only one friend on the *Bounty*—the violent, hotheaded Matthew Quintal. McCoy, who had once worked in a distillery, had experimented tirelessly and had finally achieved success in a months-long quest to distill alcohol from a native root called *Ti* (*Cordyline terminalis*), but his unrestrained enthusiasm over his discovery resulted in his almost constant stupefaction. Ultimately, McCoy staggered over the edge of a cliff while in a drunken haze, dying on impact with the rocky coastline below.

When the American ship *Topaz* under the command of Captain Mayhew Folger reached Pitcairn in 1808, there remained but one surviving mutineer, Alexander Smith, also known as "Restless Jack" Adams. The second generation of Pitcairn's inhabitants had been living peaceably, fortified by the instruction of Adams, who had brought a Bible to the island and who took the education of the children as his solemn responsibility. After such violent origins, Pitcairn became one of the most abstemious, cooperative, and peaceful communities in the Pacific.

We pick up the Pitcairn story over a century later, in December of 1900. The *Pyrenees*, a 2,234-ton, four-masted, steel bark from Glasgow, carrying wheat and barley, was under the command of Capt. Robert Bryce. Its cargo on fire, the *Pyrenees* called at Pitcairn with the hope of beaching the ship in order to save what they could of cargo, vessel, and crew. Unfortunately, there is nowhere on the island to beach a ship of that size safely—ironically, one of the very reasons the island was chosen by the mutineers in 1790.

One of the island's inhabitants, James Russell McCoy, learning of their plight, came aboard and suggested that the captain make for Mangareva, about a day's sail away, where it was much easier and safer to beach the ship. Fifty-five-year-old McCoy, great-grandson of *Bounty* mutineer William McCoy (and, through his mother, also a relative of Fletcher Christian), was a deeply spiritual man who had joined with most of the other residents of Pitcairn in a mass conversion to Seventh Day Adventism in 1890. A practical and effective leader, McCoy had been elected Magistrate on Pitcairn. He served with credit in political offices through his sixty-second year, finally devoting his later years to missionary work away from Pitcairn. Faced with the *Pyrenees* crisis, McCoy unhesitatingly accepted the challenge and successfully guided the ship to Mangareva, a twenty-eight-hour voyage. There the vessel was successfully beached and the fire extinguished.[4]

Supplied with some of this information, London's genius transforms the details by introducing his larger concepts, changing an exciting episode into an epic quest. Altering the captain's name from Bryce to Davenport, London opens "The Seed of McCoy" with the appearance of the *Pyrenees* off the coast of Pitcairn, her cargo of wheat on fire and the ship in imminent danger of total combustion. In the fiction as in the historical record, it is Captain Davenport's intention to run the ship aground to try to save her crew. They will find the task far from easy.

Perhaps the most interesting feature of "The Seed of McCoy" is the light it seems to shed on the vigorous imagination of its author. Taking an incident that was, no doubt, harrowing enough for its participants, but really little more than an exciting anecdote of South Seas lore, London crafted it into a great deal more. Weaving biblical allusions into the story of the mutiny on the *Bounty*, London was able to create a mythic tale of sin and redemption, in which the wickednesses of the mutinous McCoy are expiated by the selflessness of his calmly heroic great-grandson.

On February 25, 1908, the day after London completed the manuscript of his novel *Martin Eden*, the author began writing "The Seed of McCoy." At nearly 11,000 words, it is one of the longest of his Pacific tales. On March 25, London mailed the finished story to his stateside agent, Charmian's aunt, Ninetta Eames. She submitted it to several magazines before it was accepted by *Century* and published in April 1909. London received $750 for this story—a record matched by none of the other stories in the present collection. The illustrations are by W. J. Aylward, who also had done the pictures for London's 1904 classic *The Sea-Wolf*.

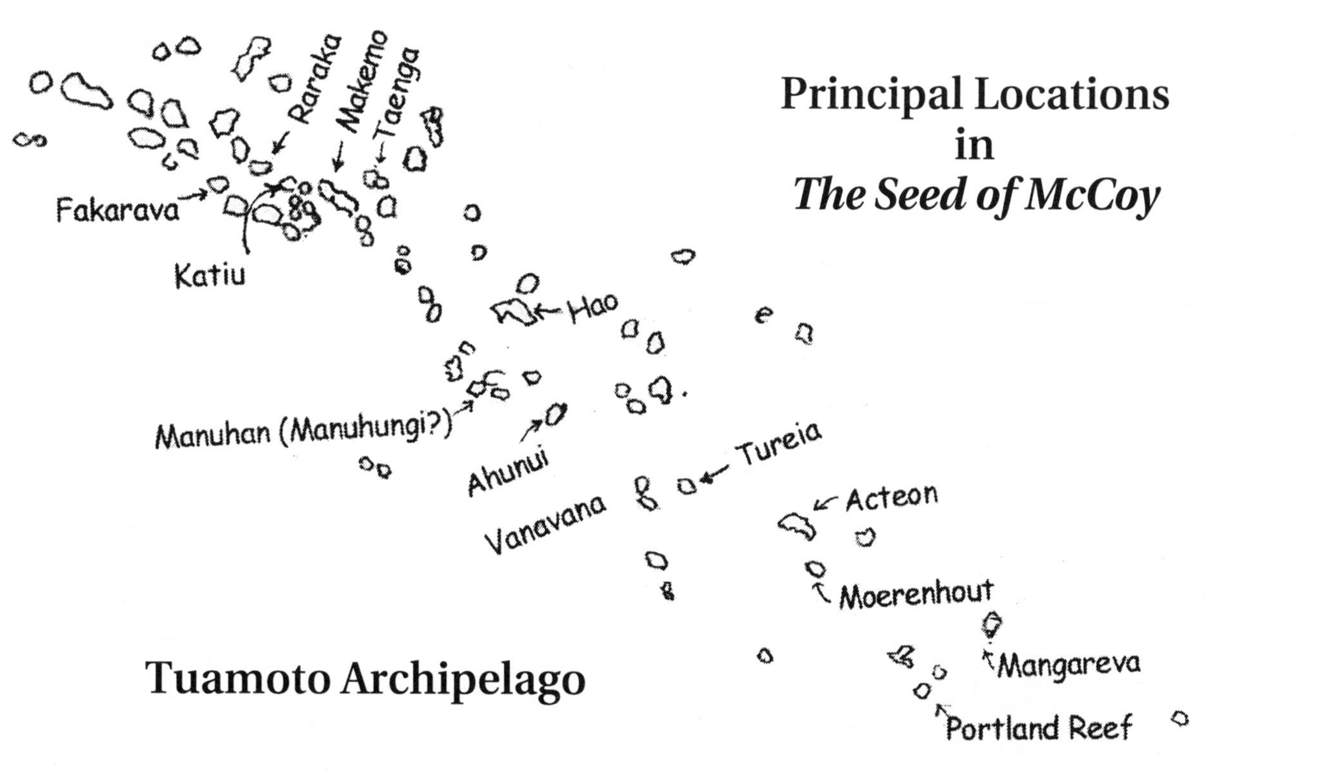
Principal Locations
in
The Seed of McCoy
Tuamoto Archipelago
Fakarava
Katiu
Raraka
Makemo
Taenga
Hao
Manuhan (Manuhungi?)
Ahunui
Vanavana
Tureia
Acteon
Moerenhout
Mangareva
Portland Reef
Pitcairn Island

THE SEED OF McCOY

The *Pyrenees*, her iron sides pressed low in the water by her cargo of wheat, rolled sluggishly, and made it easy for the man who was climbing aboard from out a tiny outrigger canoe. As his eyes came level with the rail, so that he could see inboard, it seemed to him that he saw a dim, almost indiscernible haze. It was more like an illusion, like a blurring film that had spread abruptly over his eyes. He felt an inclination to brush it away, and the same instant he thought that he was growing old and that it was time to send to San Francisco for a pair of spectacles.

As he came over the rail he cast a glance aloft at the tall masts, and, next, at the pumps. They were not working. There seemed nothing the matter with the big ship, and he wondered why she had hoisted the signal of distress. He thought of his happy islanders, and hoped it was not disease. Perhaps the ship was short of water or provisions. He shook hands with the captain whose gaunt face and care-worn eyes made no secret of the trouble, whatever it was. At the same moment the newcomer was aware of a faint, indefinable smell. It seemed like that of burnt bread, but different.

He glanced curiously about him. Twenty feet away a weary-faced sailor was calking the deck. As his eyes lingered on the man, he saw suddenly arise from under his hands a faint spiral of haze that curled and twisted and was gone. By now he had reached the deck. His bare feet were pervaded by a dull warmth that quickly penetrated the thick calluses. He knew now the nature of the ship's distress. His eyes roved swiftly forward, where the full crew of weary-faced sailors regarded him eagerly. The glance from his liquid brown eyes swept over them like a benediction, soothing them, rapping them about as in the mantle of a great peace. "How long has she been afire, Captain?" he asked in a voice so gentle and unperturbed that it was as the cooing of a dove.

At first the captain felt the peace and content of it stealing in upon him; then the consciousness of all that he had gone through and was going through smote him, and he was resentful. By what right did this ragged beachcomber, in dungaree trousers and a cotton shirt, suggest such a thing as peace and content to him and his overwrought, exhausted soul? The captain did not reason this; it was the unconscious process of emotion that caused his resentment.

"Fifteen days," he answered shortly. "Who are you?"

"My name is McCoy," came the answer in tones that breathed tenderness and compassion.

"I mean, are you the pilot?"

McCoy passed the benediction of his gaze over the tall, heavy-shouldered man with the haggard, unshaven face who had joined the captain.

"I am as much a pilot as anybody," was McCoy's answer. "We are all pilots here, Captain, and I know every inch of these waters."

But the captain was impatient.

"What I want is some of the authorities. I want to talk with them, and blame quick."

"Then I'll do just as well."

Again that insidious suggestion of peace, and his ship a raging furnace beneath his feet! The captain's eyebrows lifted impatiently and nervously, and his fist clenched as if he were about to strike a blow with it.

"Who in hell are you?" he demanded.

"I am the chief magistrate," was the reply in a voice that was still the softest and gentlest imaginable.

The tall, heavy-shouldered man broke out in a harsh laugh that was partly amusement, but mostly hysterical. Both he and the captain regarded McCoy with incredulity and amazement. That this barefooted beachcomber should possess such high-sounding dignity was inconceivable. His cotton shirt, unbuttoned, exposed a grizzled chest and the fact that there was no undershirt beneath. A worn straw hat failed to hide the ragged gray hair. Halfway down his chest descended an untrimmed patriarchal beard. In any slop shop, two shillings would have outfitted him complete as he stood before them.

"Any relation to the McCoy of the *Bounty*?" the captain asked.

"He was my great-grandfather."

"Oh," the captain said, then bethought himself. "My name is Davenport, and this is my first mate, Mr. Konig."

They shook hands.

"And now to business." The captain spoke quickly, the urgency of a great haste pressing his speech. "We've been on fire for over two weeks. She's ready to break all hell loose any moment. That's why I held for Pitcairn. I want to beach her, or scuttle her, and save the hull."

"Then you made a mistake, Captain," said McCoy. "You should have slacked away for Mangareva. There's a beautiful beach there, in a lagoon where the water is like a mill pond."

"But we're here, ain't we?" the first mate demanded. "That's the point. We're here, and we've got to do something."

McCoy shook his head kindly.

"You can do nothing here. There is no beach. There isn't even anchorage."

"Gammon!" said the mate.[5] "Gammon!" he repeated loudly, as the captain signaled him to be more soft spoken. "You can't tell me that sort of stuff. Where d'ye keep your own boats, hey—your schooner, or cutter, or whatever you have? Hey? Answer me that."

McCoy smiled as gently as he spoke. His smile was a caress, an embrace that surrounded the tired mate and sought to draw him into the quietude and rest of McCoy's tranquil soul.

"We have no schooner or cutter," he replied. "And we carry our canoes to the top of the cliff."

"You've got to show me," snorted the mate. "How d'ye get around to the other islands, heh? Tell me that."

"We don't get around. As governor of Pitcairn, I sometimes go. When I was younger, I was away a great deal—sometimes on the trading schooners, but mostly on the missionary brig. But she's gone now, and we depend on passing vessels. Sometimes we have had as high as six calls in one year. At other times, a year, and even longer, has gone by without one passing ship. Yours is the first in seven months."

"And you mean to tell me—" the mate began.

But Captain Davenport interfered.

"Enough of this. We're losing time. What is to be done, Mr. McCoy?"

The old man turned his brown eyes, sweet as a woman's, shoreward, and both captain and mate followed his gaze around from the lonely rock of Pitcairn to the crew clustering forward and waiting anxiously for the announcement of a decision. McCoy did not hurry. He thought smoothly and slowly, step by step, with the certitude of a mind that was never vexed or outraged by life.

"The wind is light now," he said finally. "There is a heavy current setting to the westward."

"That's what made us fetch to leeward," the captain interrupted, desiring to vindicate his seamanship.

"Yes, that is what fetched you to leeward," McCoy went on. "Well, you can't work up against this current today. And if you did, there is no beach. Your ship will be a total loss."

He paused, and captain and mate looked despair at each other.

"But I will tell you what you can do. The breeze will freshen tonight around midnight—see those tails of clouds and that thickness to windward, beyond the point there? That's where she'll come from, out of the southeast, hard. It is three hundred miles to Mangareva. Square away for it. There is a beautiful bed for your ship there."

The mate shook his head.

"Come in to the cabin, and we'll look at the chart," said the captain.

McCoy found a stifling, poisonous atmosphere in the pent cabin. Stray waftures of invisible gases bit his eyes and made them sting. The deck was hotter, almost unbearably hot to his bare feet. The sweat poured out of his body. He looked almost with apprehension about him. This malignant, internal heat was astounding. It was a marvel that the cabin did not burst into flames. He had a feeling as if of being in a huge bake oven where the heat might at any moment increase tremendously and shrivel him up like a blade of grass.

As he lifted one foot and rubbed the hot sole against the leg of his trousers, the mate laughed in a savage, snarling fashion.

"The anteroom of hell," he said. "Hell herself is right down there under your feet."[6]

"It's hot!" McCoy cried involuntarily, mopping his face with a bandana handkerchief.

"Here's Mangareva," the captain said, bending over the table and pointing to a black speck in the midst of the white blankness of the chart. "And here, in between, is another island. Why not run for that?"

McCoy did not look at the chart.

"That's Crescent Island," he answered. "It is uninhabited, and it is only two or three feet above water. Lagoon, but no entrance. No, Mangareva is the nearest place for your purpose."

"Mangareva it is, then," said Captain Davenport, interrupting the mate's growling objection. "Call the crew aft, Mr. Konig."

The sailors obeyed, shuffling wearily along the deck and painfully endeavoring to make haste. Exhaustion was evident in every movement. The cook came out of his galley to hear, and the cabin boy hung about near him.

When Captain Davenport had explained the situation and announced his intention of running for Mangareva, an uproar broke out. Against a background of throaty rumbling arose inarticulate cries of rage, with here and there a distinct curse, or word, or phrase. A shrill Cockney voice soared and dominated for a moment, crying: "Gawd! After bein' in 'ell for fifteen days—an' now e wants us to sail this floatin' 'ell to sea again?"

The captain could not control them, but McCoy's gentle presence seemed to rebuke and calm them, and the muttering and cursing died away, until the full crew, save here and there an anxious face directed at the captain, yearned dumbly toward the green clad peaks and beetling coast of Pitcairn.

Soft as a spring zephyr was the voice of McCoy: "Captain, I thought I heard some of them say they were starving."

"Ay," was the answer, "and so we are. I've had a sea biscuit and a spoonful of salmon in the last two days. We're on whack.[7] You see, when we discovered the fire, we battened down immediately to suffocate the fire. And then we found how little food there was in the pantry. But it was too late. We didn't dare break out the lazarette. Hungry? I'm just as hungry as they are."

He spoke to the men again, and again the throat rumbling and cursing arose, their faces convulsed and animal-like with rage. The second and third mates had joined the captain, standing behind

When Captain Davenport had explained the situation . . . an uproar arose.

him at the break of the poop. Their faces were set and expressionless; they seemed bored, more than anything else, by this mutiny of the crew. Captain Davenport glanced questioningly at his first mate, and that person merely shrugged his shoulders in token of his helplessness.

"You see," the captain said to McCoy, "you can't compel sailors to leave the safe land and go to sea on a burning vessel. She has been their floating coffin for over two weeks now. They are worked out, and starved out, and they've got enough of her. We'll beat up for Pitcairn."

But the wind was light, the *Pyrenees'* bottom was foul, and she could not beat up against the strong westerly current. At the end of two hours she had lost three miles. The sailors worked eagerly, as if by main strength they could compel the *Pyrenees* against the adverse elements. But steadily, port tack and starboard tack, she sagged off to the westward. The captain paced restlessly up and down, pausing occasionally to survey the vagrant smoke wisps and to trace them back to the portions of the deck from which they sprang. The carpenter was engaged constantly in attempting to locate such places, and, when he succeeded, in calking them tighter and tighter.

"Well, what do you think?" the captain finally asked McCoy, who was watching the carpenter with all a child's interest and curiosity in his eyes.

McCoy looked shoreward, where the land was disappearing in the thickening haze.

"I think it would be better to square away for Mangareva. With that breeze that is coming, you'll be there tomorrow evening."

"But what if the fire breaks out? It is liable to do it any moment."

"Have your boats ready in the falls. The same breeze will carry your boats to Mangareva if the ship burns out from under."

Captain Davenport debated for a moment, and then McCoy heard the question he had not wanted to hear, but which he knew was surely coming.

"I have no chart of Mangareva. On the general chart it is only a fly speck. I would not know where to look for the entrance into the lagoon. Will you come along and pilot her in for me?"

McCoy's serenity was unbroken.

"Yes, Captain," he said, with the same quiet unconcern with which he would have accepted an invitation to dinner; "I'll go with you to Mangareva."

Again the crew was called aft, and the captain spoke to them from the break of the poop.

"We've tried to work her up, but you see how we've lost ground. She's setting off in a two-knot current. This gentleman is the Honorable McCoy, Chief Magistrate and Governor of Pitcairn Island. He will come along with us to Mangareva. So you see the situation is not so dangerous. He would not make such an offer if he thought he was going to lose his life. Besides, whatever risk there is, if he of his own free will come on board and take it, we can do no less. What do you say for Mangareva?"

This time there was no uproar. McCoy's presence, the surety and calm that seemed to radiate from him, had had its effect. They conferred with one another in low voices. There was little urging. They were virtually unanimous, and they shoved the Cockney out as their spokesman. That worthy was overwhelmed with consciousness of the heroism of himself and his mates, and with flashing eyes he cried:

"By Gawd! If 'e will, we will!"

The crew mumbled its assent and started forward.

"One moment, Captain," McCoy said, as the other was turning to give orders to the mate. "I must go ashore first."

Mr. Konig was thunderstruck, staring at McCoy as if he were a madman.

"Go ashore!" the captain cried. "What for? It will take you three hours to get there in your canoe."

McCoy measured the distance of the land away, and nodded.

"Yes, it is six now. I won't get ashore till nine. The people cannot be assembled earlier than ten. As the breeze freshens up tonight, you can begin to work up against it, and pick me up at daylight tomorrow morning."

"In the name of reason and common sense," the captain burst forth, "what do you want to assemble the people for? Don't you realize that my ship is burning beneath me?"

McCoy was as placid as a summer sea, and the other's anger produced not the slightest ripple upon it.

"Yes, Captain," he cooed in his dove-like voice. "I do realize that your ship is burning. That is why I am going with you to Mangareva. But I must get permission to go with you. It is our custom. It is an important matter when the governor leaves the island. The people's interests are at stake, and so they have the right to vote their permission or refusal. But they will give it, I know that."

"Are you sure?"

"Quite sure."

"Then if you know they will give it, why bother with getting it? Think of the delay—a whole night."

"It is our custom," was the imperturbable reply. "Also, I am the governor, and I must make arrangements for the conduct of the island during my absence."

"But it is only a twenty-four-hour run to Mangareva," the captain objected. "Suppose it took you six times that long to return to windward; that would bring you back by the end of a week."

McCoy smiled his large, benevolent smile.

"Very few vessels come to Pitcairn, and when they do, they are usually from San Francisco or from around the Horn. I shall be fortunate if I get back in six months. I may be away a year, and I may have to go to San Francisco in order to find a vessel that will bring me back. My father once left Pitcairn to be gone three months, and two years passed before he could get back. Then, too, you are short of food. If you have to take to the boats, and the weather comes up bad, you may be days in reaching land. I can bring off two canoe loads of food in the morning. Dried bananas will be best. As the breeze freshens, you beat up against it. The nearer you are, the bigger loads I can bring off. Goodby."

He held out his hand. The captain shook it, and was reluctant to let go. He seemed to cling to it as a drowning sailor clings to a life buoy.

"How do I know you will come back in the morning?" he asked.

"Yes, that's it!" cried the mate. "How do we know but what he's skinning out to save his own hide?"

McCoy did not speak. He looked at them sweetly and benignantly, and it seemed to them that they received a message from his tremendous certitude of soul.

The captain released his hand, and, with a last sweeping glance that embraced the crew in its benediction, McCoy went over the rail and descended into his canoe.

The wind freshened, and the *Pyrenees*, despite the foulness of her bottom, won half a dozen miles away from the westerly current. At daylight, with Pitcairn three miles to windward, Captain Davenport made out two canoes coming off to him. Again McCoy clambered up the side and dropped over the rail to the hot deck. He was followed by many packages of dried bananas, each package wrapped in dry leaves.

"Now, Captain," he said, "swing the yards and drive for dear life. You see, I am no navigator," he explained a few minutes later, as he stood by the captain aft, the latter with gaze wandering from aloft to overside as he estimated the *Pyrenees*' speed. "You must fetch her to Mangareva. When you have picked up the land, then I will pilot her in. What do you think she is making?"

"Eleven," Captain Davenport answered, with a final glance at the water rushing past.

"Eleven. Let me see, if she keeps up that gait, we'll sight Mangareva between eight and nine o'clock tomorrow morning. I'll have her on the beach by ten or by eleven at latest. And then your troubles will be all over."

It almost seemed to the captain that the blissful moment had already arrived, such was the persuasive convincingness of McCoy. Captain Davenport had been under the fearful strain of navigating his burning ship for over two weeks, and he was beginning to feel that he had had enough.

A heavier flaw of wind struck the back of his neck and whistled by his ears. He measured the weight of it, and looked quickly overside.

"The wind is making all the time," he announced. "The old girl's doing nearer twelve than eleven right now. If this keeps up, we'll be shortening down tonight."

All day the *Pyrenees*, carrying her load of living fire, tore across the foaming sea. By nightfall, royals and topgallantsails were in, and she flew on into the darkness, with great, crested seas roaring after her. The auspicious wind had had its effect, and fore and aft a visible brightening was apparent. In the second dog-watch some careless soul started a song, and by eight bells the whole crew was singing.

Captain Davenport had his blankets brought up and spread on top the house.

"I've forgotten what sleep is," he explained to McCoy. "I'm all in. But give me a call at any time you think necessary."

At three in the morning he was aroused by a gentle tugging at his arm. He sat up quickly, bracing himself against the skylight, stupid yet from his heavy sleep. The wind was thrumming its war song in the rigging, and a wild sea was buffeting the *Pyrenees*. Amidships she was wallowing first one rail under and then the other, flooding the waist more often than not. McCoy was shouting something he could not hear. He reached out, clutched the other by the shoulder, and drew him close so that his own ear was close to the other's lips.

"It's three o'clock," came McCoy's voice, still retaining its dove-like quality, but curiously muffled, as if from a long way off. "We've run two hundred and fifty. Crescent Island is only thirty miles away, somewhere there dead ahead. There's no lights on it. If we keep running, we'll pile up, and lose ourselves as well as the ship."

"What d' ye think—heave to?"

"Yes; heave to till daylight. It will only put us back four hours."

So the *Pyrenees*, with her cargo of fire, was hove to, bitting the teeth of the gale and fighting and smashing the pounding seas. She was a shell, filled with a conflagration, and on the outside of the shell, clinging precariously, the little motes of men, by pull and haul, helped her in the battle.

"It is most unusual, this gale," McCoy told the captain, in the lee of the cabin. "By rights there should be no gale at this time of the year. But everything about the weather has been unusual. There has been a stoppage of the trades, and now it's howling right out of the trade quarter." He waved his hand into the darkness, as if his vision could dimly penetrate for hundreds of miles. "It is off to the westward. There is something big making off there somewhere—a hurricane or something. We're lucky to be so far to the eastward. But this is only a little blow," he added. "It can't last. I can tell you that much."

By daylight the gale had eased down to normal. But daylight revealed a new danger. It had come on thick. The sea was covered by a fog, or, rather, by a pearly mist that was fog-like in density, in so far as it obstructed vision, but that was no more than a film on the sea, for the sun shot it through and filled it with a glowing radiance. The deck of the *Pyrenees* was making more smoke than on the preceding day, and the cheerfulness of officers and crew had vanished. In the lee of the galley the cabin boy could be heard whimpering. It was his first voyage, and the fear of death was at his heart. The captain wandered about like a lost soul, nervously chewing his mustache, scowling, unable to make up his mind what to do.

"What do you think?" he asked, pausing by the side of McCoy, who was making a breakfast off fried bananas and a mug of water.

McCoy finished the last banana, drained the mug, and looked slowly around. In his eyes was a smile of tenderness as he said: "Well, Captain, we might as well drive as burn. Your decks are not going to hold out forever. They are hotter this morning. You haven't a pair of shoes I can wear? It is getting uncomfortable for my bare feet."

The *Pyrenees* shipped two heavy seas as she was swung off and put once more before it, and the first mate expressed a desire to have all that water down in the hold, if only it could be introduced without taking off the hatches. McCoy ducked his head into the binnacle and watched the course set.

"I'd hold her up some more, Captain," he said. "She's been making drift when hove to."

"I've set it to a point higher already," was the answer. "Isn't that enough?"

"I'd make it two points, Captain. This bit of a blow kicked that westerly current ahead faster than you imagine."

Captain Davenport compromised on a point and a half, and then went aloft, accompanied by McCoy and the first mate, to keep a lookout for land. Sail had been made, so that the *Pyrenees* was doing ten knots. The following sea was dying down rapidly. There was no break in the pearly fog, and by ten o'clock Captain Davenport was growing nervous. All hands were at their stations, ready, at the first warning of land ahead, to spring like fiends to the task of bringing the *Pyrenees* up on the wind. That land ahead, a surf-washed outer reef, would be perilously close when it revealed itself in such a fog.

Another hour passed. The three watchers aloft stared intently into the pearly radiance. "What if we miss Mangareva?" Captain Davenport asked abruptly.

McCoy, without shifting his gaze, answered softly: "Why, let her drive, captain. That is all we can do. All the Paumotus are before us. We can drive for a thousand miles through reefs and atolls. We are bound to fetch up somewhere."

"Then drive it is." Captain Davenport evidenced his intention of descending to the deck. "We've missed Mangareva.[8] God knows where the next land is. I wish I'd held her up that other half-point," he confessed a moment later. "This cursed current plays the devil with a navigator."

"The old navigators called the Paumotus the Dangerous Archipelago," McCoy said, when they had regained the poop. "This very current was partly responsible for that name."

"I was talking with a sailor chap in Sydney, once," said Mr. Konig. "He'd been trading in the Paumotus. He told me insurance was eighteen per cent. Is that right?"

McCoy smiled and nodded.

"Except that they don't insure," he explained. "The owners write off twenty per cent of the cost of their schooners each year."

"My God!" Captain Davenport groaned. "That makes the life of a schooner only five years!" He shook his head sadly, murmuring, "Bad waters! Bad waters!"

Again they went into the cabin to consult the big general chart; but the poisonous vapors drove them coughing and gasping on deck.

"Here is Moerenhout Island." Captain Davenport pointed it out on the chart, which he had spread on the house. "It can't be more than a hundred miles to leeward."

"A hundred and ten." McCoy shook his head doubtfully. "It might be done, but it is very difficult. I might beach her, and then again I might put her on the reef. A bad place, a very bad place."

"We'll take the chance," was Captain Davenport's decision, as he set about working out the course.

Sail was shortened early in the afternoon, to avoid running past in the night; and in the second dog-watch the crew manifested its regained cheerfulness. Land was so very near, and their troubles would be over in the morning.

But morning broke clear, with a blazing tropic sun. The southeast trade had swung around to the eastward, and was driving the *Pyrenees* through the water at an eight-knot clip. Captain Davenport worked up his dead reckoning, allowing generously for drift, and announced Moerenhout Island to be not more than ten miles off. The *Pyrenees* sailed the ten miles; she sailed ten miles more; and the lookouts at the three mastheads saw naught but the naked, sun-washed sea.

"But the land is there, I tell you," Captain Davenport shouted to them from the poop.

McCoy smiled soothingly, but the captain glared about him like a madman, fetched his sextant, and took a chronometer sight.

"I knew I was right, he almost shouted, when he had worked up the observation. "Twenty-one, fifty-five, south; one-thirty-six, two, west. There you are. We're eight miles to windward yet. What did you make it out, Mr. Konig?"

The first mate glanced at his own figures, and said in a low voice: "Twenty-one, fifty-five all right; but my longitude's one-thirty-six, forty-eight. That puts us considerably to leeward—"

But Captain Davenport ignored his figures with so contemptuous a silence as to make Mr. Konig grit his teeth and curse savagely under his breath.

"Keep her off," the captain ordered the man at the wheel. "Three points—steady there, as she goes!"

Then he returned to his figures and worked them over. The sweat poured from his face. He chewed his mustache, his lips, and his pencil, staring at the figures as a man might at a ghost. Suddenly, with a fierce, muscular outburst, he crumpled the scribbled paper in his fist and crushed it under foot. Mr. Konig grinned vindictively and turned away, while Captain Davenport leaned against the cabin and for half an hour spoke no word, contenting himself with gazing to leeward with an expression of musing hopelessness on his face.

"Mr. McCoy," he broke silence abruptly. "The chart indicates a group of islands, but not how many, off there to the north'ard, or nor'-nor'westward, about forty miles—the Acteon Islands. What about them?"

"There are four, all low," McCoy answered. "First to the southeast is Matuerui—no people, no entrance to the lagoon. Then comes Tenarunga. There used to be about a dozen people there, but they may be all gone now. Anyway, there is no entrance for a ship—only a boat entrance, with a fathom of water. Vehauga and Teua-raro are the other two. No entrances, no people, very low. There is no bed for the *Pyrenees* in that group. She would be a total wreck."

"Listen to that!" Captain Davenport was frantic. "No people! No entrances! What in the devil are islands good for?

"Well, then," he barked suddenly, like an excited terrier, "the chart gives a whole mess of islands off to the nor'west. What about them? What one has an entrance where I can lay my ship?"

McCoy calmly considered. He did not refer to the chart. All these islands, reefs, shoals, lagoons, entrances, and distances were marked on the chart of his memory. He knew them as the city dweller knows his buildings, streets, and alleys.

"Papakena and Vanavana are off there to the westward, or west-nor'westward a hundred miles and a bit more," he said. "One is uninhabited, and I heard that the people on the other had gone off to Cadmus Island. Anyway, neither lagoon has an entrance.

Ahunui is another hundred miles on to the nor'west. No entrance, no people."

"Well, forty miles beyond them are two islands?" Captain Davenport queried, raising his head from the chart.

McCoy shook his head.

"Paros and Manuhungi—no entrances, no people. Nengo-Nengo is forty miles beyond them, in turn, and it has no people and no entrance. But there is Hao Island. It is just the place. The lagoon is thirty miles long and five miles wide. There are plenty of people. You can usually find water. And any ship in the world can go through the entrance."

He ceased and gazed solicitously at Captain Davenport, who, bending over the chart with a pair of dividers in hand, had just emitted a low groan.

"Is there any lagoon with an entrance anywhere nearer than Hao Island?" he asked.

"No, Captain; that is the nearest."

"Well, it's three hundred and forty miles." Captain Davenport was speaking very slowly, with decision. "I won't risk the responsibility of all these lives. I'll wreck her on the Acteons. And she's a good ship, too," he added regretfully, after altering the course, this time making more allowance than ever for the westerly current.

An hour later the sky was overcast. The southeast trade still held, but the ocean was a checker board of squalls.

"We'll be there by one o'clock," Captain Davenport announced confidently. "By two o'clock at the outside. McCoy, you put her ashore on the one where the people are."

The sun did not appear again, nor, at one o'clock, was any land to be seen. Captain Davenport looked astern at the *Pyrenees*' canting wake.

"Good Lord!" he cried. "An easterly current? Look at that!"

Mr. Konig was incredulous. McCoy was noncommittal, though he said that in the Paumotus there was no reason why it should not be an easterly current. A few minutes later a squall robbed the *Pyrenees* temporarily of all her wind, and she was left rolling heavily in the trough.

"Where's that deep lead? Over with it, you there!" Captain Davenport held the lead line and watched it sag off to the northeast. "There, look at that! Take hold of it for yourself."

McCoy and the mate tried it, and felt the line thrumming and vibrating savagely to the grip of the tidal stream.

"A four-knot current," said Mr. Konig.

"An easterly current instead of a westerly," said Captain Davenport, glaring accusingly at McCoy, as if to cast the blame for it upon him.

"That is one of the reasons, Captain, for insurance being eighteen per cent in these waters," McCoy answered cheerfully. "You can never tell. The currents are always changing. There was a man who wrote books, I forget his name, in the yacht *Casco*. He missed Takaroa by thirty miles and fetched Tikei, all because of the shifting currents.[9] You are up to windward now, and you'd better keep off a few points."

"But how much has this current set me?" the captain demanded irately. "How am I to know how much to keep off?"

"I don't know, Captain," McCoy said with great gentleness. The wind returned, and the *Pyrenees*, her deck smoking and shimmering in the bright gray light, ran off dead to leeward. Then she worked back, port tack and starboard tack, crisscrossing her track, combing the sea for the Acteon Islands, which the masthead lookouts failed to sight.

Captain Davenport was beside himself. His rage took the form of sullen silence, and he spent the afternoon in pacing the poop or leaning against the weather shrouds. At nightfall, without even consulting McCoy, he squared away and headed into the northwest. Mr. Konig, surreptitiously consulting chart and binnacle, and McCoy, openly and innocently consulting the binnacle, knew that they were running for Hao Island. By midnight the squalls ceased, and the stars came out. Captain Davenport was cheered by the promise of a clear day.

"I'll get an observation in the morning," he told McCoy, "though what my latitude is, is a puzzler. But I'll use the Sumner method, and settle that. Do you know the Sumner line?"[10]

And thereupon he explained it in detail to McCoy.

The day proved clear, the trade blew steadily out of the east, and the Pyrenees just as steadily logged her nine knots. Both the captain and mate worked out the position on a Sumner line, and agreed, and at noon agreed again, and verified the morning sights by the noon sights.

"Another twenty-four hours and we'll be there," Captain Davenport assured McCoy. "It's a miracle the way the old girl's decks hold out. But they can't last. They can't last. Look at them smoke, more and more every day. Yet it was a tight deck to begin with, fresh-calked in 'Frisco. I was surprised when the fire first broke out and we battened down. Look at that!"

He broke off to gaze with dropped jaw at a spiral of smoke that coiled and twisted in the lee of the mizzenmast twenty feet above the deck.

"Now, how did that get there?" he demanded indignantly.

Beneath it there was no smoke. Crawling up from the deck, sheltered from the wind by the mast, by some freak it took form and visibility at that height. It writhed away from the mast, and for a moment overhung the captain like some threatening portent. The next moment the wind whisked it away, and the captain's jaw returned to place.

"As I was saying, when we first battened down, I was surprised. It was a tight deck, yet it leaked smoke like a sieve. And we've calked and calked ever since. There must be tremendous pressure underneath to drive so much smoke through."

That afternoon the sky became overcast again, and squally, drizzly weather set in. The wind shifted back and forth between southeast and northeast, and at midnight the *Pyrenees* was caught aback by a sharp squall from the southwest, from which point the wind continued to blow intermittently.

"We won't make Hao until ten or eleven," Captain Davenport complained at seven in the morning, when the fleeting promise of the sun had been erased by hazy cloud masses in the eastern sky. And the next moment he was plaintively demanding, "And what are the currents doing?"

Lookouts at the mastheads could report no land, and the day passed in drizzling calms and violent squalls. By nightfall a heavy sea began to make from the west. The barometer had fallen to 29.50. There was no wind, and still the ominous sea continued to increase. Soon the *Pyrenees* was rolling madly in the huge waves that marched in an unending procession from out of the darkness of the west. Sail was shortened as fast as both watches could work, and, when the tired crew had finished, its grumbling and complaining voices, peculiarly animal-like and menacing, could be heard in the darkness. Once the starboard watch was called aft to lash down and make secure, and the men openly advertised their sullenness and unwillingness. Every slow movement was a protest and a threat. The atmosphere was moist and sticky like mucilage, and in the absence of wind all hands seemed to pant and gasp for air. The sweat stood out on faces and bare arms, and Captain Davenport for one, his face more gaunt and care-worn than ever, and his eyes troubled and staring, was oppressed by a feeling of impending calamity.

"It's off to the westward," McCoy said encouragingly. "At worst, we'll be only on the edge of it."

But Captain Davenport refused to be comforted, and by the light of a lantern read up the chapter in his Epitome that related to the strategy of shipmasters in cyclonic storms. From somewhere amidships the silence was broken by a low whimpering from the cabin boy.

"Oh, shut up!" Captain Davenport yelled suddenly and with such force as to startle every man on board and to frighten the offender into a wild wail of terror.

"Mr. Konig," the captain said in a voice that trembled with rage and nerves, "will you kindly step for'ard and stop that brat's mouth with a deck mop?"

But it was McCoy who went forward, and in a few minutes had the boy comforted and asleep.

Shortly before daybreak the first breath of air began to move from out the southeast, increasing swiftly to a stiff and stiffer breeze. All hands were on deck waiting for what might be behind it.

"We're all right now, Captain," said McCoy, standing close to his shoulder. "The hurricane is to the west'ard, and we are south of it. This breeze is the in-suck. It won't blow any harder. You can begin to put sail on her."

"But what's the good? Where shall I sail? This is the second day without observations, and we should have sighted Hao Island yesterday morning. Which way does it bear, north, south, east, or what? Tell me that, and I'll make sail in a jiffy."

"I am no navigator, Captain," McCoy said in his mild way.

"I used to think I was one," was the retort, "before I got into these Paumotus."

At mid-day the cry of "Breakers ahead!" was heard from the lookout. The *Pyrenees* was kept off, and sail after sail was loosed and sheeted home. The *Pyrenees* was sliding through the water and fighting a current that threatened to set her down upon the breakers. Officers and men were working like mad, cook and cabin boy, Captain Davenport himself, and McCoy all lending a hand. It was a close shave. It was a low shoal, a bleak and perilous place over which the seas broke unceasingly, where no man could live, and on which not even sea birds could rest. The *Pyrenees* was swept within a hundred yards of it before the wind carried her clear, and at this moment the panting crew, its work done, burst out in a torrent of curses upon the head of McCoy—of McCoy who had come on board, and proposed the run to Mangareva, and lured them all away from the safety of Pitcairn Island to certain destruction in this baffling and terrible stretch of sea. But McCoy's tranquil soul was undisturbed. He smiled at them with simple and gracious benevolence, and, somehow, the exalted goodness of him seemed to penetrate to their dark and somber souls, shaming them, and from very shame stilling the curses vibrating in their throats.

"Bad waters! Bad waters!" Captain Davenport was murmuring as his ship forged clear; but he broke off abruptly to gaze at the shoal which should have been dead astern, but which was already on the *Pyrenees*' weather-quarter and working up rapidly to windward.

He sat down and buried his face in his hands. And the first mate saw, and McCoy saw, and the crew saw, what he had seen. South of the shoal an easterly current had set them down upon it; north of the shoal an equally swift westerly current had clutched the ship and was sweeping her away.

"I've heard of these Paumotus before," the captain groaned, lifting his blanched face from his hands. "Captain Moyendale told me about them after losing his ship on them. And I laughed at him behind his back. God forgive me, I laughed at him. What shoal is that?" he broke off, to ask McCoy.

"I don't know, Captain."

"Why don't you know?"

"Because I never saw it before, and because I have never heard of it. I do know that it is not charted. These waters have never been thoroughly surveyed."

"Then you don't know where we are?"

"No more than you do," McCoy said gently.

"Then you don't know where we are?"

At four in the afternoon cocoanut trees were sighted, apparently growing out of the water. A little later the low land of an atoll was raised above the sea.

"I know where we are now, Captain." McCoy lowered the glasses from his eyes. "That's Resolution Island. We are forty miles beyond Hao Island, and the wind is in our teeth."

"Get ready to beach her then. Where's the entrance?"

"There's only a canoe passage. But now that we know where we are, we can run for Barclay de Tolley. It is only one hundred and twenty miles from here, due nor'-nor'west. With this breeze we can be there by nine o'clock tomorrow morning."

Captain Davenport consulted the chart and debated with himself.

"If we wreck her here," McCoy added, "we'd have to make the run to Barclay de Tolley in the boats just the same."

The captain gave his orders, and once more the *Pyrenees* swung off for another run across the inhospitable sea.

And the middle of the next afternoon saw despair and mutiny on her smoking deck. The current had accelerated, the wind had slackened, and the Pyrenees had sagged off to the west. The lookout sighted Barclay de Tolley to the eastward, barely visible from the masthead, and vainly and for hours the *Pyrenees* tried to beat up to it. Ever, like a mirage, the cocoanut trees hovered on the horizon, visible only from the masthead. From the deck they were hidden by the bulge of the world.

Again Captain Davenport consulted McCoy and the chart. Makemo lay seventy-five miles to the southwest. Its lagoon was thirty miles long, and its entrance was excellent. When Captain Davenport gave his orders, the crew refused duty. They announced that they had had enough of hell fire under their feet. There was the land. What if the ship could not make it? They could make it in the boats. Let her burn, then. Their lives amounted to something to them. They had served faithfully the ship, now they were going to serve themselves.

They sprang to the boats, brushing the second and third mates out of the way, and proceeded to swing the boats out and to prepare to lower away. Captain Davenport and the first mate, revolvers in hand, were advancing to the break of the poop, when McCoy, who had climbed on top of the cabin, began to speak.

He spoke to the sailors, and at the first sound of his dovelike, cooing voice they paused to hear. He extended to them his own ineffable serenity and peace. His soft voice and simple thoughts flowed out to them in a magic stream, soothing them against their wills. Long forgotten things came back to them, and some remembered lullaby songs of childhood and the content and rest of the mother's arm at the end of the day. There was no more trouble, no more danger, no more irk, in all the world. Everything was as it should be, and it was only a matter of course that they should turn their backs upon the land and put to sea once more with hell fire hot beneath their feet.

McCoy spoke simply; but it was not what he spoke. It was his personality that spoke more eloquently than any word he could utter. It was an alchemy of soul occultly subtile and profoundly deep—a mysterious emanation of the spirit, seductive, sweetly humble, and terribly imperious. It was illumination in the dark crypts of their souls, a compulsion of purity and gentleness vastly greater than that which resided in the shining, death-spitting revolvers of the officers.

The men wavered reluctantly where they stood, and those who had loosed the turns made them fast again. Then one, and then another, and then all of them, began to sidle awkwardly away.

McCoy's face was beaming with childlike pleasure as he descended from the top of the cabin. There was no trouble. For that matter there had been no trouble averted. There never had been any trouble, for there was no place for such in the blissful world in which he lived.

"You hypnotized 'em," Mr. Konig grinned at him, speaking in a low voice.

"Those boys are good," was the answer. "Their hearts are good. They have had a hard time, and they have worked hard, and they will work hard to the end."

Mr. Konig had not time to reply. His voice was ringing out orders, the sailors were springing to obey, and the *Pyrenees* was paying slowly off from the wind until her bow should point in the direction of Makemo.

The wind was very light, and after sundown almost ceased. It was insufferably warm, and fore and aft men sought vainly to sleep. The deck was too hot to lie upon, and poisonous vapors, oozing through the seams, crept like evil spirits over the ship, stealing into the nostrils and windpipes of the unwary and causing fits of sneezing and coughing. The stars blinked lazily in the dim vault overhead; and the full moon, rising in the east, touched with its light the myriads of wisps and threads and spidery films of smoke that intertwined and writhed and twisted along the deck, over the rails, and up the masts and shrouds.

"Tell me," Captain Davenport said, rubbing his smarting eyes, "what happened with that *Bounty* crowd after they reached Pitcairn? The account I read said they burnt the *Bounty*, and that they were not discovered until many years later. But what happened in the meantime? I've always been curious to know. They were men with their necks in the rope. There were some native men, too. And then there were women. That made it look like trouble right from the jump."

"There was trouble," McCoy answered. "They were bad men. They quarreled about the women right away. One of the mutineers, Williams, lost his wife. All the women were Tahitian women. His wife fell from the cliffs when hunting sea birds. Then he took the wife of one of the native men away from him. All the native men were made very angry by this, and they killed off nearly all the mutineers. Then the mutineers that escaped killed off all the native men. The women helped. And the natives killed each other. Everybody killed everybody. They were terrible men.

"Timiti was killed by two other natives while they were combing his hair in friendship. The white men had sent them to do it. Then the white men killed them. The wife of Tullaloo killed him in a cave because she wanted a white man for husband. They were very wicked. God had hidden His face from them. At the end of two years all the native men were murdered, and all the white men except four. They were Young, John Adams, McCoy, who was my great-grandfather, and Quintal. He was a very bad man, too. Once, just because his wife did not catch enough fish for him, he bit off her ear."

"They were a bad lot!" Mr. Konig exclaimed.

"Yes, they were very bad," McCoy agreed and went on serenely cooing of the blood and lust of his iniquitous ancestry. "My great-grandfather escaped murder in order to die by his own hand. He made a still and manufactured alcohol from the roots of the ti-plant. Quintal was his chum, and they got drunk together all the time. At last McCoy got delirium tremens, tied a rock to his neck, and jumped into the sea.

"Quintal's wife, the one whose ear he bit off, also got killed by falling from the cliffs. Then Quintal went to Young and demanded his wife, and went to Adams and demanded his wife. Adams and Young were afraid of Quintal. They knew he would kill them. So they killed him, the two of them together, with a hatchet. Then Young died. And that was about all the trouble they had."

"I should say so," Captain Davenport snorted. "There was nobody left to kill."

"You see, God had hidden His face," McCoy said.[11]

By morning no more than a faint air was blowing from the eastward, and, unable to make appreciable southing by it, Captain

Davenport hauled up full-and-by on the port track. He was afraid of that terrible westerly current which had cheated him out of so many ports of refuge. All day the calm continued, and all night, while the sailors, on a short ration of dried banana, were grumbling. Also, they were growing weak and complaining of stomach pains caused by the straight banana diet. All day the current swept the *Pyrenees* to the westward, while there was no wind to bear her south. In the middle of the first dogwatch, cocoanut trees were sighted due south, their tufted heads rising above the water and marking the low-lying atoll beneath.

"That is Taenga Island," McCoy said. "We need a breeze tonight, or else we'll miss Makemo."

"What's become of the southeast trade?" the captain demanded. "Why don't it blow? What's the matter?"

"It is the evaporation from the big lagoons—there are so many of them," McCoy explained. "The evaporation upsets the whole system of trades. It even causes the wind to back up and blow gales from the southwest. This is the Dangerous Archipelago, Captain."

Captain Davenport faced the old man, opened his mouth, and was about to curse, but paused and refrained. McCoy's presence was a rebuke to the blasphemies that stirred in his brain and trembled in his larynx. McCoy's influence had been growing during the many days they had been together. Captain Davenport was an autocrat of the sea, fearing no man, never bridling his tongue, and now he found himself unable to curse in the presence of this old man with the feminine brown eyes and the voice of a dove. When he realized this, Captain Davenport experienced a distinct shock. This old man was merely the seed of McCoy, of McCoy of the *Bounty*, the mutineer fleeing from the hemp that waited him in England, the McCoy who was a power for evil in the early days of blood and lust and violent death on Pitcairn Island.

Captain Davenport was not religious, yet in that moment he felt a mad impulse to cast himself at the other's feet[12]—and to say he knew not what. It was an emotion that so deeply stirred him, rather than a coherent thought, and he was aware in some vague way of his own unworthiness and smallness in the presence of this other man who possessed the simplicity of a child and the gentleness of a woman.

Of course he could not so humble himself before the eyes of his officers and men. And yet the anger that had prompted the blasphemy still raged in him. He suddenly smote the cabin with his clenched hand and cried:

"Look here, old man, I won't be beaten. These Paumotus have cheated and tricked me and made a fool of me. I refuse to be beaten. I am going to drive this ship, and drive and drive and drive clear through the Paumotus to China but what I find a bed for her. If every man deserts, I'll stay by her. I'll show the Paumotus. They can't fool me. She's a good girl, and I'll stick by her as long as there's a plank to stand on. You hear me?"

"And I'll stay with you, Captain," McCoy said.

During the night, light, baffling airs blew out of the south, and the frantic captain, with his cargo of fire, watched and measured his westward drift and went off by himself at times to curse softly so that McCoy should not hear.

Daylight showed more palms growing out of the water to the south.

"That's the leeward point of Makemo," McCoy said. "Katiu is only a few miles to the west. We may make that."

But the current, sucking between the two islands, swept them to the northwest, and at one in the afternoon they saw the palms of Katiu rise above the sea and sink back into the sea again.

A few minutes later, just as the captain had discovered that a new current from the northeast had gripped the *Pyrenees*, the masthead lookouts raised cocoanut palms in the northwest.

"It is Raraka," said McCoy. "We won't make it without wind. The current is drawing us down to the southwest. But we must watch out. A few miles farther on a current flows north and turns in a circle to the northwest. This will sweep us away from Fakarava, and Fakarava is the place for the *Pyrenees* to find her bed."

"They can sweep all they da—all they well please," Captain Davenport remarked with heat. "We'll find a bed for her somewhere just the same." But the situation on the *Pyrenees* was reaching a culmination. The deck was so hot that it seemed an increase of a few degrees would cause it to burst into flames. In many places even the heavy-soled shoes of the men were no protection, and they were compelled to step lively to avoid scorching their feet. The smoke had increased and grown more acrid. Every man on board was suffering from inflamed eyes, and they coughed and strangled like a crew of tuberculosis patients. In the afternoon the boats were swung out and equipped. The last several packages of dried bananas were stored in them, as well as the instruments of the officers. Captain Davenport even put the chronometer into the longboat, fearing the blowing up of the deck at any moment.

All night this apprehension weighed heavily on all, and in the first morning light, with hollow eyes and ghastly faces, they stared at one another as if in surprise that the *Pyrenees* still held together and that they still were alive.

Walking rapidly at times, and even occasionally breaking into an undignified hop-skip-and-run, Captain Davenport inspected his ship's deck.

"It is a matter of hours now, if not of minutes," he announced on his return to the poop.

The cry of land came down from the masthead. From the deck the land was invisible, and McCoy went aloft, while the captain took advantage of the opportunity to curse some of the bitterness out of his heart. But the cursing was suddenly stopped by a dark line on the water which he sighted to the northeast. It was not a squall, but a regular breeze—the disrupted trade wind, eight points out of its direction but resuming business once more.

"Hold her up, Captain," McCoy said as soon as he reached the poop. "That's the easterly point of Fakarava, and we'll go in through the passage full-tilt, the wind abeam, and every sail drawing."

At the end of an hour, the cocoanut trees and the low-lying land were visible from the deck. The feeling that the end of the *Pyrenees*' resistance was imminent weighed heavily on everybody. Captain Davenport had the three boats lowered and dropped short astern, a man in each to keep them apart. The *Pyrenees* closely skirted the shore, the surf-whitened atoll a bare two cable lengths away.

And a minute later the land parted, exposing a narrow passage and the lagoon beyond, a great mirror, thirty miles in length and a third as broad.

"Now, Captain."

For the last time the yards of the *Pyrenees* swung around as she obeyed the wheel and headed into the passage. The turns had scarcely been made, and nothing had been coiled down, when the men and mates swept back to the poop in panic terror. Nothing had happened, yet they averred that something was going to happen. They could not tell why. They merely knew that it was about to happen. McCoy started forward to take up his position on the bow in order to con the vessel in; but the captain gripped his arm and whirled him around.

"Do it from here," he said. "That deck's not safe. What's the matter?" he demanded the next instant. "We're standing still."

McCoy smiled.

"You are bucking a seven-knot current, Captain," he said. "That is the way the full ebb runs out of this passage."

At the end of another hour the *Pyrenees* had scarcely gained her length, but the wind freshened and she began to forge ahead.

"Better get into the boats, some of you," Captain Davenport commanded.

His voice was still ringing, and the men were just beginning to move in obedience, when the amidship deck of the *Pyrenees*, in a mass of flame and smoke, was flung upward into the sails and rigging, part of it remaining there and the rest falling into the sea. The wind being abeam was what had saved the men crowded aft. They made a blind rush to gain the boats, but McCoy's voice, carrying its convincing message of vast calm and endless time, stopped them.

"Take it easy," he was saying. "Everything is all right. Pass that boy down somebody, please."

The man at the wheel had forsaken it in a funk, and Captain Davenport had leaped and caught the spokes in time to prevent the ship from yawing in the current and going ashore.

"Better take charge of the boats," he said to Mr. Konig. "Tow one of them short, right under the quarter. . . . When I go over, it'll be on the jump."

Mr. Konig hesitated, then went over the rail and lowered himself into the boat.

"Keep her off half a point, Captain."

Captain Davenport gave a start. He had thought he had the ship to himself.

"Ay, ay; half a point it is," he answered.

Amidships the *Pyrenees* was an open flaming furnace, out of which poured an immense volume of smoke which rose high above the masts and completely hid the forward part of the ship. McCoy, in the shelter of the mizzen-shrouds, continued his difficult task of conning the ship through the intricate channel. The fire was working aft along the deck from the seat of explosion, while the soaring tower of canvas on the mainmast went up and vanished in a sheet of flame. Forward, though they could not see them, they knew that the head-sails were still drawing.

"If only she don't burn all her canvas off before she makes inside," the captain groaned.

"She'll make it," McCoy assured him with supreme confidence. "There is plenty of time. She is bound to make it. And once inside, we'll put her before it; that will keep the smoke away from us and hold back the fire from working aft."

A tongue of flame sprang up the mizzen, reached hungrily for the lowest tier of canvas, missed it, and vanished. From aloft a burning shred of rope stuff fell square on the back of Captain Davenport's neck. He acted with the celerity of one stung by a bee as he reached up and brushed the offending fire from his skin.

"How is she heading, Captain?"

"Nor'west by west."

"Keep her west-nor'west."

Captain Davenport put the wheel up and steadied her.

"West by north, Captain."

"West by north she is."

"And now west."

Slowly, point by point, as she entered the lagoon, the *Pyrenees* described the circle that put her before the wind; and point by point, with all the calm certitude of a thousand years of time to spare, McCoy chanted the changing course.

"Another point, Captain."

"A point it is."

Captain Davenport whirled several spokes over, suddenly reversing and coming back one to check her.

"Steady."

"Steady she is—right on it."

Despite the fact that the wind was now astern, the heat was so intense that Captain Davenport was compelled to steal sidelong glances into the binnacle, letting go the wheel now with one hand, now with the other, to rub or shield his blistering cheeks.

McCoy's beard was crinkling and shriveling and the smell of it, strong in the other's nostrils, compelled him to look toward McCoy with sudden solicitude. Captain Davenport was letting go the spokes alternately with his hands in order to rub their blistering backs against his trousers. Every sail on the mizzenmast vanished in a rush of flame, compelling the two men to crouch and shield their faces.

"Now," said McCoy, stealing a glance ahead at the low shore, "four points up, Captain, and let her drive."

Shreds and patches of burning rope and canvas were falling about them and upon them. The tarry smoke from a smouldering piece of rope at the captain's feet set him off into a violent coughing fit, during which he still clung to the spokes.

The *Pyrenees* struck, her bow lifted and she ground ahead gently to a stop. A shower of burning fragments, dislodged by the shock, fell about them. The ship moved ahead again and struck a second time. She crushed the fragile coral under her keel, drove on, and struck a third time.

"Hard over," said McCoy. "Hard over?" he questioned gently, a minute later.

"She won't answer," was the reply.

"All right. She is swinging around." McCoy peered over the side. "Soft, white sand. Couldn't ask better. A beautiful bed."

As the *Pyrenees* swung around her stern away from the wind, a fearful blast of smoke and flame poured aft. Captain Davenport deserted the wheel in blistering agony. He reached the painter of the boat that lay under the quarter, then looked for McCoy, who was standing aside to let him go down.

"You first," the captain cried, gripping him by the shoulder and almost throwing him over the rail. But the flame and smoke were too terrible, and he followed hard after McCoy, both men wriggling on the rope and sliding down into the boat together. A sailor in the bow, without waiting for orders, slashed the painter through with his sheath knife. The oars, poised in readiness, bit into the water, and the boat shot away.

"A beautiful bed, Captain," McCoy murmured, looking back.

"Ay, a beautiful bed, and all thanks to you," was the answer.

The three boats pulled away for the white beach of pounded coral, beyond which, on the edge of a cocoanut grove, could be seen a half dozen grass houses and a score or more of excited natives, gazing wide-eyed at the conflagration that had come to land.

The boats grounded and they stepped out on the white beach.

"And now," said McCoy, "I must see about getting back to Pitcairn."

Notes

1. Charmian London, *The Log of the Snark* (New York, Macmillan, 1915), 180.
2. See Russ Kingman, *Jack London: A Definitive Chronology* (Middletown, CA: David Rejl, 1992), 87, and James Williams, "Jack London's Works by Date of Composition." In a letter to his church's leaders, McCoy tells his own story:

> The ship's cargo was discovered to be on fire 15 days previous to her arrival at Pitcairn. The captain's intention was to run her on the island in order to save the crew, if possible. Owing to strong, contrary winds and heavy seas onshore, I found it impossible to carry the captain's plans into effect, and planned, or advised, that she be taken to Mangareva, Gambier Islands. At first the ship's crew refused to come, knowing it was a great risk, and that the fire might break through the deck at any moment. When the captain asked me to pilot them (to Mangareva) and I gave my consent, the ship's company was made willing to come; for they saw that I was willing to risk my life for their sake. It was after dark when I landed from the ship (back on Pitcairn). A public meeting was called in the schoolroom, and I told my people of my intention to pilot the ship to Mangareva, if they would consent to my leaving them for a few weeks or perhaps for a few months. After an hour's talking and advising the people, and reminding them of the time when they had shipwrecked men on the island and of the trouble made by them, I asked that all who were willing for me to leave the island for humanity's sake should raise their right hand. The majority were in favor of my going. I told them that I was not taking my life into my own hands as some might suppose; neither did I consider the big and strong fire that would be burning underneath me every day and night; but I did consider and realize that the strong "everlasting arms" would be underneath me. Jesus left His Father's throne and His bright home above for humanity's sake. Why not we? There was no sleeping in Pitcairn that night. While I was attending to family affairs, the women were cooking food for the distressed ship's company, the men were gathering potatoes, fowls, bananas, pumpkins, etc. and at 6 a.m., I bade farewell to home and people, and sailed with a strong and fair wind for

> Mangareva, a distance of 296 miles (about). On Sunday morning (after 28 hours at sea) we failed to get the chains from the hold of the burning ship to anchor her, so we ran her on the beach (under Mangareva's Mount Duff) and saved ourselves, our effects, and a few stores. Two days later the fire broke out from the hold, and now she is all in flames and will continue to be so until her cargo of wheat and barley is burned up. . . . If I cannot get a vessel here (in Mangareva) or in Tahiti to take me back to Pitcairn, I will have to go to San Francisco and take a merchant vessel, as I did before, and risk making a long voyage before being on my way home again. . . . (Ford, Herbert. *Pitcairn—Port of Call* [Angwin, CA: Hawser Titles, 1996], 135–36.)

3. Boswell, James. *The Life of Samuel Johnson, LL.D.* (London: J. M. Dent, 1926), 230. Johnson's statements were made in 1759.
4. In 1905, the ship was salvaged by Captains J. E. Thayer and Porter, rechristened the *Manga Reva*, and chartered by the Sugar Factors Company of Honolulu. By one of those remarkable coincidences that proverbially surpass fiction, the ship that had been saved by a descendant of the *Bounty*'s crew went on itself to become the scene of a mutiny in the United States in the fall of 1913. After a history of adventures that exceeded that of most vessels, in 1917 she was reported missing in the Atlantic, presumed to have been sunk by German submarines.
5. An expression meaning "Nonsense!" The term comes from thieves' slang: A gammon is any diversionary technique used by a pickpocket to misdirect the "mark's" attention.
6. In contrast to the serenity of McCoy's assurance and confidence, the crew's mood is understandably hellish. Taking a cue from the historical McCoy's self-identification with Jesus, London uses many references to Christian ideas and images. He suggests the messianic properties of the pilot McCoy, who voluntarily comes on board not merely to offer his life to save the sailors from burning to death, but perhaps also to expiate, through his positive actions, the sins of his fathers. The metaphor of seed in the title suggests not only the genetic successor of the original mutineer, but also the cargo itself. That the historical *Pyrenees* was carrying wheat perhaps awakened London's interest in extending the metaphor from planting to harvest and finally to baking. (McCoy "had the feeling as of being in a huge bake-oven.") However, here it is not baking, but on fire. The wheat, under normal situations, would present the promise of bread and, given the abundance of religious material in the tale, hint at the bread of life, the Eucharist.

   The elasticity of the metaphor increases as London cites the burning wheat through frequent references to "hellfire" and "malignant heat" below decks. It was, the text assures, "the anteroom of hell." Thus the cargo is at once the promise of food and life as well as the threat of death and the implication of hell. By linking the metaphor to McCoy's family story, London reminds us that Jesus, too, uses seed as a metaphor: "He who sows the good seed is the Son of Man. The field is the world; the good seed the sons of the kingdom; the weeds, the sons of the wicked one; and the enemy who sowed them is the devil. But the harvest is the end of the world, and the reapers are the angels. Therefore, just as the weeds are gathered up and burnt with fire, so will it be at the end of the world. The Son of Man will send forth his angels, and they will gather out of his kingdom all scandals, and those who work iniquity, and cast them into the furnace of fire, where there will be the weeping and the gnashing of teeth" (Matt. 13: 37–43). In Mark 4: 3–9, Jesus also refers to the seed as metaphor. London turns this to his narrative advantage as he ties McCoy to his violent progenitors: his ancestors had fallen onto harsh ground, and the savage isolation of Pitcairn, coupled with their frustrated lusts, had led them to evil and violence. However, some of the seed had fallen on ground that enabled a virtuous and heroic strain to flourish into this beachcomber-redeemer, come now out of the legendary past of South Seas lore into the sordid present as an agent of salvation, atoning for wickedness committed generations ago.

7. The men on the *Pyrenees* are hungry and have been placed "on whack"—the barest minimum ration of hardtack and water. Ironically, they sail on water that they can neither drink nor use to put out the fire as it burns up the grain that could have fed them.

8. To make McCoy's achievement even more impressive, London takes the burning *Pyrenees* beyond nearby Mangareva, embarking on a fearful tour of the Tuamoto Archipelago. Each island they pass seems impossible for them to use as a harbor; each island brings the panicking sailors closer to the ship's inevitable explosion. The accompanying map is a copy of one from the Londons' own collection, and may well have been the one Jack had before him as he wrote, though his use of variant spellings of island names suggests that he was working from memory or from a chart that no longer exists in the currently held map collection. According to Milo Shepard, Jack's grandnephew, during WWII the U.S. Navy, finding itself without adequate maps of the region, confiscated the majority of the Londons' charts.

9. In chapter 17 of *The Cruise of the Snark*, London identified the writer on the *Casco* as Robert Louis Stevenson.

10. The Sumner line was discovered in 1837 by American Captain Thomas Sumner. It is a navigational procedure involving the plotting of three lines on a chart that together can indicate a ship's position when more conventional methods cannot be used with certainty. London learned of this method in his often-consulted *Sailing Directions* as well as in John Davis, *Sun's True Bearing or Azimuth Tables* (London: J. D. Potter, 1900).

11. McCoy is paraphrasing Psalm 104: 29.

12. Though he makes no claim to supernatural knowledge, faith in McCoy's leadership grows gradually in the crew, and McCoy exerts a chastening and reforming spiritual power over Davenport and the men. The captain realizes that he doesn't want to swear in McCoy's presence, and the men actually come to believe, despite every evidence of their senses and all their quantity of experience, that McCoy has the power to save them—to bring them to a safe harbor—"a beautiful bed." McCoy's moral presence is so pronounced that it has effects on others as well as on him.

An Introduction to "The Chinago"

"The Chinago" and "The Whale Tooth" are companion stories that illustrate London's use of darkly ironic humor to illuminate the ruthless exploitation of nonwhite people by white capitalist interlopers. In one story, a person of color, a Chinese coolie, is caught up in the harrow of European efforts to colonize and exploit the resources of a remote island. In the other, a white man becomes the victim of his own impulse to proselytize the benighted heathen of Fiji. Both stories depict victims of the clash of cultures, and in both an innocent man winds up dead because the world's varying races seem incapable of mutual understanding. As we have noted in the general introduction, modern literary criticism suggests a new way of reading these stories, a way that allows the reader to find a profoundly layered series of misread texts, of misunderstood data, all related to the inability of characters to interpret their situation and all tending to promote violence because of the ways their disparate cultures have taught them to perceive reality.

For example, the first part of "The Chinago" is framed by a trial—theoretically a search for Truth; however, from the main character's perspective, the process is unintelligible because it is in a language he cannot understand. Inside the frame of the judicial proceedings are his reflections and memories as well as his plans and anticipations. Sure of his innocence, he looks forward to a rich and contented future back home in China. After the verdict, the second part of the story concerns the efforts of the innocent but convicted prisoners to adjust to their new condition. The third section of the story details the final sets of misinterpretations as the unfortunate victim of a genuinely blind justice is mistakenly led to his execution, trying to explain that his execution is a case of mistaken identity.

London develops this theme of fatal misunderstanding, making each section of the story contain references to botched interpretations. Modern critics are frequently interested in any signs or symbols that invite an interpretive response, and the word "text" has taken on an expansion in recent decades. Throughout both "The Chinago" and "The Whale Tooth," texts are represented as creations mistakenly interpreted and acted upon. Whether they are spoken, written down, remembered, imagined, or predicted, these varying kinds of interpretable materials run counter to the facts of the characters' experience.

Particularly in "The Chinago" London offers up a labyrinth of spoken testimonies, written texts, and unspoken recollections conveyed by a distant and objective narrator with selectively limited omniscience. A fairly complete list of all the texts (written and otherwise) mentioned within the narrative is almost numbing: testimony, statements, law, contracts, judgments, proceedings, signatures, indentures, meditations, riddles, certificates, reports, insults, curses, signals, marks, sentences, maxims, orders, jokes, pictures, recollections, reprimands, passages, instructions, and tracts.

"The Chinago" has received probably the warmest reception of all the stories in this volume, with the exception of "The Red One." Citing its "building of an atmosphere, the telling of a narrative, and the development of irony," renowned London authority King Hendricks has called it "the greatest story of London's career."[1]

Written between April 4 and 12, 1908, while the *Snark* sailed from Raiatea to Tahaa, then on to Bora Bora, "The Chinago" was first published without illustrations in *Harper's Monthly* for July, 1910.

THE CHINAGO[2]

The coral waxes, the palm grows, but man departs.
— Tahitian proverb

Ah Cho did not understand French. He sat in the crowded court room, very weary and bored, listening to the unceasing, explosive French that now one official and now another uttered. It was just so much gabble to Ah Cho, and he marvelled at the stupidity of the Frenchmen who took so long to find out the murderer of Chung Ga, and who did not find him at all. The five hundred coolies on the plantation knew that Ah San had done the killing, and here was Ah San not even arrested. It was true that all the coolies had agreed secretly not to testify against one another; but then, it was so simple, the Frenchmen should have been able to discover that Ah San was the man. They were very stupid, these Frenchmen.

Ah Cho had done nothing of which to be afraid. He had had no hand in the killing. It was true he had been present at it, and Schemmer,[3] the overseer on the plantation, had rushed into the barracks immediately afterward and caught him there, along with four or five others; but what of that? Chung Ga had been stabbed only twice. It stood to reason that five or six men could not inflict two stab wounds. At the most, if a man had struck but once, only two men could have done it.

So it was that Ah Cho reasoned, when he, along with his four companions, had lied and blocked and obfuscated in their statements to the court concerning what had taken place. They had heard the sounds of the killing, and, like Schemmer, they had run to the spot. They had got there before Schemmer—that was all. True, Schemmer had testified that, attracted by the sound of quarrelling as he chanced to pass by, he had stood for at least five minutes outside; that then, when he entered, he found the prisoners already inside; and that they had not entered just before, because he had been standing by the one door to the barracks. But what of that? Ah Cho and his four fellow-prisoners had testified that Schemmer was mistaken. In the end they would be let go. They were all confident of that. Five men could not have their heads cut off for two stab wounds. Besides, no foreign devil had seen the killing. But these Frenchmen were so stupid. In China, as Ah Cho well knew, the magistrate would order all of them to the torture and learn the truth. The truth was very easy to learn under torture. But these Frenchmen did not torture—bigger fools they! Therefore they would never find out who killed Chung Ga.

But Ah Cho did not understand everything. The English Company that owned the plantation had imported into Tahiti, at great expense, the five hundred coolies. The stockholders were clamoring for dividends, and the Company had not yet paid any; wherefore the Company did not want its costly contract laborers to start the practice of killing one another. Also, there were the French, eager and willing to impose upon the Chinagos the virtues and excellences of French law. There was nothing like setting an example once in a while; and, besides, of what use was New Caledonia except to send men to live out their days in misery and pain in payment of the penalty for being frail and human?

Ah Cho did not understand all this. He sat in the court room and waited for the baffled judgment that would set him and his comrades free to go back to the plantation and work out the terms of their contracts. This judgment would soon be rendered. Proceedings were drawing to a close. He could see that. There was no more testifying, no more gabble of tongues. The French devils were tired, too, and evidently waiting for the judgment. And as he waited he remembered back in his life to the time when he had signed the contract and set sail in the ship for Tahiti. Times had been hard in his seacoast village, and when he indentured himself to labor for five years in the South Seas at fifty cents Mexican a day, he had thought himself fortunate. There were men in his village who toiled a whole year for ten dollars Mexican, and there were women who made nets all the year round for five dollars, while in the houses of shopkeepers there were maid-servants who received four dollars for a year of service. And here he was to receive fifty cents a day; for one day, only one day, he was to receive that princely sum! What if the work were hard? At the end of the five years he would return home—that was in the contract—and he would never have to work again. He would be a rich man for life, with a house of his own, a wife, and children growing up to venerate him. Yes, and back of the house he would have a small garden, a place of meditation and repose, with goldfish in a tiny lakelet, and wind bells tinkling in the several trees, and there would be a high wall all around so that his meditation and repose should be undisturbed. Well, he had worked out three of those five years. He was already a wealthy man (in his own country), through his earnings, and only two years more intervened between the cotton plantation on Tahiti and the meditation and repose that awaited him. But just now he was losing money because of the unfortunate accident of being present at the killing of Chung Ga. He had lain three weeks in prison, and for each day of those three weeks he had lost fifty cents. But now judgment would soon be given, and he would go back to work.

Ah Cho was twenty-two years old. He was happy and good-natured, and it was easy for him to smile. While his body was slim in the Asiatic way, his face was rotund. It was round, like the moon, and it irradiated a gentle complacence and a sweet kindliness of spirit that was unusual among his countrymen. Nor did his looks belie him. He never caused trouble, never took part in wrangling. He did not gamble. His soul was not harsh enough for the soul that must belong to a gambler. He was content with little things and simple pleasures. The hush and quiet in the cool of the day after the blazing toil in the cotton field was to him an infinite satisfaction. He could sit for hours gazing at a solitary flower and philosophizing about the mysteries and riddles of being. A blue heron on a tiny crescent of sandy beach, a silvery splatter of flying fish, or a sunset of pearl and rose across the lagoon, could entrance him to all forgetfulness of the procession of wearisome days and of the heavy lash of Schemmer.

Schemmer, Karl Schemmer, was a brute, a brutish brute. But he earned his salary. He got the last particle of strength out of the five hundred slaves; for slaves they were until their term of years was up. Schemmer worked hard to extract the strength from those five hundred sweating bodies and to transmute it into bales of fluffy cotton ready for export. His dominant, iron-clad, primeval brutishness was what enabled him to effect the transmutation. Also, he was assisted by a thick leather belt, three inches wide and a yard in length, with which he always rode and which, on occasion, could come down on the naked back of a stooping coolie with a report like a pistol-shot.[4] These reports were frequent when Schemmer rode down the furrowed field.

Once, at the beginning of the first year of contract labor, he had killed a coolie with a single blow of his fist. He had not exactly crushed the man's head like an egg-shell, but the blow had been sufficient to addle what was inside, and, after being sick for a week, the man had died. But the Chinese had not complained to the French devils that ruled over Tahiti. It was their own lookout. Schemmer was their problem. They must avoid his wrath as they avoided the venom of the centipedes that lurked in the grass or crept into the sleeping quarters on rainy nights. The Chinagos—such they were called by the indolent, brown-skinned island folk—saw to it that they did not displease Schemmer too greatly. This was equivalent to rendering up to him a full measure of efficient toil. That blow of Schemmer's fist had been worth thousands of dollars to the Company, and no trouble ever came of it to Schemmer.

The French, with no instinct for colonization, futile in their childish playgame of developing the resources of the island, were only too glad to see the English Company succeed. What matter of Schemmer and his redoubtable fist? The Chinago that died? Well, he was only a Chinago. Besides, he died of sunstroke, as the doctor's certificate attested. True, in all the history of Tahiti no one had ever died of sunstroke. But it was that, precisely that, which made the death of this Chinago unique. The doctor said as much in his report. He was very candid. Dividends must be paid, or else one more failure would be added to the long history of failure in Tahiti.

There was no understanding these white devils. Ah Cho pondered their inscrutableness as he sat in the court room waiting the judgment. There was no telling what went on at the back of their minds. He had seen a few of the white devils. They were all alike—the officers and sailors on the ship, the French officials, the several white men on the plantation, including Schemmer. Their minds all moved in mysterious ways there was no getting at. They grew angry without apparent cause, and their anger was always dangerous. They were like wild beasts at such times. They worried about little things, and on occasion could out-toil even a Chinago. They were not temperate as Chinagos were temperate; they were gluttons, eating prodigiously and drinking more prodigiously. A Chinago never knew when an act would please them or arouse a storm of wrath. A Chinago could never tell. What pleased one time, the very next time might provoke an outburst of anger. There was a curtain behind the eyes of the white devils that screened the backs of their minds from the Chinago's gaze. And then, on top of it all, was that terrible efficiency of the white devils, that ability to do things, to make things go, to work results, to bend to their wills all creeping, crawling things, and the powers of the very elements themselves. Yes, the white men were strange and wonderful, and they were devils. Look at Schemmer.

Ah Cho wondered why the judgment was so long in forming. Not a man on trial had laid hand on Chung Ga. Ah San alone had killed him. Ah San had done it, bending Chung Ga's head back with one hand by a grip of his queue, and with the other hand, from behind, reaching over and driving the knife into his body. Twice had he driven it in. There in the court room, with closed eyes, Ah Cho saw the killing acted over again—the squabble, the vile words bandied back and forth, the filth and insult flung upon venerable ancestors, the curses laid upon unbegotten generations, the leap of Ah San, the grip on the queue of Chung Ga, the knife that sank twice into his flesh, the bursting open of the door, the irruption of Schemmer, the dash for the door, the escape of Ah San, the flying belt of Schemmer that drove the rest into the corner, and the firing of the revolver as a signal that brought help to Schemmer. Ah Cho shivered as he lived it over. One blow of the belt had bruised his cheek, taking off some of the skin. Schemmer had pointed to the bruises when, on the witness-stand, he had identified Ah Cho. It was only just now that the marks had become no longer visible. That had been a blow. Half an inch nearer the centre and it would have taken out his eye. Then Ah Cho forgot the whole happening in a vision he caught of the garden of meditation and repose that would be his when he returned to his own land.

He sat with impassive face, while the magistrate rendered the judgment. Likewise were the faces of his four companions impassive. And they remained impassive when the interpreter explained that the five of them had been found guilty of the murder of Chung Ga, and that Ah Chow should have his head cut off, Ah Cho serve twenty years in prison in New Caledonia, Wong Li twelve years, and Ah Tong ten years. There was no use in getting excited about it. Even Ah Chow remained expressionless as a mummy, though it was his head that was to be cut off. The magistrate added a few words, and the interpreter explained that Ah Chow's face having been most severely bruised by Schemmer's strap had made his identification so positive that, since one man must die, he might as well be that man. Also, the fact that Ah Cho's face likewise had been severely bruised, conclusively proving his presence at the murder and his undoubted participation, had merited him the twenty years of penal servitude. And down to the ten years of Ah Tong, the proportioned reason for each sentence was explained. Let the Chinagos take the lesson to heart, the Court said finally, for they must learn that the law would be fulfilled in Tahiti though the heavens fell.

The five Chinagos were taken back to jail. They were not shocked nor grieved. The sentences being unexpected was quite what they were accustomed to in their dealings with the white devils. From them a Chinago rarely expected more than the unexpected. The heavy punishment for a crime they had not committed was no stranger than the countless strange things that white devils did. In the weeks that followed, Ah Cho often contemplated Ah Chow with mild curiosity. His head was to be cut off by the guillotine that was being erected on the plantation. For him there would be no declining years, no gardens of tranquillity. Ah Cho philosophized and speculated about life and death. As for himself, he was not perturbed. Twenty years were merely twenty years. By that much was his garden removed from him—that was all. He was young, and the patience of Asia was in his bones. He could wait those twenty years, and by that time the heats of his blood would be assuaged and he would be better fitted for that garden of calm delight. He thought of a name for it; he would call it The

Garden of the Morning Calm. He was made happy all day by the thought, and he was inspired to devise a moral maxim on the virtue of patience, which maxim proved a great comfort, especially to Wong Li and Ah Tong. Ah Chow, however, did not care for the maxim. His head was to be separated from his body in so short a time that he had no need for patience to wait for that event. He smoked well, ate well, slept well, and did not worry about the slow passage of time.

Cruchot was a gendarme. He had seen twenty years of service in the colonies, from Nigeria and Senegal to the South Seas, and those twenty years had not perceptibly brightened his dull mind. He was as slow-witted and stupid as in his peasant days in the south of France. He knew discipline and fear of authority, and from God down to the sergeant of gendarmes the only difference to him was the measure of slavish obedience which he rendered. In point of fact, the sergeant bulked bigger in his mind than God, except on Sundays when God's mouthpieces had their say. God was usually very remote, while the sergeant was ordinarily very close at hand.

Cruchot it was who received the order from the Chief Justice to the jailer commanding that functionary to deliver over to Cruchot the person of Ah Chow. Now, it happened that the Chief Justice had given a dinner the night before to the captain and officers of the French man-of-war. His hand was shaking when he wrote out the order, and his eyes were aching so dreadfully that he did not read over the order. It was only a Chinago's life he was signing away, anyway. So he did not notice that he had omitted the final letter in Ah Chow's name.[5] The order read "Ah Cho," and, when Cruchot presented the order, the jailer turned over to him the person of Ah Cho. Cruchot took that person beside him on the seat of a wagon, behind two mules, and drove away.

Ah Cho was glad to be out in the sunshine. He sat beside the gendarme and beamed. He beamed more ardently than ever when he noted the mules headed south toward Atimaono. Undoubtedly Schemmer had sent for him to be brought back. Schemmer wanted him to work. Very well, he would work well. Schemmer would never have cause to complain. It was a hot day. There had been a stoppage of the trades. The mules sweated, Cruchot sweated, and Ah Cho sweated. But it was Ah Cho that bore the heat with the least concern. He had toiled three years under that sun on the plantation. He beamed and beamed with such genial good nature that even Cruchot's heavy mind was stirred to wonderment.

"You are very funny," he said at last.

Ah Cho nodded and beamed more ardently. Unlike the magistrate, Cruchot spoke to him in the Kanaka tongue, and this, like all Chinagos and all foreign devils, Ah Cho understood.

"You laugh too much," Cruchot chided. "One's heart should be full of tears on a day like this."

"I am glad to get out of the jail."

"Is that all?" The gendarme shrugged his shoulders.

"Is it not enough?" was the retort.

"Then you are not glad to have your head cut off?"

Ah Cho looked at him in abrupt perplexity and said:

"Why, I am going back to Atimaono to work on the plantation for Schemmer. Are you not taking me to Atimaono?"

Cruchot stroked his long mustaches reflectively. "Well, well," he said finally, with a flick of the whip at the off mule, "so you don't know?"

"Know what?" Ah Cho was beginning to feel a vague alarm. "Won't Schemmer let me work for him any more?"

"Not after to-day." Cruchot laughed heartily. It was a good joke. "You see, you won't be able to work after to-day. A man with his head off can't work, eh?" He poked the Chinago in the ribs, and chuckled.

Ah Cho maintained silence while the mules trotted a hot mile. Then he spoke: "Is Schemmer going to cut off my head?"

Cruchot grinned as he nodded.

"It is a mistake," said Ah Cho, gravely. "I am not the Chinago that is to have his head cut off. I am Ah Cho. The honorable judge has determined that I am to stop twenty years in New Caledonia."

The gendarme laughed. It was a good joke, this funny Chinago trying to cheat the guillotine. The mules trotted through a cocoanut grove and for half a mile beside the sparkling sea before Ah Cho spoke again.

"I tell you I am not Ah Chow. The honorable judge did not say that my head was to go off."

"Don't be afraid," said Cruchot, with the philanthropic intention of making it easier for his prisoner. "It is not difficult to die that way." He snapped his fingers. "It is quick—like that. It is not like hanging on the end of a rope and kicking and making faces for five minutes. It is like killing a chicken with a hatchet. You cut its head off, that is all. And it is the same with a man. Pouf!—it is over. It doesn't hurt. You don't even think it hurts. You don't think. Your head is gone, so you cannot think. It is very good. That is the way I want to die—quick, ah, quick. You are lucky to die that way. You might get the leprosy and fall to pieces slowly, a finger at a time, and now and again a thumb, also the toes.[6] I knew a man who was burned by hot water. It took him two days to die. You could hear him yelling a kilometre away. But you? Ah! so easy! Chck!—the knife cuts your neck like that. It is finished. The knife may even tickle. Who can say? Nobody who died that way ever came back to say."

He considered this last an excruciating joke, and permitted himself to be convulsed with laughter for half a minute. Part of his mirth was assumed, but he considered it his humane duty to cheer up the Chinago.

"But I tell you I am Ah Cho," the other persisted. "I don't want my head cut off."

Cruchot scowled. The Chinago was carrying the foolishness too far.

"I am not Ah Chow—" Ah Cho began.

"That will do," the gendarme interrupted. He puffed up his cheeks and strove to appear fierce.

"I tell you I am not—" Ah Cho began again.

"Shut up!" bawled Cruchot.

After that they rode along in silence. It was twenty miles from Papeete to Atimaono, and over half the distance was covered by the time the Chinago again ventured into speech.

"I saw you in the court room, when the honorable judge sought after our guilt," he began. "Very good. And do you remember that Ah Chow, whose head is to be cut off—do you remember that he—Ah Chow—was a tall man? Look at me."

He stood up suddenly, and Cruchot saw that he was a short man. And just as suddenly Cruchot caught a glimpse of a memory picture of Ah Chow, and in that picture Ah Chow was tall. To the gendarme all Chinagos looked alike. One face was like another. But between tallness and shortness he could differentiate, and he knew that he had the wrong man beside him on the seat.[7] He pulled up the mules abruptly, so that the pole shot ahead of them, elevating their collars.

"You see, it was a mistake," said Ah Cho, smiling pleasantly.

But Cruchot was thinking. Already he regretted that he had stopped the wagon. He was unaware of the error of the Chief Justice, and he had no way of working it out; but he did know that he had been given this Chinago to take to Atimaono and that it was his duty to take him to Atimaono. What if he was the wrong man and they cut his head off? It was only a Chinago when all was said, and what was a Chinago, anyway? Besides, it might not be a mistake. He did not know what went on in the minds of his superiors. They knew their business best. Who was he to do their thinking for them? Once, in the long ago, he had attempted to think for them, and the sergeant had said: "Cruchot, you are a fool! The quicker you know that, the better you will get on. You are not to think; you are to obey and leave thinking to your betters." He smarted under the recollection. Also, if he turned back to Papeete, he would delay the execution at Atimaono, and if he were wrong in turning back, he would get a reprimand from the sergeant who was waiting for the prisoner. And, furthermore, he would get a reprimand at Papeete as well.[8]

He touched the mules with the whip and drove on. He looked at his watch. He would be half an hour late as it was, and the sergeant was bound to be angry. He put the mules into a faster trot. The more Ah Cho persisted in explaining the mistake, the more stubborn Cruchot became. The knowledge that he had the wrong man did not make his temper better. The knowledge that it was through no mistake of his confirmed him in the belief that the wrong he was doing was the right. And, rather than incur the displeasure of the sergeant, he would willingly have assisted a dozen wrong Chinagos to their doom.

As for Ah Cho, after the gendarme had struck him over the head with the butt of the whip and commanded him in a loud voice to shut up, there remained nothing for him to do but to shut up. The long ride continued in silence. Ah Cho pondered the strange ways of the foreign devils. There was no explaining them. What they were doing with him was of a piece with everything they did. First they found guilty five innocent men, and next they cut off the head of the man that even they, in their benighted ignorance, had deemed meritorious of no more than twenty years' imprisonment. And there was nothing he could do. He could only sit idly and take what these lords of life measured out to him. Once, he got in a panic, and the sweat upon his body turned cold; but he fought his way out of it. He endeavored to resign himself to his fate by remembering and repeating certain passages from the "Yin Chih Wen" ("The Tract of the Quiet Way"); but, instead, he kept seeing his dream-garden of meditation and repose. This bothered him, until he abandoned himself to the dream and sat in his garden listening to the tinkling of the wind-bells in the several trees. And lo! sitting thus, in the dream, he was able to remember and repeat the passages from "The Tract of the Quiet Way."

So the time passed nicely until Atimaono was reached and the mules trotted up to the foot of the scaffold, in the shade of which stood the impatient sergeant. Ah Cho was hurried up the ladder of the scaffold. Beneath him on one side he saw assembled all the coolies of the plantation. Schemmer had decided that the event would be a good object-lesson, and so had called in the coolies from the fields and compelled them to be present. As they caught sight of Ah Cho they gabbled among themselves in low voices. They saw the mistake; but they kept it to themselves. The inexplicable white devils had doubtlessly changed their minds. Instead of taking the life of one innocent man, they were taking the life of another innocent man. Ah Chow or Ah Cho—what did it matter which? They could never understand the white dogs any more than could the white dogs understand them. Ah Cho was going to have his head cut off, but they, when their two remaining years of servitude were up, were going back to China.

Schemmer had made the guillotine himself. He was a handy man, and though he had never seen a guillotine, the French officials had explained the principle to him. It was on his suggestion that they had ordered the execution to take place at Atimaono instead of at Papeete. The scene of the crime, Schemmer had argued, was the best possible place for the punishment, and, in addition, it would have a salutary influence upon the half-thousand Chinagos on the plantation. Schemmer had also volunteered to act as executioner, and in that capacity he was now on the scaffold, experimenting with the instrument he had made. A banana tree, of the size and consistency of a man's neck, lay under the guillotine. Ah Cho watched with fascinated eyes. The German, turning a small crank, hoisted the blade to the top of the little derrick he had rigged. A jerk on a stout piece of cord loosed the blade and it dropped with a flash, neatly severing the banana trunk.

"How does it work?" The sergeant, coming out on top the scaffold, had asked the question.

"Beautifully," was Schemmer's exultant answer. "Let me show you."

Again he turned the crank that hoisted the blade, jerked the cord, and sent the blade crashing down on the soft tree. But this time it went no more than two-thirds of the way through.

The sergeant scowled. "That will not serve," he said.

Schemmer wiped the sweat from his forehead. "What it needs is more weight," he announced. Walking up to the edge of the scaffold, he called his orders to the blacksmith for a twenty-five-pound piece of iron. As he stooped over to attach the iron to the broad top of the blade, Ah Cho glanced at the sergeant and saw his opportunity.

"The honorable judge said that Ah Chow was to have his head cut off," he began.

The sergeant nodded impatiently. He was thinking of the fifteen-mile ride before him that afternoon, to the windward side of the island, and of Berthe, the pretty half-caste daughter of Lafiere, the pearl-trader, who was waiting for him at the end of it. "Well, I am not Ah Chow. I am Ah Cho. The honorable jailer has made a mistake. Ah Chow is a tall man, and you see I am short."

The sergeant looked at him hastily and saw the mistake. "Schemmer!" he called, imperatively. "Come here."

The German grunted, but remained bent over his task till the chunk of iron was lashed to his satisfaction. "Is your Chinago ready?" he demanded.

"Look at him," was the answer. "Is he the Chinago?"

Schemmer was surprised. He swore tersely for a few seconds, and looked regretfully across at the thing he had made with his own hands and which he was eager to see work. "Look here," he said finally, "we can't postpone this affair. I've lost three hours' work already out of those five hundred Chinagos. I can't afford to lose it all over again for the right man. Let's put the performance through just the same. It is only a Chinago."

The sergeant remembered the long ride before him, and the pearl-trader's daughter, and debated with himself.

"They will blame it on Cruchot—if it is discovered," the German urged. "But there's little chance of its being discovered. Ah Chow won't give it away, at any rate."

"The blame won't lie with Cruchot, anyway," the sergeant said. "It must have been the jailer's mistake."

"Then let's go on with it. They can't blame us. Who can tell one Chinago from another? We can say that we merely carried out instructions with the Chinago that was turned over to us. Besides, I really can't take all those coolies a second time away from their labor."

They spoke in French, and Ah Cho, who did not understand a word of it, nevertheless knew that they were determining his destiny. He knew, also, that the decision rested with the sergeant, and he hung upon that official's lips.

"All right," announced the sergeant. "Go ahead with it. He is only a Chinago."

"I'm going to try it once more, just to make sure." Schemmer moved the banana trunk forward under the knife, which he had hoisted to the top of the derrick.

Ah Cho tried to remember maxims from "The Tract of the Quiet Way." "Live in concord," came to him; but it was not applicable. He was not going to live. He was about to die. No, that would not do. "Forgive malice"—yes, but there was no malice to forgive. Schemmer and the rest were doing this thing without malice. It was to them merely a piece of work that had to be done, just as clearing the jungle, ditching the water, and planting cotton were pieces of work that had to be done. Schemmer jerked the cord, and Ah Cho forgot "The Tract of the Quiet Way." The knife shot down with a thud, making a clean slice of the tree.

"Beautiful!" exclaimed the sergeant, pausing in the act of lighting a cigarette. "Beautiful, my friend."

Schemmer was pleased at the praise.

"Come on, Ah Chow," he said, in the Tahitian tongue.

"But I am not Ah Chow—" Ah Cho began.

"Shut up!" was the answer. "If you open your mouth again, I'll break your head."

The overseer threatened him with a clenched fist, and he remained silent. What was the good of protesting? Those foreign devils always had their way. He allowed himself to be lashed to the vertical board that was the size of his body. Schemmer drew the buckles tight—so tight that the straps cut into his flesh and hurt. But he did not complain. The hurt would not last long. He felt the board tilting over in the air toward the horizontal, and closed his eyes. And in that moment he caught a last glimpse of his garden of meditation and repose. It seemed to him that he sat in the garden. A cool wind was blowing, and the bells in the several trees were tinkling softly. Also, birds were making sleepy noises, and from beyond the high wall came the subdued sound of village life.

Then he was aware that the board had come to rest, and from muscular pressures and tensions he knew that he was lying on his back. He opened his eyes. Straight above him he saw the suspended knife blazing in the sunshine. He saw the weight which had been added, and noted that one of Schemmer's knots had slipped. Then he heard the sergeant's voice in sharp command. Ah Cho closed his eyes hastily. He did not want to see that knife descend. But he felt it—for one great fleeting instant. And in that instant he remembered Cruchot and what Cruchot had said. But Cruchot was wrong. The knife did not tickle. That much he knew before he ceased to know.[9]

Notes

1. King Hendricks, "Jack London: Master Craftsman of the Short Story," Thirty-third Faculty Honor Lecture (Logan, Utah: Utah State University, April, 1966), 24.
2. Thanks to the internet research efforts of a colleague, Mr. Timothy Carlson, we have been able to learn that "Chinago" is an Anglicized version of a Chinese expression of contempt for indentured laborers: "Chinese Dog." Thanks further to information from one of our students, Geoffrey Wong (and with apologies to our Chinese-speaking readers), we can roughly transliterate the original term as "Chung-GWA-Gkow?"; however, for purposes of reference, probably "Chin-AH-go" is close to the pronunciation London would have heard.
3. The cruelty of Schemmer, the German overseer, is magnified in the character of Max Bunster in "Mauki."
4. At the time of the arrest (see below), Schemmer's belt had flown out to brand Ah Cho and, to a worse extent, Ah Chow. Schemmer uses these marks, in fact, to identify the accused in court, since to him no doubt all Chinagos look alike. We are perhaps invited to see the marks on flesh as words or signifiers on a page. Like other misinterpreted texts, the wounds are accepted as truthful evidence that leads to a false conclusion. After three weeks in jail, Ah Chow still possesses this signifier of his guilt most clearly, so he is the one who is sentenced to die. The

healing of the wounds indicates an erasure of the text; thus the skin of the Chinagos becomes a palimpsest ready for the next text to be "written" by Schemmer.

5. This is perhaps the most striking example of an unstable text and a clear example of what Vincent Leitch means when he says, "The word and the referent are incorrigibly different" (*Deconstructive Criticism: An Advanced Introduction.* [New York: Colombia University Press, 1983], 50). Here, the smallest unit of text, unmeaningful in itself yet at once signifier and signified, marks not only the difference between one human being and another but actually between life and death.
6. Misreading Ah Cho's simple statement of a bureaucratic slip-up for a panicky state of denial, Cruchot begins to speculate on the relative pains of alternative forms of death. He specifically mentions that it would be preferable to experience decapitation in an instant to, for example, the lingering death of leprosy, in which one might "fall to pieces slowly, a finger at a time, and now and again a thumb, also the toes," ironically not unlike a word or name that loses its being as one letter is omitted or lost.
7. Even the unreflecting Cruchot recognizes that, whatever the mistake, it wasn't his. And here the final irony presents itself: In the presence of two realities, Cruchot opts to obey the printed text, even though he knows it is wrong. After all, "he is only a Chinago," so in a sense all texts are alike to those who blindly accept their authority. Similarly, when Schemmer sees the mistake, he too will think of several reasons—several layers of reality—more significant than true justice to proceed with the execution.
8. One may suppose it a simple matter to return Ah Cho and collect Ah Chow, but the hardened poststructuralist might argue that the intended text cannot be retrieved anyway; further, anything signified (here, Ah Cho) remains undifferentiated and unrecognizable from *the* signified (all the other Chinagos).
9. The guillotine becomes the final instrument to deconstruct the text as it cuts the being of Ah Cho just as the judge's pen stroke initiated the deconstruction of Ah Chow's name. The guillotine also is an effort to close off interpretation of the text since it ends the narrative.

An Introduction to "The Whale Tooth"

"The Whale Tooth" offers a splendid example of London's ability to take actual characters and incidents and shape them to his own darkly satirical designs. The story of John Starhurst, a Pentecostal missionary, is based on the 1867 murder and consumption of the real-life Methodist missionary, the Rev. Thomas Baker, who had entered the dark fastnesses of the Fijian wilderness to bring the light of Protestantism to the benighted heathens.

Baker had an unfortunate run-in with Ra Undreundre, an important and powerful Fijian chief. Having handed Ra Undreundre a comb, Baker later tried to retrieve it, but the comb was lodged in the chief's hair. Baker unthinkingly touched the chief's head, a grave taboo. According to historical accounts, the villagers killed Baker, ate parts of him, and then sent the remaining parts of his body as gifts to influential leaders on the island. True to London's story, the cannibals saved his boots, possibly as a trophy. (One of the boots is on display in the museum at Suva.)

In what has to be more than coincidence, Herbert Spencer (whose works London read voraciously) wrote about the Fijian chief in an 1890 issue of *The Nineteenth Century* magazine. In a passage that exhibits some of the few examples of dry wit of which Spencer has ever been accused, the philosopher and anthropologist describes the Olympian career of Ra Undreundre:

> Life in Fiji at the time... must have been something worse than uncomfortable. One of the people who passed near the string of nine hundred stones [The number of stones varies according to source—editors' note], with which Ra Undreundre recorded the number of human victims he had devoured, must have had unpleasant waking thoughts and occasionally horrible dreams. A man who had lost some fingers for breaches of ceremony, or had seen his neighbor killed by a chief for behavior not sufficiently respectful, and who remembered how King Tanoa cut off his cousin's arm, cooked it and ate it in his presence, and then had him cut to pieces, must not infrequently have had "a bad quarter of an hour." Nor could creeping sensations have failed to run through any women who heard Tui Thakan eulogizing his dead son for cruelty, and saying that "he could kill his own wives if they offended him, and eat them afterwards." Happiness could not have been general in a society where there was a liability to be one among the ten whose lifeblood baptized the decks of a new canoe—a society in which the killing even of unoffending persons was no crime but a glory; and in which everyone knew that his neighbor's restless ambition was to be an acknowledged murderer. Still there must have been some moderation in murdering even in Fiji. Or must we hesitate to conclude that unlimited murder would have caused extinction of the society?[1]

Other missionaries and visitors to Fiji during the nineteenth century recorded many other gruesome accounts of barbarity. It is fair to note, however, that cannibalism in Fiji likely ended after the midpoint of the century as the islands were Christianized. So painful was the memory of the murder of Rev. Baker that in October 2003 the inhabitants of the remote village of Nabutautau, high in the hills of Viti Levu, offered a formal apology to Baker's descendants. Believing that a curse had fallen upon them as a result of their village ancestors' consumption of the unlucky Baker, the Fijians invited eleven of the missionary's descendants to Nabutautau for a ceremony. They offered to Baker's relatives gifts of cows, specially woven mats, and (with special irony for readers of London's story) carved sperm whale teeth. This unique ceremonial event contained so much human interest quality that newspapers worldwide carried reports. (See, for example, the on-line editions of the *BBC News*, United Kingdom edition, and the United Press International for October 14, 2003.)

In London's reworking of the historical facts, a good deal of ironic humor arises from the effort to make clear to the reader the perspectives of contending sides, the Christian and the heathen. As a result, the reader is better informed about the actual facts than is Starhurst, the missionary in Fiji, where the time-honored cannibalistic practices are carried on with cheerful and unabandoned gusto. But these islanders, unrepentant ritual murderers though they may be, are also people bound by their own concepts of dignity, respect, and honor, concepts completely lacking in the whites of "The Chinago." Just as Spencer's essay uses Ra Undreundre's accomplishments as a springboard for a discussion of "Absolute Political Ethics," London's narrator deftly outlines the coherent value system of the islanders, marked by the text of stones, each of which symbolically represents the literal ingestion of an enemy. Naively, Starhurst will present a contradictory text—the Bible—interpreted by his own values and perceptions of the world, values and perceptions formed by his adherence to a text that he believes is so infallible that he entrusts his very life to it.

If "The Chinago" demonstrates that fatal misunderstandings can arise from ignorance of the truth and foolish reliance on untrustworthy texts, "The Whale Tooth" sardonically explores the parallel possibility that it can also be disastrous to be quite sure of the Absolute truth and invincibility afforded by an Absolute text. "The Chinago" is a tale that grows out of one of the two great reasons for white European presence in the South Seas—commercial exploitation; "The Whale Tooth" examines the other great reason—the Christian missionary impulse to show that accurate perception of the world is only reliably provided by one, true, immutable and sacred text. Ah Cho loses his head because he understands too little; Starhurst loses his feet because he strides too far.

After a bout with malaria, Jack wrote "The Whale Tooth" in July of 1908 during a visit to Pennduffryun, a large copra plantation on Guadalcanal. Originally entitled "The Mission of John Starhurst," the story first appeared in the January 1910 edition of *Sunset* magazine. A generic beach scene served as the only illustration. The artist is unknown.

THE WHALE TOOTH[2]

It was in the early days in Fiji, when John Starhurst arose in the mission house at Rewa Village and announced his intention of carrying the gospel throughout all Viti Levu.[3] Now Viti Levu means the "Great Land," it being the largest island in a group composed of many large islands, to say nothing of hundreds of small ones. Here and there on the coasts, living by most precarious tenure, was a sprinkling of missionaries, traders, bêche-de-mer fishers, and whaleship deserters. The smoke of the hot ovens arose under their windows, and the bodies of the slain were dragged by their doors on the way to the feasting.

The Lotu, or the Worship, was progressing slowly, and, often, in crablike fashion. Chiefs, who announced themselves Christians and were welcomed into the body of the chapel, had a distressing habit of backsliding in order to partake of the flesh of some favorite enemy. Eat or be eaten had been the law of the land; and eat or be eaten promised to remain the law of the land for a long time to come. There were chiefs, such as Tanoa, Tuiveikoso, and Tuikilakila, who had literally eaten hundreds of their fellow men. But among these gluttons Ra Undreundre ranked highest. Ra Undreundre lived at Takiraki. He kept a register of his gustatory exploits. A row of stones outside his house marked the bodies he had eaten. This row was two hundred and thirty paces long, and the stones in it numbered eight hundred and seventy-two. Each stone represented a body. The row of stones might have been longer, had not Ra Undreundre unfortunately received a spear in the small of his back in a bush skirmish on Somo Somo and been served up on the table of Naungavuli, whose mediocre string of stones numbered only forty-eight.[4]

The hard-worked, fever-stricken missionaries stuck doggedly to their task, at times despairing, and looking forward for some special manifestation, some outburst of Pentecostal fire that would bring a glorious harvest of souls. But cannibal Fiji had remained obdurate. The frizzle-headed man-eaters were loath to leave their fleshpots so long as the harvest of human carcasses was plentiful. Sometimes, when the harvest was too plentiful, they imposed on the missionaries by letting the word slip out that on such a day there would be a killing and a barbecue. Promptly the missionaries would buy the lives of the victims with stick tobacco, fathoms of calico, and quarts of trade beads. Natheless the chiefs drove a handsome trade in thus disposing of their surplus live meat. Also, they could always go out and catch more.

It was at this juncture that John Starhurst proclaimed that he would carry the Gospel from coast to coast of the Great Land, and that he would begin by penetrating the mountain fastnesses of the headwaters of the Rewa River. His words were received with consternation.[5]

The native teachers wept softly. His two fellow missionaries strove to dissuade him. The King of Rewa warned him that the mountain dwellers would surely kai-kai him—kai-kai meaning "to eat"—and that he, the King of Rewa, having become Lotu, would be put to the necessity of going to war with the mountain dwellers. That he could not conquer them he was perfectly aware. That they might come down the river and sack Rewa Village he was likewise perfectly aware. But what was he to do? If John Starhurst persisted in going out and being eaten, there would be a war that would cost hundreds of lives.

Later in the day a deputation of Rewa chiefs waited upon John Starhurst. He heard them patiently, and argued patiently with them, though he abated not a whit from his purpose. To his fellow missionaries he explained that he was not bent upon martyrdom; that the call had come for him to carry the Gospel into Viti Levu, and that he was merely obeying the Lord's wish.

To the traders, who came and objected most strenuously of all, he said: "Your objections are valueless. They consist merely of the damage that may be done your businesses. You are interested in making money, but I am interested in saving souls. The heathen of this dark land must be saved."

John Starhurst was not a fanatic. He would have been the first man to deny the imputation. He was eminently sane and practical.

He was sure that his mission would result in good, and he had private visions of igniting the Pentecostal spark in the souls of the mountaineers and of inaugurating a revival that would sweep down out of the mountains and across the length and breadth of the Great Land from sea to sea and to the isles in the midst of the sea. There were no wild lights in his mild gray eyes, but only calm resolution and an unfaltering trust in the Higher Power that was guiding him.

One man only he found who approved of his project, and that was Ra Vatu, who secretly encouraged him and offered to lend him guides to the first foothills. John Starhurst, in turn, was greatly pleased by Ra Vatu's conduct. From an incorrigible heathen, with a heart as black as his practices, Ra Vatu was beginning to emanate light. He even spoke of becoming Lotu. True, three years before he had expressed a similar intention, and would have entered the church had not John Starhurst entered objection to his bringing his four wives along with him. Ra Vatu had had economic and ethical objections to monogamy. Besides, the missionary's hair-splitting objection had offended him; and, to prove that he was a free agent and a man of honor, he had swung his huge war club over Starhurst's head. Starhurst had escaped by rushing in under the club and holding on to him until help arrived. But all that was now forgiven and forgotten. Ra Vatu was coming into the church, not merely as a converted heathen, but as a converted polygamist as well. He was only waiting, he assured Starhurst, until his oldest wife, who was very sick, should die.

John Starhurst journeyed up the sluggish Rewa in one of Ra Vatu's canoes. This canoe was to carry him for two days, when, the head of navigation reached, it would return. Far in the distance, lifted into the sky, could be seen the great smoky mountains that marked the backbone of the Great Land. All day John Starhurst gazed at them with eager yearning.

Sometimes he prayed silently. At other times he was joined in prayer by Narau, a native teacher, who for seven years had been Lotu, ever since the day he had been saved from the hot oven by

Dr. James Ellery Brown at the trifling expense of one hundred sticks of tobacco, two cotton blankets, and a large bottle of painkiller. At the last moment, after twenty hours of solitary supplication and prayer, Narau's ears had heard the call to go forth with John Starhurst on the mission to the mountains.

"Master, I will surely go with thee," he had announced.

John Starhurst had hailed him with sober delight. Truly, the Lord was with him thus to spur on so broken-spirited a creature as Narau.

"I am indeed without spirit, the weakest of the Lord's vessels," Narau explained, the first day in the canoe.

"You should have faith, stronger faith," the missionary chided him.

Another canoe journeyed up the Rewa that day. But it journeyed an hour astern, and it took care not to be seen. This canoe was also the property of Ra Vatu. In it was Erirola, Ra Vatu's first cousin and trusted henchman; and in the small basket that never left his hand was a whale tooth. It was a magnificent tooth, fully six inches long, beautifully proportioned, the ivory turned yellow and purple with age. This tooth was likewise the property of Ra Vatu; and in Fiji, when such a tooth goes forth, things usually happen. For this is the virtue of the whale tooth: Whoever accepts it cannot refuse the request that may accompany it or follow it. The request may be anything from a human life to a tribal alliance, and no Fijian is so dead to honor as to deny the request when once the tooth has been accepted. Sometimes the request hangs fire, or the fulfilment is delayed, with untoward consequences.[6]

High up the Rewa, at the village of a chief, Mongondro by name, John Starhurst rested at the end of the second day of the journey. In the morning, attended by Narau, he expected to start on foot for the smoky mountains that were now green and velvety with nearness. Mongondro was a sweet-tempered, mild-mannered little old chief, short-sighted and afflicted with elephantiasis, and no longer inclined toward the turbulence of war. He received the missionary with warm hospitality, gave him food from his own table, and even discussed religious matters with him. Mongondro was of an inquiring bent of mind, and pleased John Starhurst greatly by asking him to account for the existence and beginning of things. When the missionary had finished his summary of the

Creation according to Genesis, he saw that Mongondro was deeply affected. The little old chief smoked silently for some time. Then he took the pipe from his mouth and shook his head sadly.

"It cannot be," he said. "I, Mongondro, in my youth, was a good workman with the adze. Yet three months did it take me to make a canoe—a small canoe, a very small canoe. And you say that all this land and water was made by one man—"

"Nay, was made by one God, the only true God," the missionary interrupted.

"It is the same thing," Mongondro went on, "that all the land and all the water, the trees, the fish, and bush and mountains, the sun, the moon, and the stars, were made in six days! No, no. I tell you that in my youth I was an able man, yet did it require me three months for one small canoe. It is a story to frighten children with; but no man can believe it."

"I am a man," the missionary said.

"True, you are a man. But it is not given to my dark understanding to know what you believe."

"I tell you, I do believe that everything was made in six days."

"So you say, so you say," the old cannibal murmured soothingly.

It was not until after John Starhurst and Narau had gone off to bed that Erirola crept into the chief's house, and, after diplomatic speech, handed the whale tooth to Mongondro.

The old chief held the tooth in his hands for a long time. It was a beautiful tooth, and he yearned for it. Also, he divined the request that must accompany it. "No, no; whale teeth were beautiful," and his mouth watered for it, but he passed it back to Erirola with many apologies.

In the early dawn John Starhurst was afoot, striding along the bush trail in his big leather boots, at his heels the faithful Narau, himself at the heels of a naked guide lent him by Mongondro to show the way to the next village, which was reached by midday. Here a new guide showed the way. A mile in the rear plodded Erirola, the whale tooth in the basket slung on his shoulder. For two days more he brought up the missionary's rear, offering the tooth to the village chiefs. But village after village refused the tooth. It followed so quickly the missionary's advent that they divined the request that would be made, and would have none of it.

They were getting deep into the mountains, and Erirola took a secret trail, cut in ahead of the missionary, and reached the stronghold of the Buli of Gatoka. Now the Buli was unaware of John Starhurst's imminent arrival. Also, the tooth was beautiful—an extraordinary specimen, while the coloring of it was of the rarest order. The tooth was presented publicly. The Buli of Gatoka, seated on his best mat, surrounded by his chief men, three busy fly-brushers at his back, deigned to receive from the hand of his herald the whale tooth presented by Ra Vatu and carried into the mountains by his cousin, Erirola. A clapping of hands went up at the acceptance of the present, the assembled headman, heralds, and fly-brushers crying aloud in chorus:

"A! woi! woi! woi! A! woi! woi! woi! A tabua levu! woi! woi! A mudua, mudua, mudua!"

"Soon will come a man, a white man," Erirola began, after the proper pause. "He is a missionary man, and he will come today. Ra Vatu is pleased to desire his boots. He wishes to present them to his good friend, Mongondro, and it is in his mind to send them with the feet along in them, for Mongondro is an old man and his teeth are not good. Be sure, O Buli, that the feet go along in the boots. As for the rest of him, it may stop here."

The delight in the whale tooth faded out of the Buli's eyes, and he glanced about him dubiously. Yet had he already accepted the tooth.

"A little thing like a missionary does not matter," Erirola prompted.

"No, a little thing like a missionary does not matter," the Buli answered, himself again. "Mongondro shall have the boots. Go, you young men, some three or four of you, and meet the missionary on the trail. Be sure you bring back the boots as well."

"It is too late," said Erirola. "Listen! He comes now."

Breaking through the thicket of brush, John Starhurst, with Narau close on his heels, strode upon the scene. The famous boots, having filled in wading the stream, squirted fine jets of water at every step. Starhurst looked about him with flashing eyes. Upborne by an unwavering trust, untouched by doubt or fear, he exulted in all he saw. He knew that since the beginning of time he was the first white man ever to tread the mountain stronghold of Gatoka.

The grass houses clung to the steep mountain side or overhung the rushing Rewa. On either side towered a mighty precipice.

At the best, three hours of sunlight penetrated that narrow gorge. No cocoanuts nor bananas were to be seen, though dense, tropic vegetation overran everything, dripping in airy festoons from the sheer lips of the precipices and running riot in all the crannied ledges. At the far end of the gorge the Rewa leaped eight hundred feet in a single span, while the atmosphere of the rock fortress pulsed to the rhythmic thunder of the fall.

From the Buli's house, John Starhurst saw emerging the Buli and his followers.

"I bring you good tidings," was the missionary's greeting.

"Who has sent you?" the Buli rejoined quietly.

"God."

"It is a new name in Viti Levu," the Buli grinned. "Of what islands, villages, or passes may he be chief?"

"He is the chief over all islands, all villages, all passes," John Starhurst answered solemnly. "He is the Lord over heaven and earth, and I am come to bring His word to you."

"Has he sent whale teeth?" was the insolent query.

"No, but more precious than whale teeth is the—"

"It is the custom, between chiefs, to send whale teeth," the Buli interrupted. "Your chief is either a niggard, or you are a fool, to come empty-handed into the mountains. Behold, a more generous than you is before you."

So saying, he showed the whale tooth he had received from Erirola.

Narau groaned.

"It is the whale tooth of Ra Vatu," he whispered to Starhurst. "I know it well. Now are we undone."

"A gracious thing," the missionary answered, passing his hand through his long beard and adjusting his glasses. "Ra Vatu has arranged that we should be well received."

But Narau groaned again, and backed away from the heels he had dogged so faithfully.

"Ra Vatu is soon to become Lotu," Starhurst explained, "and I have come bringing the Lotu to you."

"I want none of your Lotu," said the Buli, proudly. "And it is in my mind that you will be clubbed this day."

The Buli nodded to one of his big mountaineers, who stepped forward, swinging a club. Narau bolted into the nearest house, seeking to hide among the women and mats; but John Starhurst sprang in under the club and threw his arms around his executioner's neck. From this point of vantage he proceeded to argue. He was arguing for his life, and he knew it; but he was neither excited nor afraid.

"It would be an evil thing for you to kill me," he told the man. "I have done you no wrong, nor have I done the Buli wrong."

So well did he cling to the neck of the one man that they dared not strike with their clubs. And he continued to cling and to dispute for his life with those who clamored for his death.

"I am John Starhurst," he went on calmly. "I have labored in Fiji for three years, and I have done it for no profit. I am here among you for good. Why should any man kill me? To kill me will not profit any man."

The Buli stole a look at the whale tooth. He was well paid for the deed.

The missionary was surrounded by a mass of naked savages, all struggling to get at him. The death song, which is the song of the oven, was raised, and his expostulations could no longer be heard. But so cunningly did he twine and wreathe his body about his captor's that the death blow could not be struck. Erirola smiled, and the Buli grew angry.

"Away with you!" he cried. "A nice story to go back to the coast—a dozen of you and one missionary, without weapons, weak as a woman, overcoming all of you."

"Wait, O Buli," John Starhurst called out from the thick of the scuffle, "and I will overcome even you. For my weapons are Truth and Right, and no man can withstand them."

"Come to me, then," the Buli answered, "for my weapon is only a poor miserable club, and, as you say, it cannot withstand you."

The group separated from him, and John Starhurst stood alone, facing the Buli, who was leaning on an enormous, knotted warclub.[7]

"Come to me, missionary man, and overcome me," the Buli challenged.

"Even so will I come to you and overcome you," John Starhurst made answer, first wiping his spectacles and settling them properly, then beginning his advance.

The Buli raised the club and waited.

"In the first place, my death will profit you nothing," began the argument.

"I leave the answer to my club," was the Buli's reply.

And to every point he made the same reply, at the same time watching the missionary closely in order to forestall that cunning run-in under the lifted club. Then, and for the first time, John Starhurst knew that his death was at hand. He made no attempt to run in. Bareheaded, he stood in the sun and prayed aloud—the mysterious figure of the inevitable white man, who, with Bible, bullet, or rum bottle, has confronted the amazed savage in his every stronghold. Even so stood John Starhurst in the rock fortress of the Buli of Gatoka.

"Forgive them, for they know not what they do," he prayed. "O Lord! Have mercy upon Fiji. Have compassion for Fiji. O Jehovah, hear us for His sake, Thy Son, whom Thou didst give that through Him all men might also become Thy children. From Thee we came, and our mind is that to Thee we may return. The land is dark, O Lord, the land is dark. But Thou art mighty to save. Reach out Thy hand, O Lord, and save Fiji, poor cannibal Fiji."[8]

The Buli grew impatient.

"Now will I answer thee," he muttered, at the same time swinging his club with both hands.

Narau, hiding among the women and the mats, heard the impact of the blow and shuddered. Then the death song arose, and he knew his beloved missionary's body was being dragged to the oven as he heard the words:

"Drag me gently. Drag me gently."

"For I am the champion of my land."

"Give thanks! Give thanks! Give thanks!"

Next, a single voice arose out of the din, asking:

"Where is the brave man?'

A hundred voices bellowed the answer:

"Gone to be dragged into the oven and cooked."

"Where is the coward?" the single voice demanded.

"Gone to report!" the hundred voices bellowed back. "Gone to report! Gone to report!"

Narau groaned in anguish of spirit. The words of the old song were true. He was the coward, and nothing remained to him but to go and report.

Notes

1. Herbert Spencer, "Absolute Political Ethics," *The Nineteenth Century* (Jan. 1890): 119.
2. Placed at the beginning of the magazine appearance of the story was a Fijian aphorism:

A mate na-rawarawa:
Me bula—na ka ni cava?
A mate ne cegu.

Death is easy:
Of what use is life?
To die is rest.

3. In "The Whale Tooth," as in "The Chinago," interior texts are crucial to a firm understanding of the clash between white and aboriginal cultures. If the first and last sentences of "The Chinago" deal with knowing, the first and last sentences of "The Whale Tooth" deal directly with texts. The first sentence mentions the Gospel, a text that will be carried by a white man into the interior of Fiji. The last sentence (the last word actually) mentions Narau's report, a text not yet composed, that a Fijian will carry to the outside world. And in between these two texts lie others, including the great whale tooth itself carrying its grim humor and irony.
4. There is fine economy here, as the narrative implies that the Fijians regard Ra Undreundre not as an abominable mass murderer but as an admirable victor in many battles, the owner of a fine display of trophies, and a community leader struck down ("unfortunately") by an unseasoned upstart. London further challenges the anticipated and likely reactions of his readers' interpretations of the grisly cenotaphic text of stones as he points out the connections between the practices of the cannibals, who ritually devour their "favorite enemy" and the Christians who (though in low-church Protestantism metaphorically) devour the incarnation of their God.
5. The notion of the ambiguity of the missionary is also embedded in two of London's other South Sea narratives, "The House of Pride" and "Good Bye, Jack." In both of these stories missionaries have come with "the lofty purpose of teaching the kanakas the true religion, the worship of the one only genuine and undeniable God, [but] the missionary who came to give the bread of life remained to gobble up the whole heathen feast."

6. Though the narrative of Jack London's story does not tell us that the tooth has been carved or written on, it is undeniably a kind of text, since it impels its viewers/readers toward interpretation. As it arrives in close temporal proximity to the arrival of the missionary, the savvy island chiefs easily conclude that acceptance of the tooth will obligate them to kill Starhurst. Mongondro, for example, hands it back to Erirola with "many apologies." But Starhurst, who has had a "calling"—an unusual sort of extratextual interpretive awareness—has no idea that this whale tooth is at first following him and finally preceding him. The reader knows that Starhurst is moving inexorably closer to his own inevitable destruction, like Oedipus when he decides to leave Corinth to make a new home for himself in Thebes. But unlike his classical predecessor, Starhurst himself will never experience anagnorisis—a character's sudden awareness of his unwitting involvement in a fate-ridden design. Only Starhurst's islander companion, the converted Christian Narau, will live to interpret with an understanding as complete as the story's reader.
7. The Fijians had a tool culture that included over thirty varieties of war clubs and a set of values that disdained the use of pointed weapons when dispatching an opponent. (See, for example, John Fowler, "Fiji: The Warrior Archipelago," http://www.tribalsite.com/articles/fiji.htm, 2.)
8. Just as Ah Cho, when he realizes his death is imminent, remembers passages from "The Tract of the Quiet Way," John Starhurst, when he sees the Buli's raised club, finds comfort in the faith his text provides. In "The Chinago" the narrative ends with the abrupt drop of the blade of the guillotine, but "The Whale Tooth" does not end with the drop of the club. London suggests that the story will be retold by Narau, who escapes Starhurst's fate by hiding in a native hut among the women. Narau hears the death song (yet another text) and listens to the words. The reader is left to speculate about the accuracy of the absent and not-yet-composed text—Narau's report.

With this perspective, the tales may be seen to present the kind of subject matter that anticipates by a generation and a half the academic discussions of postmodern critics. The one thread that seems to run through all of our contemporary poststructuralist conflicts is the unreliability of texts—whatever they might be—to mediate meaning—whatever that is—from "writer" to "reader." Whether it was his intention to do so or not, few writers at the turn of the twentieth century could have more clearly set forth the basic issues that vex literary criticism today than did Jack London in "The Chinago" and "The Whale Tooth" in 1908.

An Introduction to "The Heathen"

In the first flush of new love, during the summer of 1903, Jack London wrote a curious letter to Charmian Kittredge, not focused specifically on their relationship but rather serving as a kind of confession of a long-held fantasy of male friendship. He wrote:

> I had dreamed of the great Man-Comrade. I, who have been comrades with many men, and a good comrade I believe, have never had a comrade at all, and in the deeper significance of it have never been able to be the comrade I was capable of being. Always it was here this one failed, and there that one failed until all failed.... It was plain that it was not possible. I could never hope to find that comradeship, that closeness, that sympathy and understanding, whereby the man and I might merge and become one for love and life.
>
> How can I say what I mean? This man should be so much one with me that we could never misunderstand. He should love the flesh, as he should the spirit, honoring and loving each and giving each its due. There should be in him both fact and fancy. He should be practical in-so-far as the mechanics of life were concerned; and fanciful, imaginative, sentimental where the thrill of life was concerned. He should be delicate and tender, brave and game, sensitive as

> he pleased in the soul of him, and in the body of him unfearing and unwitting of pain. He should be warm with glow of great adventure, unafraid of the harshnesses of life and its evils, and knowing all its harshness and evil.
>
> Do you see...the man I am trying to picture for you?—an all-around man, who could weep over a strain of music, a bit of verse, and who could grapple with the fiercest life and fight good-naturedly or like a fiend as the case might be . . . —the man who could live at the same time in the realms of fancy and of fact; who, knowing the frailties and weaknesses of life, could look with frank fearless eyes upon them; a man who had no smallnesses and meannesses, who could sin greatly, perhaps, but who could as greatly forgive. . . . [1]

Though certain idealizing transformations obviously took place in the process of turning fact to fiction, London is believed to have been inspired to write this story because of a friendship with an islander named Tehei. (London cues our pronunciations in his *Cruise of the Snark*, and, as nonspeakers of Pacific languages, we have found this helpful: Tay-hay-ee.) Tehei was a Polynesian, a native of the island of Tahaa (Tah-hah-ah), just north of Raiatea (Ra-ee-ah-tay-ah). They first met when he showed the Londons around his island neighborhood and introduced them to some local customs. Tehei and London took to each other at once, and the author invited the islander as a guest passenger on the *Snark* on April 4, 1908. Bihaura (Bee-ah-oo-rah), Tehei's wife, accompanied them as well. The first stop on their jaunt was Bora Bora, which of course would become the home island of Otoo (O-to-o) in the story. One day during the voyage—on April 15, in fact—Tehei told Jack he wanted to sail with him on the *Snark*'s ambitious round-the-world cruise.

London was touched by this gesture, seeing it as a frank expression of trust and a devoted act of willing comradeship. However, Jack was bothered by the one-sidedness of such an arrangement, since Tehei had become not only a friend but an able shipmate as well. Finally, London said he'd only allow Tehei to continue with them if he would accept a salary. Tehei quickly agreed, and so, for $12 a month, Tehei signed on as a member of the crew of the *Snark*. He could speak almost no English, but he worked hard to learn it. They sailed on to Guadalcanal, where, on July 7, they anchored to go ashore and visit the white managers of one of the Solomon Islands' biggest copra plantations, Penduffryn.

No sooner were they safely back at Penduffryn than they decided to sail for Ontong Java Atoll. Unfortunately, after they set out, Jack and Charmian realized they had left their charts at the plantation. Lost at sea for several days, the *Snark* could easily have drifted in these waters indefinitely except for a stroke of good luck. It was Tehei who first spotted Ontong Java, crying, "Lan' ho!" on September 17.

On Ontong, they met the colorful adventurer Harold Markham and the Malaitan serial fugitive who became the source for the hero of "Mauki." The party then sailed back to Guadalcanal, from which, after much soul-searching, they decided to interrupt the voyage of the *Snark* and take a steamer to Sydney, where the complex of tropical illnesses that afflicted London might be treated in a hospital. Tehei appears to have been left at Penduffryn, and we have been unable to trace his subsequent career.

Though the real-life friendship between London and Tehei has none of the life-altering glamour of the relationship that exists in "The Heathen," it nonetheless indicates the patchwork inconsistency of Jack's racial thinking. Nothing in the fictional or the real-life relationships suggests that either Charley or London felt any concerns about a color line between Polynesians and whites, though such a line certainly exists in the minds of many other whites, and there is in the story a clear-cut distinction made in the characterization of Melanesians. In the end, it is possible that Jack London used the interracial issue because it would emphasize for his audiences the transcendent nature of the idealized friendship about which he had for so long fantasized.

Though knocked down by an attack of malaria, Jack worked on "The Heathen," completing the first draft on July 15, 1908. A series of parties and hijinks followed on Guadalcanal, culminating in a bizarre experiment in which the group decided to try hashish mixed with butter and spread on bread. Though the others became satisfactorily stupefied, Jack apparently only became violently sick. By August 2, despite illnesses and misadventures, Jack completed the polishing of "The Heathen" and submitted it for publication. Submitted to ten magazines, it finally saw print in

London Magazine a little over a year later, followed by its American appearance in *Everybody's* in August of 1910. The illustrations are by the brilliant maritime artist Anton Otto Fischer.

THE HEATHEN

I met him first in a hurricane. And though we had been through the hurricane on the same schooner, it was not until the schooner had gone to pieces under us that I first laid eyes on him. Without doubt I had seen him with the rest of the Kanaka crew on board, but I had not consciously been aware of his existence, for the *Petite Jeanne* was rather overcrowded. In addition to her eight or ten Kanaka sea men, her white captain, mate, and supercargo, and her six cabin passengers, she sailed from Rangiroa with something like eighty-five deck passengers—Paumotuans and Tahitians, men, women, and children, each with a trade-box, to say nothing of sleeping-mats, blankets, and clothes-bundles.

The pearling season in the Paumotus was over, and all hands were returning to Tahiti. The six of us cabin passengers were pearl-buyers. Two were Americans, one was Ah Choon, the whitest Chinese I have ever known, one was a German, one was a Polish Jew, and I completed the half-dozen.

It had been a prosperous season. Not one of us had cause for complaint, nor one of the eighty-five deck passengers either. All had done well, and all were looking forward to a rest-off and a good time in Papeete.

Of course the *Petite Jeanne* was overloaded. She was only seventy tons, and she had no right to carry a tithe of the mob she had on board.

Beneath her hatches she was crammed and jammed with pearl shell and copra. Even the trade-room was packed full of shell. It was a miracle that the sailors could work her. There was no

moving about the decks. They simply climbed back and forth along the rails.

In the night-time they walked upon the sleepers, who carpeted the deck, two deep, I'll swear. Oh, and there were pigs and chickens on deck, and sacks of yams, while every conceivable place was festooned with strings of drinking cocoanuts and bunches of bananas. On both sides, between the fore and main shrouds, guys had been stretched, just low enough for the fore-boom to swing clear; and from each of these guys at least fifty bunches of bananas were suspended.

It promised to be a messy passage, even if we did make it in the two or three days that would have been required if the southeast trades had been blowing fresh. But they weren't blowing fresh. After the first five hours, the trade died away in a dozen gasping fans. The calm continued all that night and the next day—one of those glaring, glossy calms when the very thought of opening one's eyes to look at it is sufficient to cause a headache.

The second day a man died, an Easter Islander, one of the best divers that season in the lagoon. Smallpox, that is what it was, though how smallpox could come on board when there had been no known cases ashore when we left Rangiroa is beyond me. There it was, though, smallpox, a man dead, and three others down on their backs.

There was nothing to be done. We could not segregate the sick, nor could we care for them. We were packed like sardines. There was nothing to do but die—that is, there was nothing to do after the night that followed the first death. On that night, the mate, the supercargo, the Polish Jew, and four native divers sneaked away in the large whaleboat. They were never heard of again. In the morning the captain promptly scuttled the remaining boats, and there we were.

That day there were two deaths; the following day three; then it jumped to eight. It was curious to see how we took it. The natives, for instance, fell into a condition of dumb, stolid fear. The captain—Oudouse, his name was, a Frenchman—became very nervous and voluble.

The German, the two Americans, and myself bought up all the Scotch whisky and proceeded to drink. The theory was beautiful—namely, if we kept ourselves soaked in alcohol, every smallpox germ that came into contact with us would immediately be scorched to a cinder. And the theory worked, though I must confess that neither Captain Oudouse nor Ah Choon was attacked by the disease either. The Frenchman did not drink at all, while Ah Choon restricted himself to one drink daily.

It was a pretty time. The sun, going into northern declination, was straight overhead. There was no wind, except for frequent squalls, which blew fiercely for from five minutes to half an hour, and wound up by deluging us with rain. After each squall, the awful sun would come out, drawing clouds of steam from the soaked decks.

The steam was not nice. It was the vapor of death, freighted with millions and millions of germs. We always took another drink when we saw it going up from the dead and dying, and usually we took two or three more drinks, mixing them exceptionally stiff. Also, we made it a rule to take an additional several each time they hove the dead over to the sharks that swarmed about us.

We had a week of it, and then the whisky gave out. It was just as well, or I shouldn't be alive now. It took a sober man to pull through what followed, as you will agree when I mention the little fact that only two men did pull through. The other man was the Heathen—at least that was what I heard Captain Oudouse call him at the moment I first became aware of the Heathen's existence. But to come back.

It was at the end of the week, with the whiskey gone, and the pearl-buyers sober, that I happened to glance at the barometer that hung in the cabin companion-way. Its normal register in the Paumotus was 29.90, and it was quite customary to see it vacillate between 29.85 and 30.00, or even 30.05; but to see it, as I saw it, down to 29.62, was sufficient to sober the most drunken pearl-buyer that ever incinerated smallpox microbes in Scotch whiskey.

I called Captain Oudouse's attention to it, only to be informed that he had watched it going down for several hours. There was little to do, but that little he did very well, considering the circumstances. He took off the light sails, shortened right down to storm canvas, spread life-lines, and waited for the wind. His mistake lay in what he did after the wind came. He hove to on the port tack, which was the right thing to do south of the Equator, if—and there was the rub—if one were not in the direct path of the hurricane.

We were in the direct path. I could see that by the steady increase of the wind and the equally steady fall of the barometer. I wanted to turn and run with the wind on the port quarter until the barometer ceased falling, and then to heave to. We argued till he was reduced to hysteria, but budge he would not. The worst of it was that I could not get the rest of the pearl-buyers to back me up. Who was I, anyway, to know more about the sea and its ways than a properly qualified captain? was what was in their minds, I knew.

Of course, the sea rose with the wind, frightfully, and I shall never forget the first three seas the *Petite Jeanne* shipped. She had

The women and children, the bananas and cocoanuts, the pigs and trade-boxes, the sick and the dying, were swept along in a solid, screeching, groaning mass.

fallen off, as vessels do when hove to, and the first sea made a clean breach. The lifelines were only for the strong and well, and little good were they even for these when the women and children, the bananas and cocoanuts, the pigs and trade-boxes, the sick and the dying, were swept along in a solid, screeching, groaning mass.

The second sea filled the *Petite Jeanne's* decks flush with the rails, and, as her stern sank down and her bow tossed skyward, all the miserable dunnage of life and luggage poured aft. It was a human torrent. They came head-first, feet-first, sidewise, rolling over and over, twisting, squirming, writhing, and crumpling up. Now and again one or another caught a grip on a stanchion or a rope, but the weight of the bodies behind tore such grips loose.

One man I noticed fetch up, head on and square on, with the starboard-bitt. His head cracked like an egg. I saw what was coming, sprang on top the cabin, and from there into the mainsail itself. Ah Choon and one of the Americans tried to follow me, but I was one jump ahead of them. The American was swept away and over the stern like a piece of chaff. Ah Choon caught a spoke of the wheel and swung in behind it. But a strapping Rarotonga vahine (woman)—she must have weighed two hundred and fifty—brought up against him and got an arm around his neck. He clutched the Kanaka steersman with his other hand. And just at that moment the schooner flung down to starboard.

The rush of bodies and the sea that was coming along the port runway between the cabin and the rail, turned abruptly and poured to starboard. Away they went, vahine, Ah Choon, and steersman; and I swear I saw Ah Choon grin at me with philosophic resignation as he cleared the rail and went under.

The third sea—the biggest of the three—did not do so much damage. By the time it arrived, nearly everybody was in the rigging. On deck perhaps a dozen gasping, half-drowned, and half-stunned wretches were rolling about or attempting to crawl into safety. They went by the board, as did the wreckage of the two remaining boats. The other pearl-buyers and myself, between seas, managed to get about fifteen women and children into the cabin and battened down. Little good it did the poor creatures in the end.

Wind? Out of all my experiences I could not have believed it possible for the wind to blow as it did. There is no describing it. How can one describe a nightmare? It was the same way with that wind. It tore the clothes off our bodies. I say tore them off, and I mean it. I am not asking you to believe it. I am merely telling something that I saw and felt. There are times when I do not believe it myself. I went through it, and that is enough. One could not face that wind and live. It was a monstrous thing, and the most monstrous thing about it was that it increased and continued to increase.

Imagine countless millions and billions of tons of sand. Imagine this sand tearing along at ninety, a hundred, a hundred and twenty, or any other number of miles per hour. Imagine, further, this sand to be invisible, impalpable, yet to retain all the weight and density of sand. Do all this, and you may get a vague inkling of what that wind was like. Perhaps sand is not the right comparison. Consider it mud, invisible, impalpable, but heavy as mud. Nay, it goes beyond that. Consider every molecule of air to be a mud-bank in itself. Then try to imagine the multitudinous impact of mud-banks—no, it is beyond me. Language may be adequate to express the ordinary conditions of life, but it cannot possibly express any of the conditions of so enormous a blast of wind. It would have been better had I stuck by my original intention of not attempting a description.

I will say this much: The sea, which had risen at first, was beaten down by that wind. More—it seemed as if the whole ocean had been sucked up in the maw of the hurricane and hurled on through that portion of space which previously had been occupied by the air.

Of course, our canvas had gone long before. But Captain Oudouse had on the *Petite Jeanne* something I had never before seen on a South Sea schooner—a sea-anchor. It was a conical canvas bag, the mouth of which was kept open by a huge hoop of iron. The sea-anchor was bridled something like a kite, so that it bit into the water as a kite bites into the air—but with a difference. The sea-anchor remained just under the surface of the ocean, in a perpendicular position. A long line, in turn, connected it with the schooner. As a result, the *Petite Jeanne* rode bow-on to the wind and to what little sea there was.

The situation really would have been favorable, had we not been in the path of the storm. True, the wind itself tore our canvas out of the gaskets, jerked out our topmasts, and made a raffle of our running gear; but still we would have come through nicely had we not been square in front of the advancing storm-center. That was what fixed us. I was in a state of stunned, numbed, paralyzed collapse from enduring the impact of the wind, and I think I was just about ready to give up and die when the center smote us. The blow we received was an absolute lull. There was not a breath of air. The effect on one was sickening.

Remember that for hours we had been at terrific muscular tension, withstanding the awful pressure of that wind. And then, suddenly, the pressure was removed. I know that I felt as though I were about to expand, to fly apart in all directions. It seemed as if every atom composing my body was repelling every other atom, and was on the verge of rushing off irresistibly into space. But that lasted only for a moment. Destruction was upon us.

In the absence of the wind and pressure the sea rose. It jumped, it leaped, it soared straight toward the clouds. Remember, from every point of the compass that inconceivable wind was blowing in toward the center of calm. The result was that the seas sprang up from every point of the compass. There was no wind to check them. They popped up like corks released from the bottom of a pail of water. There was no system to them, no stability. They were hollow, maniacal seas. They were eighty feet high at the least. They were not seas at all. They resembled no sea a man had ever seen.

They were splashes, monstrous splashes, that is all, splashes that were eighty feet high. Eighty! They were more than eighty. They went over our mastheads. They were spouts, explosions. They were drunken. They fell anywhere, anyhow. They jostled one another, they collided. They rushed together and collapsed upon one another, or fell apart like a thousand waterfalls all at once. It was no ocean any man ever dreamed of, that hurricane-center. It was confusion thrice confounded. It was anarchy. It was a hell-pit of sea water gone mad.

The *Petite Jeanne*? I don't know. The Heathen told me afterward that he did not know. She was literally torn apart, ripped wide open, beaten into a pulp, smashed into kindling wood, annihilated. When I came to, I was in the water, swimming automatically, though I was about two-thirds drowned. How I got there I had no recollection. I remembered seeing the *Petite Jeanne* fly to pieces at what must have been the instant that my own consciousness was buffeted out of me. But there I was, with nothing to do but make the best of it, and in that best there was little promise. The wind was blowing again, the sea was much smaller and more regular, and I knew that I had passed through the center. Fortunately, there were no sharks about. The hurricane had dissipated the ravenous horde that had surrounded the death ship and fed off the dead.

It was about midday when the *Petite Jeanne* went to pieces, and it must have been two hours afterward when I picked up with one of her hatch-covers. Thick rain was driving at the time; and it was the merest chance that flung me and the hatch-cover together. A short length of line was trailing from the rope handle; and I knew that I was good for a day at least, if the sharks did not return. Three hours later, possibly a little longer, sticking close to the cover and, with closed eyes, concentrating my whole soul upon the task of breathing in enough air to keep me going and, at the same time, to avoid breathing in enough water to drown me, it seemed to me that I heard voices. The rain had ceased, and wind and sea were easing marvelously. Not twenty feet away from me, on another hatch-cover, were Captain Oudouse and the Heathen. They were fighting over the possession of the cover—at least the Frenchman was.

"Paien noir!" I heard him scream, and at the same time I saw him kick the Kanaka.

Now, Captain Oudouse had lost all his clothes except his shoes, and they were heavy brogans. It was a cruel blow, for it caught the Heathen on the mouth and the point of the chin, half-stunning him. I looked for him to retaliate, but he contented himself with swimming about forlornly, a safe ten feet away. Whenever a fling of the sea threw him closer, the Frenchman, hanging on with his hands, kicked out at him with both feet. Also, at the moment of delivering each kick, he called the Kanaka a black heathen.

"For two centimes I'd come over there and drown you, you white beast!" I yelled.

The only reason I did not go was that I felt too tired. The very thought of the effort to swim over was nauseating. So I called to the Kanaka to come to me, and proceeded to share the hatch-cover with him. Otoo, he told me his name was (pronounced o-to-o); also he told me that he was a native of Bora Bora, the most westerly of the Society Group. As I learned afterward, he had got the hatch-cover first, and, after some time, encountering Captain Oudouse, had offered to share it with him, and had been kicked off for his pains.

And that was how Otoo and I first came together. He was no fighter. He was all sweetness and gentleness, a love-creature though he stood nearly six feet tall and was muscled like a gladiator. He was no fighter, but he was also no coward. He had the heart of a lion, and in the years that followed I have seen him run risks that I would never dream of taking. What I mean is that, while he was no fighter, and while he always avoided precipitating a row, he never ran away from trouble when it started. And it was " 'Ware shoal!" when once Otoo went into action. I shall never forget what he did to Bill King. It occurred in German Samoa. Bill King was hailed the champion heavyweight of the American navy. He was a big brute of a man, a veritable gorilla, one of those hard-hitting, rough-housing chaps, and clever with his fists as well. He picked the quarrel, and he kicked Otoo twice and struck him once before Otoo felt it to be necessary to fight. I don't think it lasted four minutes, at the end of which time Bill King was the unhappy possessor of four broken ribs, a broken fore-arm, and a dislocated shoulder-blade. Otoo knew nothing of scientific boxing. He was merely a man-handler, and Bill King was something like three months in recovering from the bit of man-handling he received that afternoon on Apia beach.

But I am running ahead of my yarn. We shared the hatch-cover between us. We took turn and turn about, one lying flat on the cover and resting, while the other, submerged to the neck, merely held on with his hands. For three days and nights, spell and spell, on the cover and in the water, we drifted over the ocean. Toward the last I was delirious most of the time, and there were times, too, when I heard Otoo babbling and raving in his native tongue. Our continuous immersion prevented us from dying of thirst, though the sea water and the sunshine gave us the prettiest imaginable combination of salt pickle and sunburn. In the end, Otoo saved my life; for I came to, lying on the beach twenty feet from the water, sheltered from the sun by a couple of cocoanut leaves. No one but Otoo could have dragged me there and stuck up the leaves for shade. He was lying beside me. I went off again, and the next time I came around it was cool and starry night and Otoo was pressing a drinking cocoanut to my lips.

We were the sole survivors of the *Petite Jeanne.* Captain Oudouse must have succumbed to exhaustion, for several days later his hatch-cover drifted ashore without him. Otoo and I lived with the natives of the atoll for a week, when we were rescued by a French cruiser and taken to Tahiti. In the meantime, however, we had performed the ceremony of exchanging names. In the South Seas such a ceremony binds two men closer together than blood-brothership. The initiative had been mine, and Otoo was rapturously delighted when I suggested it.[2]

"It is well," he said, in Tahitian. "For we have been mates together for three days on the lips of Death."

"But Death stuttered," I smiled.

"It was a brave deed you did, master," he replied, "and Death was not vile enough to speak."

"Why do you 'master' me?" I demanded, with a show of hurt feelings. "We have exchanged names. To you I am Otoo. To me you are Charley. And between you and me, forever and forever, you

We took turn and turn about, one lying flat on the cover and resting, while the other merely held on with his hands.

shall be Charley and I shall be Otoo. It is the way of the custom. And when we die, if it does happen that we live again, somewhere beyond the stars and the sky, still shall you be Charley to me and I Otoo to you."

"Yes, master," he answered, his eyes luminous and soft with joy.

"There you go!" I cried indignantly.

"What does it matter what my lips utter?" he argued. "They are only my lips. But I shall think Otoo always. Whenever I think of myself I shall think of you. Whenever men call me by name I shall think of you. And beyond the sky and beyond the stars always and forever you shall be Otoo to me. Is it well, master?"

I hid my smile and answered that it was well.

We parted at Papeete. I remained ashore to recuperate, and he went on in a cutter to his own island, Bora Bora. Six weeks later he was back. I was surprised, for he had told me of his wife and said that he was returning to her and would give over sailing on far voyages.

"Where do you go, master?" he asked, after our first greetings.

"Whenever I think of myself, I shall think of you. Whenever men call me by name I shall think of you. Is it well, master?"

I shrugged my shoulders. It was a hard question. "To all the world," was my answer. "All the world, all the sea, and all the islands that are in the sea."

"I will go with you," he said simply. "My wife is dead."

I never had a brother; but from what I have seen of other men's brothers I doubt if any man ever had one who was to him what Otoo was to me. He was brother, and father and mother as well. And this I know—I lived a straighter and a better man because of Otoo. I had to live straight in Otoo's eyes. Because of him I dared not tarnish myself. He made me his ideal, compounding me, I fear, chiefly out of his own love and worship; and there were times when I stood close to the steep pitch of hell and would have taken the plunge had not the thought of Otoo restrained me. His pride in me entered into me until it became one of the major rules in my personal code to do nothing that would diminish that pride of his.

Naturally, I did not learn right away what his feelings were toward me. He never criticised, never censured, and slowly the exalted place I held in his eyes dawned upon me, and slowly I grew to comprehend the hurt I could inflict upon him by being anything less than my best.

For seventeen years we were together. For seventeen years he was at my shoulder, watching while I slept, nursing me through fever and wounds, aye, and receiving wounds in fighting for me. He signed on the same ships with me, and together we ranged the Pacific from Hawaii to Sydney Head and from Torres Strait to the Galapagos. We blackbirded from the New Hebrides and the Line Islands over to the westward, clear through the Louisiades, New Britain, New Ireland, and New Hanover. We were wrecked three times—in the Gilberts, in the Santa Cruz group, and in the Fijis. And we traded and salved wherever a dollar promised in the way of pearl and pearl shell, copra, bêche-de-mer, hawkbill turtle shell, and stranded wrecks.

It began in Papeete, immediately after his announcement that he was going with me over all the sea and the islands in the midst thereof. There was a club in those days in Papeete, where the pearlers, traders, captains, and South Sea adventurers foregathered. The play ran high and the drink ran high, and I am very much afraid that I kept later hours than were becoming or proper. No matter what the hour was when I left the club, there was Otoo waiting to see me safely home. At first I smiled. Next I chided him. Then I told him flatly I stood in need of no wet-nursing. After that I did not see him when I came out of the club. Quite by accident, a week or so later, I discovered that he still saw me home, lurking across the street among the shadows of the mango trees. What could I do? I know what I did do.

Insensibly I began to keep better hours. On wet and stormy nights, in the thick of the folly and the fun, the thought would come to me of Otoo keeping his dreary vigil under the dripping mangoes. Truly, he made me a better man. Yet he was not strait-laced. And he knew nothing of common Christian morality. All the people on Bora Bora were Christians. But he was a heathen, the only unbeliever on the island, a gross materialist who believed that when he died he was dead. He believed merely in fair play and square-dealing. Petty meanness, in his code, was almost as serious as wanton homicide, and I am sure that he respected a murderer more than a man given to small practices.

Concerning me, personally, he objected to my doing anything that was hurtful to me. Gambling was all right. He was an ardent gambler himself. But late hours, he explained, were bad for one's health. He had seen men who did not take care of themselves die of fever. He was no teetotaler, and welcomed a stiff nip any time when it was wet work in the boats. On the other hand, he believed in liquor in moderation. He had seen many men killed or disgraced by squareface or Scotch.

Otoo had my welfare always at heart. He thought ahead for me, weighed my plans and took a greater interest in them than I did myself. At first, when I was unaware of this interest of his in my affairs, he had to divine my intentions, as, for instance, at Papeete, when I contemplated going partners with a knavish fellow countryman on a guano venture. I did not know he was a knave. Nor did any white man in Papeete. Neither did Otoo know; but he saw how thick we were getting and found out for me, and that without my asking. Native sailors from the ends of the seas knock about on the beach in Tahiti, and Otoo, suspicious merely, went among them till he had gathered sufficient data to justify his suspicions. Oh, it was a nice history, that of Randolph Waters! I couldn't believe it when Otoo first narrated it, but when I sheeted it home to Waters he gave in without a murmur and got away on the first steamer to Auckland.

At first, I am free to confess, I resented Otoo's poking his nose into my business. But I knew that he was wholly unselfish, and soon I had to acknowledge his wisdom and discretion. He had his eyes open always to my main chance, and he was both keen-sighted and far-sighted. In time he became my counselor, until he knew more of my business than I did myself. He really had my interest at heart more than I did. Mine was the magnificent carelessness of youth, for I preferred romance to dollars, and adventure to a comfortable billet with all night in. So it was well that I had some one to look out for me. I know that if it had not been for Otoo, I should not be here to-day.

Of numerous instances, let me give one. I had had some experience in blackbirding before I went pearling in the Paumotus. Otoo and I were on the beach in Samoa—we really were on the beach and hard aground—when my chance came to go as a recruiter on a blackbird brig. Otoo signed on before the mast, and for the next half-dozen years, in as many ships, we knocked about the wildest portions of Melanesia. Otoo saw to it that he always pulled stroke-oar in my boat. Our custom, in recruiting labor, was to land the recruiter on the beach. The covering boat always lay on its oars several hundred feet off shore, while the recruiter's boat, also lying on its oars, kept afloat on the edge of the beach. When I landed with my trade goods, leaving my steering sweep apeak, Otoo left his stroke position and came into the stern sheets, where a Winchester lay ready to hand under a flap of canvas. The boat's crew was also armed, the Sniders concealed under canvas flaps that ran the length of the gunwales. While I was busy arguing and persuading the woolly-headed cannibals to come and labor on the Queensland plantations Otoo kept watch. And often and often his low voice warned me of suspicious actions and impending treachery. Sometimes it was the quick shot from his rifle, knocking a nigger over, that was the first warning I received.[3] And in my rush to the boat his hand was always there to jerk me flying aboard. Once, I remember, on Santa Anna, the boat grounded just as the trouble began. The covering boat was dashing to our assistance, but the several score of savages would have wiped us out before it arrived. Otoo took a flying leap ashore, dug both hands into the trade goods, and scattered tobacco, beads, tomahawks, knives, and calicoes in all directions.

This was too much for the woolly-heads. While they scrambled for the treasures, the boat was shoved clear and we were aboard and forty feet away. And I got thirty recruits off that very beach in the next four hours.

The particular instance I have in mind was on Malaita, the most savage island in the easterly Solomons. The natives had been remarkably friendly; and how were we to know that the whole village had been taking up a collection for over two years with which to buy a white man's head? The beggars are all head-hunters, and they especially esteem that of a white man. The fellow who captured the head would receive the whole collection. As I say, they appeared very friendly, and this day I was fully a hundred yards down the beach from the boat. Otoo had cautioned me, and, as usual when I did not heed him, I came to grief.

The first I knew, a cloud of spears sailed out of the mangrove swamp at me. At least a dozen were sticking into me. I started to run, but tripped over one that was fast in my calf and went down. The woolly-heads made a run for me, each with a long-handled, fantail tomahawk with which to hack off my head. They were so eager for the prize that they got in one another's way. In the confusion I avoided several hacks by throwing myself right and left on the sand.

Then Otoo arrived—Otoo the man-handler. In some way he had got hold of a heavy war-club, and at close quarters it was a far more efficient weapon than a rifle. He was right in the thick of them, so that they could not spear him, while their tomahawks seemed worse than useless. He was fighting for me, and he was in a true Berserker rage. The way he handled that club was amazing. Their skulls squashed like overripe oranges. It was not until he had driven them back, picked me up in his arms, and started to run, that he received his first wounds. He arrived in the boat with four spear-thrusts, got his Winchester, and with it got a man for every shot. Then we pulled aboard the schooner and doctored up.

Seventeen years we were together. He made me. I should today be a supercargo, a recruiter, or a memory, if it had not been for him.

"You spend your money, and you go out and get more," he said, one day. "It is easy to get money, now. But when you get old, your money will be spent and you will not be able to go out and get more. I know, master. I have studied the way of white men. On the beaches are many old men who were young once and who could get money just like you. Now they are old, and they have nothing, and they wait about for the young men like you to come ashore and buy drinks for them.

"The black boy is a slave on the plantations. He gets twenty dollars a year. He works hard. The overseer does not work hard. He rides a horse and watches the black boy work. He gets twelve hundred dollars a year. I am a sailor on the schooner. I get fifteen dollars a month. That is because I am a good sailor. I work hard.

The captain has a double awning and drinks beer out of long bottles. I have never seen him haul a rope or pull an oar. He gets one hundred and fifty dollars a month. I am a sailor. He is a navigator. Master, I think it would be very good for you to know navigation."

Otoo spurred me on to it. He sailed with me as second mate on my first schooner, and he was far prouder of my command than was I myself. Later on it was:

"The captain is well paid, master, but the ship is in his keeping and he is never free from the burden. It is the owner who is better paid, the owner who sits ashore with many servants and turns his money over."

"True, but a schooner costs five thousand dollars—an old schooner at that," I objected. "I should be an old man before I saved five thousand dollars."

"There be short ways for white men to make money," he went on, pointing ashore at the cocoanut-fringed beach.

We were in the Solomons at the time, picking up a cargo of ivory-nuts along the east coast of Guadalcanar.

"Between this river mouth and the next it is two miles," he said. "The flat land runs far back. It is worth nothing now. Next year—who knows!—or the year after—men will pay much money for that land. The anchorage is good. Big steamers can lie close up. You can buy the land four miles deep from the old chief for ten thousand sticks of tobacco, ten bottles of squareface, and a Snider, which will cost you maybe one hundred dollars. Then you place the deed with the commissioner, and the next year, or the year after, you sell and become the owner of a ship."

I followed his lead, and his words came true, though in three years instead of two. Next came the grass-lands deal on Guadalcanar—twenty thousand acres on a governmental nine hundred and ninety-nine years' lease at a nominal sum. I owned the lease for precisely ninety days, when I sold it to the Moonlight Soap crowd for half a fortune. Always it was Otoo who looked ahead and saw the opportunity. He was responsible for the salving of the *Doncaster*—bought in at auction for five hundred dollars and clearing fifteen thousand after every expense was paid. He led me into the Savaii plantation and the cocoa venture on Upolu.

We did not go seafaring so much as in the old days now. I was too well off. I married and my standard of living rose; but Otoo remained the same old-time Otoo, moving about the house or trailing through the office, his wooden pipe in his mouth, a shilling undershirt on his back, and a four-shilling lava-lava about his loins. I could not get him to spend money. There was no way of repaying him except with love, and God knows he got that in full measure from all of us. The children worshiped him, and if he had been spoilable my wife would surely have been his undoing.

The children! He really was the one who showed them the way of their feet in the world practical. He began by teaching them to walk. He sat up with them when they were sick. One by one, when they were scarcely toddlers, he took them down to the lagoon and made them into amphibians. He taught them more than I ever knew of the habits of fish and the ways of catching them. In the bush it was the same thing. At seven, Tom knew more woodcraft than I ever dreamed existed. At six, Mary went over the Sliding Rock without a quiver—and I have seen strong men balk at that feat. And when Frank had just turned six he could bring up shillings from the bottom in three fathoms.

"My people in Bora Bora do not like heathen; they are all Christians; and I do not like Bora Bora Christians," he said one day, when I, with the idea of getting him to spend some of the money that was rightfully his, had been trying to persuade him to make a visit to his own island in one of our schooners—a special voyage that I had hoped to make a record-breaker in the matter of prodigal expense.

I say one of *our* schooners, though legally, at the time, they belonged to me. I struggled long with him to enter into partnership.

"We have been partners from the day the *Petite Jeanne* went down," he said at last. "But if your heart so wishes, then shall we become partners by the law. I have no work to do, yet are my expenses large. I drink and eat and smoke in plenty—it costs much, I know. I do not pay for the playing of billiards, for I play on your table; but still the money goes. Fishing on the reef is only a rich man's pleasure. It is shocking, the cost of hooks and cotton line. Yes, it is necessary that we be partners by the law. I need the money. I shall get it from the head clerk in the office."

So the papers were made out and recorded. A year later I was compelled to complain.

"Charley," said I, "you are a wicked old fraud, a miserly skin-flint, a miserable land-crab. Behold, your share for the year in all our partnership has been thousands of dollars. The head clerk has given me this paper. It says that during the year you have drawn just eighty-seven dollars and twenty cents."

"Is there any owing me?" he asked anxiously.

"I tell you thousands and thousands," I answered.

His face brightened as with an immense relief.

"It is well," he said. "See that the head-clerk keeps good account of it. When I want it, I shall want it, and there must not be a cent missing. If there is," he added fiercely, after a pause, "it must come out of the clerk's wages."

And all the time, as I afterward learned, his will, drawn up by Carruthers and making me sole beneficiary, lay in the American consul's safe.

But the end came as the end must come to all human associations. It occurred in the Solomons, where our wildest work had been done in the wild young days, and where we were once more—principally on a holiday, incidentally to look after our holdings on Florida Island and to look over the pearling possibilities of the Mboli Pass. We were lying at Savo, having run in to trade for curios. Now Savo is alive with sharks. The custom of the woolly-heads of burying their dead in the sea did not tend to discourage the sharks from making the adjacent waters a hang-out. It was my luck to be coming aboard in a tiny, overloaded, native canoe, when the thing capsized. There were four woolly heads and myself in it, or rather, hanging to it. The schooner was a hundred yards away. I was just hailing for a boat when one of the woolly-heads began to scream. Holding on to the end of the canoe, both he and that portion of the canoe were dragged under several times. Then he loosed his clutch and disappeared. A shark had got him.

The three remaining niggers tried to climb out of the water upon the bottom of the canoe. I yelled and cursed and struck at the nearest with my fist, but it was no use. They were in a blind funk. The canoe could barely have supported one of them. Under the three it up-ended and rolled sidewise, throwing them back into the water.

I abandoned the canoe and started to swim toward the schooner, expecting to be picked up by the boat before I got there. One of the niggers elected to come with me, and we swam along silently, side by side, now and again putting our faces into the water and peering about for sharks. The screams of the men who stayed by the canoe informed us that they were taken. I was peering into the water when I saw a big shark pass directly beneath me. He was fully sixteen feet in length. I saw the whole thing. He got the woolly-head by the middle and away he went, the poor devil, head, shoulders, and arms out of water all the time, screeching in a heart-rending way. He was carried along in this fashion for several hundred feet, when he was dragged beneath the surface.

I swam doggedly on, hoping that that was the last unattached shark. But there was another. Whether it was one that had attacked the natives earlier, or whether it was one that had made a good meal elsewhere, I do not know. At any rate, he was not in such haste as the others. I could not swim so rapidly now, for a large part of my effort was devoted to keeping track of him. I was watching him when he made his first attack. By good luck I got both hands on his nose, and, though his momentum nearly shoved me under, I managed to keep him off. He veered clear and began circling about again. A second time I escaped him by the same maneuver. The third rush was a miss on both sides. He sheered at the moment my hands should have landed on his nose, but his sandpaper hide—I had on a sleeveless undershirt—scraped the skin off one arm from elbow to shoulder.

By this time I was played out and gave up hope. The schooner was still two hundred feet away. My face was in the water and I was watching him maneuver for another attempt, when I saw a brown body pass between us. It was Otoo.

"Swim for the schooner, master," he said, and he spoke gayly, as though the affair was a mere lark. "I know sharks. The shark is my brother."

I obeyed, swimming slowly on, while Otoo swam about me, keeping always between me and the shark, foiling his rushes and encouraging me.

"The davit-tackle carried away, and they are rigging the falls," he explained a minute or so later, and then went under to head off another attack.

By the time the schooner was thirty feet away I was about done for. I could scarcely move. They were heaving lines at us from on board, but these continually fell short. The shark, finding that it was receiving no hurt, had become bolder. Several times it nearly got me, but each time Otoo was there just the moment before it was too late. Of course Otoo could have saved himself any time. But he stuck by me.

"Good by, Charley, I'm finished," I just managed to gasp.

I knew that the end had come and that the next moment I should throw up my hands and go down.

But Otoo laughed in my face, saying:

"I will show you a new trick. I will make that shark damn sick."

He dropped in behind me, where the shark was preparing to come at me.

"A little more to the left," he next called out. "There is a line there on the water. To the left, master—to the left!"

I changed my course and struck out blindly. I was by that time barely conscious. As my hand closed on the line I heard an exclamation from on board. I turned and looked. There was no sign of Otoo. The next instant he broke surface. Both hands were off at the wrist, the stumps spouting blood.

"Otoo," he called softly, and I could see in his gaze the love that thrilled in his voice. Then, and then only, at the very last of all our years, he called me by that name.

"Good by, Otoo," he called.

Then he was dragged under, and I was hauled aboard, where I fainted in the captain's arms.

And so passed Otoo, who saved me and made me a man, and who saved me in the end. We met in the maw of a hurricane and parted in the maw of a shark, with seventeen intervening years of comradeship the like of which I dare to assert have never befallen two men, the one brown and the other white. If Jehovah be from His high place watching every sparrow fall, not least in His Kingdom shall be Otoo, the one heathen of Bora Bora. And if there be no place for him in that Kingdom, then will I have none of it.[4]

Notes

1. Jack London. *Letters*, vol. 1, 370–71.
2. London remained intrigued by this idea and returned to it in the 1911 story, "The Devils of Fuatino," in which the redoubtable Captain David Grief has also exchanged names with a Polynesian youth named Mauriri.
3. As London's readers have come to acquire a keenness of consciousness about race that has now surpassed even the author's own, they have tended to find in "The Heathen" the sort of representation they have expected to find. In the early 1940s, when this story found its way into

fiction anthologies and high school textbooks, it was admired for its fiercely detailed picture of a storm at sea and for its courageous examination of a friendship that transcended cultural and racial differences. While the first of these strengths in this story remains for us to admire half a century afterward, it is nowadays impossible for us to read the account of the friendship between Charley and Otoo so simply. There was already a degree of awareness of this problem at the time of the mid-century anthologies, indicated by certain editorial changes in London's language. For example, fiction anthology editors (at Doubleday in 1945 and 1953 and later in 1962 and 1964 at Fawcett) omitted the word "nigger" from Charley's characterizations of Solomon Islanders or substituted for it what apparently seemed to them to be a less insensitive term: "woolyheads." (The sensitivity of these editors was, however, selective: They apparently didn't notice or didn't care, and so they retained Charley's stirring encomium about his friend, Ah Choon—"the whitest Chinese I have ever known.") By the 1970s, as editors began to see the complexity of the ideas about race embedded in "The Heathen," it simply became easier to drop the story from collections altogether. Today, like much of London's short fiction set in the Pacific, it remains powerful, touching, disturbing, and largely ignored.

4. The editors have retrieved the last sentence of the story from the magazine version (*Everybody's Magazine*, August, 1910), though it occurs in none of the subsequent publications of "The Heathen." Furthermore, entire paragraphs not in *Everybody's* were included when the story was published as part of *South Sea Tales* (Macmillan, 1911). We have opted to use the text from the first edition, assuming that it represents London's final version, but this conclusion is too striking to omit. The complete text of "The Heathen" in its original magazine form is available at the Jack London Web site, http://sunsite.berkeley.edu/London/Writings/SouthSea/heathen.html. It is tempting to suppose that this sentence was cut because of its antireligious sentiment; however, there are several passages in the story in which Otoo freely expresses his heathen, anti-Christian opinions. Perhaps London intended to show that, as a result of his long friendship with Otoo, Charley too had become a heathen, a term that for him had become honorific.

An Introduction to "The Terrible Solomons"

The phrase "the inevitable white man" is used several times in London's Pacific fiction, and it is fraught with ironic implications. By failing to examine these ironies, some readers have been led to think along lines that are almost the precise opposite of what the stories actually seem to be about. London makes it clear that it is not the search for scientific knowledge, nor an existential drive to discover the essence of life, nor a quest to extend their nations' political influence that has really brought Europeans to the Pacific. Instead, it is greed that is the call the white colonialists have answered. However disguised by reference to selfless service under "the White Man's Burden," greed has become the underlying, rationalized fact behind the commission of inhuman atrocities. The rapacious white opportunists believe that their own inevitability is a state of being, not a moral choice, an attitude that leads many of London's characters "inevitably" to corruption and death.

In "The Terrible Solomons," the character of Captain Malu is probably based on a combination of actual people Jack met in the islands, likely including Captain Jansen of the *Minota,* as well as other experienced veterans in the Solomons. Malu and his friends, who have survived all of the islands' threats against long life, from fevers to tomahawks, see in the fresh-faced and imaginative tourist Bertie Arkwright an opportunity to exercise what remains of their sense of humor. They rumor, insinuate, hint, imply, suggest, and thereby create fearful dangers and narrow escapes—which they trust Bertie will imaginatively magnify into an increasingly unbearable horror. Working further on the theme of interpretation introduced in "The Chinago," London has these practical jokers plan to create texts that Bertie will certainly misread. Starting from a simple, old fictional chestnut, the "cowboys tease the dude" scenario, London goes on to analyze the psychology of misinterpretation itself.

A careful reading of this intriguing story demonstrates how far-reaching are London's intellectual underpinnings. For example, London pointedly cites the Romantic poet William Wordsworth (1770–1850) twice in the narrative. Wordsworth's understanding of the psychology of the imagination provides a perfect background to allow the author to show exactly how Bertie's mind is working. Wordsworth suggests that it is the function of the poet to take "incidents and situations from common life . . . and . . . throw over them a certain coloring of the imagination, whereby ordinary things should be presented to the mind in an unusual aspect." Certainly then poor Bertie Arkwright plays the poet with his tourist's visit to the Solomons.

Considered in this light, the curious thing about this adventure story is that it is precisely not an adventure story. Had there really been cannibal attacks, mutinies, poison plots, and murders on a remote jungle island—had there really been a handful of rough-and-tumble, gin-soaked hardies clad in pith helmets, canvas shoes, and tropical suits, risking their necks in a struggle against naked savagery, "The Terrible Solomons" would have qualified. Instead, there is a complete absence of these features—that is, outside the romantically charged brain of Bertie Arkwright. This is not the exotic; it is the artifice of exoticism, methodically presented to the reader as exactly the opposite of the expectations aroused by the title, effectively serving as an erased adventure story.

Within twelve days after completing "The Terrible Solomons," London began work on his South Seas novel *Adventure*, in which these savage occurrences do actually happen. "The Terrible Solomons" thus serves to erase a work not yet composed—a whimsical paradox that ought to warm the heart of the most thoroughgoing contemporary literary critic.

The story was written in September of 1908, while the *Snark*'s skipper and crew put up with cockroach infestations and miserable illnesses, as the Londons continued their exploration of the "terrible" Solomon Islands. It first appeared in *Hampton's* magazine in March of 1910, illustrated with ink drawings by Charles Sarka.

THE TERRIBLE SOLOMONS

There is no gainsaying that the Solomons are a hard-bitten bunch of islands. On the other hand, there are worse places in the world. But to the new chum who has no constitutional understanding of men and life in the rough, the Solomons may indeed prove terrible.

It is true that fever and dysentery are perpetually on the walk-about, that loathsome skin diseases abound, that the air is saturated with a poison that bites into every pore, cut, or abrasion and plants malignant ulcers, and that many strong men who escape dying there return as wrecks to their own countries. It is also true that the natives of the Solomons are a wild lot, with a hearty appetite for human flesh and a fad for collecting human heads. Their highest instinct of sportsmanship is to catch a man with his back turned and to smite him a cunning blow with a tomahawk that severs the spinal column at the base of the brain.[1] It is equally true that on some islands, such as Malaita, the profit and loss account of social intercourse is calculated in homicides. Heads are a medium of exchange, and white heads are extremely valuable. Very often a dozen villages make a jack-pot, which they fatten moon by moon, against the time when some brave warrior presents a white man's head, fresh and gory, and claims the pot.

All the foregoing is quite true, and yet there are white men who have lived in the Solomons a score of years and who feel homesick when they go away from them. A man needs only to be careful—and lucky—to live a long time in the Solomons; but he must also be of the right sort. He must have the hallmark of the inevitable white man stamped upon his soul. He must be inevitable. He must have a certain grand carelessness of odds, a certain colossal self-satisfaction, and a racial egotism that convinces him that one white is better than a thousand niggers every day in the week, and that on Sunday he is able to clean out two thousand niggers. For such are the things that have made the white man inevitable. Oh, and one other thing—the white man who wishes to be inevitable, must not merely despise the lesser breeds and think a lot of himself; he must also fail to be too long on imagination. He must not understand too well the instincts, customs, and mental processes of the blacks, the yellows, and the browns; for it is not in such fashion that the white race has tramped its royal road around the world.

Bertie Arkwright was not inevitable. He was too sensitive, too finely strung, and he possessed too much imagination. The world was too much with him. He projected himself too quiveringly into his environment. Therefore, the last place in the world for him to come was the Solomons. He did not come, expecting to stay. A five weeks' stop-over between steamers, he decided, would satisfy the call of the primitive he felt thrumming the strings of his being. At least, so he told the lady tourists on the *Makembo*, though in different terms; and they worshipped him as a hero, for they were lady tourists and they would know only the safety of the steamer's deck as she threaded her way through the Solomons.[2]

There was another man on board, of whom the ladies took no notice. He was a little shriveled wisp of a man, with a withered skin the color of mahogany. His name on the passenger list does not matter, but his other name, Captain Malu, was a name for niggers to conjure with, and to scare naughty pickaninnies to righteousness from New Hanover to the New Hebrides. He had farmed savages and savagery, and from fever and hardship, the crack of Sniders and the lash of the overseers, had wrested five millions of money in the form of bêche-de-mer, sandalwood, pearl-shell and turtle-shell, ivory nuts and copra, grasslands, trading stations, and plantations. Captain Malu's little finger, which was broken, had more inevitableness in it than Bertie Arkwright's whole carcass. But then, the lady tourists had nothing by which to judge save appearances, and Bertie certainly was a fine-looking man.[3]

Bertie talked with Captain Malu in the smoking room, confiding to him his intention of seeing life red and bleeding in the Solomons. Captain Malu agreed that the intention was ambitious and honorable. It was not until several days later that he became interested in Bertie, when that young adventurer insisted on showing him an automatic 44-caliber pistol. Bertie explained the mechanism and demonstrated by slipping a loaded magazine up the hollow butt.

"It is so simple," he said. He shot the outer barrel back along the inner one. "That loads it and cocks it, you see. And then all I have to do is pull the trigger, eight times, as fast as I can quiver my finger. See that safety clutch. That's what I like about it. It is safe. It is positively fool-proof." He slipped out the magazine. "You see how safe it is."

As he held it in his hand, the muzzle came in line with Captain Malu's stomach. Captain Malu's blue eyes looked at it unswervingly.

"Would you mind pointing it in some other direction?" he asked.

"It's perfectly safe," Bertie assured him. "I withdrew the magazine. It's not loaded now, you know."

"A gun is always loaded."

"But this one isn't."

"Turn it away just the same."

Captain Malu's voice was flat and metallic and low, but his eyes never left the muzzle until the line of it was drawn past him and away from him.

"I'll bet a fiver it isn't loaded," Bertie proposed warmly.

The other shook his head.

"Then I'll show you."

Bertie started to put the muzzle to his own temple with the evident intention of pulling the trigger.

"Just a second," Captain Malu said quietly, reaching out his hand. "Let me look at it."

He pointed it seaward and pulled the trigger. A heavy explosion followed, instantaneous with the sharp click of the mechanism that flipped a hot and smoking cartridge sidewise along the deck.

Bertie's jaw dropped in amazement.

"I slipped the barrel back once, didn't I?" he explained. "It was silly of me, I must say."

He giggled flabbily, and sat down in a steamer chair. The blood had ebbed from his face, exposing dark circles under his eyes. His hands were trembling and unable to guide the shaking cigarette to his lips. The world was too much with him, and he saw himself with dripping brains prone upon the deck.[4]

"Really," he said, ". . . really."

"It's a pretty weapon," said Captain Malu, returning the automatic to him.

The Commissioner was on board the *Makembo,* returning from Sydney, and by his permission a stop was made at Ugi to land a missionary. And at Ugi lay the ketch *Arla,* Captain Hansen, skipper. Now the *Arla* was one of many vessels owned by Captain Malu, and it was at his suggestion and by his invitation that Bertie went aboard the *Arla* as guest for a four days' recruiting cruise on the coast of Malaita. Thereafter the *Arla* would drop him at Reminge Plantation (also owned by Captain Malu), where Bertie could remain for a week, and then be sent over to Tulagi, the seat of government, where he would become the Commissioner's guest. Captain Malu was responsible for two other suggestions, which given, he disappears from this narrative. One was to Captain Hansen, the other to Mr. Harriwell, manager of Reminge Plantation. Both suggestions were similar in tenor, namely, to give Mr. Bertram Arkwright an insight into the rawness and redness of life in the Solomons. Also, it is whispered that Captain Malu mentioned that a case of Scotch would be coincidental with any particularly gorgeous insight Mr. Arkwright might receive.

"Yes, Swartz always was too pig-headed. You see, he took four of his boat's crew to Tulagi to be flogged—officially, you know—then started back with them in the whaleboat. It was pretty squally, and the boat capsized just outside. Swartz was the only one drowned. Of course, it was an accident."

"Was it? Really?" Bertie asked, only half-interested, staring hard at the black man at the wheel.

Ugi had dropped astern, and the *Arla* was sliding along through a summer sea toward the wooded ranges of Malaita. The helmsman who so attracted Bertie's eyes sported a ten penny nail, stuck skewerwise through his nose. About his neck was a string of pants buttons. Thrust through holes in his ears were a can opener, the broken handle of a toothbrush, a clay pipe, the

"Was it really?" Bertie asked, staring at the black man at the wheel.

brass wheel of an alarm clock, and several Winchester rifle cartridges. On his chest, suspended from around his neck hung the half of a china plate. Some forty similarly appareled blacks lay about the deck, fifteen of which were boat's crew, the remainder being fresh labor recruits.

"Of course it was an accident," spoke up the *Arla's* mate, Jacobs, a slender, dark-eyed man who looked more a professor than a sailor. "Johnny Bedip nearly had the same kind of accident. He was bringing back several from a flogging, when they capsized him. But he knew how to swim as well as they, and two of them were drowned. He used a boat stretcher and a revolver. Of course it was an accident."

"Quite common, them accidents," remarked the skipper. "You see that man at the wheel, Mr. Arkwright? He's a man eater. Six months ago, he and the rest of the boat's crew drowned the then captain of the *Arla*. They did it on deck, sir, right aft there by the mizzen-traveler."

"The deck was in a shocking state," said the mate.

"Do I understand—?" Bertie began.

"Yes, just that," said Captain Hansen. "It was an accidental drowning."

"But on deck—?"

"Just so. I don't mind telling you, in confidence, of course, that they used an axe."

"This present crew of yours?"

Captain Hansen nodded.

"The other skipper always was too careless," explained the mate. "He but just turned his back, when they let him have it."

"We haven't any show down here," was the skipper's complaint. "The government protects a nigger against a white every time. You can't shoot first. You've got to give the nigger first shot, or else the government calls it murder and you go to Fiji. That's why there's so many drowning accidents."[5]

Dinner was called, and Bertie and the skipper went below, leaving the mate to watch on deck.

"Keep an eye out for that black devil, Auiki," was the skipper's parting caution. "I haven't liked his looks for several days."

"Right O," said the mate.

Dinner was part way along, and the skipper was in the middle of his story of the cutting out of the *Scottish Chiefs*.

"Yes," he was saying, "she was the finest vessel on the coast. But when she missed stays, and before ever she hit the reef, the canoes started for her. There were five white men, a crew of twenty Santa Cruz boys and Samoans, and only the supercargo escaped. Besides, there were sixty recruits. They were all *kai-kai'd. Kai-kai* ?—oh, I beg your pardon. I mean they were eaten. Then there was the *James Edwards*, a dandy-rigged—"

But at that moment there was a sharp oath from the mate on deck and a chorus of savage cries. A revolver went off three times, and then was heard a loud splash. Captain Hansen had sprung up the companionway on the instant, and Bertie's eyes had been fascinated by a glimpse of him drawing his revolver as he sprang. Bertie went up more circumspectly, hesitating before he put his head above the companionway slide. But nothing happened. The mate was shaking with excitement, his revolver in his hand. Once he startled, and half-jumped around, as if danger threatened his back.

"One of the natives fell overboard," he was saying, in a queer tense voice.

"He couldn't swim."

"Who was it?" the skipper demanded.

"Auiki," was the answer.

"But I say, you know, I heard shots," Bertie said, in trembling eagerness, for he scented adventure, and adventure that was happily over with.

The mate whirled upon him, snarling:

"It's a damned lie. There ain't been a shot fired. The nigger fell overboard."

Captain Hansen regarded Bertie with unblinking, lack-luster eyes.

"I—I thought—" Bertie was beginning.

"Shots?" said Captain Hansen, dreamily. "Shots? Did you hear any shots, Mr. Jacobs?"

"Not a shot," replied Mr. Jacobs.

The skipper looked at his guest triumphantly, and said:

"Evidently an accident. Let us go down, Mr. Arkwright, and finish dinner."

Bertie slept that night in the captain's cabin, a tiny stateroom off the main cabin. The for'ard bulkhead was decorated with a stand of rifles. Over the bunk were three more rifles. Under the bunk was a big drawer, which, when he pulled it out, he found filled with ammunition, dynamite, and several boxes of detonators. He elected to take the settee on the opposite side. Lying conspicuously on the small table was the *Arla*'s log. Bertie did not know that it had been especially prepared for the occasion by Captain Malu, and he read therein how on September 21, two boat's crew had fallen overboard and been drowned. Bertie read between the lines and knew better. He read how the *Arla*'s whale boat had been bushwhacked at Su'u and had lost three men; of how the skipper discovered the cook stewing human flesh on the galley fire—flesh purchased by the boat's crew ashore in Fui; of how an accidental discharge of dynamite, while signaling, had killed another boat's crew; of night attacks; ports fled from between the dawns; attacks by bushmen in mangrove swamps and by fleets of salt-water men in the larger passages. One item that occurred with monotonous frequency was death by dysentery. He noticed with alarm that two white men had so died—guests, like himself, on the *Arla*.

"I say, you know," Bertie said next day to Captain Hansen. "I've been glancing through your log."

The skipper displayed quick vexation that the log had been left lying about.

"And all that dysentery, you know, that's all rot, just like the accidental drownings," Bertie continued. "What does dysentery really stand for?"

The skipper openly admired his guest's acumen, stiffened himself to make indignant denial, then gracefully surrendered.

"You see, it's like this, Mr. Arkwright. These islands have got a bad enough name as it is. It's getting harder every day to sign on white men. Suppose a man is killed. The company has to pay through the nose for another man to take the job. But if the man merely dies of sickness, it's all right. The new chums don't mind disease. What they draw the line at is being murdered. I thought the skipper of the *Arla* had died of dysentery when I took his billet. Then it was too late. I'd signed the contract."[6]

"Besides," said Mr. Jacobs, "there's altogether too many accidental drownings anyway. It don't look right. It's the fault of the government. A white man hasn't a chance to defend himself from the niggers."

"Yes, look at the *Princess* and that Yankee mate," the skipper took up the tale. "She carried five white men besides a government agent. The captain, the agent, and the supercargo were ashore in the two boats. They were killed to the last man. The mate and bosun, with about fifteen of the crew—Samoans and Tongans—were on board. A crowd of niggers came off from shore. First thing the mate knew, the boson and the crew were killed in the first rush. The mate grabbed three cartridge belts and two Winchesters and skinned up to the cross-trees. He was the sole survivor, and you can't blame him for being mad. He pumped one rifle till it got so hot he couldn't hold it, then he pumped the other. The deck was black with niggers. He cleaned them out. He dropped them as they went over the rail, and he dropped them as fast as they picked up their paddles. Then they jumped into the water and started to swim for it, and being mad, he got half a dozen more. And what did he get for it?"

"Seven years in Fiji," snapped the mate.

"The government said he wasn't justified in shooting after they'd taken to the water," the skipper explained.

"And that's why they die of dysentery nowadays," the mate added.

"Just fancy," said Bertie, as he felt a longing for the cruise to be over.[7]

Later on in the day he interviewed the black who had been pointed out to him as a cannibal. This fellow's name was Sumasai. He had spent three years on a Queensland plantation. He had been to Samoa, and Fiji, and Sydney; and as a boat's crew had been on recruiting schooners through New Britain, New Ireland, New Guinea, and the Admiralties. Also, he was a wag, and he had taken a line on his skipper's conduct. Yes, he had eaten many men. How many? He could not remember the tally. Yes, white men, too; they were very good, unless they were sick. He had once eaten a sick one.

"My word!" he cried, at the recollection. "Me sick plenty along him. My belly walk about too much."

Bertie shuddered, and asked about heads. Yes, Sumasai had several hidden ashore, in good condition, sun-dried, and smoke-cured. One was of the captain of a schooner. It had long whiskers. He would sell it for two quid. Black men's heads he would sell for one quid. He had some pickaninny heads, in poor condition, that he would let go for ten bob.

Five minutes afterward, Bertie found himself sitting on the companionway-slide alongside a black with a horrible skin disease. He sheered off, and on inquiry was told that it was leprosy. He hurried below and washed himself with antiseptic soap. He took many antiseptic washes in the course of the day, for every native on board was afflicted with malignant ulcers of one sort or another.

As the *Arla* drew in to an anchorage in the midst of mangrove swamps, a double row of barbed wire was stretched around above her rail. That looked like business, and when Bertie saw the shore canoes alongside, armed with spears, bows and arrows, and Sniders, he wished more earnestly than ever that the cruise was over.

That evening the natives were slow in leaving the ship at sundown. A number of them checked the mate when he ordered them ashore. "Never mind, I'll fix them," said Captain Hansen, diving below.

When he came back, he showed Bertie a stick of dynamite attached to a fish hook. Now it happens that a paper-wrapped bottle of chlorodyne with a piece of harmless fuse projecting can fool anybody. It fooled Bertie, and it fooled the natives. When Captain Hansen lighted the fuse and hooked the fish hook into the tail end

He started for'ard, and the natives in his path took headers over the barbed wire at every jump.

of a native's loin cloth, that native was smitten with so an ardent a desire for the shore that he forgot to shed the loin cloth. He started for'ard, the fuse sizzling and spluttering at his rear, the natives in his path taking headers over the barbed wire at every jump. Bertie was horror-stricken. So was Captain Hansen. He had forgotten his twenty-five recruits, on each of which he had paid thirty shillings advance. They went over the side along with the shore-dwelling folk and followed by him who trailed the sizzling chlorodyne bottle.

Bertie did not see the bottle go off; but the mate opportunely discharging a stick of real dynamite aft where it would harm nobody, Bertie would have sworn in any admiralty court to a nigger blown to flinders. The flight of the twenty-five recruits had actually cost the *Arla* forty pounds, and, since they had taken to the bush, there was no hope of recovering them. The skipper and his mate proceeded to drown their sorrow in cold tea. The cold tea was in whiskey bottles, so Bertie did not know it was cold tea they were mopping up. All he knew was that the two men got very drunk and argued eloquently and at length as to whether the exploded nigger should be reported as a case of dysentery or as an accidental drowning. When they snored off to sleep, he was the only white man left, and he kept a perilous watch till dawn, in fear of an attack from shore and an uprising of the crew.

Three more days the *Arla* spent on the coast, and three more nights the skipper and the mate drank overfondly of cold tea, leaving Bertie to keep the watch. They knew he could be depended upon, while he was equally certain that if he lived, he would report their drunken conduct to Captain Malu. Then the Arla dropped anchor at Reminge Plantation, on Guadalcanar, and Bertie landed on the beach with a sigh of relief and shook hands with the manager. Mr. Harriwell was ready for him.

"Now you mustn't be alarmed if some of our fellows seem downcast," Mr. Harriwell said, having drawn him aside in confidence. "There's been talk of an outbreak, and two or three suspicious signs I'm willing to admit, but personally I think it's all poppycock."

"How—how many blacks have you on the plantation?" Bertie asked, with a sinking heart.

"We're working four hundred just now," replied Mr. Harriwell, cheerfully; "but the three of us, with you, of course, and the skipper and mate of the *Arla*, can handle them all right."

Bertie turned to meet one McTavish, the storekeeper, who scarcely acknowledged the introduction, such was his eagerness to present his resignation.

"It being that I'm a married man, Mr. Harriwell, I can't very well afford to remain on longer. Trouble is working up, as plain as the nose on your face. The niggers are going to break out, and there'll be another Hohono horror here."

"What's a Hohono horror?" Bertie asked, after the storekeeper had been persuaded to remain until the end of the month.

"Oh, he means Hohono Plantation, on Ysabel," said the manager. "The niggers killed the five white men ashore, captured the schooner, killed the captain and mate, and escaped in a body to Malaita. But I always said they were careless on Hohono. They won't catch us napping here. Come along, Mr. Arkwright, and see our view from the veranda."

Bertie was too busy wondering how he could get away to Tulagi to the Commissioner's house, to see much of the view. He was still wondering, when a rifle exploded very near to him, behind his back. At the same moment his arm was nearly dislocated, so eagerly did Mr. Harriwell drag him indoors.

"I say, old man, that was a close shave," said the manager, pawing him over to see if he had been hit. "I can't tell you how sorry I am. But it was broad daylight, and I never dreamed."

Bertie was beginning to turn pale.

"They got the other manager that way," McTavish vouchsafed. "And a dashed fine chap he was. Blew his brains out all over the veranda. You noticed that dark stain there between the steps and the door?"

Bertie was ripe for the cocktail which Mr. Harriwell pitched in and compounded for him; but before he could drink it, a man in riding trousers and puttees entered.

"What's the matter now?" the manager asked, after one look at the newcomer's face. "Is the river up again?"

"River be blowed—it's the niggers. Stepped out of the cane grass, not a dozen feet away, and whopped at me. It was a Snider, and he shot from the hip. Now what I want to know is where'd he get that Snider?—Oh, I beg pardon. Glad to know you, Mr. Arkwright."

"Mr. Brown is my assistant," explained Mr. Harriwell. "And now let's have that drink."

"But where'd he get that Snider?" Mr. Brown insisted. "I always objected to keeping those guns on the premises."

"They're still there," Mr. Harriwell said, with a show of heat.

Mr. Brown smiled incredulously.

"Come along and see," said the manager.

Bertie joined the procession into the office, where Mr. Harriwell pointed triumphantly at a big packing case in a dusty corner.

"Well, then where did the beggar get that Snider?" harped Mr. Brown.

But just then McTavish lifted the packing case. The manager started, then tore off the lid. The case was empty. They gazed at one another in horrified silence. Harriwell drooped wearily.

Then McVeigh cursed.

"What I contended all along—the house-boys are not to be trusted."

"It does look serious," Harriwell admitted, "but we'll come through it all right. What the sanguinary niggers need is a shaking up. Will you gentlemen please bring your rifles to dinner, and will you, Mr. Brown, kindly prepare forty or fifty sticks of dynamite. Make the fuses good and short. We'll give them a lesson. And now, gentlemen, dinner is served."

One thing that Bertie detested was rice and curry, so it happened that he alone partook of an inviting omelet. He had quite finished his plate, when Harriwell helped himself to the omelet. One mouthful he tasted, then spat out vociferously.

"That's the second time," McTavish announced ominously.

Harriwell was still hawking and spitting.

"Second time, what?" Bertie quavered.

"Poison," was the answer. "That cook will be hanged yet."

"That's the way the bookkeeper went out at Cape March," Brown spoke up. "Died horribly. They said on the Jessie that they heard him screaming three miles away."

"I'll put the cook in irons," sputtered Harriwell. "Fortunately we discovered it in time."

Bertie sat paralyzed. There was no color in his face. He attempted to speak, but only an inarticulate gurgle resulted. All eyed him anxiously.

"Don't say it, don't say it," McTavish cried in a tense voice.

"Yes, I ate it, plenty of it, a whole plateful!" Bertie cried explosively, like a diver suddenly regaining breath.

The awful silence continued half a minute longer, and he read his fate in their eyes.

"Maybe it wasn't poison after all," said Harriwell, dismally.

"Call in the cook," said Brown.

In came the cook, a grinning black boy, nose-spiked and ear-plugged.

"Here, you, Wi-wi, what name that?" Harriwell bellowed, pointing accusingly at the omelet.

Wi-wi was very naturally frightened and embarrassed.

"Him good fella *kai-kai*," he murmured apologetically.

"Make him eat it," suggested McTavish. "That's a proper test."

Harriwell filled a spoon with the stuff and jumped for the cook, who fled in panic.

"That settles it," was Brown's solemn pronouncement. "He won't eat it."

"Mr. Brown, will you please go and put the irons on him?" Harriwell turned cheerfully to Bertie. "It's all right, old man, the

"That settles it," said Brown.
"He won't eat it!"

Commissioner will deal with him, and if you die, depend upon it, he will be hanged."

"Don't think the government'll do it," objected McTavish.

"But gentlemen, gentlemen," Bertie cried. "In the meantime think of me."

Harriwell shrugged his shoulders pityingly.

"Sorry, old man, but it's a native poison, and there are no known antidotes for native poisons. Try and compose yourself and if—"

Two sharp reports of a rifle from without interrupted the discourse, and Brown, entering, reloaded his rifle and sat down to table.

"The cook's dead," he said. "Fever. A rather sudden attack."

"I was just telling Mr. Arkwright that there are no antidotes for native poisons—"

"Except gin," said Brown.

Harriwell called himself an absent-minded idiot and rushed for the gin bottle.

"Neat, man, neat," he warned Bertie, who gulped down a tumbler two-thirds full of the raw spirits, and coughed and choked from the angry bite of it till the tears ran down his cheeks.

Harriwell took his pulse and temperature, made a show of looking out for him, and doubted that the omelet had been poisoned. Brown and McTavish also doubted; but Bertie discerned an insincere ring in their voices. His appetite had left him, and he took his own pulse stealthily under the table. There was no question but what it was increasing, but he failed to ascribe it to the gin he had taken. McTavish, rifle in hand, went out on the veranda to reconnoiter.

"They're massing up at the cook-house," was his report.[8] "And they've no end of Sniders. My idea is to sneak around on the other side and take them in flank. Strike the first blow, you know. Will you come along, Brown?"

Harriwell ate on steadily, while Bertie discovered that his pulse had leaped up five beats. Nevertheless, he could not help jumping when the rifles began to go off. Above the scattering of Sniders could be heard the pumping of Brown's and McTavish's Winchesters—all against a background of demoniacal screeching and yelling.

"They've got them on the run," Harriwell remarked, as voices and gunshots faded away in the distance.

Scarcely were Brown and McTavish back at the table when the latter reconnoitered.

"They've got dynamite," he said.

"Then let's charge them with dynamite," Harriwell proposed.

Thrusting half a dozen sticks each into their pockets and equipping themselves with lighted cigars, they started for the door. And just then it happened. They blamed McTavish for it afterward, and he admitted that the charge had been a trifle excessive. But at any rate it went off under the house, which lifted up cornerwise and settled back on its foundations. Half the china on the table was shattered, while the eight-day clock stopped. Yelling for vengeance, the three men rushed out into the night, and the bombardment began.

When they returned, there was no Bertie. He had dragged himself away to the office, barricaded himself in, and sunk upon the floor in a gin-soaked nightmare, wherein he died a thousand deaths while the valorous fight went on around him. In the morning, sick and headachey from the gin, he crawled out to find the sun still in the sky and God presumably in heaven, for his hosts were alive and uninjured.

Harriwell pressed him to stay on longer, but Bertie insisted on sailing immediately on the *Arla* for Tulagi, where, until the following steamer day, he stuck close by the Commissioner's house.[9] There were lady tourists on the outgoing steamer, and Bertie was again a hero, while Captain Malu, as usual, passed unnoticed. But Captain Malu sent back from Sydney two cases of the best Scotch whiskey on the market, for he was not able to make up his mind as to whether it was Captain Hansen or Mr. Harriwell who had given Bertie Arkwright the more gorgeous insight into life in the Solomons.

Notes

1. London's fondness for telling stories that have multiple levels of meaning is once again evidenced, as the narrator tells us humorously of the nature of the challenge that confronts white men in the Solomons. As London knew, steel tomahawks were not native to the Solomons but were supplied originally by white traders, and some historians state that the practice of head-hunting itself had been suspended by the islanders for over a generation before the white man came to the islands and encouraged its reestablishment as a medium of trade. In fact, the full hypocrisy of the narrator's sneer at the islanders' customs is not clear to us until we read a few pages further and see that the burden of the plot of this tale is the distinctly unsportsmanlike conspiracy to attack Bertie, the main character, from behind—a conspiracy planned and executed by whites against one of their own.
2. The Londons were given lunch on the *Makambo* on August 22, 1908, just a few days before Jack began writing "The Terrible Solomons." The ship was named after a tiny island neighbor to Ghavutu, about 500 meters from Tulaghi Island in the Ngele Islands. Makambo was the headquarters of the Burns Philp Company, the most powerful capitalist operation in the South Seas. Though they would not invest deeply in sightseeing excursions until after the Londons' visit, Burns Philp was

already testing the tourist market in the late nineteenth century. By the 1920s, the company owned a monopoly on luxury voyages, allowing urban-weary Australians to get a glimpse of the exotic "cannibal isles." Before World War II, Lever Brothers also headquartered on Makambo.

3. In his ignorance of the challenges of this wilderness, Bertie resembles another London character, Percy Cuthfert, one of the tenderfeet of "In a Far Country" (published in 1899). Cuthfert is, at first, an eager participant in a party making an audacious journey to the Klondike in search of gold. London describes Cuthfert as suffering from "an abnormal development of sentimentality, [which] he mistook for the true spirit of romance and adventure." Cuthfert and his partner Weatherbee, like Bertie Arkwright, are unprepared for the strange and hostile environment in which they find themselves. In both stories London uses large doses of humor in developing narrative and character. However, the lessons learned by the characters provide different results. Bertie Arkwright survives the hazing of veterans experienced in living in the savage Solomons, presumably to return to civilization corrupted by the failure to face his own cowardice, choosing once again to pose as an adventurer, while Percy Cuthfert's and Carter Weatherbee's lesson in living in the unforgiving winter of the Northland ends in their untragic deaths.

Captain Malu, in "The Terrible Solomons," also has his parallel with a character in "In a Far Country." The small and wizened Sloper, whose "weight was probably ninety pounds, with the heavy hunting knife thrown in," is London's "inevitable white man" of the north. Sloper is "the incarnation of Teutonic stubbornness" and is drawn to the Northland by the same inborn trait that draws London's assemblage of white men to the Pacific—their "inevitableness."

The Yankee Sloper, "yellow and weak, fleeing from a South American fever-hole" has journeyed "nonstop across the zones" to pursue possible riches in the Klondike. Both Sloper's and Captain Malu's superiority is directly linked by London to their vast experience in their respective environments and not their physical strength or stature. The small Captain Malu, for example, has in his "little finger, which was broken, ...more inevitableness ...than Bertie Arkwright's whole carcass." Sloper is imaginative enough to predict correctly the ultimate demise of the lazy Cuthfert and Weatherbee; Malu, however, chooses not to imagine—or perhaps cannot imagine—Bertie Arkwright's comeuppance. Though Sloper can envision the destiny of Cuthfert and Weatherbee, Malu must control the details of an elaborate joke, have it acted out, and finally hear a full report from Hansen and Harriwell of any "gorgeous insights" Bertie might obtain.

The apparent joke, which is the narrative burden of the rest of the plot, is probably more complicated than it seems, since it in fact constitutes the rejection of an individual by the many, admirable perhaps to Social Darwinists, but hardly funny to a committed socialist—or to a true sportsman. More odious still, it is also a betrayal of the brotherhood of man, the importance of which is often stressed in the Northland stories. For example, Sloper and the rest of the party of prospectors leave Cuthfert and Weatherbee on their own only after making sure the two men have adequate shelter and more than adequate supplies.

4. Bertie's literary imagination is described in terms cited once through Shakespeare and twice through Wordsworth. Like the speaker in William Wordsworth's sonnet, Bertie wishes to escape the ennui of modern life and come to feel life dynamically, romantically:

The world is too much with us; late and soon,
Getting and spending, we lay waste our powers;
Little we see in nature that is ours;
We have given our hearts away, a sordid boon!

This sea that bares her bosom to the moon,
The winds that will be howling at all hours
And are up-gather'd now like sleeping flowers,
For this, for every thing, we are out of tune;

It moves us not.—Great God! I'd rather be
A Pagan suckled in a creed outworn,—
So might I, standing on this pleasant lea,

Have glimpses that would make me less forlorn;
Have sight of Proteus rising from the sea;
Or hear old Triton blow his wreathed horn.

London's allusion to Wordsworth is not accidental—it is an invitation to look at his story through the prism of Romanticism, and so we might also find it appropriate to recall in "Tintern Abbey" Wordsworth's interest in "all the mighty world/Of eye, and ear—both what they half-create/And what perceive," a fine introduction to the process of misinterpretation through which Bertie passes.

5. Whether in historical fact such fictional reports were actually submitted is neither confirmed nor denied by the text, since the claim is itself lodged in a fiction specifically created for Bertie to misread. Bertie goes on to assemble various clues that lead him to make false conclusions. The reader, however, is aware that this is a whole world of terror and excitement unseen by Bertie, one that consists entirely of fictions purposely constructed to mislead their intended "reader."

Bertie next consults the *Arla*'s log, which has been conveniently left out for him to peruse. London here lightly touches on a series of issues that invite deconstructive analysis. A ship's log, of course, is always expected to be a literal and accurate account of a vessel's day-to-day location, condition, and other relevant details; however, this log is a fiction, one devised by the now-absent Captain Malu, who has added to—or substituted for—the real log. Here, too, Bertie finds the record of terrifying violence concealed with the cover-up language: "Bertie read between the lines and knew better." This is followed by more outrageous fictions, which must have occasioned the wizened Captain Malu some amusement in the spinning.

6. The skipper goes on to justify the fraudulent log by telling a story that London would, only three weeks later, expand into "The Inevitable White Man"—the story of a not-very-bright sharpshooter named Saxtorph who shoots down a boatload of mutinous blacks. Captain Hansen avers that, because Saxtorph was sentenced to serve seven

years in the government prison on Fiji, all other blackbirders have since decided to turn in false reports of all deaths, just to avoid troublesome legal inquiries.

Docker, in *The Blackbirders* ([Sydney: Angus and Robertson, 1970], 71, 112, 114, 219, 223–24, 232, 239, 263–64) tells of several parliamentary inquiries into the procedures involved in labor recruiting between 1869 and 1906, noting the thorough approach taken by investigators and the often severe punishments that were handed out to miscreants.

7. The piling up of vivid details, the most grisly of which are concealed in the midst of a routine list of maritime activities, ending in the direct application of these events to the intended reader's own future, lends both verisimilitude and urgency to Bertie's interpretation. But now that Bertie knows what he thinks he knows, the skipper—a gifted thespian, apparently—lets the greenhorn in on the "meaning" of the text. Because Bertie has been reading between the lines, he guesses that "dysentery" is a code for something else. In coming to this conclusion, which the author-conspirators have fully predicted, Bertie ends up exactly wrong. He has read the lie only as a superficial lie, unaware of its real nature.

8. The level of cooperation between the white plantation owners and the black laborers to stage an uprising for Bertie's edification may seem improbable, but there is some evidence that natives on their home islands were accustomed to put on shows for passing tourist ships. As they saw the vessels come close to their island, they would assemble on the shore and produce spontaneous, crude parodies of traditional dances. On later occasions, it was suspected that sometimes native "attacks" on passing tourist ships were subsidized by the shipping lines themselves in order to add a little zest to the passengers' experience. (See Ngaire Douglas, *They Came for Savages: 100 Years of Tourism in Melanesia* [Lismore, New South Wales, Australia: Southern Cross University Press, 1996].) If this was a part of their home custom, it might not be surprising to find that their sense of humor could allow them to do something similar, perhaps even finding such pastimes a welcome break from their toils. As evidence of the natives' willingness to play such roles, we have included among London's photos in this book a picture of a "cannibal capture" of a white prisoner, recreated by Melanesians for the *Snark*'s cameraman, Martin Johnson.

9. Having created for Bertie the "gorgeous insight" that Captain Malu had charged the conspirators to manufacture, Bertie's tormentors let him go back to the comparatively urban safety of Tulagi, the Solomons' capital—which boasted at the time the story was written a store, a Chinese carpenter's shop, and a government hospital. (We do not know why the island is spelled "Tulaghi" and the city "Tulagi," nor can we account for its pronunciation, which is actually "Too-LAR-gee.")

Jack London at the wheel of the *Roamer*.

The *Minota* sets out on a blackbirding adventure.

Rare dustjacket for an early reprint of *South Sea Tales*.

Jack and Charmian aboard the *Mariposa*.

Jack and Charmian aboard the *Snark*.

Solomon Islanders.

Solomon Islands bowman.

During palavers, whites were never far from their guns nor islanders far from their shields.

Cannibals "capture" a white man, a scene recreated for the *Snark*'s crew and camera by enthusiastic islanders.

The immaculate white duck suit and pith helmet were rarely found among the older South Seas hands.

Islanders in canoes pull alongside a whaleboat.

An Introduction to "Mauki"

"Mauki" is an important story for London readers to reexamine. At the time of its inspiration, Jack and Charmian had been lost in the South Seas, wandering for days in the *Snark*, unable to find their bearings. They had unwittingly left their navigational charts at Penduffryn copra plantation on Guadalcanal. On September 17, Jack finally sighted Lord Howe Atoll, and they made land there the next day. There they met Harold Markham, the white trader on Lord Howe; he introduced the Londons to his cook, a Solomon Islander named Mauki. The man was serving several sentences for offenses against the white overlords, including escape, theft, and murder—part of a record of casually committed, horrible crimes. Not surprisingly, Jack found the man's account of his life fascinating, and even though Jack was suffering greatly from several physical ailments, he was excited enough to frame a short story around the cook's exploits. Inspired by the cook's story, Jack began to write "Mauki" on October 5, eighteen days after their first interview.

London's dry, objective narration serves perfectly to counterpoint the violence of the narrative. He carefully develops the experiences of a down-and-outer who is living human life in what must be the most sordid of possible naturalistic environments. Mauki is first a little boy captured by cannibals from the interior of his own island, then a virtual slave working for white plantation managers, and finally a man who recaptures his dignity and becomes master of his own fate. He thus serves as a splendid example of Jack London's interest in portraying characters who have emerged from wretchedness to become self-determined heroes.[1]

At the turn of the twentieth century, editors and readers would have seen the story as unappealing and even disturbing because of its apparently insouciant celebration of an unregenerate black cannibal hero. Popular fiction writers of the period (including G. A. Henty, Rudyard Kipling, H. Rider Haggard, A. Conan Doyle, John Buchan, Arthur O. Friel, Talbot Mundy, A. E. W. Mason, Richard Harding Davis, P. C. Wren, and Edgar Rice Burroughs) tended to valorize Anglo-Saxon colonialist adventurers, often obliquely suggesting the notion that it was the heroes' whiteness itself that accounted for their success.

Indeed, the story's publication history indicates that magazine editors were unconvinced of the commercial value of this and a surprising number of other London stories written at the height of his popularity. "Mauki" was submitted to eleven of the leading magazines of the day before it was accepted by *Hampton's*. It may have been that other factors entered into the editors' repeated rejections, but it is reasonable to suppose that the story's indelicate subject matter considered in 1908 might have been judged as objectionable. *Hampton's Magazine* was probably the most likely venue for the story in any case. Though apparently not a convinced socialist himself, its owner and editor, Benjamin B. Hampton, was confident that there was profit to be made in accounts of social injustices. In his career as an editor and publisher, he therefore sought to keep alive the politically radical, confrontational, and muckraking school of journalism, when most of his contemporaries felt that such material was old-fashioned by 1910. Appropriately for *Hampton's* target audience, Mauki's story exposes the kind of capitalistic atrocities the socialists were most incensed about. The story first appeared in the December 1909 issue, illustrated by the artist Maynard Dixon, who had earlier done the art for London's first published book, *Son of the Wolf*. Dixon was best known for his pictures of the American West, including his work on books by Francis Parkman and Robert Service. He also illustrated Clarence Mulford's popular Hopalong Cassidy stories.

MAUKI

He weighed one hundred and ten pounds. His hair was kinky and negroid, and he was black. He was peculiarly black. He was neither blue-black nor purple-black, but plum-black. His name was Mauki, and he was the son of a chief. He had three *tambos*. *Tambo* is Melanesian for *taboo*, and is first cousin to that Polynesian word. Mauki's three tambos were as follows: first, he must never shake hands with a woman, nor have a woman's hand touch him or any of his personal belongings; secondly, he must never eat clams nor any food from a fire in which clams had been cooked; thirdly, he must never touch a crocodile, nor travel in a canoe that carried any part of a crocodile even if as large as a tooth.

Of a different black were his teeth, which were deep black, or, perhaps better, lamp-black. They had been made so in a single night, by his mother, who had compressed about them a powdered mineral which was dug from the landslide back of Port Adams.[2] Port Adams is a salt-water village on Malaita, and Malaita is the most savage island in the Solomons—so savage that no traders nor planters have yet gained a foothold on it; while, from the time of the earliest bêche-de-mer fishers and sandalwood traders down to the latest labor recruiters equipped with automatic rifles and gasoline engines, scores of white adventurers have been passed out by tomahawks and soft-nosed Snider bullets. So Malaita remains today, in the twentieth century, the stamping ground of the labor recruiters, who farm its coasts for laborers who engage and contract themselves to toil on the plantations of the neighboring and more

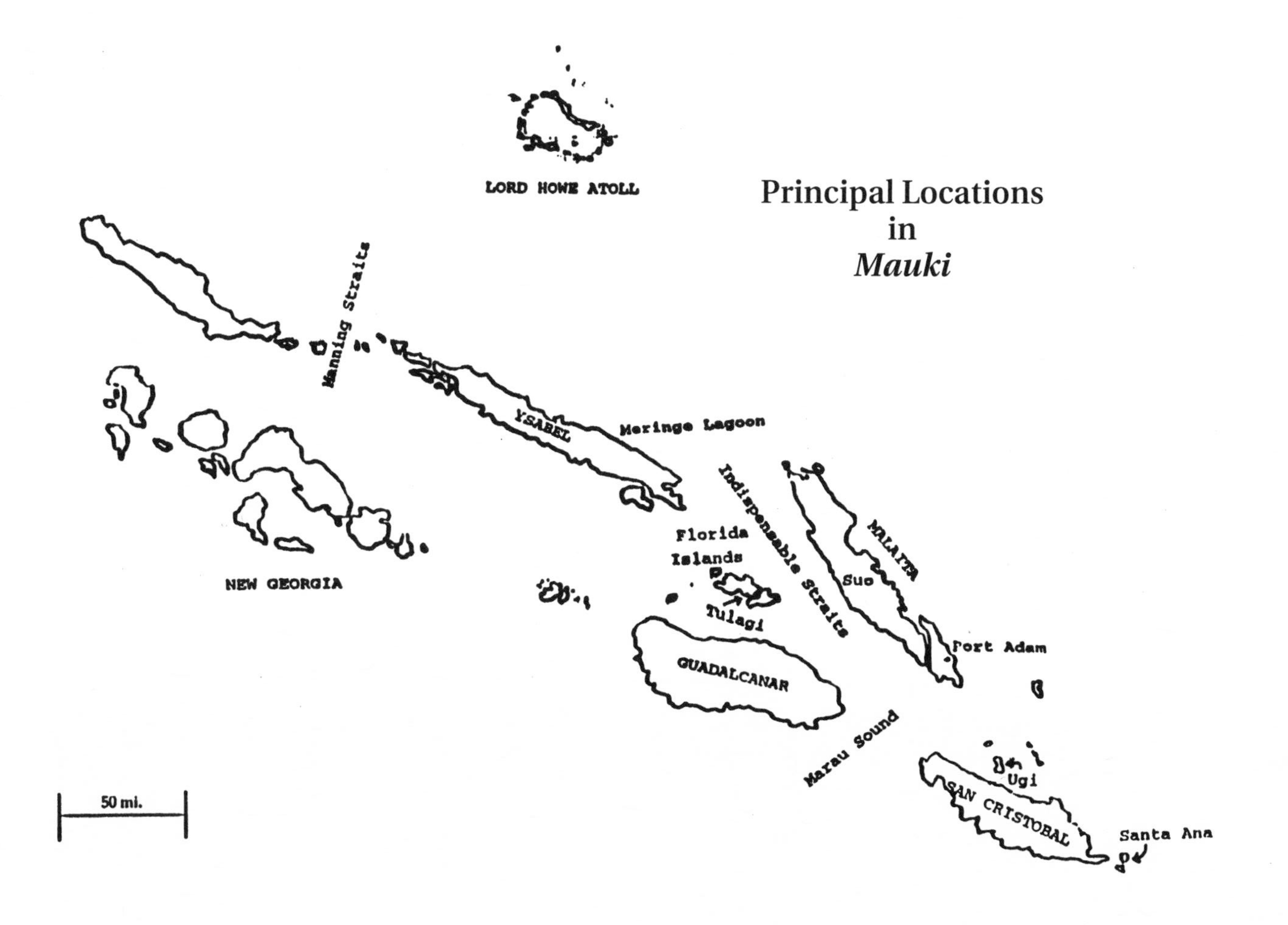
LORD HOWE ATOLL
Principal Locations in *Mauki*
Manning Straits
YSABEL
Meringe Lagoon
NEW GEORGIA
Indispensable Straits
Florida Islands
Tulagi
MALAITA
Suo
Port Adam
GUADALCANAR
Marau Sound
Ugi
SAN CRISTOBAL
Santa Ana
50 mi.

civilized islands for a wage of thirty dollars a year.[3] The natives of those neighboring and more civilized islands have themselves become too civilized to work on plantations.

Mauki's ears were pierced, not in one place, nor two places, but in a couple of dozen places. In one of the smaller holes he carried a clay pipe. The larger holes were too large for such use. The bowl of the pipe would have fallen through. In fact, in the largest hole in each ear he habitually wore round wooden plugs that were an even four inches in diameter. Roughly speaking, the circumference of said holes was twelve and one-half inches. Mauki was catholic in his tastes. In the various smaller holes he carried such things as empty rifle cartridges, horseshoe nails, copper screws, pieces of string, braids of sennit, strips of green leaf, and, in the cool of the day, scarlet hibiscus flowers. From which it will be seen that pockets were not necessary to his well-being. Besides, pockets were impossible, for his only wearing apparel consisted of a piece of calico several inches wide. A pocket knife he wore in his hair, the blade snapped down on a kinky lock. His most prized possession was the handle of a china cup, which he suspended from a ring of turtle-shell, which, in turn, was passed through the partition-cartilage of his nose.[4]

But in spite of embellishments, Mauki had a nice face. It was really a pretty face, viewed by any standard, and for a Melanesian it was a remarkably good-looking face. Its one fault was its lack of strength. It was softly effeminate, almost girlish. The features were small, regular, and delicate. The chin was weak, and the mouth was weak. There was no strength nor character in the jaws, forehead, and nose. In the eyes only could be caught any hint of the unknown quantities that were so large a part of his make-up and that other persons could not understand. These unknown quantities were pluck, pertinacity, fearlessness, imagination, and cunning; and when they found expression in some consistent and striking action, those about him were astounded.[5] Mauki's father was chief over the village at Port Adams, and thus, by birth a salt-water man, Mauki was half amphibian. He knew the way of the fishes and oysters, and the reef was an open book to him. Canoes, also, he knew. He learned to swim when he was a year old. At seven years he could hold his breath a full minute and swim straight down to bottom through thirty feet of water. And at seven years he was stolen by the bushmen, who cannot even swim and who are afraid of salt water.[6] Thereafter Mauki saw the sea only from a distance, through rifts in the jungle and from open spaces on the high mountain sides. He became the slave of old Fanfoa, head chief over a score of scattered bush-villages on the range-lips of Malaita, the smoke of which, on calm mornings, is about the only evidence the seafaring white men have of the teeming interior population. For the whites do not penetrate Malaita. They tried it once, in the days when the search was on for gold, but they always left their heads behind to grin from the smoky rafters of the bushmen's huts.

When Mauki was a young man of seventeen, Fanfoa got out of tobacco. He got dreadfully out of tobacco.[7] It was hard times in all his villages. He had been guilty of a mistake. Suo was a harbor so small that a large schooner could not swing at anchor in it. It was surrounded by mangroves that overhung the deep water. It was a trap, and into the trap sailed two white men in a small ketch. They were after recruits, and they possessed much tobacco and trade-goods, to say nothing of three rifles and plenty of ammunition. Now there were no salt-water men living at Suo, and it was there that the bushmen could come down to the sea. The ketch did a splendid traffic. It signed on twenty recruits the first day. Even old Fanfoa signed on. And that same day the score of new recruits chopped off the two white men's heads, killed the boat's crew, and burned the ketch. Thereafter, and for three months, there was tobacco and trade-goods in plenty and to spare in all the bush-villages. Then came the man-of-war that threw shells for miles into the hills, frightening the people out of their villages and into the deeper bush. Next the man-of-war sent landing parties ashore. The villages were all burned, along with the tobacco and trade-stuff. The cocoanuts and bananas were chopped down, the taro gardens uprooted, and the pigs and chickens killed.

It taught Fanfoa a lesson, but in the meantime he was out of tobacco. Also, his young men were too frightened to sign on with the recruiting vessels. That was why Fanfoa ordered his slave, Mauki, to be carried down and signed on for half a case of tobacco advance, along with knives, axes, calico, and beads, which he would pay for with his toil on the plantations. Mauki was sorely frightened when they brought him on board the schooner. He was a lamb led to the slaughter. White men were ferocious creatures.

They had to be, or else they would not make a practice of venturing along the Malaita coast and into all harbors, two on a schooner, when each schooner carried from fifteen to twenty blacks as boat's crew, and often as high as sixty or seventy black recruits. In addition to this, there was always the danger of the shore population, the sudden attack and the cutting off of the schooner and all hands. Truly, white men must be terrible. Besides, they were possessed of such devil-devils—rifles that shot very rapidly many times, things of iron and brass that made the schooners go when there was no wind, and boxes that talked and laughed just as men talked and laughed. Ay, and he had heard of one white man whose particular devil-devil was so powerful that he could take out all his teeth and put them back at will.[8]

Down into the cabin they took Mauki. On deck, the one white man kept guard with two revolvers in his belt. In the cabin the other white man sat with a book before him, in which he inscribed strange marks and lines. He looked at Mauki as though he had been a pig or a fowl, glanced under the hollows of his arms, and wrote in the book. Then he held out the writing stick and Mauki just barely touched it with his hand, in so doing pledging himself to toil for three years on the plantations of the Moongleam Soap Company.[9] It was not explained to him that the will of the ferocious white men would be used to enforce the pledge, and that, behind all, for the same use, was all the power and all the warships of Great Britain.

Other blacks there were on board, from unheard-of far places, and when the white man spoke to them, they tore the long feather from Mauki's hair, cut that same hair short, and wrapped about his waist a lava-lava of bright yellow calico.

After many days on the schooner, and after beholding more land and islands than he had ever dreamed of, he was landed on New Georgia, and put to work in the field clearing jungle and cutting cane grass. For the first time he knew what work was. Even as a slave to Fanfoa he had not worked like this. And he did not like work. It was up at dawn and in at dark, on two meals a day. And the food was tiresome. For weeks at a time they were given nothing but sweet potatoes to eat, and for weeks at a time it would be nothing but rice. He cut out the cocoanut from the shells day after day; and for long days and weeks he fed the fires that smoked the copra,

If the white men told a boy they would knock seven bells out of him, seven bells were knocked out of him.

till his eyes got sore and he was set to felling trees. He was a good axe-man, and later he was put in the bridge-building gang. Once, he was punished by being put in the road-building gang. At times he served as boat's crew in the whale-boats, when they brought in copra from distant beaches or when the white men went out to dynamite fish.

Among other things he learned bêche-de-mer English, with which he could talk with all white men, and with all recruits who otherwise would have talked in a thousand different dialects. Also, he learned certain things about the white men, principally that they kept their word. If they told a boy he was going to receive a stick of tobacco, he got it. If they told a boy they would knock seven bells out of him if he did a certain thing, when he did that thing seven bells invariably were knocked out of him. Mauki did not know what seven bells were, but they occurred in bêche-de-mer, and he imagined them to be the blood and teeth that sometimes accompanied the process of knocking out seven bells. One other thing he learned: no boy was struck or punished unless he did wrong. Even when the white men were drunk, as they were frequently, they never struck unless a rule had been broken.

Mauki did not like the plantation. He hated work, and he was the son of a chief. Furthermore, it was ten years since he had been stolen from Port Adams by Fanfoa, and he was homesick. He was even homesick for the slavery under Fanfoa. So he ran away. He struck back into the bush, with the idea of working southward to the beach and stealing a canoe in which to go home to Port Adams. But the fever got him, and he was captured and brought back more dead than alive.

A second time he ran away, in the company of two Malaita boys. They got down the coast twenty miles, and were hidden in the hut of a Malaita freeman, who dwelt in that village. But in the dead of night two white men came, who were not afraid of all the village people and who knocked seven bells out of the three runaways, tied them like pigs, and tossed them into the whale-boat. But the man in whose house they had hidden—seven times seven bells must have been knocked out of him from the way the hair, skin, and teeth flew, and he was discouraged for the rest of his natural life from harboring runaway laborers.

For a year Mauki toiled on. Then he was made a house-boy, and had good food and easy times, with light work in keeping the house clean and serving the white men with whiskey and beer at all hours of the day and most hours of the night. He liked it, but he liked Port Adams more. He had two years longer to serve, but two years were too long for him in the throes of homesickness. He had grown wiser with his year of service, and, being now a house-boy, he had opportunity. He had the cleaning of the rifles, and he knew where the key to the store-room was hung. He planned the escape, and one night ten Malaita boys and one boy from San Cristoval sneaked from the barracks and dragged one of the whale-boats down to the beach. It was Mauki who supplied the key that opened the padlock on the boat, and it was Mauki who equipped the boat with a dozen Winchesters, an immense amount of ammunition, a case of dynamite with detonators and fuse, and ten cases of tobacco.

The northwest monsoon was blowing, and they fled south in the night-time, hiding by day on detached and uninhabited islets, or dragging their whale-boat into the bush on the large islands. Thus they gained Guadalcanar, skirted halfway along it, and crossed the Indispensable Straits to Florida Island. It was here that they killed the San Cristoval boy, saving his head and cooking and eating the rest of him. The Malaita coast was only twenty miles away, but the last night a strong current and baffling winds prevented them from gaining across. Daylight found them still several miles from their goal. But daylight brought a cutter, in which were two white men, who were not afraid of eleven Malaita men armed with twelve rifles. Mauki and his companions were carried back to Tulagi, where lived the great white master of all the white men. And the great white master held a court, after which, one by one, the runaways were tied up and given twenty lashes each, and sentenced to a fine of fifteen dollars. Then they were sent back to New Georgia, where the white men knocked seven bells out of them all around and put them to work. But Mauki was no longer house-boy. He was put in the road-making gang. The fine of fifteen dollars had been paid by the white men from whom he had run away, and he was told that he would have to work it out, which meant six months' additional toil. Further, his share of the stolen tobacco earned him another year of toil.

Port Adams was now three years and a half away, so he stole a canoe one night, hid on the islets in Manning Straits, passed through the Straits, and began working along the eastern coast of Ysabel, only to be captured, two-thirds of the way along, by the white men on Meringe Lagoon. After a week, he escaped from them and took to the bush. There were no bush natives on Ysabel, only salt-water men, who were all Christians. The white men put up a reward of five hundred sticks of tobacco, and every time Mauki ventured down to the sea to steal a canoe he was chased by the salt-water men. Four months of this passed, when, the reward having been raised to a thousand sticks, he was caught and sent back to New Georgia and the road-building gang. Now a thousand sticks are worth fifty dollars, and Mauki had to pay the reward himself, which required a year and eight months' labor. So Port Adams was now five years away.

His homesickness was greater than ever, and it did not appeal to him to settle down and be good, work out his four years, and go

Every time Mauki ventured down to the sea he was chased by the salt-water men.

home. The next time, he was caught in the very act of running away. His case was brought before Mr. Haveby, the island manager of the Moongleam Soap Company, who adjudged him an incorrigible. The Company had plantations on the Santa Cruz Islands, hundreds of miles across the sea, and there it sent its Solomon Islands' incorrigibles. And there Mauki was sent, though he never arrived. The schooner stopped at Santa Anna, and in the night Mauki swam ashore, where he stole two rifles and a case of tobacco from the trader and got away in a canoe to Cristoval. Malaita was now to the north, fifty or sixty miles away. But when he attempted the passage, he was caught by a light gale and driven back to Santa Anna, where the trader clapped him in irons and held him against the return of the schooner from Santa Cruz. The two rifles the trader recovered, but the case of tobacco was charged up to Mauki at the rate of another year. The sum of years he now owed the Company was six.

On the way back to New Georgia, the schooner dropped anchor in Marau Sound, which lies at the southeastern extremity of Guadalcanar. Mauki swam ashore with handcuffs on his wrists and got away to the bush. The schooner went on, but the Moongleam trader ashore offered a thousand sticks, and to him Mauki was brought by the bushmen with a year and eight months tacked on to his account. Again, and before the schooner called in, he got away, this time in a whale-boat accompanied by a case of the trader's tobacco. But a northwest gale wrecked him upon Ugi, where the Christian natives stole his tobacco and turned him over to the Moongleam trader who resided there. The tobacco the natives stole meant another year for him, and the tale was now eight years and a half.

"We'll send him to Lord Howe," said Mr. Haveby. "Bunster is there, and we'll let them settle it between them. It will be a case, I imagine, of Mauki getting Bunster, or Bunster getting Mauki, and good riddance in either event."

If one leaves Meringe Lagoon, on Ysabel, and steers a course due north, magnetic, at the end of one hundred and fifty miles he will lift the pounded coral beaches of Lord Howe above the sea. Lord Howe is a ring of land some one hundred and fifty miles in circumference, several hundred yards wide at its widest, and towering in places to a height of ten feet above sea-level. Inside this ring of sand is a mighty lagoon studded with coral patches. Lord Howe belongs to the Solomons neither geographically nor ethnologically. It is an atoll, while the Solomons are high islands; and its people and language are Polynesian, while the inhabitants of the Solomons are Melanesian. Lord Howe has been populated by the westward Polynesian drift which continues to this day, big outrigger canoes being washed upon its beaches by the southeast trade. That there has been a slight Melanesian drift in the period of the northwest monsoon, is also evident.

Nobody ever comes to Lord Howe, or Ontong-Java as it is sometimes called. Thomas Cook & Son do not sell tickets to it, and tourists do not dream of its existence. Not even a white missionary has landed on its shore. Its five thousand natives are as peaceable as they are primitive. Yet they were not always peaceable. The Sailing Directions speak of them as hostile and treacherous. But the men who compile the Sailing Directions have never heard of the change that was worked in the hearts of the inhabitants, who, not many years ago, cut off a big bark and killed all hands with the exception of the second mate. This survivor carried the news to his brothers. The captains of three trading schooners returned with him to Lord Howe. They sailed their vessels right into the lagoon and proceeded to preach the white man's gospel that only white men shall kill white men and that the lesser breeds must keep hands off. The schooners sailed up and down the lagoon, harrying and destroying. There was no escape from the narrow sand-circle, no bush to which to flee. The men were shot down at sight, and there was no avoiding being sighted. The villages were burned, the canoes smashed, the chickens and pigs killed, and the precious cocoanut-trees chopped down. For a month this continued, when the schooners sailed away; but the fear of the white man had been seared into the souls of the islanders and never again were they rash enough to harm one.[10]

Max Bunster was the one white man on Lord Howe, trading in the pay of the ubiquitous Moongleam Soap Company.[11] And the Company billeted him on Lord Howe, because, next to getting rid of him, it was the most out-of-the-way place to be found. That the Company did not get rid of him was due to the difficulty of finding another man to take his place. He was a strapping big German, with something wrong in his brain. Semi-madness would be a charitable statement of his condition. He was a bully and a coward, and a thrice-bigger savage than any savage on the island. Being a coward, his brutality was of the cowardly order. When he first went into the Company's employ, he was stationed on Savo. When a consumptive colonial was sent to take his place, he beat him up with his fists and sent him off a wreck in the schooner that brought him.

Mr. Haveby next selected a young Yorkshire giant to relieve Bunster. The Yorkshire man had a reputation as a bruiser and preferred fighting to eating. But Bunster wouldn't fight. He was a regular little lamb—for ten days, at the end of which time the Yorkshire man was prostrated by a combined attack of dysentery and fever. Then Bunster went for him, among other things getting him down and jumping on him a score or so of times. Afraid of what would happen when his victim recovered, Bunster fled away in a cutter to Guvutu, where he signalized himself by beating up a young Englishman already crippled by a Boer bullet through both hips.

Then it was that Mr. Haveby sent Bunster to Lord Howe, the falling-off place. He celebrated his landing by mopping up half a case of gin and by thrashing the elderly and wheezy mate of the schooner which had brought him. When the schooner departed, he called the kanakas down to the beach and challenged them to throw him in a wrestling bout, promising a case of tobacco to the one who succeeded. Three kanakas he threw, but was promptly thrown by a fourth, who, instead of receiving the tobacco, got a bullet through his lungs.

And so began Bunster's reign on Lord Howe. Three thousand people lived in the principal village; but it was deserted, even in broad day, when he passed through. Men, women, and children fled before him. Even the dogs and pigs got out of the way, while the king was not above hiding under a mat. The two prime ministers lived in terror of Bunster, who never discussed any moot subject, but struck out with his fists instead.

And to Lord Howe came Mauki, to toil for Bunster for eight long years and a half. There was no escaping from Lord Howe. For better or worse, Bunster and he were tied together. Bunster weighed two hundred pounds. Mauki weighed one hundred and ten. Bunster was a degenerate brute. But Mauki was a primitive savage. While both had wills and ways of their own.

Mauki had no idea of the sort of master he was to work for. He had had no warnings, and he had concluded as a matter of course that Bunster would be like other white men, a drinker of much whiskey, a ruler and a lawgiver who always kept his word and who never struck a boy undeserved. Bunster had the advantage. He knew all about Mauki, and gloated over the coming into possession of him. The last cook was suffering from a broken arm and a dislocated shoulder, so Bunster made Mauki cook and general house-boy.

And Mauki soon learned that there were white men and white men. On the very day the schooner departed he was ordered to buy a chicken from Samisee, the native Tongan missionary. But Samisee had sailed across the lagoon and would not be back for three days. Mauki returned with the information. He climbed the steep stairway (the house stood on piles twelve feet above the sand), and entered the living-room to report. The trader demanded the chicken. Mauki opened his mouth to explain the missionary's absence. But Bunster did not care for explanations. He struck out with his fist. The blow caught Mauki on the mouth and lifted him into the air. Clear through the doorway he flew, across the narrow veranda, breaking the top railing, and down to the ground. His lips were a contused, shapeless mass, and his mouth was full of blood and broken teeth.

"That'll teach you that back talk don't go with me," the trader shouted, purple with rage, peering down at him over the broken railing.

Mauki had never met a white man like this, and he resolved to walk small and never offend. He saw the boat-boys knocked about, and one of them put in irons for three days with nothing to eat for the crime of breaking a rowlock while pulling. Then, too, he heard the gossip of the village and learned why Bunster had taken a third wife—by force, as was well known. The first and second wives lay in the graveyard, under the white coral sand, with slabs of coral rock at head and feet. They had died, it was said, from beatings he had given them. The third wife was certainly ill-used, as Mauki could see for himself.

But there was no way by which to avoid offending the white man, who seemed offended with life. When Mauki kept silent, he was struck and called a sullen brute. When he spoke, he was struck for giving back talk. When he was grave, Bunster accused him of plotting and gave him a thrashing in advance; and when he strove to be cheerful and to smile, he was charged with sneering at his lord and master and given a taste of stick. Bunster was a devil. The village would have done for him, had it not remembered the lesson of the three schooners. It might have done for him anyway, if there had been a bush to which to flee. As it was, the murder of the white men, of any white man, would bring a man-of-war that would kill the offenders and chop down the precious cocoanut-trees.

Then there were the boat-boys, with minds fully made up to drown him by accident at the first opportunity to capsize the cutter. Only Bunster saw to it that the boat did not capsize.

Mauki was of a different breed, and, escape being impossible while Bunster lived, he was resolved to get the white man. The trouble was that he could never find a chance. Bunster was always on guard. Day and night his revolvers were ready to hand. He permitted nobody to pass behind his back, as Mauki learned after having been knocked down several times. Bunster knew that he had more to fear from the good-natured, even sweet-faced, Malaita boy than from the entire population of Lord Howe; and it gave added zest to the programme of torment he was carrying out. And Mauki walked small, accepted his punishments, and waited.

All other white men had respected his *tambos*, but not so Bunster. Mauki's weekly allowance of tobacco was two sticks. Bunster passed them to his woman and ordered Mauki to receive them from her hand. But this could not be, and Mauki went without his tobacco. In the same way he was made to miss many a meal, and to go hungry many a day. He was ordered to make chowder out of the big clams that grew in the lagoon. This he could not do, for clams were *tambo*. Six times in succession he refused to touch the clams, and six times he was knocked senseless. Bunster knew that the boy would die first, but called his refusal mutiny, and would have killed him had there been another cook to take his place.

One of the trader's favorite tricks was to catch Mauki's kinky locks and bat his head against the wall. Another trick was to catch Mauki unawares and thrust the live end of a cigar against his flesh. This Bunster called vaccination, and Mauki was vaccinated a number of times a week. Once, in a rage, Bunster ripped the cup handle from Mauki's nose, tearing the hole clear out of the cartilage.

"Oh, what a mug!" was his comment, when he surveyed the damage he had wrought.

The skin of a shark is like sandpaper, but the skin of a ray fish is like a rasp. In the South Seas the natives use it as a wood file in smoothing down canoes and paddles. Bunster had a mitten made of ray fish skin. The first time he tried it on Mauki, with one sweep of the hand it fetched the skin off his back from neck to armpit. Bunster was delighted. He gave his wife a taste of the mitten, and tried it out thoroughly on the boat-boys. The prime ministers came in for a stroke each, and they had to grin and take it for a joke.

"Laugh, damn you, laugh!" was the cue he gave.

Mauki came in for the largest share of the mitten. Never a day passed without a caress from it. There were times when the loss of so much cuticle kept him awake at night, and often the half-healed surface was raked raw afresh by the facetious Mr. Bunster. Mauki continued his patient wait, secure in the knowledge that sooner or later his time would come. And he knew just what he was going to do, down to the smallest detail, when the time did come.

One morning Bunster got up in a mood for knocking seven bells out of the universe. He began on Mauki, and wound up on Mauki, in the interval knocking down his wife and hammering all the boat-boys. At breakfast he called the coffee slops and threw the scalding contents of the cup into Mauki's face. By ten o'clock Bunster was shivering with ague, and half an hour later he was burning with fever. It was no ordinary attack. It quickly became pernicious, and developed into black-water fever. The days passed, and he grew weaker and weaker, never leaving his bed. Mauki waited and watched, the while his skin grew intact once more. He ordered the boys to beach the cutter, scrub her bottom, and give her a general overhauling. They thought the order emanated from Bunster, and they obeyed. But Bunster at the time was lying unconscious and giving no orders. This was Mauki's chance, but still he waited.

When the worst was past, and Bunster lay convalescent and conscious, but weak as a baby, Mauki packed his few trinkets, including the china cup handle, into his trade box. Then he went over to the village and interviewed the king and his two prime ministers.

"This fella Bunster, him good fella you like too much?" he asked.

They explained in one voice that they liked the trader not at all. The ministers poured forth a recital of all the indignities and wrongs that had been heaped upon them. The king broke down and wept. Mauki interrupted rudely.

"You savve me—me big fella marster my country. You no like 'm this fella white marster. Me no like 'm. Plenty good you put hundred cocoanut, two hundred cocoanut, three hundred cocoanut along cutter. Him finish, you go sleep 'm good fella. Altogether kanaka sleep 'm good fella. Bime by big fella noise along house, you no savve hear 'm that fella noise. You altogether sleep strong fella too much."

In like manner Mauki interviewed the boat-boys. Then he ordered Bunster's wife to return to her family house. Had she refused, he would have been in a quandary, for his tambo would not have permitted him to lay hands on her.

The house deserted, he entered the sleeping-room, where the trader lay in a doze. Mauki first removed the revolvers, then placed the ray fish mitten on his hand. Bunster's first warning was a stroke of the mitten that removed the skin the full length of his nose.

"Good fella, eh?" Mauki grinned, between two strokes, one of which swept the forehead bare and the other of which cleaned off one side of his face. "Laugh, damn you, laugh."

Mauki did his work thoroughly, and the kanakas, hiding in their houses, heard the "big fella noise" that Bunster made and continued to make for an hour or more.

When Mauki was done, he carried the boat compass and all the rifles and ammunition down to the cutter, which he proceeded to ballast with cases of tobacco. It was while engaged in this that a hideous, skinless thing came out of the house and ran screaming down the beach till it fell in the sand and mowed and gibbered under the scorching sun. Mauki looked toward it and hesitated. Then he went over and removed the head, which he wrapped in a mat and stowed in the stern-locker of the cutter.

So soundly did the kanakas sleep through that long hot day that they did not see the cutter run out through the passage and head south, close-hauled on the southeast trade. Nor was the cutter ever sighted on that long tack to the shores of Ysabel, and during the tedious head-beat from there to Malaita. He landed at Port Adams with a wealth of rifles and tobacco such as no one man had ever possessed before. But he did not stop there. He had taken a white man's head, and only the bush could shelter him. So back he went to the bush-villages, where he shot old Fanfoa and half a dozen of the chief men, and made himself the chief over all the villages. When his father died, Mauki's brother ruled in Port Adams, and, joined together, salt-water men and bushmen, the resulting combination was the strongest of the ten score fighting tribes of Malaita.

More than his fear of the British government was Mauki's fear of the all-powerful Moongleam Soap Company; and one day a message came up to him in the bush, reminding him that he owed the Company eight and one-half years of labor. He sent back a favorable answer, and then appeared the inevitable white man, the captain of the schooner, the only white man during Mauki's reign who ventured the bush and came out alive. This man not only came out, but he brought with him seven hundred and fifty dollars in gold sovereigns—the money price of eight years and a half of labor plus the cost price of certain rifles and cases of tobacco.

At such times the hush of death falls on the village.

Mauki no longer weighs one hundred and ten pounds. His stomach is three times its former girth, and he has four wives. He has many other things—rifles and revolvers, the handle of a china cup, and an excellent collection of bushmen's heads. But more precious than the entire collection is another head, perfectly dried and cured, with sandy hair and a yellowish beard, which is kept wrapped in the finest of fibre lava-lavas. When Mauki goes to war with villages beyond his realm, he invariably gets out this head, and, alone in his grass palace, contemplates it long and solemnly. At such times the hush of death falls on the village, and not even a pickaninny dares make a noise. The head is esteemed the most powerful devil-devil on Malaita, and to the possession of it is ascribed all of Mauki's greatness.

Notes

1. In his novel *Martin Eden*, which was completed during the voyage of the *Snark*, London has his main character call for an aesthetic based on the examination of "saints in slime":

> He knew life, its foulness as well as its fairness, its greatness in spite of the slime that infested it, and by God he was going to have his say on it to the world. Saints in heaven—how could they be anything but fair and pure? No praise to them. But saints in slime—ah, that was the everlasting wonder! That was what made life worth while. To see moral grandeur rising out of cesspools of iniquity; to rise himself and first glimpse beauty, faint and far, through mud-dripping eyes; to see out of weakness, and frailty, and viciousness, and all abysmal brutishness, arising strength, and truth, and high spiritual endowment. . . . (168)

2. Mauki's home town is referred to as "Port Adams" in the story and his trips to "Suo" and "Santa Anna" are mentioned, though the actual places are "Port Adam," "Sa'a," and "Santa Ana."
3. It was claimed that a white man's life expectancy could be measured in minutes should he venture too far from the beaches when landing on Malaita, allegedly the most savage island in the Solomons. The Kwaio people, who to this day live in the interior, have been on the island for at least twenty-five centuries, perhaps longer. In London's day, they lived as they had always—in an intimidating atmosphere that glorified daily violence, often escalating to murder, hired killings, vendettas, and ruthless executions. Nevertheless, by the 1870s Malaita had become one of the most popular sites for the blackbirders to gather "recruits." Blackbirders resorted so frequently to trickery, kidnapping, and even killing the natives that the Kwaios eventually deemed it only prudent to massacre all white people who arrived on Malaita. For example, four years after London's visit to the island, two *ramos* (powerful and respected Kwaio bounty hunters) killed the first emissary from the South Sea Evangelical Mission.
4. Mauki's physical description, with every detail of body decoration, is strictly true to island custom. The importance of his *tambos* to the management of his life demonstrates a subtle knowledge of the restrictions imposed upon the typical South Sea islander—even down to the mere fact that *taboo* is pronounced *tambo* in Melanesia.
5. Charmian recorded the meeting with the real-life Mauki on Ontong Java Atoll in her personal log: "The third and last member of Markham's household is a mild-faced Solomon Island cook, who, despite his deceptive weak prettiness, is deservedly serving an aggregation of sentences that cover eight years, for murders, escapes in hand cuffs, thefts of whaleboats—a history of bloodcurdling crimes and reprisals too long to go in here, but which so tickles Jack's fancy that he intends making a short story of it, to be called 'Mauki,' and including it in his collection of

South Sea Tales" (*The Log of the Snark*, 445).

6. London's knowledge of Malaitan tribal relations is also demonstrated in the tale. For example, the raid that results in Mauki's kidnapping and removal from his boyhood life on the beach was (and to some extent still is) typical of the adversarial relationships among the various populations on the island. So fierce were the Kwaio bushmen who lived in the mountainous interior of the island that the "salt-water people," who dwelt along the shoreline, remained for centuries in daily fear of raids. A unique feature of Malaitan life even today is that the island is surrounded in turn by artificial islands made up of chunks of coral that the salt-water people have taken out piece by piece to build platforms for homes. Because the bushmen still dread salt water, the ocean moats that surround these homes are still used to protect the inhabitants from Kwaio invasions.
7. Fanfoa's devotion to tobacco, which ultimately leads to the deaths of several people, shows London's awareness of the tremendous value then placed on tobacco by the Malaitans. Fanfoa sold Mauki for half a case of tobacco and a few other items. Fanfoa's desperation at being "dreadfully out of tobacco" is an indication of the dependency of the Solomon Islanders in general on tobacco. Even young children smoked throughout the islands, becoming addicted early. Osa Johnson (who also knew the real Mauki very well, meeting him nine years after London did) observed that most people in the Solomons would give their dearest possession for tobacco, which was supplied in sticks by white traders.
8. This reference may allude to the reaction that ensued whenever London removed and then replaced his own false teeth for the islanders' amusement. (What is believed to be London's upper plate is currently in a drawer at the Jack London State Park.)
9. Though the text does not tell us the true identity of the "Moongleam Soap Company," Levers Pacific Plantations, Ltd., (later, Lever Brothers) seems a promising candidate. One of the first companies to become involved in Solomon Islands copra production, a large Levers plantation was located on the northern tip of the New Georgia group. Traders could take unprocessed dried copra and sell it to the British and American soap manufacturers. On some islands, the copra was further rendered into coconut oil and shipped as liquid in barrels. The first islanders to be recruited for labor on plantations had been treated humanely—an impulse reflected by the managers' provision of three meals a day for the workmen, when in fact at home the islanders usually had only two meals a day. Once the laborers got used to the increased amount of food, in most places it was too late to go back to two meals; however, on New Georgia, plantation managers succeeded in saving money by serving cheap sweet potatoes twice a day. It is here Mauki learns bêche-de-mer English, a pidgin dialect that even today allows islanders to converse throughout the Solomons.
10. See London's story "Yah! Yah! Yah!" for a more detailed treatment of this episode.
11. Osa Johnson, in her *Bride in the Solomons* (Boston: Houghton Mifflin, 1944), tells of her later friendship with Mauki in 1917, and though she never met Bunster, she takes his existence for granted. She does not confirm, however, the name London used in his recounting of Mauki's

adventures. After "Bunster," other whites used Ontong Java as their base, including Harold Markham, the likely inspiration for London's character Captain David Grief. In the autumn of 1908, when the Londons visited the atoll, they met two other European traders, a Mr. McNicoll and his boss, Mr. Oberg (Charmian London, *The Log of the Snark,* 463). For an account of the relations between the islanders and their new overlords, see "Yah! Yah! Yah!"

An Introduction to "Yah! Yah! Yah!"

As in several other tales in this volume, colonialist power is effectively subverted in "Yah! Yah! Yah!" As the frame story opens, the narrator and an islander have worked out a fair trade for a pair of cowrie shells and have sealed their agreement with a day's fishing together. Each participant in the bargain wants an item that is valued in the other's culture: cowries and tobacco sticks. It is the essence of a satisfactory bargain that each participant thinks he's taken advantage of the other's foolishness, and the act itself irresistibly weakens the relationship of dominance and subordination.

But London pushes the idea further. The value of shells as currency comes from the island culture, but these shells are coveted by the white man. Tobacco was introduced to the Pacific by the white invaders, but it is Oti, the islander, who wants it. This breakdown of clear-cut divisions of desire sets the stage for the next subversion. During their discussion, Oti emerges as the narrator's superior at fishing and diving, and possesses knowledge that the narrator requires in order to interpret correctly the true nature of Ontong Java's sadistic overseer, McAllister—a person of the narrator's own race. Moreover, McAllister, while embodying the power of life and death over the whole atoll, certainly can be seen as traumatized by his relationship with the Other, clearly evidenced by his alcoholism as well as by his loss of all human sympathies. The text places the narrator in the space between Oti and McAllister, truly identifying with neither. In short, this story is more complex than it first might appear:

It may be interpreted as a representation of the racial Other in an unusual light, as a sympathetic depiction of an interracial friendship in an atmosphere of absolute oppression, and as a subversion of the colonialist project it at first might seem to be championing.

Most of this story is true. Jack London learned the story of "Oolong"—actually Ontong Java Atoll, or Lord Howe Atoll—in the autumn of 1908. On October 31, 1908, he wrote with pride to his sister, Eliza Shepard, "We picked up an orange cowrie, at Lord Howe Island, in fine condition. It cost me $1.15 in trade goods to get from the native. A pair of good orange cowries is worth $25.00 in Sydney. So you see, I was lucky. I'll bet you haven't one in your collection. Charmian will mail the orange cowrie, or express it, to you from Sydney."[1] London was gleaning considerable information on this particular section of the voyage of the *Snark*, and it would not be at all unusual if the discussion between the narrator and Oti took place substantially as the story says. Though Jack thought that the story scared off editors because of its frank depiction of the violence and depravity of the action, "Just the same," he says in a letter of May 14, 1910, "'Yah! Yah! Yah!' is a cracking good short story. It is absolutely true, absolutely real, and it absolutely happened. I know; I've been there, and I have sailed that lagoon where the natives were hunted."[2] On this island, with its sick, fearful, enslaved inhabitants and the grim and ruthless white overlord, London found the seed of an idea for a short story that would truthfully expose some of the darkness in the heart of this fallen Pacific paradise.

Composed in the week after London wrote the companion story "Mauki," it was rejected by thirteen American magazines from its first submission on October 20, 1908, until its acceptance by *Columbian Magazine* on September 6, 1910. *Columbian* assigned the illustrations to the least skillful of all Jack's visualizers, W. B. Stewart. Benjamin B. Hampton, owner and editor of *Hampton's Magazine*, had recently also assumed editorship of *Columbian*. Hampton had also been London's last resort in placing both "The Terrible Solomons" and "Mauki" after they, too, had been rejected by many better-paying magazines. Jack was offered and accepted the unusually low fee of $150.00. No British magazine wanted it.

"YAH! YAH! YAH!"

He was a whiskey-guzzling Scotchman, and he downed his whiskey neat, beginning with his first tot punctually at six in the morning, and thereafter repeating it at regular intervals throughout the day till bedtime, which was usually midnight. He slept but five hours out of the twenty-four, and for the remaining nineteen hours he was quietly and decently drunk. During the eight weeks I spent with him on Oolong Atoll, I never saw him draw a sober breath. In fact, his sleep was so short that he never had time to sober up. It was the most beautiful and orderly perennial drunk I have ever observed.

McAllister was his name. He was an old man, and very shaky on his pins. His hand trembled as with a palsy, especially noticeable when he poured his whiskey, though I never knew him to spill a drop. He had been twenty-eight years in Melanesia, ranging from German New Guinea to the German Solomons, and so thoroughly had he become identified with that portion of the world, that he habitually spoke in that bastard lingo called "bêche-de-mer." Thus, in conversation with me, *sun he come up* meant sunrise; *kai-kai he stop* meant that dinner was served; and *belly belong me walk about* meant that he was sick at his stomach. He was a small man, and a withered one, burned inside and outside by ardent spirits and ardent sun. He was a cinder, a bit of a clinker of a man, a little animated clinker, not yet quite cold, that moved stiffly and by starts and jerks like an automaton. A gust of wind would have blown him away. He weighed ninety pounds.

No one loved him,
while he loved
only whiskey.

But the immense thing about him was the power with which he ruled. Oolong Atoll was one hundred and forty miles in circumference. One steered by compass course in its lagoon. It was populated by five thousand Polynesians, all strapping men and women, many of them standing six feet in height and weighing a couple of hundred pounds. Oolong was two hundred and fifty miles from the nearest land. Twice a year a little schooner called to collect copra. The one white man on Oolong was McAllister, petty trader and unintermittent guzzler; and he ruled Oolong and its six thousand savages with an iron hand. He said come, and they came, go, and they went. They never questioned his will nor judgment. He was cantankerous as only an aged Scotchman can be, and interfered continually in their personal affairs. When Nugu, the king's daughter, wanted to marry Haunau from the other end of the atoll, her father said yes; but McAllister said no, and the marriage never came off. When the king wanted to buy a certain islet in the lagoon from the chief priest, McAllister said no. The king was in debt to the Company to the tune of 180,000 cocoanuts, and until that was paid he was not to spend a single cocoanut on anything else.

And yet the king and his people did not love McAllister. In truth, they hated him horribly, and, to my knowledge, the whole population, with the priests at the head, tried vainly for three months to pray him to death. The devil-devils they sent after him were awe-inspiring, but since McAllister did not believe in devil-devils, they were without power over him. With drunken Scotchmen all signs fail. They gathered up scraps of food which had touched his lips, an empty whiskey bottle, a cocoanut from which he had drunk, and even his spittle, and performed all kinds of deviltries over them. But McAllister lived on. His health was superb. He never caught fever; nor coughs nor colds; dysentery passed him by; and the malignant ulcers and vile skin diseases that attack blacks and whites alike in that climate never fastened upon him. He must have been so saturated with alcohol as to defy the lodgment of germs. I used to imagine them falling to the ground in showers of microscopic cinders as fast as they entered his whiskey-sodden aura. No one loved him, not even germs, while he loved only whiskey, and still he lived.

I was puzzled. I could not understand six thousand natives putting up with that withered shrimp of a tyrant. It was a miracle that he had not died suddenly long since. Unlike the cowardly Melanesians, the people were high-stomached and warlike. In the big graveyard, at head and feet of the graves, were relics of past sanguinary history—blubber-spades, rusty old bayonets and cutlasses, copper bolts, rudder-irons, harpoons, bomb guns, bricks that could have come from nowhere but a whaler's trying-out furnace, and old brass pieces of the sixteenth century that verified the traditions of the early Spanish navigators. Ship after ship had come to grief on Oolong. Not thirty years before, the whaler *Blennerdale*, running into the lagoon for repair, had been cut off with all hands. In similar fashion had the crew of the *Gasket*, a sandalwood trader, perished. There was a big French bark, the *Toulon*, becalmed off the atoll, which the islanders boarded after a sharp tussle and wrecked in the Lipau Passage, the captain and a handful of sailors escaping in the longboat. Then there were the Spanish pieces, which told of the loss of one of the early explorers. All this, of the vessels named, is a matter of history, and is to be found in the *South Pacific Sailing Directory*.[3] But that there was other history, unwritten, I was yet to learn. In the meantime I puzzled why six thousand primitive savages let one degenerate Scotch despot live.

One hot afternoon McAllister and I sat on the veranda looking out over the lagoon, with all its wonder of jeweled colors. At our backs, across the hundred yards of palm-studded sand, the outer surf roared on the reef. It was dreadfully warm. We were in four degree south latitude and the sun was directly overhead, having crossed the Line a few days before on its journey south. There was no wind—not even a catspaw. The season of the southeast trade was drawing to an early close, and the northwest monsoon had not yet begun to blow.

"They can't dance worth a damn," said McAllister.

I had happened to mention that the Polynesian dances were superior to the Papuan, and this McAllister had denied, for no other reason than his cantankerousness. But it was too hot to argue, and I said nothing. Besides, I had never seen the Oolong people dance.

"I'll prove it to you," he announced, beckoning to the black New Hanover boy, a labor recruit, who served as cook and general house servant. "Hey, you, boy, you tell 'm one fella king come along me."

The boy departed, and back came the prime minister, perturbed, ill at ease, and garrulous with apologetic explanation. In short, the king slept, and was not to be disturbed.

"King he plenty strong fella sleep," was his final sentence.

McAllister was in such a rage that the prime minister incontinently fled, to return with the king himself. They were a magnificent pair, the king especially, who must have been all of six feet three inches in height. His features had the eagle-like quality that is so frequently found in those of the North American Indian. He had been molded and born to rule. His eyes flashed as he listened, but right meekly he obeyed McAllister's command to fetch a couple of hundred of the best dancers, male and female, in the village.

They were a magnificent pair, the king especially, who must have been six feet three inches in height.

And dance they did, for two mortal hours, under that broiling sun. They did not love him for it, and little he cared, in the end dismissing them with abuse and sneers.

The abject servility of those magnificent savages was terrifying. How could it be? What was the secret of his rule? More and more I puzzled as the days went by, and though I observed perpetual examples of his undisputed sovereignty, never a clew was there as to how it was.

One day I happened to speak of my disappointment in failing to trade for a beautiful pair of orange cowries. The pair was worth five pounds in Sydney if it was worth a cent. I had offered two hundred sticks of tobacco to the owner, who had held out for three hundred.

When I casually mentioned the situation, McAllister immediately sent for the man, took the shells from him, and turned them over to me. Fifty sticks were all he permitted me to pay for them. The man accepted the tobacco and seemed overjoyed at getting off so easily. As for me, I resolved to keep a bridle on my tongue in the future. And still I mulled over the secret of McAllister's power. I even went to the extent of asking him directly, but all he did was to cock one eye, look wise, and take another drink.

One night I was out fishing in the lagoon with Oti, the man who had been mulcted of the cowries. Privily, I had made up to him an additional hundred and fifty sticks, and he had come to regard me with a respect that was almost veneration, which was curious, seeing that he was an old man, twice my age at least.

"What name you fella kanaka all the same pickaninny?" I began on him. "This fella trader he one fella. You fella kanaka plenty fella too much. You fella kanaka just like 'm dog—plenty fright along that fella trader. He no eat you fella. He no get 'm teeth along him. What name you too much fright?"

"S'pose plenty fella kanaka kill 'm?" he asked.

"He die," I retorted. "You fella kanaka kill 'm plenty fella white man long time before. What name you fright this fella white man?"

"Yes, we kill 'm plenty," was his answer. "My word! Any amount! Long time before. One time, me young fella too much, one big fella ship he stop outside. Wind he no blow. Plenty fella kanaka we get 'm canoe, plenty fella canoe, we go catch 'm that fella ship. My word—we catch 'm big fella fight. Two, three white men shoot like hell. We no fright. We come alongside, we go up side, plenty fella, maybe I think fifty-ten (five hundred). One fella white Mary (woman) belong that fella ship. Never before I see 'm white Mary. Bime by plenty white man finish. One fella skipper he no die. Five fella, six fella white man no die. Skipper he sing out. Some fella white man he fight. Some fella white man he lower away boat. After that, all together over the side they go. Skipper he sling white Mary down. After that they washee (row) strong fella plenty too much. Father belong me, that time he strong fella. He throw 'm one fella spear. That fella spear he go in one side that white Mary. He no stop. My word, he go out other side that fella Mary. She finish. Me no fright. Plenty kanaka too much no fright."

Old Oti's pride had been touched, for he suddenly stripped down his lava-lava and showed me the unmistakable scar of a bullet. Before I could speak, his line ran out suddenly. He checked it and attempted to haul in, but found that the fish had run around a coral branch. Casting a look of reproach at me for having beguiled him from his watchfulness, he went over the side, feet first, turning over after he got under and following his line down to bottom. The water was ten fathoms. I leaned over and watched the play of his feet, growing dim and dimmer, as they stirred the wan phosphorescence into ghostly fires. Ten fathoms—sixty feet—it was nothing to him, an old man, compared with the value of a hook and line. After what seemed five minutes, though it could not have been more than a minute, I saw him flaming whitely upward. He broke surface and dropped a ten pound rock cod into the canoe, the line and hook intact, the latter still fast in the fish's mouth.

"It may be," I said remorselessly. "You no fright long ago. You plenty fright now along that fella trader."

"Yes, plenty fright," he confessed, with an air of dismissing the subject. For half an hour we pulled up our lines and flung them out in silence. Then small fish-sharks began to bite, and after losing a hook apiece, we hauled in and waited for the sharks to go their way.

"I speak you true," Oti broke into speech, "then you savve we fright now."

I lighted up my pipe and waited, and the story that Oti told me in atrocious bêche-de-mer I here turn into proper English. Otherwise, in spirit and order of narrative, the tale is as it fell from Oti's lips.

"It was after that that we were very proud. We had fought many times with the strange white men who live upon the sea, and always we had beaten them. A few of us were killed, but what was that compared with the stores of wealth of a thousand thousand kinds that we found on the ships? And then one day, maybe twenty years ago, or twenty-five, there came a schooner right through the passage and into the lagoon. It was a large schooner with three masts. She had five white men and maybe forty boat's crew, black fellows from New Guinea and New Britain; and she had come to fish bêche-de-mer. She lay at anchor across the lagoon from here, at Pauloo, and her boats scattered out everywhere, making camps on the beaches where they cured the bêche-de-mer. This made them weak by dividing them, for those who fished here and those

Before I could speak, his line ran out suddenly.

on the schooner at Pauloo were fifty miles apart, and there were others farther away still.

"Our king and headmen held council, and I was one in the canoe that paddled all afternoon and all night across the lagoon, bringing word to the people of Pauloo that in the morning we would attack the fishing camps at the one time and that it was for them to take the schooner. We who brought the word were tired with the paddling, but we took part in the attack. On the schooner were two white men, the skipper and the second mate, with half a dozen black boys. The skipper with three boys we caught on shore and killed, but first eight of us the skipper killed with his two revolvers. We fought close together, you see, at hand grapples.

"The noise of our fighting told the mate what was happening, and he put food and water and a sail in the small dingy, which was so small that it was no more than twelve feet long. We came down upon the schooner, a thousand men, covering the lagoon with our canoes. Also, we were blowing conch shells, singing war songs, and striking the sides of the canoes with our paddles. What chance had one white man and three black boys against us? No chance at all, and the mate knew it.

"White men are hell. I have watched them much, and I am an old man now, and I understand at last why the white men have taken to themselves all the islands in the sea. It is because they are hell. Here are you in the canoe with me. You are hardly more than a boy. You are not wise, for each day I tell you many things you do not know. When I was a little pickaninny, I knew more about fish and the ways of fish than you know now. I am an old man, but I swim down to the bottom of the lagoon, and you cannot follow me. What are you good for, anyway? I do not know, except to fight. I have never seen you fight, yet I know that you are like your brothers and that you will fight like hell. Also, you are a fool, like your brothers. You do not know when you are beaten. You will fight until you die, and then it will be too late to know that you are beaten.

"Now behold what this mate did. As we came down upon him, covering the sea and blowing our conches, he put off from the schooner in the small boat, along with the three black boys, and rowed for the passage. There again he was a fool, for no wise man would put out to sea in so small a boat. The sides of it were not four inches above the water. Twenty canoes went after him, filled with two hundred young men. We paddled five fathoms while his black boys were rowing one fathom. He had no chance, but he was a fool. He stood up in the boat with a rifle, and he shot many times. He was not a good shot, but as we drew close many of us were wounded and killed. But still he had no chance.

"I remember that all the time he was smoking a cigar. When we were forty feet away and coming fast, he dropped the rifle, lighted a stick of dynamite with the cigar, and threw it at us. He lighted another and another, and threw them at us very rapidly, many of them. I know now that he must have split the ends of the fuses and stuck in match heads, because they lighted so quickly. Also, the fuses were very short. Sometimes the dynamite sticks went off in the air, but most of them went off in the canoes. And each time they went off in a canoe, that canoe was finished. Of the twenty canoes, the half were smashed to pieces. The canoe I was in was so smashed, and likewise the two men who sat next to me. The dynamite fell between them. The other canoes turned and ran away. Then that mate yelled, 'Yah! Yah! Yah!' at us. Also he went at us again with his rifle, so that many were killed through the back as they fled away. And all the time the black boys in the boat went on rowing. You see, I told you true, that mate was hell.

"Nor was that all. Before he left the schooner, he set her on fire, and fixed up all the powder and dynamite so that it would go off at one time. There were hundreds of us on board, trying to put out the fire, heaving up water from overside, when the schooner blew up. So that all we had fought for was lost to us, besides many more of us being killed. Sometimes, even now, in my old age, I have bad dreams in which I hear that mate yell, 'Yah! Yah! Yah!' In a voice of thunder he yells, 'Yah! Yah! Yah!' But all those in the fishing camps were killed.

"The mate went out of the passage in his little boat, and that was the end of him we made sure, for how could so small a boat, with four men in it, live on the ocean? A month went by, and then, one morning, between two rain squalls, a schooner sailed in through our passage and dropped anchor before the village. The king and the headmen made big talk, and it was agreed that we would take the schooner in two or three days. In the meantime, as it was our custom always to appear friendly, we went off to her in canoes, bringing strings of cocoanuts, fowls, and pigs, to trade. But when we were alongside, many canoes of us, the men on board began to shoot us with rifles, and as we paddled away I saw the mate who had gone to sea in the little boat spring upon the rail and dance and yell, 'Yah! Yah! Yah!'

"That afternoon they landed from the schooner in three small boats filled with white men. They went right through the village, shooting every man they saw. Also they shot the fowls and pigs. We who were not killed got away in canoes and paddled out into the lagoon. Looking back, we could see all the houses on fire. Late in the afternoon we saw many canoes coming from Nihi, which is the village near the Nihi Passage in the northeast. They were all that were left, and like us their village had been burned by a second schooner that had come through Nihi Passage.

"We stood on in the darkness to the westward for Pauloo, but in the middle of the night we heard women wailing and then we ran into a big fleet of canoes. They were all that were left of Pauloo, which likewise was in ashes, for a third schooner had come in through the Pauloo Passage. You see, that mate, with his black boys, had not been drowned. He had made the Solomon Islands, and there told his brothers of what we had done in Oolong. And all his brothers had said they would come and punish us, and there they were in the three schooners, and our three villages were wiped out.

"And what was there for us to do? In the morning the two schooners from windward sailed down upon us in the middle of the lagoon. The trade wind was blowing fresh, and by scores of canoes they ran us down. And the rifles never ceased talking. We scattered like flying fish before the bonita, and there were so many of us that we escaped by thousands, this way and that, to the islands on the rim of the atoll.

"And thereafter the schooners hunted us up and down the lagoon. In the nighttime we slipped past them. But the next day, or in two days or three days, the schooners would be coming back, hunting us toward the other end of the lagoon. And so it went. We no longer counted nor remembered our dead. True, we were many and they were few. But what could we do? I was in one of the twenty canoes filled with men who were not afraid to die. We attacked the smallest schooner. They shot us down in heaps. They threw dynamite into the canoes, and when the dynamite gave out, they threw hot water down upon us. And the rifles never ceased talking. And those whose canoes were smashed were shot as they swam away. And the mate danced up and down upon the cabin top and yelled, 'Yah! Yah! Yah!'

"Every house on every smallest island was burned. Not a pig nor a fowl was left alive. Our wells were defiled with the bodies of the slain, or else heaped high with coral rock. We were twenty-five thousand on Oolong before the three schooners came. Today we are five thousand. After the schooners left, we were but three thousand, as you shall see.

"At last the three schooners grew tired of chasing us back and forth. So they went, the three of them, to Nihi, in the northeast. And then they drove us steadily to the west. Their nine boats were in the water as well. They beat up every island as they moved along. They drove us, drove us, drove us day by day. And every night the three schooners and the nine boats made a chain of watchfulness that stretched across the lagoon from rim to rim, so that we could not escape back.

"They could not drive us forever that way, for the lagoon was only so large, and at last all of us that yet lived were driven upon the last sand bank to the west. Beyond lay the open sea. There were ten thousand of us, and we covered the sand bank from the lagoon edge to the pounding surf on the other side. No one could lie down. There was no room. We stood hip to hip and shoulder to shoulder. Two days they kept us there, and the mate would climb up in the rigging to mock us and yell, 'Yah! Yah! Yah!' till we were well sorry that we had ever harmed him or his schooner a month before. We had no food, and we stood on our feet two days and nights. The little babies died, and the old and weak died, and the wounded died. And worst of all, we had no water to quench our thirst, and for two days the sun beat down on us, and there was no shade. Many men and women waded out into the ocean and were drowned, the surf casting their bodies back on the beach. And there came a pest of flies. Some men swam to the sides of the schooners, but they were shot to the last one. And we that lived were very sorry that in our pride we tried to take the schooner with the three masts that came to fish for bêche-de-mer.

"On the morning of the third day came the skippers of the three schooners and that mate in a small boat. They carried rifles, all of them, and revolvers, and they made talk. It was only that they were weary of killing us that they had stopped, they told us. And we told them that we were sorry, that never again would we harm a white man, and in token of our submission we poured sand upon our heads. And all the women and children set up a great wailing for water, so that for some time no man could make himself heard. Then we were told our punishment. We must fill the three schooners with copra and bêche-de-mer. And we agreed, for we wanted water, and our hearts were broken, and we knew that we

"Two days they kept us there, and the mate would climb up in the rigging to mock us and yell 'Yah! Yah! Yah!'"

were children at fighting when we fought with white men who fight like hell.

"And when all the talk was finished, the mate stood up and mocked us, and yelled, 'Yah! Yah! Yah!' After that we paddled away in our canoes and sought water.

"And for weeks we toiled at catching bêche-de-mer and curing it, in gathering the cocoanuts and turning them into copra. By day and night the smoke rose in clouds from all the beaches of all the islands of Oolong as we paid the penalty of our wrongdoing. For in those days of death it was burned clearly on all our brains that it was very wrong to harm a white man.

"By and by, the schooners full of copra and bêche-de-mer and our trees empty of cocoanuts, the three skippers and that mate called us all together for a big talk. And they said they were very glad that we had learned our lesson, and we said for the ten-thousandth time that we were sorry and that we would not do it again. Also, we poured sand upon our heads. Then the skippers said that it was all very well, but just to show us that they did not forget us, they would send a devil-devil that we would never forget and that we would always remember any time we might feel like harming a white man. After that the mate mocked us one more time and yelled, 'Yah! Yah! Yah!' Then six of our men, whom we thought long dead, were put ashore from one of the schooners, and the schooners hoisted their sails and ran out through the passage for the Solomons.

"The six men who were put ashore were the first to catch the devil-devil the skippers sent back after us."

"A great sickness came," I interrupted, for I recognized the trick. The schooner had had measles on board, and the six prisoners had been deliberately exposed to it.

"Yes, a great sickness," Oti went on. "It was a powerful devil-devil. The oldest man had never heard of the like. Those of our priests that yet lived we killed because they could not overcome the devil-devil. The sickness spread. I have said that there were ten thousand of us that stood hip to hip and shoulder to shoulder on the sandbank. When the sickness left us, there were three thousand yet alive. Also, having made all our cocoanuts into copra, there was a famine.

"That fella trader," Oti concluded, "he like 'm that much dirt. He like 'm clam he die *kai-kai* (meat) he stop, stink 'm any amount. He like 'm one fella dog, one sick fella dog plenty fleas stop along him. We no fright along that fella trader. We fright because he white man. We savve plenty too much no good kill white man. That one fella sick dog trader he plenty brother stop along him, white men like 'm you fight like hell. We no fright that damn trader. Some time he made kanaka plenty cross along him and kanaka want 'm kill 'm, kanaka he think devil-devil and kanaka he hear that fella mate sing out, 'Yah! Yah! Yah!' and kanaka no kill 'm."

Oti baited his hook with a piece of squid, which he tore with his teeth from the live and squirming monster, and hook and bait sank in white flames to the bottom.

"Shark walk about he finish," he said. "I think we catch 'm plenty fella fish."

His line jerked savagely. He pulled it in rapidly, hand under hand, and landed a big gasping rock cod in the bottom of the canoe.

"Sun he come up, I make 'm that dam fella trader one present big fella fish," said Oti.[4]

Notes

1. Labor, Earle, Robert C. Leitz III, and I. Milo Shepard, eds., *The Letters of Jack London,* (Stanford: Stanford University Press, 1988), 2: 769.
2. Ibid., 2: 890.
3. London's copy of this book, which is frequently mentioned in his Pacific stories, is in the collection at the Huntington Library. Its actual title is *Pacific Islands, Volume I. Sailing Directions for the South East, North East and North Coasts of New Guinea, Also for the Louisade and Solomon Islands, the Bismark Archipelago, and the Caroline and Mariana Islands.* Chapter 6, which deals particularly with this geographic area, does not contain the information that the narrator claims is there.
4. The inhumanity that London has Oti straightforwardly describe was true not only of Ontong Java's history; it was a sinister pattern, used with chilling frequency by the white invaders, apparently pioneered in the exploitation of the New Hebrides. In the early decades of the nineteenth century, members of the upper class in China enjoyed the scent of sandalwood incense. More than two thousand miles away, Australian farmers sought to establish a world-class system of cotton production. On the other side of the planet, in America, sincere and earnest individuals began to develop groups within Protestant congregations, giving voice to a calling to take the word of God to those they thought to be the ignorant and degraded savages of the South Seas. These far-flung and seemingly isolated facts were to effect life-altering changes in many hundreds of thousands of people who had dwelt till then in isolation from the benefits of civilization on the many tiny islands that dot the South Pacific.

   Robert Towns, a prominent Queensland entrepreneur, learned in 1845 that sandalwood had been discovered on the island of Erromango in the New Hebrides, today called Vanuatu. Towns, motivated by news of a strong Chinese market—fifty Australian pounds for each ton of what was to the islanders a useless and damaging plant—sent his vessel *Elizabeth* to Erromango with orders to glut her hold with sandalwood. Arriving in September, the adventurers were pleased by the enthusiastic greeting of the islanders, who expressed a cheerful willingness to give the white men as much of the stuff as they could carry. No sooner had the first boat crew set foot on the island, however, than the islanders set upon them and murdered them with ruthless efficiency. Undaunted, Towns sent two more expeditions to Erromango. In the week following the incident, the *Elizabeth* managed to get a load of sandalwood despite the murder of two more white men, and soon afterward, another skipper managed to return safely with more than a hundred tons of it. Within the next few years, rumors of fortunes to be made on Erromango swept through the South Seas. Sandalwooders risked death as they crowded toward the island—death, or perhaps worse, for the Erromangans were infamous as cannibals.

Meanwhile, from 1839 onward, missionaries began their efforts to make Protestants out of the Erromangans. Throughout the South Pacific, virtually the first goal of these modest white invaders was to convince islanders of the virtues of clothing to conceal the nakedness of which the natives had as yet not learned to be ashamed. The islanders shrugged agreeably, put on the clothes, and wore them without washing till they rotted and fell off. Well-intentioned though these earnest believers may have been, the missionaries carried with them diseases for which the islanders had no resistance, and the rotting rags, which the missionaries seemed so set on their wearing, proved to be perfect for the collection of myriads of odd germs. In 1842, because of an epidemic of dysentery, the Erromangans looked narrowly at the strange teachers on their island. Concluding correctly that there must be a connection between the missionaries' arrival and the appalling disease rate, the Erromangans killed all of the Christian intruders.

Until the discovery of sandalwood, the Erromangans had succeeded in establishing a reputation that had served to keep white men away. Though Towns was reputedly cautious and fair with islanders, his competitors, who sensed easy money, were not. They thronged to Erromango to gather their loads, and then, in order to make it more difficult for any subsequent rival party of sandalwooders, they would depart firing volleys into the island at every beach village they spotted. In a final act of retribution for all the resistance the sandalwooders had experienced, one of Towns' partners, James Paddon, gathered up some natives from the neighboring island of Tanna. Paddon, it is alleged, knew that the men were coming down with measles, and he thought it a good object lesson to drop the infected party off on Erromango. The resulting epidemic killed thousands in that January of 1861.

Such lore from past generations was still circulating throughout the islands when Jack and Charmian London arrived in the *Snark* at the island of Tasman, just after their visit to nearby Ontong Java Atoll in the Autumn of 1908. There they met, Charmian recalls in *The Log of the Snark*, "Mr. McNicoll, a small, hardbitten Scotsman, who holds power of life and death over the rapidly diminishing handful of almost pure Polynesians on this privately-owned island. He is only here temporarily, having come to help the manager, Mr. Oberg, to suppress an uprising of the natives consequent upon a scourge of dysentery introduced by Oberg's Black Papuan boat crew" (463). Charmian was prescient about the fragility of the islanders' health; in the generation that followed the visit of the *Snark*, the population of the atolls fell from 5500 to below 600 in 1939, when the area was closed to outsiders.

An Introduction to "The Inevitable White Man"

"The Inevitable White Man" combines humor and horror in an unlikely and perhaps unpalatable mix. The frame story is a parody of the "clubland" tale identified by critic Richard Usborne in his entertaining study *Clubland Heroes.*[1] The typical cast of characters in the clubland story is a half-dozen educated, well-to-do gentlemen gathered in a rather upper-crust British sportsman's-adventurer's-explorer's clubroom. As they sip their drinks and smoke lingeringly through the evening, they reminisce about past adventures they have witnessed as personal tragedies, wars they have helped fight, or colonial enterprises that have flung them to exotic corners of the world.

In a humorous contrast to these formal expectations, Jack London's scruffy and weather-beaten South Seas discussants are the old salt Woodward, Charley Roberts, and an unnamed narrator. Here, in the humble pub in far-off Samoa, the characters repeatedly slam down a concoction called the "Abu Hamed," which, Roberts tells the narrator, was the invention of "the Stevens [sic] who was responsible for 'With Kitchener to Kartoun [sic],'[2] and who passed out at the siege of Ladysmith" during the Boer War.[3]

In clubland fiction, one of the gentlemen usually makes a general observation, which offers the occasion for one of the characters to tell a story that either supports or undermines the original point. In "The Inevitable White Man," the originating observation is as follows: "Half the trouble is the stupidity of the whites. . . . If the white man would lay himself out a bit to understand the workings of the black man's mind, most of the messes would be avoided." Woodward disagrees, stating that his experience indicates that white men who are the first to understand islander customs and practices are also the first to be eaten by the cannibals. And off the narrative goes, as the racist Woodward tries to defend his thesis by telling a story more horrible than he ever understands.

In addition to being a parody of clubland fiction, "The Inevitable White Man" also reflects London's experimentation with the tall tale, a popular and peculiarly American folklore genre that originated in colonial times and flourished during the expansion of the Western frontier. In the tall tale, characters and action are greatly exaggerated for comic effect. Among the best-known tall-tale characters are Mike Fink, the legendary flatboatman; Paul Bunyan, the giant lumberjack of Minnesota; frontiersmen Davy Crockett and Daniel Boone; and that six-shootin', bronc-ridin' cowboy as big as Texas, Pecos Bill. Most tall tales are so obviously exaggerated that the broadness of the humor and the depiction of comic character become immediately apparent. Note, for example, London's description of Captain Woodward's scars and how he got them.

Though the tall tale's exaggerations are usually for comic effect, London's subtle take on the genre undermines and subverts our expectations. Indeed, while there are very funny parts to "The Inevitable White Man," juxtaposed to them is the horrific main episode. Nowhere is London's bitter take on the interaction of the races more violent.

Like so many of London's stories, this one was inspired by real people and real experience. In fact, Charley Roberts, the name of the bartender in the story, was one of Jack's friends whom he met during the *Snark* voyage, and perhaps this is an actual character study. A colorful turf character, the real Roberts had had his brushes with the law. Kicked off the race tracks of England, America, Australia, and even New Zealand, Roberts had withdrawn to the comparative peace of Apia, hoping to continue horseracing without the intrusive oversight of the authorities.

"The Inevitable White Man" was composed in mid-October 1908, while Jack was suffering terribly from exotic ailments.[4] It was typed by Charmian on the *Snark* on the 17th through the 19th.

Despite its complexity and interest, the story was put together rapidly. After eleven months and a dozen rejections, it was finally accepted a year later by *Black Cat* for a mere $50 and published without illustrations in the issue for November of 1910. It was later published in book form by MacMillan in *South Sea Tales* in 1911.

THE INEVITABLE WHITE MAN

"The black will never understand the white, nor the white the black, as long as black is black and white is white."

So said Captain Woodward.[5] We sat in the parlor of Charley Roberts' pub in Apia, drinking long Abu Hameds compounded and shared with us by the aforesaid Charley Roberts, who claimed the recipe direct from Stevens, famous for having invented the Abu Hamed at a time when he was spurred on by Nile thirst—the Stevens who was responsible for "With Kitchener to Kartoun," and who passed out at the siege of Ladysmith.

Captain Woodward, short and squat, elderly, burned by forty years of tropic sun, and with the most beautiful liquid brown eyes I ever saw in a man, spoke from a vast experience. The crisscross of scars on his bald pate bespoke a tomahawk intimacy with the black, and of equal intimacy was the advertisement, front and rear, on the right side of his neck, where an arrow had at one time entered and been pulled clean through. As he explained, he had been in a hurry on that occasion—the arrow impeded his running—and he felt that he could not take the time to break off the head and pull out the shaft the way it had come in. At the present moment he was commander of the *Savaii*, the big steamer that recruited labor from the westward for the German plantations on Samoa.

"Half the trouble is the stupidity of the whites," said Roberts, pausing to take a swig from his glass and to curse the Samoan bar-boy in affectionate terms. "If the white man would lay himself out a bit to understand the workings of the black man's mind, most of the messes would be avoided."

"I've seen a few who claimed they understood niggers," Captain Woodward retorted, "and I always took notice that they were the first to be *kai-kai'd* (eaten). Look at the missionaries in New Guinea and the New Hebrides—the martyr isle of Erromanga [sic] and all the rest.[6] Look at the Austrian expedition that was cut to pieces in the Solomons, in the bush of Guadalcanar. And look at the traders themselves, with a score of years' experience, making their brag that no nigger would ever get them, and whose heads to this day are ornamenting the rafters of the canoe houses. There was old Johnny Simons—twenty-six years on the raw edges of Melanesia, swore he knew the niggers like a book and that they'd never do for him, and he passed out at Marovo Lagoon, New Georgia, had his head sawed off by a black Mary (woman) and an old nigger with only one leg, having left the other leg in the mouth of a shark while diving for dynamited fish. There was Billy Watts, horrible reputation as a nigger killer, a man to scare the devil. I remember lying at Cape Little, New Ireland you know, when the niggers stole half a case of trade-tobacco—cost him about three dollars and a half. In retaliation he turned out, shot six niggers, smashed up their war canoes and burned two villages. And it was at Cape Little, four years afterward, that he was jumped along with fifty Buku boys he had with him fishing bêche-de-mer. In five minutes they were all dead, with the exception of three boys who got away in a canoe. Don't talk to me about understanding the nigger. The white man's mission is to farm the world, and it's a big enough job cut out for him. What time has he got left to understand niggers anyway?"[7]

"Just so," said Roberts. "And somehow it doesn't seem necessary, after all, to understand the niggers. In direct proportion to the white man's stupidity is his success in farming the world—"

"And putting the fear of God into the nigger's heart," Captain Woodward blurted out. "Perhaps you're right, Roberts. Perhaps it's his stupidity that makes him succeed, and surely one phase of his stupidity is his inability to understand the niggers. But there's one thing sure, the white has to run the niggers whether he understands them or not. It's inevitable. It's fate."

"And of course the white man is inevitable—it's the niggers' fate," Roberts broke in. "Tell the white man there's pearl shell in some lagoon infested by ten-thousand howling cannibals, and he'll head there all by his lonely, with half a dozen kanaka divers and a tin alarm clock for chronometer, all packed like sardines on a commodious, five-ton ketch. Whisper that there's a gold strike at the North Pole, and that same inevitable white-skinned creature will set out at once, armed with pick and shovel, a side of bacon, and the latest patent rocker—and what's more, he'll get there. Tip it off to him that there's diamonds on the red-hot ramparts of hell, and Mr. White Man will storm the ramparts and set old Satan himself to pick-and-shovel work. That's what comes of being stupid and inevitable."

"But I wonder what the black man must think of the—the inevitableness," I said.

Captain Woodward broke into quiet laughter. His eyes had a reminiscent gleam.

"I'm just wondering what the niggers of Malu thought and still must be thinking of the one inevitable white man we had on board when we visited them in the *Duchess*," he explained.

Roberts mixed three more Abu Hameds.

"That was twenty years ago. Saxtorph was his name. He was certainly the most stupid man I ever saw, but he was as inevitable as death. There was only one thing that chap could do, and that was shoot. I remember the first time I ran into him—right here in Apia, twenty years ago. That was before your time, Roberts. I was sleeping at Dutch Henry's hotel, down where the market is now. Ever heard of him? He made a tidy stake smuggling arms in to the rebels, sold out his hotel, and was killed in Sydney just six weeks afterward in a saloon row.

"But Saxtorph. One night I'd just got to sleep, when a couple of cats began to sing in the courtyard. It was out of bed and up window, water jug in hand. But just then I heard the window of the next room go up. Two shots were fired, and the window was closed. I fail to impress you with the celerity of the transaction. Ten seconds at the outside. Up went the window, bang bang went the revolver, and down went the window. Whoever it was, he had never stopped to see the effect of his shots. He knew. Do you follow me?—he *knew*. There was no more cat concert, and in the morning there lay the two offenders, stone dead. It was marvelous to me. It still is marvelous. First, it was starlight, and Saxtorph shot without drawing a bead; next, he shot so rapidly that the two reports were like a double report; and finally, he knew he had hit his marks without looking to see.

"Two days afterward he came on board to see me. I was mate, then, on the *Duchess*, a whacking big one-hundred-and-fifty-ton schooner, a blackbirder. And let me tell you that blackbirders were blackbirders in those days.[8] There weren't any government protection for *us*, either. It was rough work, give and take, if we were finished, and nothing said, and we ran niggers from every south sea island they didn't kick us off from. Well, Saxtorph came on board, John Saxtorph was the name he gave. He was a sandy little man, hair sandy, complexion sandy, and eyes sandy, too. Nothing striking about him. His soul was as neutral as his color scheme. He said he was strapped and wanted to ship on board. Would go cabin boy, cook, supercargo, or common sailor. Didn't know anything about any of the billets, but said that he was willing to learn. I didn't want him, but his shooting had so impressed me that I took him as common sailor, wages three pounds per month.

"He was willing to learn all right, I'll say that much. But he was constitutionally unable to learn anything. He could no more box the compass than I could mix drinks like Roberts here. And as for steering, he gave me my first gray hairs. I never dared risk him at the wheel when we were running in a big sea, while full-and-by and close-and-by were insoluble mysteries. Couldn't ever tell the difference between a sheet and a tackle, simply couldn't. The fore-throat-jig and the jib-jig were all one to him. Tell him to slack off the mainsheet, and before you know it, he'd drop the peak. He fell overboard three times, and he couldn't swim. But he was always cheerful, never seasick, and he was the most willing man I ever knew. He was an uncommunicative soul. Never talked about himself. His history, so far as we were concerned, began the day he signed on the *Duchess*. Where he learned to shoot, the stars alone can tell. He was a Yankee—that much we knew from the twang in his speech. And that was all we ever did know.

"And now we begin to get to the point. We had bad luck in the New Hebrides, only fourteen boys for five weeks, and we ran up before the southeast for the Solomons. Malaita, then as now, was good recruiting ground, and we ran into Malu, on the northwestern corner. There's a shore reef and an outer reef, and a mighty nervous anchorage; but we made it all right and fired off our dynamite as a signal to the niggers to come down and be recruited. In three days we got not a boy. The niggers came off to us in their canoes by hundreds, but they only laughed when we showed them beads and calico and hatchets and talked of the delights of plantation work in Samoa.

"On the fourth day there came a change. Fifty-odd boys signed on and were billeted in the main-hold, with the freedom of the deck, of course. And of course, looking back, this wholesale signing on was suspicious, but at the time we thought some powerful chief had removed the ban against recruiting. The morning of the fifth day our two boats went ashore as usual—one to cover the other, you know, in case of trouble. And, as usual, the fifty niggers on board were on deck, loafing, talking, smoking, and sleeping. Saxtorph and myself, along with four other sailors, were all that were left on board. The two boats were manned with Gilbert Islanders. In the one were the captain, the supercargo, and the recruiter. In the other, which was the covering boat and which lay off shore a hundred yards, was the second mate. Both boats were well-armed, though trouble was little expected.

"Four of the sailors, including Saxtorph, were scraping the poop rail. The fifth sailor, rifle in hand, was standing guard by the water-tank just for'ard of the mainmast. I was for'ard, putting in the finishing licks on a new jaw for the fore-gaff. I was just reaching for my pipe where I had laid it down, when I heard a shot from shore. I straightened up to look. Something struck me on the back of the head, partially stunning me and knocking me to the deck. My first thought was that something had carried away aloft; but even as I went down, and before I struck the deck, I heard the devil's own tattoo of rifles from the boats, and twisting sidewise, I caught a glimpse of the sailor who was standing guard. Two big niggers were holding his arms, and a third nigger from behind was braining him with a tomahawk.

"I can see it now, the water-tank, the mainmast, the gang hanging on to him, the hatchet descending on the back of his head, and all under the blazing sunlight. I was fascinated by that growing vision of death. The tomahawk seemed to take a horribly long time to come down. I saw it land, and the man's legs give under him as he crumpled. The niggers held him up by sheer strength while he was hacked a couple of times more. Then I got two more hacks on the head and decided that I was dead. So did the brute that was hacking me. I was too helpless to move, and I lay there and watched them removing the sentry's head. I must say they did it slick enough. They were old hands at the business.

"The rifle firing from the boats had ceased, and I made no doubt that they were finished off and that the end had come to everything. It was only a matter of moments when they would return for my head. They were evidently taking the heads from the sailors aft. Heads are valuable on Malaita, especially white heads. They have the place of honor in the canoe houses of the salt-water natives. What particular decorative effect the bushmen get out of them I didn't know, but they prize them just as much as the salt-water crowd.

"I had a dim notion of escaping, and I crawled on hands and knees to the winch, where I managed to drag myself to my feet. From there I could look aft and see three heads on top the cabin—the heads of three sailors I had given orders to for months. The niggers saw me standing, and started for me. I reached for my revolver, and found they had taken it. I can't say that I was scared. I've been near to death several times, but it never seemed easier than right then. I was half-stunned, and nothing seemed to matter.

"The leading nigger had armed himself with a cleaver from the galley, and he grimaced like an ape as he prepared to slice me down. But the slice was never made. He went down on the deck all of a heap, and I saw the blood gush from his mouth. In a dim way I heard a rifle go off and continue to go off. Nigger after nigger went down. My senses began to clear, and I noted that there was never a miss. Every time that the rifle went off a nigger dropped. I sat down on deck beside the winch and looked up. Perched in the crosstrees was Saxtorph. How he had managed it I can't imagine, for he had carried up with him two Winchesters and I don't know how many bandoliers of ammunition; and he was now doing the one only thing in this world that he was fitted to do.

"I've seen shooting and slaughter, but I never saw anything like that. I sat by the winch and watched the show. I was weak and faint, and it seemed to be all a dream. Bang, bang, bang, bang, went his rifle, and thud, thud, thud, thud, went the niggers to the deck. It was amazing to see them go down. After their first rush to get me, when about a dozen had dropped, they seemed paralyzed; but he never left off pumping his gun. By this time canoes and the two boats arrived from shore, armed with Sniders, and with Winchesters which they had captured in the boats. The fusillade they let loose on Saxtorph was tremendous. Luckily for him the niggers are only good at close range. They are not used to putting the gun to their shoulders. They wait until they are right on top of a man, and then they shoot from the hip. When his rifle got too hot, Saxtorph changed off. That had been his idea when he carried two rifles up with him.

"The astounding thing was the rapidity of his fire. Also, he never made a miss. If ever anything was inevitable, that man was. It was the swiftness of it that made the slaughter so appalling. The niggers did not have time to think. When they did manage to think, they went over the side in a rush, capsizing the canoes of course. Saxtorph never let up. The water was covered with them, and plump, plump, plump, he dropped his bullets into them. Not a single miss, and I could hear distinctly the thud of every bullet as it buried in human flesh.

"The niggers spread out and headed for the shore, swimming. The water was carpeted with bobbing heads, and I stood up, as in a dream, and watched it all—the bobbing heads and the heads that ceased to bob. Some of the long shots were magnificent. Only one man reached the beach, but as he stood up to wade ashore, Saxtorph got him. It was beautiful. And when a couple of niggers ran down to drag him out of the water, Saxtorph got them, too.

"I thought everything was over then, when I heard the rifle go off again. A nigger had come out of the cabin companion on the run for the rail and gone down in the middle of it. The cabin must have been full of them. I counted twenty. They came up one at a time and jumped for the rail. But they never got there. It reminded me of trapshooting. A black body would pop out of the companion, bang would go Saxtorph's rifle, and down would go the black body. Of course, those below did not know what was happening on deck, so they continued to pop out until the last one was finished off.

"Saxtorph waited a while to make sure, and then came down on deck. He and I were all that were left of the *Duchess*'s complement, and I was pretty well to the bad, while he was helpless now that the shooting was over. Under my direction he washed out my scalp wounds and sewed them up. A big drink of whiskey braced me to make an effort to get out. There was nothing else to do. All the rest were dead. We tried to get up sail, Saxtorph hoisting and I holding the turn. He was once more the stupid lubber. He couldn't hoist worth a cent, and when I fell in a faint, it looked all up with us.

"When I came to, Saxtorph was sitting helplessly on the rail, waiting to ask me what he should do. I told him to overhaul the wounded and see if there were any able to crawl. He gathered together six. One, I remember, had a broken leg; but Saxtorph said his arms were all right. I lay in the shade, brushing the flies off and directing operations, while Saxtorph bossed his hospital gang. I'll be blessed if he didn't make those poor niggers heave at every rope on the pin-rails before he found the halyards. One of them let go the rope in the midst of the hoisting and slipped down to the deck dead; but Saxtorph hammered the others and made them stick by the job. When the fore and main were up, I told him to knock the shackle out of the anchor chain and let her go. I had had myself helped aft to the wheel, where I was going to make a shift at steering. I can't guess how he did it, but instead of knocking the shackle out, down went the second anchor, and there we were doubly moored.

"In the end he managed to knock both shackles out and raise the staysail and jib, and the *Duchess* filled away for the entrance. Our decks were a spectacle. Dead and dying niggers were everywhere. They were wedged away some of them in the most inconceivable places. The cabin was full of them where they had crawled off the deck and cashed in. I put Saxtorph and his graveyard gang to work heaving them overside, and over they went, the living and the dead. The sharks had fat pickings that day. Of course our four murdered sailors went the same way. Their heads, however, we put in a sack with weights, so that by no chance should they drift on the beach and fall into the hands of the niggers.

"Our five prisoners I decided to use as crew, but they decided otherwise. They watched their opportunity and went over the side. Saxtorph got two in mid-air with his revolver, and would have shot the other three in the water if I hadn't stopped him. I was sick of the slaughter, you see, and besides, they'd helped work the schooner out. But it was mercy thrown away, for the sharks got the three of them.

"I had brain fever or something after we got clear of the land. Anyway, the *Duchess* lay hove to for three weeks, when I pulled myself together and we jogged on with her to Sydney. Anyway those niggers of Malu learned the everlasting lesson that it is not good to monkey with a white man. In their case, Saxtorph was certainly inevitable."[9]

Charley Roberts emitted a long whistle and said:

"Well I should say so. But whatever became of Saxtorph?"

"He drifted into seal hunting and became a crackerjack. For six years he was high line of both the Victoria and San Francisco fleets. The seventh year his schooner was seized in Bering Sea by a Russian cruiser, and all hands, so the talk went, were slammed into the Siberian salt mines. At least I've never heard of him since."

"Farming the world," Roberts muttered. "Farming the world. Well here's to them. Somebody's got to do it—farm the world, I mean."

Captain Woodward rubbed the criss-crosses on his bald head.

"I've done my share of it," he said. "Forty years now. This will be my last trip. Then I'm going home to stay."

"I'll wager the wine you don't," Roberts challenged. "You'll die in the harness, not at home."

Captain Woodward promptly accepted the bet, but personally I think Charley Roberts has the best of it.

Notes

1. Richard Usborne, *Clubland Heroes* (London: Barrie and Jenkins, 1953).
2. General Horatio Herbert Kitchener (1850–1916) indeed had been sent into the Sudan by the British government in 1898, charged with the task of reclaiming Khartoum, avenging the death of the gallant adventurer General "Chinese" Gordon, and executing the Islamic fundamentalist warlord known as the Khalifa.
3. George W. Steevens did indeed publish a record of his 1896 adventures in the Sudan entitled *With Kitchener to Khartoum* (Edinburgh:

Blackwood, 1898), telling of the Anglo-Egyptian army attack on Khartoum. Steevens may well have died in the defense of Ladysmith, South Africa, during the devastating Boer siege, which lasted 118 days from October 1899 to February 28, 1900. London thus links his characters, cultural washouts though they may be, with recent and heroic events in British colonial history, and they certainly suffer in the comparison: the only connection the characters share with the vaulting ambitions of empire is the "Abu Hamed" drink. These characters' only brush with military greatness is at least three times removed from the valiant battlefields of the great national struggles of their time and is commemorated only in the bottom of a (no doubt) dirty cocktail glass.

Unfortunately, the Abu Hamed has, we are sad to admit, resisted our efforts to learn its recipe or even to verify its existence, though its authenticity is suggested by the fact that the city of Abu Hamed in the Sudan, down the Nile from Khartoum, had served both Gordon and Kitchener as military bases.

4. In a letter to his editor at Macmillan, Jack states that he has "just returned from voyage on *Snark* up to Lord Howe and Tasman Islands [respectively known today as Ontong Java and Nukumanu Atoll]. All of us were sick and fevers were high. Tahitian [see the introduction to "The Heathen"] nearly died and the Jap cook went crazy, and all the time I've been the sickest of anybody on board. I have accumulated several new and alarming diseases—two of which have been utterly unheard of by any white man I have met in the Solomons. Have 20,000 words written on a short Solomons' Island novel [*Adventure*]" (Jack London, in *The Letters of Jack London*, ed. Labor, Earle, Robert C. Leitz III, and I. Milo Shepard [Stanford, CA: Stanford University Press, 1988, 2: 754–55].)

5. In her study *Jack London: A Study of the Short Fiction* (New York: Twayne, 1999), Jeanne C. Reesman says that Captain Woodward is based on the colorful Captain Jansen, of the *Minota*, a labor recruiting vessel. The interior story tells of a recruiting adventure that happens on the northwestern tip of Malaita at a place called Maluu ("Malu" in the story) twenty years before in the blackbirding heyday of the late 1880s.

6. Woodward is making a reference to H. A. Robertson's *Erromanga: The Martyr Isle* (London: Hodder and Stoughton, 1902), a book London had in his library. For a more complete discussion of Erromangan history see footnote 2 to "Yah! Yah! Yah!"

7. Citing anecdotes that seem to him conclusive, Woodward argues that the psychology of the blacks is inscrutable. His culminating example is complicated by London's subtle twist, which actually subverts Woodward's point about the inscrutability of blacks. Read superficially by most for the past three generations as a celebration of white ruthlessness, "The Inevitable White Man" is actually a vivid picture of the psychology and the logic underlying the colonial and commercial exploitation of the period.

8. While the practice was outlawed around 1904, some few rascals could still make a handsome and exciting living by bootlegging recruits. London's friend Jansen was one of them as was the brave, pistol-packing Captain Keller, who (as we describe in the general introduction) had rescued Jack and Charmian from the cannibals at Maluu in 1908. Unfortunately, Captain Keller would not live to become the old salt Woodward managed to become: Keller, Jack learned, "came to his death

[several years later] by having his head chopped off and smoke-cured by the cannibal head-hunters of the Solomon Islands" (Labor et al., *Letters*, 3: 1599).

9. In relating the episode of the battle aboard the blackbirding ship *Duchess*, the narrator offers no evaluation of the characters' relative culpability, leaving such judgments up to the reader. Saxtorph may have his own stupidity as a possible excuse for his cold-bloodedness, not to mention a very ethical sense of duty and a proper responsibility to help defend his fellow crew members from a very real threat. Because of a long history of negative experiences with blackbirders and treacherous traders, the natives do indeed have plans to kill the sailors. This is another example of London's interest in presenting and exploring the moral ambiguities of both parties involved in the colonialist project.

An Introduction to "The Red One"

Throughout London's late short story "The Red One," the recurring image of the human head becomes an emblem for the complicated ways people from different cultures come to know things, which in turn symbolically show the fatal consequences of the human impulse to interpret meaning according to the interpreter's cultural limitations. And, running like a thread of allusions and symbols through the fabric of the text is the notion that the acquisition of knowledge will lead to death—especially in the green hell that is the poisonous interior of Guadalcanal.

Bassett, the main character whose biases supply the narrative perspective, sees the world through the artificially ordered frameworks of Western science. Another expert on knowing is the island "devil-devil doctor, priest, or medicine man" Ngurn, whose hobby is the "curing" of heads—a grimly charming pun that links decapitation with improved thinking. Finally, there is Balatta, an ignorant, terrified, and superstitious island woman who rejects everything she "knows" for the sake of her increasingly obsessive love for the European scientist.

Racist, sexist, sexless, imperialist, empiricist, and scientific trivialist, the relentless lepidopterist Bassett seems to have been endowed by his creator with a nearly complete kit of traits necessary to being one of those "inevitable white men" of London's South Sea tales. (Bassett is, uncharacteristically, not an alcoholic.)

Finding himself on the island of Guadalcanal in the captivity of a tribe of head-hunting cannibals, suffering from a hatchet wound in his head, and knocked flat by a jungle fever, Bassett has only an uncertain and fluctuating consciousness. His tenuous condition provides a frame of only dubious reliability as he tries to recall the details of his experiences over what he believes must have been several months. Though uncertain of the truth of many of his perceptions because of his head wound and the fever, Bassett has become fascinated by an eerie, reverberating sound coming from the island interior. In what quickly becomes an obsessive drive to learn the source of this weird song, Bassett displays, flourishes, and luxuriates in every Western prejudice, shortcoming, and stereotype, as these same shortcomings limit and direct his interpretations. In contrast to Bassett's shaky puzzlement, the islanders know very well the origin of the sound: it proceeds from a great, red, spherical object too massive to have been constructed by mere human ingenuity or engineering, an object that tradition tells them has fallen from the stars.

The gap between Ngurn's religious primitive and Bassett's modern rational systems of interpreting experiences provides the text with its many opportunities for ironic parody as well as biting satire. More than that, however, his interest in the rift between humanism and science allows London to show characters caught—like Bassett's butterflies—in epistemological frameworks, struggling to perceive radically different worlds. London first alerts us to the need to look for ironic subtexts in the very location of the story itself: a quest for knowledge will take place on an island in a group named for the biblical king who personified wisdom.

In "The Red One" London explores the implications and difficulties inherent in the quest for reliable—or worthwhile—knowledge, detailing the limitations with which race, religion, culture, and language, among other forces, constrict our perceptions and direct our understandings. Finally, and ironically, the passionately desired attainment of knowledge is inevitably connected to death; London shows us that Bassett's rationalistic obsession with "knowing" the Red One hurries him inexorably toward the fate of all humanity. But London's humanism and skepticism does not seem to condemn Bassett to a blank void of existential Nothingness. Instead, Bassett has two visions at the moment of his own death: in the first, thematically connected and culturally derived, Bassett reverts to myth-based metaphors as he imagines that he "sees" fellow-victim Medusa, whose special and terrible powers survive the loss of her body; in the second, he cross-culturally and perhaps presciently envisions his own head "always turning, in the Devil-Devil house beside the breadfruit tree," perhaps in death attaining some yet unguessed but serene truth from the whispered wisdom of Ngurn.

"The Red One" was composed in May, 1916, during the Londons' last visit to Hawaii, apparently on the beach at Waikiki, five months before Jack's death. Charmian sold it to *Cosmopolitan*, where it was published in the issue for October 1918, and it became the lead story in Macmillan's hardcover *The Red One* in the same year. The illustrations (among the most effective of all to grace Jack's short stories) are by G. Patrick Nelson.

THE RED ONE[1]

THERE it was! The abrupt liberation of sound! As he timed it with his watch, Bassett likened it to the trump of an archangel. Walls of cities, he meditated, might well fall down before so vast and compelling a summons. For the thousandth time vainly he tried to analyse the tone-quality of that enormous peal that dominated the land far into the strong-holds of the surrounding tribes. The mountain gorge which was its source rang to the rising tide of it until it brimmed over and flooded earth and sky and air. With the wantonness of a sick man's fancy, he likened it to the mighty cry of some Titan of the Elder World vexed with misery or wrath. Higher and higher it arose, challenging and demanding in such profounds of volume that it seemed intended for ears beyond the narrow confines of the solar system. There was in it, too, the clamour of protest in that there were no ears to hear and comprehend its utterance.[2]

—Such the sick man's fancy. Still he strove to analyse the sound. Sonorous as thunder was it, mellow as a golden bell, thin and sweet as a thrummed taut cord of silver—no; it was none of these, nor a blend of these. There were no words nor semblances in his vocabulary and experience with which to describe the totality of that sound.

Time passed. Minutes merged into quarters of hours, and quarters of hours into half-hours, and still the sound persisted, ever changing from its initial vocal impulse yet never receiving fresh impulse—fading, dimming, dying as enormously as it had sprung into being. It became a confusion of troubled mutterings and babblings and colossal whisperings.[3] Slowly it withdrew, sob by sob, into whatever great bosom had birthed it, until it whimpered deadly whispers of wrath and as equally seductive whispers of delight, striving still to be heard, to convey some cosmic secret, some understanding of infinite import and value. It dwindled to a ghost of sound that had lost its menace and promise, and became a thing that pulsed on in the sick man's consciousness for minutes after it had ceased. When he could hear it no longer, Bassett glanced at his watch. An hour had elapsed ere that archangel's trump had subsided into tonal nothingness.

Was this, then, *his* dark tower?—Bassett pondered, remembering his Browning and gazing at his skeleton-like and fever-wasted hands. And the fancy made him smile—of Childe Roland bearing a slug-horn to his lips with an arm as feeble as his was.[4] Was it months, or years, he asked himself, since he first heard that mysterious call on the beach at Ringmanu? To save himself he could not tell. The long sickness had been most long. In conscious count of time he knew of months, many of them; but he had no way of estimating the long intervals of delirium and stupor. And how fared Captain Bateman of the blackbirder *Nari* he wondered; and had Captain Bateman's drunken mate died of delirium tremens yet?

From which vain speculations, Bassett turned idly to review all that had occurred since that day on the beach of Ringmanu when he first heard the sound and plunged into the jungle after it. Sagawa had protested. He could see him yet, his queer little monkeyish face eloquent with fear, his back burdened with specimen cases, in his hands Bassett's butterfly net and naturalist's shot-gun, as he quavered, in bêche-de-mer English: "Me fella too much fright along bush. Bad fella boy, too much stop'm along bush."

Bassett smiled sadly at the recollection. The little New Hanover boy had been frightened, but had proved faithful, following him without hesitancy into the bush in the quest after the source of the wonderful sound. No fire-hollowed tree-trunk, that, throbbing war through the jungle depths, had been Bassett's conclusion. Erroneous had been his next conclusion, namely, that the source or cause could not be more distant than an hour's walk, and that he would easily be back by mid-afternoon to be picked up by the *Nari*'s whale-boat.

"That big fella noise no good, all the same devil-devil," Sagawa had adjudged. And Sagawa had been right. Had he not had his head hacked off within the day? Bassett shuddered. Without doubt Sagawa had been eaten as well by the "bad fella boys too much" that stopped along the bush. He could see him, as he had last seen him, stripped of the shot-gun and all the naturalist's gear of his master, lying on the narrow trail where he had been decapitated barely the moment before. Yes, within a minute the thing had happened. Within a minute, looking back, Bassett had seen him trudging patiently along under his burdens. Then Bassett's own trouble had come upon him. He looked at the cruelly healed stumps of the first and second fingers of his left hand, then rubbed them softly into the indentation in the back of his skull. Quick as had been the flash of the long-handled tomahawk, he had been quick enough to duck away his head and partially to deflect the stroke with his up-flung hand. Two fingers and a hasty scalp-wound had been the price he paid for his life.

With one barrel of his ten-gauge shot-gun he had blown the life out of the bushman who had so nearly got him; with the other barrel he had peppered the bushmen bending over Sagawa, and had the pleasure of knowing that the major portion of the charge had gone into the one who leaped away with Sagawa's head. Everything had occurred in a flash. Only himself, the slain bushman, and what remained of Sagawa, were in the narrow, wild-pig run of a path. From the dark jungle on either side came no rustle of movement or sound of life. And he had suffered distinct and dreadful shock. For the first time in his life he had killed a human being, and he knew nausea as he contemplated the mess of his handiwork.

Then had begun the chase. He retreated up the pig-run before his hunters, who were between him and the beach. How many there were, he could not guess. There might have been one, or a hundred, for aught he saw of them. That some of them took to the trees and travelled along through the jungle roof he was certain; but at the most he never glimpsed more than an occasional flitting of shadows. No bow-strings twanged that he could hear; but every little while, whence discharged he knew not, tiny arrows whispered past him or struck tree-boles and fluttered to the ground beside him. They were bone-tipped and feather shafted, and the feathers, torn from the breasts of humming-birds, iridesced like jewels.

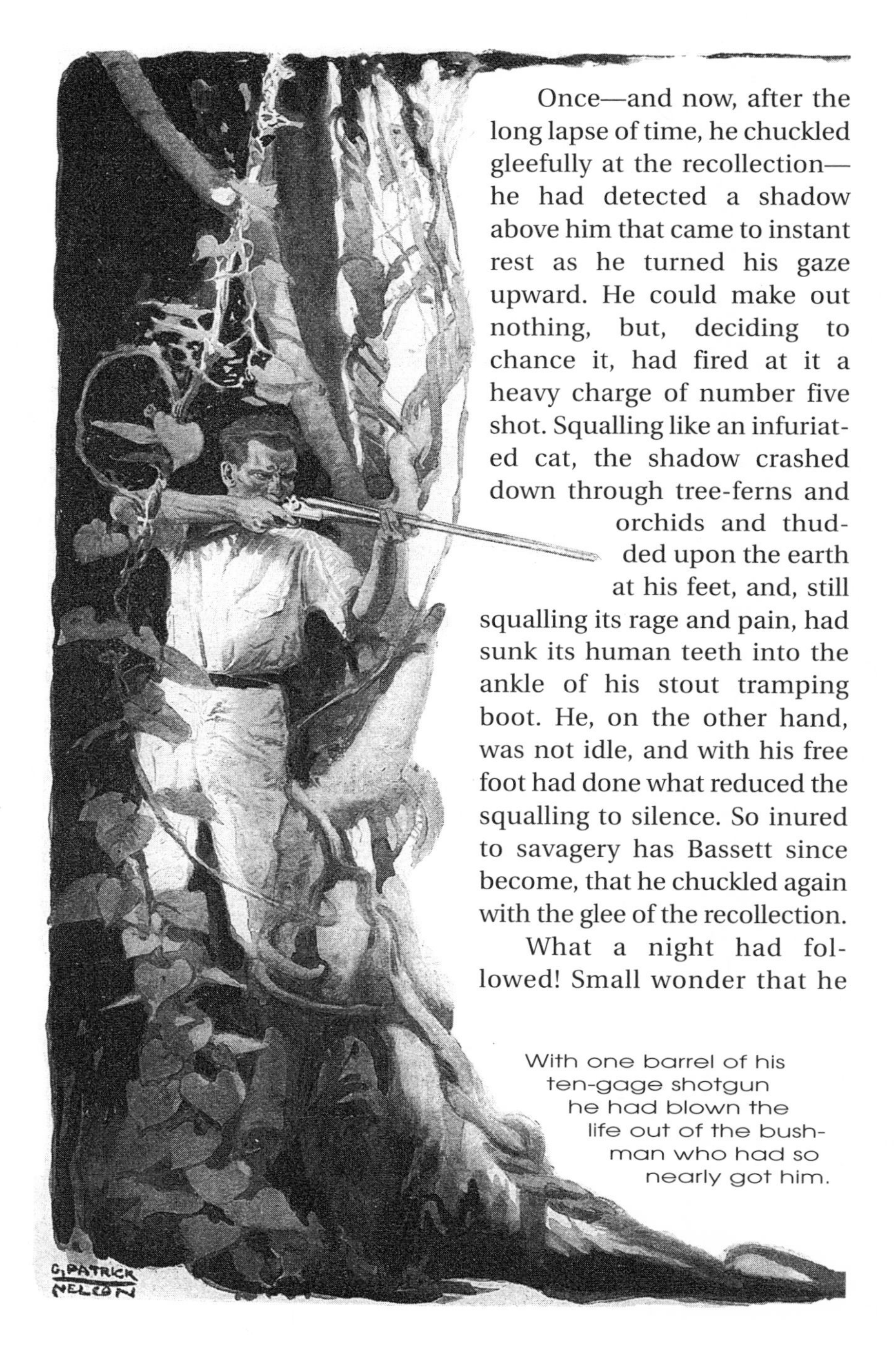

Once—and now, after the long lapse of time, he chuckled gleefully at the recollection—he had detected a shadow above him that came to instant rest as he turned his gaze upward. He could make out nothing, but, deciding to chance it, had fired at it a heavy charge of number five shot. Squalling like an infuriated cat, the shadow crashed down through tree-ferns and orchids and thudded upon the earth at his feet, and, still squalling its rage and pain, had sunk its human teeth into the ankle of his stout tramping boot. He, on the other hand, was not idle, and with his free foot had done what reduced the squalling to silence. So inured to savagery has Bassett since become, that he chuckled again with the glee of the recollection.

What a night had followed! Small wonder that he

With one barrel of his ten-gage shotgun he had blown the life out of the bushman who had so nearly got him.

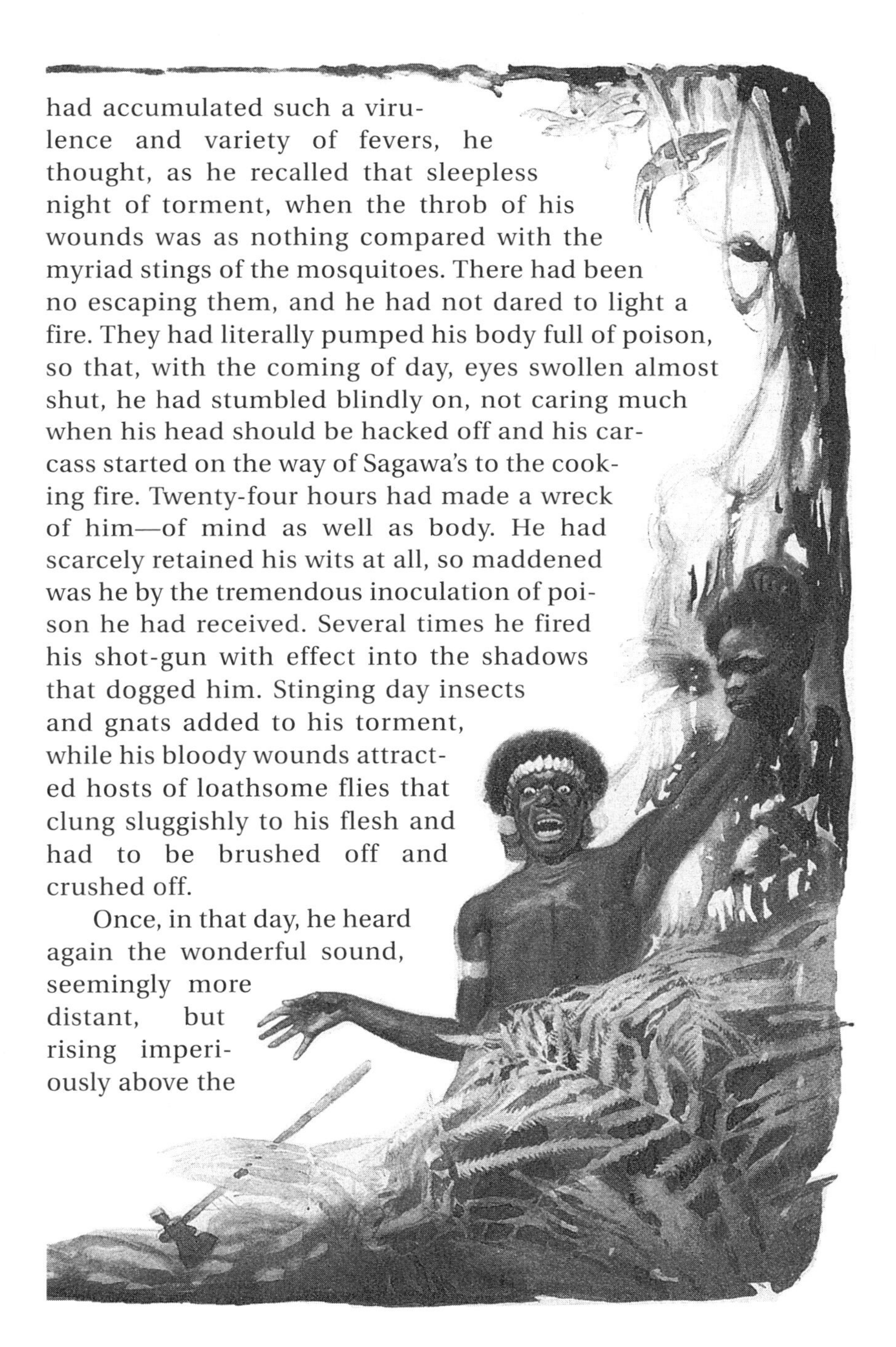

had accumulated such a virulence and variety of fevers, he thought, as he recalled that sleepless night of torment, when the throb of his wounds was as nothing compared with the myriad stings of the mosquitoes. There had been no escaping them, and he had not dared to light a fire. They had literally pumped his body full of poison, so that, with the coming of day, eyes swollen almost shut, he had stumbled blindly on, not caring much when his head should be hacked off and his carcass started on the way of Sagawa's to the cooking fire. Twenty-four hours had made a wreck of him—of mind as well as body. He had scarcely retained his wits at all, so maddened was he by the tremendous inoculation of poison he had received. Several times he fired his shot-gun with effect into the shadows that dogged him. Stinging day insects and gnats added to his torment, while his bloody wounds attracted hosts of loathsome flies that clung sluggishly to his flesh and had to be brushed off and crushed off.

Once, in that day, he heard again the wonderful sound, seemingly more distant, but rising imperiously above the nearer war-drums in the bush. Right there was where he had made his mistake. Thinking that he had passed beyond it and that, therefore, it was between him and the beach of Ringmanu, he had worked back toward it when in reality he was penetrating deeper and deeper into the mysterious heart of the unexplored island. That night, crawling in among the twisted roots of a banyan tree, he had slept from exhaustion while the mosquitoes had had their will of him.

Followed days and nights that were vague as nightmares in his memory. One clear vision he remembered was of suddenly finding himself in the midst of a bush village and watching the old men and children fleeing into the jungle. All had fled but one. From close at hand and above him, a whimpering as of some animal in pain and terror had startled him. And looking up he had seen her—a girl, or young woman rather, suspended by one arm in the cooking sun. Perhaps for days she had so hung. Her swollen, protruding tongue spoke as much. Still alive, she gazed at him with eyes of terror. Past help, he decided, as he noted the swellings of her legs which advertised that the joints had been crushed and the great bones broken. He resolved to shoot her, and there the vision terminated. He could not remember whether he had or not, any more than could he remember how he chanced to be in that village, or how he succeeded in getting away from it.

Many pictures, unrelated, came and went in Bassett's mind as he reviewed that period of his terrible wanderings. He remembered invading another village of a dozen houses and driving all before him with his shot-gun save, for one old man, too feeble to flee, who spat at him and whined and snarled as he dug open a ground-oven and from amid the hot stones dragged forth a roasted pig that steamed its essence deliciously through its green-leaf wrappings. It was at this place that a wantonness of savagery had seized upon him. Having feasted, ready to depart with a hind-quarter of the pig in his hand, he deliberately fired the grass thatch of a house with his burning glass.

But seared deepest of all in Bassett's brain, was the dank and noisome jungle. It actually stank with evil, and it was always twilight. Rarely did a shaft of sunlight penetrate its matted roof a hundred feet overhead. And beneath that roof was an aerial ooze of vegetation, a monstrous, parasitic dripping of decadent life-forms that rooted in death and lived on death. And through all this he drifted, ever pursued by the flitting shadows of the anthropophagi, themselves ghosts of evil that dared not face him in battle but that knew that, soon or late, they would feed on him. Bassett remembered that at the time, in lucid moments, he had likened himself to a wounded bull pursued by plains' coyotes too cowardly to battle with him for the meat of him, yet certain of the inevitable end of him when they would be full gorged. As the bull's horns and stamping hoofs kept off the coyotes, so his shot-gun kept off these Solomon Islanders, these twilight shades of bushmen of the island of Guadalcanal.

Came the day of the grass lands. Abruptly, as if cloven by the sword of God in the hand of God, the jungle terminated. The edge of it, perpendicular and as black as the infamy of it, was a hundred feet up and down. And, beginning at the edge of it, grew the grass—sweet, soft, tender, pasture grass that would have delighted the eyes and beasts of any husbandman and that extended, on and on, for leagues and leagues of velvet verdure, to the backbone of the great island, the towering mountain range flung up by some ancient earth-cataclysm, serrated and gullied but not yet erased by the erosive tropic rains. But the grass! He had crawled into it a dozen yards, buried his face in it, smelled it, and broken down in a fit of involuntary weeping.

And, while he wept, the wonderful sound had pealed forth—if by *peal*, he had often thought since, an adequate description could be given of the enunciation of so vast a sound melting sweet. Sweet it was, as no sound ever heard. Vast it was, of so mighty a resonance that it might have proceeded from some brazen-throated monster. And yet it called to him across that leagues-wide savannah, and was like a benediction to his long-suffering, pain-racked spirit.

He remembered how he lay there in the grass, wet-cheeked but no longer sobbing, listening to the sound and wondering that he had been able to hear it on the beach of Ringmanu. Some freak of air pressures and air currents, he reflected, had made it possible for the sound to carry so far. Such conditions might not happen again in a thousand days or ten thousand days, but the one day it had happened had been the day he landed from the *Nari* for several hours' collecting. Especially had he been in quest of the famed jungle butterfly, a foot across from wing-tip to wing-tip, as velvet-dusky of lack of colour as was the gloom of the roof, of such lofty arboreal habits that it resorted only to the jungle roof and could be brought down only by a dose of shot. It was for this purpose that Sagawa had carried the ten-gauge shot-gun.[5]

Two days and nights he had spent crawling across that belt of grass land. He had suffered much, but pursuit had ceased at the jungle-edge. And he would have died of thirst had not a heavy thunderstorm revived him on the second day.

And then had come Balatta. In the first shade, where the savannah yielded to the dense mountain jungle, he had collapsed to die. At first she had squealed with delight at sight of his helplessness, and was for beating his brain out with a stout forest branch. Perhaps it was his very utter helplessness that had appealed to her, and perhaps it was her human curiosity that made her refrain. At any rate, she had refrained, for he opened his eyes again under the impending blow, and saw her studying him intently. What especially struck her about him were his blue eyes and white skin. Coolly she had squatted on her hams, spat on his arm, and with her finger-tips scrubbed away the dirt of days and nights of muck and jungle that sullied the pristine whiteness of his skin.

And everything about her had struck him especially, although there was nothing conventional about her at all. He laughed weakly at the recollection, for she had been as innocent of garb as Eve before the fig-leaf adventure. Squat and lean at the same time, asymmetrically limbed, string-muscled as if with lengths of cordage, dirt-caked from infancy save for casual showers, she was as unbeautiful a prototype of woman as he, with a scientist's eye, had ever gazed upon. Her breasts advertised at the one time her maturity and youth; and, if by nothing else, her sex was advertised by the one article of finery with which she was adorned, namely a pig's tail, thrust though a hole in her left ear-lobe. So lately had the tail been severed, that its raw end still oozed blood that dried upon her shoulder like so much candle-droppings. And her face! A twisted and wizened complex of apish features, perforated by upturned, sky-open, Mongolian nostrils, by a mouth that sagged from a huge upper-lip and faded precipitately into a retreating chin, by peering querulous eyes that blinked as blink the eyes of denizens of monkey-cages.

Not even the water she brought him in a forest-leaf, and the ancient and half-putrid chunk of roast pig, could redeem in the slightest the grotesque hideousness of her. When he had eaten weakly for a space, he closed his eyes in order not to see her, although again and again she poked them open to peer at the blue of them. Then had come the sound. Nearer, much nearer, he knew it to be; and he knew equally well, despite the weary way he had come, that it was still many hours distant. The effect of it on her had been startling. She cringed under it, with averted face, moaning and chattering with fear. But after it had lived its full life of an hour, he closed his eyes and fell asleep with Balatta brushing the flies from him.

When he awoke it was night, and she was gone. But he was aware of renewed strength, and, by then too thoroughly inoculated by the mosquito poison to suffer further inflammation, he closed his eyes and slept an unbroken stretch till sun-up. A little later Balatta had returned, bringing with her a half-dozen women who, unbeautiful as they were, were patently not so unbeautiful as she. She evidenced by her conduct that she considered him her find, her property, and the pride she took in showing him off would have been ludicrous had his situation not been so desperate.

Later, after what had been to him a terrible journey of miles, when he collapsed in front of the devil-devil house in the shadow of the breadfruit tree, she had shown very lively ideas on the matter of retaining possession of him. Ngurn, whom Bassett was to know afterward as the devil-devil doctor, priest, or medicine man of the village, had wanted his head. Others of the grinning and chattering monkey-men, all as stark of clothes and bestial of appearance as Balatta, had wanted his body for the roasting oven. At that time he had not understood their language, if by *language* might be dignified the uncouth sounds they made to represent ideas.[6] But Bassett had thoroughly understood the matter of debate, especially when the men pressed and prodded and felt of the flesh of him as if he were so much commodity in a butcher's stall.

Balatta had been losing the debate rapidly, when the accident happened. One of the men, curiously examining Bassett's shotgun, managed to cock and pull a trigger. The recoil of the butt into the pit of the man's stomach had not been the most sanguinary result, for the charge of shot, at a distance of a yard, had blown the head of one of the debaters into nothingness.

Even Balatta joined the others in flight, and, ere they returned, his senses already reeling from the oncoming fever-attack, Bassett had regained possession of the gun. Whereupon, although his teeth chattered with the ague and his swimming eyes could scarcely see, he held on to his fading consciousness until he could intimidate the bushmen with the simple magics of compass, watch, burning glass, and matches. At the last, with due emphasis, of solemnity and awfulness, he had killed a young pig with his shotgun and promptly fainted.

Bassett flexed his arm-muscles in quest of what possible strength might reside in such weakness, and dragged himself slowly and totteringly to his feet. He was shockingly emaciated; yet, during the various convalescences of the many months of his long sickness, he had never regained quite the same degree of strength as this time. What he feared was another relapse such as he had already frequently experienced. Without drugs, without even quinine, he had managed so far to live through a combination of the most pernicious and most malignant of malarial and black-water fevers. But could he continue to endure? Such was his everlasting query. For, like the genuine scientist he was, he would not be content to die until he had solved the secret of the sound.

Supported by a staff, he staggered the few steps to the devil-devil house where death and Ngurn reigned in gloom. Almost as infamously dark and evil-stinking as the jungle was the devil-devil house—in Bassett's opinion. Yet therein was usually to be found his favourite crony and gossip, Ngurn, always willing for a yarn or a discussion, the while he sat in the ashes of death and in a slow smoke shrewdly revolved curing human heads suspended from the rafters. For, through the months' interval of consciousness of his long sickness, Bassett had mastered the psychological simplicities and lingual difficulties of the language of the tribe of Ngurn and Balatta and Gngngn—the latter the addle-headed young chief who was ruled by Ngurn, and who, whispered intrigue had it, was the son of Ngurn.

"Will the Red One speak to-day?" Bassett asked, by this time so accustomed to the old man's gruesome occupation as to take even an interest in the progress of the smoke-curing.

With the eye of an expert Ngurn examined the particular head he was at work upon.

"It will be ten days before I can say 'finish,'" he said. "Never has any man fixed heads like these."

Bassett smiled inwardly at the old fellow's reluctance to talk with him of the Red One. It had always been so. Never, by any chance, had Ngurn or any other member of the weird tribe divulged the slightest hint of any physical characteristic of the Red One. Physical the Red One must be, to emit the wonderful sound, and though it was called the Red One, Bassett could not be sure that red represented the colour of it. Red enough were the deeds and powers of it, from what abstract clues he had gleaned. Not alone, had Ngurn informed him, was the Red One more bestial powerful than the neighbour tribal gods, ever athirst for the red blood of living human sacrifices, but the neighbour gods themselves were sacrificed and tormented before him. He was the god of a dozen allied villages similar to this one, which was the central and commanding village of the federation. By virtue of the Red One many alien villages had been devastated and even wiped out, the prisoners sacrificed to the Red One. This was true to-day, and it extended back into old history carried down by word of mouth through the generations. When he, Ngurn, had been a young man, the tribes beyond the grass lands had made a war raid. In the counter raid, Ngurn and his fighting folk had made many prisoners. Of children alone over five score living had been bled white before the Red One, and many, many more men and women.

The Thunderer was another of Ngurn's names for the mysterious deity. Also at times was he called The Loud Shouter, The God-Voiced, The Bird-Throated, The One with the Throat Sweet as the Throat of the Honey-Bird, The Sun Singer, and The Star-Born.

Why The Star-Born? In vain Bassett interrogated Ngurn. According to that old devil-devil doctor, the Red One had always been, just where he was at present, for ever singing and thundering his will over men. But Ngurn's father, wrapped in decaying grass-matting and hanging even then over their heads among the smoky rafters of the devil-devil house, had held otherwise. That departed wise one had believed that the Red One came from out of the starry night, else why—so his argument had run—had the old and forgotten ones passed his name down as the Star-Born?

"I would like to have the curing of your head," Ngurn changed the subject. "It is different from any other head. No devil-devil has a head like it. Besides, I would cure it well. I would take months and months."

Bassett could not but recognize something cogent in such argument. But Ngurn affirmed the long years of his long life, wherein he had gazed upon many starry nights, yet never had he found a star on grass land or in jungle depth—and he had looked for them. True, he had beheld shooting stars (this in reply to Bassett's contention); but likewise had he beheld the phosphorescence of fungoid growths and rotten meat and fireflies on dark nights, and the flames of wood-fires and of blazing candle-nuts; yet what were flame and blaze and glow when they had flamed and blazed and glowed? Answer: memories, memories only, of things which had ceased to be, like memories of matings accomplished, of feasts forgotten, of desires that were the ghosts of desires, flaring, flaming, burning, yet unrealized in achievement of easement and satisfaction. Where was the appetite of yesterday? the roasted flesh of the wild pig the hunter's arrow failed to slay? the maid, unwed and dead ere the young man knew her?

A memory was not a star, was Ngurn's contention. How could a memory be a star? Further, after all his long life he still observed the starry night-sky unaltered. Never had he noted the absence of a single star from its accustomed place. Besides, stars were fire, and the Red One was not fire—which last involuntary betrayal told Bassett nothing.

"Will the Red One speak to-morrow?" he queried.

Ngurn shrugged his shoulders as who should say.

"And the day after?—and the day after that?" Bassett persisted.

"I would like to have the curing of your head," Ngurn changed the subject. "It is different from any other head. No devil-devil has a head like it. Besides, I would cure it well. I would take months and months. The moons would come and the moons would go, and the smoke would be very slow, and I should myself gather the materials for the curing smoke. The skin would not wrinkle. It would be as smooth as your skin now."

He stood up, and from the dim rafters, grimed with the smoking of countless heads, where day was no more than a gloom, took down a matting-wrapped parcel and began to open it.

"It is a head like yours," he said, "but it is poorly cured."

Bassett had pricked up his ears at the suggestion that it was a white man's head; for he had long since come to accept that these jungle-dwellers, in the midmost centre of the great island, had never had intercourse with white men. Certainly he had found them without the almost universal bêche-de-mer English of the west South Pacific. Nor had they knowledge of tobacco, nor of gunpowder. Their few precious knives, made from lengths of hoop-iron, and their few and more precious tomahawks from cheap trade hatchets, he had surmised they had captured in war from the bushmen of the jungle beyond the grass lands, and that they, in turn, had similarly gained them from the salt-water men who fringed the coral beaches of the shore and had contact with the occasional white men.

"The folk in the out beyond do not know how to cure heads," old Ngurn explained, as he drew forth from the filthy matting and placed in Bassett's hands an indubitable white man's head.

Ancient it was beyond question; white it was as the blond hair attested. He could have sworn it once belonged to an Englishman, and to an Englishman of long before by token of the heavy gold circlets still threaded in the withered ear-lobes.

"Now your head..." the devil-devil doctor began on his favourite topic.

"I'll tell you what," Bassett interrupted, struck by a new idea. "When I die I'll let you have my head to cure, if, first, you take me to look upon the Red One."

"I will have your head anyway when you are dead," Ngurn rejected the proposition. He added, with the brutal frankness of the savage: "Besides, you have not long to live. You are almost a dead man now. You will grow less strong. In not many months I shall have you here turning and turning in the smoke. It is pleasant, through the long afternoons, to turn the head of one you have known as well as I know you. And I shall talk to you and tell you the many secrets you want to know. Which will not matter, for you will be dead."

"Ngurn," Bassett threatened in sudden anger. "You know the Baby Thunder in the Iron that is mine." (This was in reference to his all-potent and all-awful shotgun.) "I can kill you any time, and then you will not get my head."

"Just the same, will Gngngn, or some one else of my folk get it," Ngurn complacently assured him. "And just the same will it turn here in the devil-devil house in the smoke. The quicker you slay me with your Baby Thunder, the quicker will your head turn in the smoke." And Bassett knew he was beaten in the discussion.

What was the Red One?—Bassett asked himself a thousand times in the succeeding week, while he seemed to grow stronger. What was the source of the wonderful sound? What was this Sun Singer, this Star-Born One, this mysterious deity, as bestial-conducted as the black and kinky-headed and monkey-like human beasts who worshipped it, and whose silver-sweet, bull-mouthed singing and commanding he had heard at the taboo distance for so long?

Ngurn had he failed to bribe with the inevitable curing of his head when he was dead. Gngngn, imbecile and chief that he was, was too imbecilic, too much under the sway of Ngurn, to be considered. Remained Balatta, who, from the time she found him and poked his blue eyes open to recrudescence of her grotesque female hideousness, had continued his adorer. Woman she was, and he had long known that the only way to win from her treason of her tribe was through the woman's heart of her.

Bassett was a fastidious man. He had never recovered from the initial horror caused by Balatta's female awfulness. Back in England, even at best the charm of woman, to him, had never been robust. Yet now, resolutely, as only a man can do who is capable of martyring himself for the cause of science, he proceeded to violate all the fineness and delicacy of his nature by making love to the unthinkably disgusting bushwoman.

He shuddered, but with averted face hid his grimaces and swallowed his gorge as he put his arm around her dirt-crusted shoulders and felt the contact of her rancid, oily and kinky hair with his neck and chin. But he

And the next thing he did in the singular courtship was to take her down to the stream for a vigorous scrubbing.

nearly screamed when she succumbed to that caress so at the very first of the courtship and mowed and gibbered and squealed little, queer, pig-like gurgly noises of delight. It was too much. And the next he did in the singular courtship was to take her down to the stream and give her a vigorous scrubbing.

From then on he devoted himself to her like a true swain as frequently and for as long at a time as his will could override his repugnance. But marriage, which she ardently suggested, with due observance of tribal custom, he balked at. Fortunately, taboo rule was strong in the tribe. Thus, Ngurn could never touch bone, or flesh, or hide of crocodile. This had been ordained at his birth. Gngngn was denied ever the touch of woman. Such pollution, did it chance to occur, could be purged only by the death of the offending female. It had happened once, since Bassett's arrival, when a girl of nine, running in play, stumbled and fell against the sacred chief. And the girl-child was seen no more. In whispers, Balatta told Bassett that she had been three days and nights in dying before the Red One. As for Balatta, the breadfruit was taboo to her. For which Bassett was thankful. The taboo might have been water.

For himself, he fabricated a special taboo. Only could he marry, he explained, when the Southern Cross rode highest in the sky.[7] Knowing his astronomy, he thus gained a reprieve of nearly nine months; and he was confident that within that time he would either be dead or escaped to the coast with full knowledge of the Red One and of the source of the Red One's wonderful voice. At first he had fancied the Red One to be some colossal statue, like Memnon, rendered vocal under certain temperature conditions of sunlight.[8] But when, after a war raid, a batch of prisoners was brought in and the sacrifice made at night, in the midst of rain, when the sun could play no part, the Red One had been more vocal than usual, Bassett discarded that hypothesis.

In company with Balatta, sometimes with men and parties of women, the freedom of the jungle was his for three quadrants of the compass. But the fourth quadrant, which contained the Red One's abiding place, was taboo. He made more thorough love to Balatta—also saw to it that she scrubbed herself more frequently. Eternal female she was, capable of any treason for the sake of love. And, though the sight of her was provocative of nausea and the contact of her provocative of despair, although he could not escape her awfulness in his dream-haunted nightmares of her, he nevertheless was aware of the cosmic verity of sex that animated her and that made her own life of less value than the happiness of her lover with whom she hoped to mate. Juliet or Balatta? Where was the intrinsic difference? The soft and tender product of ultra-civilization, or her bestial prototype of a hundred thousand years before her?—there was no difference.

Bassett was a scientist first, a humanist afterward. In the jungle-heart of Guadalcanal he put the affair to the test, as in the laboratory he would have put to the test any chemical reaction. He increased his feigned ardour for the bushwoman, at the same time increasing the imperiousness of his will of desire over her to be led to look upon the Red One face to face. It was the old story, he recognized, that the woman must pay, and it occurred when the two of them, one day, were catching the unclassified and unnamed little black fish, an inch long, half-eel and half-scaled, rotund with salmon-golden roe, that frequented the fresh water, and that were esteemed, raw and whole, fresh or putrid, a perfect delicacy. Prone in the muck of the decaying jungle-floor, Balatta threw herself, clutching his ankles with her hands kissing his feet and making slubbery noises that chilled his backbone up and down again. She begged him to kill her rather than exact this ultimate love-payment. She told him of the penalty of breaking the taboo of the Red One—a week of torture, living, the details of which she yammered out from her face in the mire until he realized that he was yet a tyro in knowledge of the frightfulness the human was capable of wreaking on the human.

Yet did Bassett insist on having his man's will satisfied, at the woman's risk, that he might solve the mystery of the Red One's singing, though she should die long and horribly and screaming. And Balatta, being mere woman, yielded. She led him into the forbidden quadrant. An abrupt mountain, shouldering in from the north to meet a similar intrusion from the south, tormented the stream in which they had fished into a deep and gloomy gorge. After a mile along the gorge, the way plunged sharply upward until they crossed a saddle of raw limestone which attracted his geologist's eye. Still climbing, although he paused often from sheer physical weakness, they scaled forest-clad heights until they emerged on a naked mesa or tableland. Bassett recognized the stuff of its

composition as black volcanic sand, and knew that a pocket magnet could have captured a full load of the sharply angular grains he trod upon.

And then holding Balatta by the hand and leading her onward, he came to it—a tremendous pit, obviously artificial, in the heart of the plateau. Old history, the South Seas Sailing Directions, scores of remembered data and connotations swift and furious, surged through his brain. It was Mendana who had discovered the islands and named them Solomon's, believing that he had found that monarch's fabled mines. They had laughed at the old navigator's child-like credulity; and yet here stood himself, Bassett, on the rim of an excavation for all the world like the diamond pits of South Africa.

But no diamond this that he gazed down upon. Rather was it a pearl, with the depth of iridescence of a pearl; but of a size all pearls of earth and time, welded into one, could not have totalled; and of a colour undreamed of in any pearl, or of anything else, for that matter, for it was the colour of the Red One. And the Red One himself Bassett knew it to be on the instant. A perfect sphere, full two hundred feet in diameter, the top of it was a hundred feet

And the Red One himself, Basset knew it to be on the instant—a perfect sphere, fully two hundred feet in diameter.

below the level of the rim. He likened the colour quality of it to lacquer. Indeed, he took it to be some sort of lacquer, applied by man, but a lacquer too marvellously clever to have been manufactured by the bush-folk. Brighter than bright cherry-red, its richness of colour was as if it were red builded upon red. It glowed and iridesced in the sunlight as if gleaming up from underlay under underlay of red.

In vain Balatta strove to dissuade him from descending. She threw herself in the dirt; but, when he continued down the trail that spiralled the pit-wall, she followed, cringing and whimpering her terror. That the red sphere had been dug out as a precious thing, was patent. Considering the paucity of members of the federated twelve villages and their primitive tools and methods, Bassett knew that the toil of a myriad generations could scarcely have made that enormous excavation.

He found the pit bottom carpeted with human bones, among which, battered and defaced, lay village gods of wood and stone. Some, covered with obscene totemic figures and designs, were carved from solid tree trunks forty or fifty feet in length. He noted the absence of the shark and turtle gods, so common among the shore villages, and was amazed at the constant recurrence of the helmet motive. What did these jungle savages of the dark heart of Guadalcanal know of helmets? Had Mendana's men-at-arms worn helmets and penetrated here centuries before? And if not, then whence had the bush-folk caught the motive?

Advancing over the litter of gods and bones, Balatta whimpering at his heels, Bassett entered the shadow of the Red One and passed on under its gigantic overhang until he touched it with his finger-tips. No lacquer that. Nor was the surface smooth as it should have been in the case of lacquer. On the contrary, it was corrugated and pitted, with here and there patches that showed signs of heat and fusing. Also, the substance of it was metal, though unlike any metal, or combination of metals, he had ever known. As for the colour itself, he decided it to be no application. It was the intrinsic colour of the metal itself.

He moved his finger-tips, which up to that had merely rested, along the surface, and felt the whole gigantic sphere quicken and live and respond. It was incredible! So light a touch on so vast a mass! Yet did it quiver under the finger-tip caress in rhythmic vibrations that became whisperings and rustlings and mutterings of sound—but of sound so different; so elusively thin that it was shimmeringly sibilant; so mellow that it was maddening sweet, piping like an elfin horn, which last was just what Bassett decided would be like a peal from some bell of the gods reaching earthward from across space.

He looked at Balatta with swift questioning; but the voice of the Red One he had evoked had flung her face downward and moaning among the bones. He returned to contemplation of the prodigy. Hollow it was, and of no metal known on earth, was his conclusion. It was right-named by the ones of old-time as the Star-Born. Only from the stars could it have come, and no thing of chance was it. It was a creation of artifice and mind. Such perfection of form, such hollowness that it certainly possessed, could not be the result of mere fortuitousness. A child of intelligences, remote and unguessable, working corporally in metals, it indubitably was. He stared at it in amaze, his brain a racing wild-fire of hypotheses to account for this far-journeyer who had adventured the night of space, threaded the stars, and now rose before him and above him, exhumed by patient anthropophagi, pitted and lacquered by its fiery bath in two atmospheres.

But was the colour a lacquer of heat upon some familiar metal? Or was it an intrinsic quality of the metal itself? He thrust in the blue-point of his pocket-knife to test the constitution of the stuff. Instantly the entire sphere burst into a mighty whispering, sharp with protest, almost twanging goldenly, if a whisper could possibly be considered to twang, rising higher, sinking deeper, the two extremes of the registry of sound threatening to complete the circle and coalesce into the bull-mouthed thundering he had so often heard beyond the taboo distance.

Forgetful of safety, of his own life itself, entranced by the wonder of the unthinkable and unguessable thing, he raised his knife to strike heavily from a long stroke, but was prevented by Balatta. She upreared on her own knees in an agony of terror, clasping his knees and supplicating him to desist. In the intensity of her desire to impress him, she put her forearm between her teeth and sank them to the bone.

He scarcely observed her act, although he yielded automatically to his gentler instincts and withheld the knife-hack. To him, human life had dwarfed to microscopic proportions before this colossal portent of higher life from within the distances of the sidereal universe. As had she been a dog, he kicked the ugly little bushwoman to her feet and compelled her to start with him on an encirclement of the base. Part way around, he encountered horrors. Even, among the others, did he recognize the sun-shrivelled remnant of the nine-years girl who had accidentally broken Chief Gngngn's personal taboo.[9] And, among what was left of these that had passed, he encountered what was left of one who had not yet passed. Truly had the bush-folk named themselves into the name of the Red One, seeing in him their own image which they strove to placate and please with such red offerings.

Farther around, always treading the bones and images of humans and gods that constituted the floor of this ancient charnel-house of sacrifice, he came upon the device by which the Red One was made to send his call singing thunderingly across the jungle-belts and grass-lands to the far beach of Ringmanu. Simple and primitive was it as was the Red One's consummate artifice. A great king-post, half a hundred feet in length, seasoned by centuries of superstitious care, carven into dynasties of gods, each superimposed, each helmeted, each seated in the open mouth of a crocodile, was slung by ropes, twisted of climbing vegetable parasites, from the apex of a tripod of three great forest trunks, themselves carved into grinning and grotesque adumbrations of man's modern concepts of art and god. From the striker king-post were suspended ropes of climbers to which men could apply their strength and direction. Like a battering ram, this king-post could be driven end-onward against the mighty red-iridescent sphere.

Here was where Ngurn officiated and functioned religiously for himself and the twelve tribes under him. Bassett laughed aloud, almost with madness, at the thought of this wonderful messenger, winged with intelligence across space, to fall into a bushman stronghold and be worshipped by ape-like, man-eating and head-hunting savages. It was as if God's World had fallen into the muck mire of the abyss underlying the bottom of hell; as if Jehovah's Commandments had been presented on carved stone to the monkeys of the monkey cage at the Zoo; as if the Sermon on the Mount had been preached in a roaring bedlam of lunatics.

The slow weeks passed. The nights, by election, Bassett spent on the ashen floor of the devil-devil house, beneath the ever-swinging, slow-curing heads. His reason for this was that it was taboo to the lesser sex of woman, and therefore, a refuge for him from Balatta, who grew more persecutingly and perilously loverly as the Southern Cross rode higher in the sky and marked the imminence of her nuptials. His days Bassett spent in a hammock swung under the shade of the great breadfruit tree before the devil-devil house. There were breaks in this programme, when, in the comas of his devastating fever-attacks, he lay for days and nights in the house of heads. Ever he struggled to combat the fever, to live, to continue to live, to grow strong and stronger against the day when he would be strong enough to dare the grass-lands and the belted jungle beyond, and win to the beach, and to some labour-recruiting, blackbirding ketch or schooner, and on to civilization and the men of civilization, to whom he could give news of the message from other worlds that lay, darkly worshipped by beastmen, in the black heart of Guadalcanal's midmost centre.

On the other nights, lying late under the breadfruit tree, Bassett spent long hours watching the slow setting of the western stars beyond the black wall of jungle where it had been thrust back by the clearing for the village. Possessed of more than a cursory knowledge of astronomy, he took a sick man's pleasure in speculating as to the dwellers on the unseen worlds of those incredibly remote suns, to haunt whose houses of light, life came forth, a shy visitant, from the rayless crypts of matter. He could no more apprehend limits to time than bounds to space. No subversive radium speculations had shaken his steady scientific faith in the conservation of energy and the indestructibility of matter. Always and forever must there have been stars. And surely, in that cosmic ferment, all must be comparatively alike, comparatively of the same substance, or substances, save for the freaks of the ferment. All must obey, or compose, the same laws that ran without infraction through the entire experience of man. Therefore, he argued and agreed, must worlds and life be appendages to all the suns as they were appendages to the particular of his own solar system.

Even as he lay here, under the breadfruit tree, an intelligence that stared across the starry gulfs, so must all the universe be exposed to the ceaseless scrutiny of innumerable eyes, like his, though grantedly different, with behind them, by the same token, intelligences that questioned and sought the meaning and the construction of the whole. So reasoning, he felt his soul go forth in kinship with that august company, that multitude whose gaze was forever upon the arras of infinity.

Who were they, what were they, those far distant and superior ones who had bridged the sky with their gigantic, red-iridescent, heaven-singing message? Surely, and long since, had they, too, trod the path on which man had so recently, by the calendar of the cosmos, set his feet. And to be able to send a message across the pit of space, surely they had reached those heights to which man, in tears and travail and bloody sweat, in darkness and confusion of many counsels, was so slowly struggling. And what were they on their heights? Had they won Brotherhood? Or had they learned that the law of love imposed the penalty of weakness and decay? Was strife, life? Was the rule of all the universe the pitiless rule of natural selection? And, and most immediately and poignantly, were their far conclusions, their long-won wisdoms, shut even then in the huge, metallic heart of the Red One, waiting for the first earth-man to read? Of one thing he was certain: No drop of red dew shaken from the lion-mane of some sun in torment, was the sounding sphere. It was of design, not chance, and it contained the speech and wisdom of the stars.

What engines and elements and mastered forces, what lore and mysteries and destiny-controls, might be there! Undoubtedly, since so much could be enclosed in so little a thing as the foundation stone of a public building, this enormous sphere should contain vast histories, profounds of research achieved beyond man's wildest guesses, laws and formulae that, easily mastered, would make man's life on earth, individual and collective, spring up from its present mire to inconceivable heights of purity and power. It was Time's greatest gift to blindfold, insatiable, and sky-aspiring man. And to him, Bassett, had been vouchsafed the lordly fortune to be the first to receive this message from man's interstellar kin!

No white man, much less no outland man of the other bush-tribes, had gazed upon the Red One and lived. Such the law expounded by Ngurn to Bassett. There was such a thing as blood brotherhood. Bassett, in return, had often argued in the past. But Ngurn had stated solemnly no. Even the blood brotherhood was outside the favour of the Red One. Only a man born within the tribe could look upon the Red One and live. But now, his guilty secret known only to Balatta, whose fear of immolation before the Red One fast-sealed her lips, the situation was different. What he had to do was to recover from the abominable fevers that weakened him, and gain to civilization. Then would he lead an expedition back, and, although the entire population of Guadalcanal he destroyed, extract from the heart of the Red One the message of the world from other worlds.

But Bassett's relapses grew more frequent, his brief convalescences less and less vigorous, his periods of coma longer, until he came to know, beyond the last promptings of the optimism inherent in so tremendous a constitution as his own, that he would never live to cross the grass lands, perforate the perilous coast jungle, and reach the sea. He faded as the Southern Cross rose higher in the sky, till even Balatta knew that he would be dead ere the nuptial date determined by his taboo. Ngurn made pilgrimage personally and gathered the smoke materials for the curing of Bassett's head, and to him made proud announcement and exhibition of the artistic perfectness of his intention when Bassett should be dead. As for himself, Bassett was not shocked. Too long and too deeply had life ebbed down in him to bite him with fear of its impending extinction. He continued to persist, alternating periods of unconsciousness with periods of semi-consciousness, dreamy and unreal, in which he idly wondered whether he had ever truly beheld the Red One or whether it was a nightmare fancy of delirium.

Came the day when all mists and cob-webs dissolved, when he found his brain clear as a bell, and took just appraisement of his body's weakness. Neither hand nor foot could he lift. So little control of his body did he have, that he was scarcely aware of possessing one. Lightly indeed his flesh sat upon his soul, and his soul, in its briefness of clarity, knew by its very clarity that the black of cessation was near. He knew the end was close; knew that in all truth he had with his eyes beheld the Red One, the messenger between the worlds; knew that he would never live to carry that message to the world—that message, for aught to the contrary, which might already have waited man's hearing in the heart of Guadalcanal for ten thousand years. And Bassett stirred with resolve, calling Ngurn to him, out under the shade of the breadfruit tree, and with the old devil-devil doctor discussing the terms and arrangements of his last life effort, his final adventure in the quick of the flesh.

"I know the law, O Ngurn," he concluded the matter. "Whoso is not of the folk may not look upon the Red One and live. I shall not live anyway. Your young men shall carry me before the face of the Red One, and I shall look upon him, and hear his voice, and thereupon die, under your hand, O Ngurn. Thus will the three things be satisfied: the law, my desire, and your quicker possession of my head for which all your preparations wait."

To which Ngurn consented, adding:

"It is better so. A sick man who cannot get well is foolish to live on for so little a while. Also is it better for the living that he should go. You have been much in the way of late. Not but what it was good for me to talk to such a wise one. But for moons of days we have held little talk. Instead, you have taken up room in the house of heads, making noises like a dying pig, or talking much and loudly in your own language which I do not understand. This has been a confusion to me, for I like to think on the great things of the light and dark as I turn the heads in the smoke. Your much noise has thus been a disturbance to the long-learning and hatching of the final wisdom that will be mine before I die. As for you, upon whom the dark has already brooded, it is well that you die now. And I promise you, in the long days to come when I turn your head in the smoke, no man of the tribe shall come in to disturb us. And I will tell you many secrets, for I am an old man and very wise, and I shall be adding wisdom to wisdom as I turn your head in the smoke."

So a litter was made, and, borne on the shoulders of half a dozen of the men, Bassett departed on the last little adventure that was to cap the total adventure, for him, of living. With a body of which he was scarcely aware, for even the pain had been exhausted out of it, and with a bright clear brain that accommodated him to a quiet ecstasy of sheer lucidness of thought, he lay back on the lurching litter and watched the fading of the passing world, beholding for the last time the breadfruit tree before the devil-devil house, the dim day beneath the matted jungle roof, the gloomy gorge between the shouldering mountains, the saddle of raw limestone, and the mesa of black volcanic sand.

Down the spiral path of the pit they bore him, encircling the sheening, glowing Red One that seemed ever imminent to iridesce from colour and light into sweet singing and thunder. And over bones and logs of immolated men and gods they bore him, past the horrors of other immolated ones that yet lived, to the three-king-post tripod and the huge king-post striker.[10]

Here Bassett, helped by Ngurn and Balatta, weakly sat up, swaying weakly from the hips, and with clear, unfaltering, all-seeing eyes gazed upon the Red One.

"Once, O Ngurn," he said, not taking his eyes from the sheening, vibrating surface whereon and wherein all the shades of cherry-red played unceasingly, ever a-quiver to change into sound, to become silken rustlings, silvery whisperings, golden thrummings of cords, velvet pipings of elfland, mellow distances of thunderings.

"I wait," Ngurn prompted after a long pause, the long-handled tomahawk unassumingly ready in his hand.

"Once, O Ngurn," Bassett repeated, "let the Red One speak so that I may see it speak as well as hear it. Then strike, thus, when I raise my hand; for, when I raise my hand, I shall drop my head forward and make place for the stroke at the base of my neck. But, O Ngurn, I, who am about to pass out of the light of day for ever, would like to pass with the wonder-voice of the Red One singing greatly in my ears."

"And I promise you that never will a head be so well cured as yours," Ngurn assured him, at the same time signalling the tribesmen to man the propelling ropes suspended from the king-post striker. "Your head shall be my greatest piece of work in the curing of heads."

Bassett smiled quietly to the old one's conceit, as the great carved log, drawn back through two-score feet of space, was released. The next moment he was lost in ecstasy at the abrupt and thunderous liberation of sound. But such thunder! Mellow it was with preciousness of all sounding metals. Archangels spoke in it; it was magnificently beautiful before all other sounds; it was invested with the intelligence of supermen of planets of other suns; it was the voice of God, seducing and commanding to be heard. And—the everlasting miracle of that interstellar metal! Bassett, with his own eyes, saw colour and colours transform into sound till the whole visible surface of the vast sphere was a-crawl and titillant and vaporous with what he could not tell was colour or was sound. In that moment the interstices of matter were his, and the interfusings and intermating transfusings of matter and force.

Time passed. At the last Bassett was brought back from his ecstasy by an impatient movement of Ngurn. He had quite forgotten the old devil-devil one. A quick flash of fancy brought a husky chuckle into Bassett's throat. His shot-gun lay beside him in the litter. All he had to do, muzzle to head, was to press the trigger and blow his head into nothingness.

But why cheat him? was Bassett's next thought. Head-hunting, cannibal beast of a human that was as much ape as human, nevertheless Old Ngurn had, according to his lights, played squarer than square. Ngurn was in himself a forerunner of ethics and contract, of consideration, and gentleness in man. No, Bassett decided; it would be a ghastly pity and an act of dishonour to cheat the old fellow at the last. His head was Ngurn's, and Ngurn's head to cure it would be.

And Bassett, raising his hand in signal, bending forward his head as agreed so as to expose cleanly the articulation to his taut spinal cord, forgot Balatta, who was merely a woman, a woman merely and only and undesired. He knew, without seeing, when the razor-edged hatchet rose in the air behind him. And for that instant, ere the end, there fell upon Bassett the shadows of the Unknown, a sense of impending marvel of the rending of walls before the imaginable. Almost, when he knew the blow had started and just ere the edge of steel bit the flesh and nerves it seemed that he gazed upon the serene face of the Medusa, Truth[11]—And, simultaneous with the bite of the steel on the onrush of the dark, in a flashing instant of fancy, he saw the vision of his head turning slowly, always turning, in the devil-devil house beside the breadfruit tree.[12]

Waikiki, Honolulu, May 22, 1916.

Notes

1. A fascinating distortion of and biting homage to pulp adventure and science fiction, "The Red One" also presents fruitful material for readers interested in the history of the interaction between literature and psychoanalysis. Freudian and (particularly) Jungian critics have examined the role of archetypal images that are certainly present in the text, and some scholars have followed this lead directly into the collective unconscious. Certainly the Jungian reading has been effectively defended by Riber, Brown, Campbell, and Kirsch. Moreover, Berkove has shown that London might possibly have based a work on Jungian ideas even before he read *The Psychology of the Unconscious* a month after finishing "The Red One." Jorgenson has also suggested the skeletal outline of a Freudian approach to the story, about which much more work needs to be done.

   Citing the relationship between London and one of his literary heroes, Joseph Conrad, Baskett saw close thematic and emotional connections shared by the writers' mutual interest in a main character's painful quest for knowledge through a confrontation with evil. Applying this theory to "The Red One," it is possible to see the story as a gloss on Conrad's *Heart of Darkness*, and such references as "the black heart of Guadalcanal's mid-most center" suggest allusions to the writer he perhaps most admired. Certainly throughout the South Sea stories, London seems to reflect Conrad's interest in the problematic ethics of colonialism and shares with him a profound interest in the existential abyss. (Please see the Works Consulted or Cited list for full citations of all the previously mentioned analytical sources.)

2. Bassett feels compelled to interpret the sound as an expression of frustration over the impossibility of communication. When Bassett hears within the tones of the still-unseen Red One a seductive and urgent message, he is of course extending his empathetic imagination into the unknown—and never revealed or discovered—intentions of the Red One or of its makers. Like some bush-Aquinas, Bassett later draws teleological conclusions from looking at the thing, certain that the very appearance of the object demands the supposition that it was designed by something intelligent. Where there is a watch, there must be a Watchmaker.
3. Biblical references help Bassett to organize his perceptions, though some of these associations are curiously fortuitous, as in the location of his adventure—the Solomon Islands. The islands had been named after King Solomon, perhaps because the term suggested limitless wealth, and explorers always need optimistic backers. But for this narrative the reference has another thematic relevance, as we have argued earlier, since Solomon also serves as a personification of Wisdom itself. Similarly, Bassett likens the sound made by the sphere "to the trump of an archangel" and implicitly derives an apocalyptic threat from it. His meditations directly and naturally lead him to think of Joshua's use of the destructive power of sound directed at Jericho (Josh. 5:10–21): "Walls of cities, he meditated, might well fall down before so vast and compelling a summons." And Bassett's comparison of the sound to a "rising tide" that "brimmed over and flooded earth" of course reflects the not-uncommon anxiety that the world of 1916 was very possibly in as great a danger as it was in the time of Noah. The difficulty of knowing the meaning of the sound is stressed further as Bassett notes that the sound he is trying to interpret has become "a confusion of troubled mutterings and babblings and colossal whisperings"—an allusion to the story of the Tower of Babel, a project undermined by the limitations imposed by language (Gen. 11:1–9). London's use of the word "babblings" is no random shot, but a precise connection to a biblical pun, for the Babylonian word "Babel" sounds like the Hebrew word for "confusion" (see Madeleine S. Miller and J. Lane Miller, *Harper's Bible Dictionary* [New York: Harper & Row, 1961], 55).
4. Another avenue toward interpretation is provided by the reflected light of other literary texts. Bassett's use of Robert Browning's 1852 poem "Childe Roland to the Dark Tower Came" becomes a frame for his own experience and alerts the reader to the telescoping process of reading. London not infrequently in other works uses a text within the text, perhaps as a kind of shorthand invitation to the reader to reflect on the connection between the text being read in "real life" and a text being read by the characters in the story. Certainly here the intertextualization is helpful, as there are close and intriguing parallels between Browning's nightmarish, protosurrealist narrative and the meditations of London's fever-ridden scientist. Neither Roland nor Bassett can be sure of the objectivity of their perceptions. Nature in both works is corrupt and repellent. Both the main characters are motivated by a code of ethics that they have not rationally chosen

but seem instead to have embraced existentially. Neither of them knows the meaning of the objects that are the whole point of their respective quests. Finally, both are willing to sacrifice life itself to gain their objective.

5. It is likely, though not certain, that London based his character on the exploits of Australian naturalist A. S. Meek, who was the first butterfly collector to penetrate the interior of Guadalcanal. Earlier, Meek (who worked for the Tring Museum in Queensland) had discovered the largest butterfly in the world in New Guinea. Between 1901 and 1908, Meek explored the South Seas, with several visits to the Solomons, where he netted a slightly smaller variation called *Ornithoptera victoriae*. In 1913, Meek published an account of his adventures, entitled *A Naturalist in Cannibal Land*. Meek's superiors at the museum made the claim that the naturalist was unique in his intrepid penetrations of savage island interiors, thus increasing the likelihood that he served as the model for Bassett.

   Whether or not London was thinking of Meek, what makes Bassett's lepidoptery particularly apt is the determined empiricism that motivates him, comically contrasted with the commonly perceived triviality of this branch of science, and darkly reminding us of the thematic connection between knowledge and death—again to cite Wordsworth, who notes wryly of academic analytic procedures, "We murder to dissect." Bassett seeks to understand the butterfly, but he can only do so by killing it. The amassing of knowledge demands the death of its object. Further, Bassett is not the only collecting enthusiast on Guadalcanal, as he learns at the moment that his guide, the sagacious Sagawa—the only one to advise Bassett against entering the island interior—has his head chopped off and carried away into the forest.

6. A further intellectual limitation lies in Bassett's unexamined belief in the power of language to express thoughts and communicate ideas. Postmodernists will be cheered to learn that London's working title for this story was "The Message"—which of course draws attention to the problems of language, interpretation, and (since no one in the story can translate the Red One's presumed message) the absence of text. The effort to stabilize understanding and to resolve ambiguity is thwarted rather than furthered by the necessary use of language, ultimately inadequate.

7. So powerful is Bassett's terror of this loathsome intimacy that he promises to marry her if she will violate a taboo to take him to investigate the Red One, and to consummate their relationship, but only after nine months when the Southern Cross arrives in the sky. Some measure of how keenly he feels this martyrdom of his sexuality for the sake of knowledge is indicated by his mention of the cross and the implicit allusion to the Nativity. It is clear with Whom Bassett is identifying.

8. Bassett continues his survey of prescientific frames of interpretation with a reference to other earlier, mythic systems of explanation: "He likened it to the mighty cry of some Titan of the Elder World vexed with misery or wrath." Similarly, a reference to Memnon offers the European another mythic parallel: The ancient colossus was said to emit sounds when touched by the sun's rays.

9. The editors have amended what seems to have been a typographical error in the first edition, changing "personality taboo" to "personal taboo."

10. Another filter through which Bassett interprets his experience is his subconscious mind. Before he knows anything of the origin of the sound, he flirts with the idea of Browning's phallic "dark tower," but, for the rest of the story, the images he conjures to describe the Red One are usually feminine and implicitly linked to power, secret knowledge, and cosmic Truth. Bassett's conscious feelings about sex range from indifference to revulsion. Perhaps because of his consciousness of the dangerous "otherness" of the feminine, Bassett reflexively notes the Red One's sound and later its appearance often in feminine terms, likening the sound to a woman in pain. The extraterrestrial artifact is responsive, arguing its sentience, and it is difficult to ignore the explicitly sexual nature of this response. When Bassett finds the Red One, its appearance is of a massive sphere half-buried in a great pit; Bassett tells us it is "cherry-red." Though it is made of metal, Bassett makes a startling discovery as he touches it: "He moved his fingertips... along the surface, and felt the whole gigantic sphere quicken and live and respond.... Yet did it quiver under the fingertip caress in rhythmic vibrations...."

    Bassett learns that the natives themselves seem to have made similar interpretive leaps, for though the European's first impulse is to try to cut the surface of the sphere with his little pocket knife, the islanders have realized a more ambitiously phallic project. They have erected a massive sling for a huge pole that they use as a battering ram to strike the Red One to make it "sing."

    This issue requires a great deal more examination than can be devoted to it here, and the analysis of the author's interest in, knowledge of, and literary use of specifically Freudian concepts offers a breaking field in London studies. Jack London's subscription to *The Psychoanalytic Review* only began in the autumn of 1916, while this story was composed in early May of the same year. He appears to have become interested in Freud around 1912, David Mike Hamilton's research indicates, and about the time "The Red One" was composed, London had read and annotated his copy of Freud's 1916 booklet *Three Contributions to the Theory of Sex* (see David Hamilton's *The Tools of My Trade: Annotated Books in Jack London's Library*. [Seattle: University of Washington Press, 1986], 129–30).

11. There is also another tantalizing mythic reference at the end of the story, the odd and seemingly inappropriate mention of "the Medusa, Truth." Bassett links himself with Medusa because they share the experience of decapitation, and he knows that, just as Medusa's head retained its paralytic powers after her death, so Bassett's head—though incapable of active, self-directed thought—will act out a perversely positive function as the passive recipient of another's wisdom. Finally, the European's use of the appositive "Truth" suggests that his last insight (rather like Kurtz's in a similar situation) exposes the dark inevitability of destruction and death as the ultimate and absolute reality that lies waiting at the end of the quest for knowledge.

12. London suggests throughout the story that Bassett's attainment of knowledge is somehow like the Genesis account of that earliest reckless quest for forbidden knowledge—what London calls "the fig-leaf adventure"—and Balatta is directly compared to Eve. As Genesis relates, two trees grow in Eden, the Tree of Life and beside it the Tree

of Knowledge of Good and Evil. On Guadalcanal, fast by the devil-devil hut of Ngurn, grows a breadfruit tree, and from the tree depend the oval fruits. If we take the resonance present in the word "bread-fruit" as a sufficient warrant, we may see the tree as representative not only of life but also the Eucharist: a promise, if not a guarantee, of unending life, its fruit freely available to all—all, that is, but Balatta, who, as a second Eve, is forbidden by her personal taboo to eat of the breadfruit tree. Conversely, the devil-devil hut becomes the representative of the Tree of Knowledge, and it is therefore consequently and necessarily connected to Death, its own grim fruit the cured heads that hang in the hut.

Afterword

SOME CRITICAL PERSPECTIVES ON LONDON'S PACIFIC FICTION

In this volume, in addition to the stories themselves, we wish to offer some analytic material intended to open up the complexities of the texts. Though our target audience for this collection is the ordinary intelligent reader, we realize that some readers, particularly classroom teachers coming to these stories for the first time, will wish for more analysis than others may. Therefore, we have tried here to employ several different interpretive tools, resisting wherever possible the urge to use the occasionally opaque jargon of contemporary literary criticism. These are merely approaches to the works, making what we hope are useful suggestions as to how the stories can be discussed, without asserting any claim to shut out other readings.

In a statement of aesthetic purpose in literature, developed fully in his semi-autobiographical novel *Martin Eden*, Jack London argues for the realistic depiction of life as it is really lived. Probably most of his readers have noted how successfully London managed to make his characters believable. On the other hand, it has also been no secret that Jack frequently was stumped for good plots and on a few occasions actually paid other writers for plot outlines. "The Red One," for example, was based on an idea his friend

George Sterling gave him. But the chief sources for the tales included here were actual events he heard about in the course of his adventures. The primary virtue of reworking a true story is that the plot is ready-made, and everyone appreciates how realistic the writer's fiction seems. Certainly London added to the stories from a rich imagination, and an examination of this process of creative writing based on real historical events could fruitfully begin with a glance at "The Seed of McCoy." We have already noted that the topic of race was a popular one at the beginning of the twentieth century, and that many thinkers had reached conclusions that were far different from today's notions. Considering the widespread belief that London was a racist, it is interesting to examine how the author introduces the idea of the interaction of races in this story.

Without directly discussing it, London deems it important that the main character is racially mixed, a descendent of a white sailor and a Tahitian woman. It is certain that the historical McCoy reported in his own account (cf. note 2 to "The Seed of McCoy") of the episode that he felt an identification with Christ in sacrificing himself to save the *Pyrenees*' crew. It is, however, only a guess that London wished to emphasize McCoy's racial duality as a metaphor for Christ's participation in two worlds. Fleshly, fearful, sinful whiteness blends with the spiritual, confident, altruistic islander in order to form a perfect messiah to save the microcosm of the *Pyrenees*. The original crew of the *Bounty* first got into trouble through a mutiny and hid their guilt by flying from island to island until they could find a safe place to hide, ultimately concealing their existence by burning the *Bounty*. Here, the pattern reverses itself as the modern McCoy stops a mutiny, and, as the *Pyrenees* goes from island to island, he saves a ship from burning. Instead of using the brutality and rigid regimentation characteristic of Captain Bligh's leadership, McCoy keeps everything running smoothly with words spoken in dovelike tones as his gaze passes over the crew in benediction. McCoy's smile is "a caress, an embrace that surrounded the tired mate and sought to draw him into the quietude and rest of McCoy's tranquil soul."

That McCoy is racially mixed plays a vital role in the way London develops his character. London was intrigued rather than appalled by the idea of miscegenation, which suggests something of the complexities of his thinking about the topic of race. For the convinced racist, interbreeding leads inevitably to the breakdown of the intellectual and moral structure of the world.[1] London's thoughts on race, which he believed were unambiguously supported by the historical record, were often inconsistent with his personal experience. In his virulent "from the shoulder" letters to Spiro Orfans, for example, London argues that the interbreeding of racial "mongrels" is the cause not only of the fall of empires but also of his correspondent's intellectual incapacity.[2]

For London in "The Seed of McCoy," however, it is precisely this feature of being demi-natured that prepares McCoy for the Christlike sacrifice he makes. Clarice Stasz guesses that London's interest in blending races stems from his relationship with his Santa Rosa neighbor, Luther Burbank: "London's attraction to this [idea] was more than scientific. . . . The perfect comrade would combine the feminine and masculine elements; so too, it would follow, would the perfect race be a mixture of the best of all."[3] This attitude represents one aspect of London's racial thinking that is not widely known, and it is a significant obstacle in the effort to reduce London to any conventionally understood "racist" status.

Furthermore, London was outspoken on the need for greater understanding among the races. In a letter of August 25, 1913, London speculates on the best way to eliminate the tensions between America and Japan: "I would say [that this could be accomplished] by educating the people of the United States and the people of Japan so that they will be too intelligently tolerant to respond to any call to race prejudice. . . . And . . . by realizing, in industry and government, of socialism—which last word is merely a word that stands for the actual application in the affairs of men of the theory of the Brotherhood of Man. In the meantime the nations and races are only unruly boys who have not yet grown to the stature of men. So we must expect them to do unruly and boisterous things at times. And, just as boys grow up, so the races of mankind will grow up and laugh when they look back upon their childish quarrels."[4]

Though race is revealed implicitly in "The Seed of McCoy," in "The Chinago" it is foregrounded and explicit. Because there is no cultural and linguistic common ground, none of the characters in "The Chinago" can understand each other. Set in Tahiti, the story builds on past colonial struggles for power over the large and strategically placed island, struggles primarily between Britain and France over economic and political control that introduced a warren of cultural complexities and tensions. Europeans brought in imported laborers from places as distant from each other as India and China, and linguistic confusions inevitably resulted from this interaction. Of course, how can anyone hope to penetrate the maze of cultural-textual confusion created by French law on a Pacific island worked by displaced Chinese laborers toiling under German supervision for Mexican pay on a French plantation contracted out to the British!

It may be tempting for some to read "The Chinago" as an expression of the heroic white man's urge to explore, subdue, and mold to his purposes the world he finds around him; and it would be equally alluring to regard the efforts of Christians like John Starhurst in "The Whale Tooth" to shine the light of the divine Word into the spiritually dark corners of the world as practical proof of the white man's more developed sensibility, courage, and selflessness. But it is not typical of Jack London's fictions to explore the easy or the commonplace when the opportunity arises to examine satirically the consequences of a great cultural clash. The Fijians likely regard themselves as superior to the foolishly naive white intruders, as when, for example, they use the whites' horror of literal cannibalism as an exploitable squeamishness and offer to trade surplus captives for cloth and tobacco. The islanders also believe they possess a more rational explanation for the Creation than that expounded by John Starhurst. The Fiji chief Mongondro exclaims, after hearing the Genesis account,

> "All the land and all the water, the trees, the fish, and bush and mountains, the sun, the moon and stars, were made in six days! No, no. I tell you that in my youth I was an able man, yet did it require me three months for one small canoe. It is a story to frighten children with; but no man can believe it."

This exchange with Mongondro might dissuade a less determined, less culture-bound visitor. The reader is aware that Mongondro perhaps holds the more rational and practical perspective, but John Starhurst is only reassured of the urgency of his mission. His goal, after all, is engendered by his absolute reliance on a text that he is sure will supplant native myths. Each character thinks that the other lacks the necessary tools or texts to interpret the world successfully. But if Starhurst's text, the Gospel, is the tool he hopes to introduce into the dark savagery of Fiji, the islanders are possessed of a parallel text that will provide an alternative exegesis: A whale tooth, belonging to Ra Vatu, an old enemy of Starhurst, a tardy convert to the Lotu (or the Worship), and a Machiavellian hypocrite. The tooth follows Starhurst as he ventures into the interior of Viti Levu. Not only is Starhurst ignorant of the existence of the tooth that will deconstruct his life, but he is also unaware of—and probably uninterested in—the complex network of tribal relationships symbolized by the tooth. It is an unwritten text that will provide a structure through which his voyage will be interpreted by the islanders.

This network of tribal relationships and obligations appears in another passage that is dense with possible interpretations. This element of the story reveals London's attention to offering different levels of meaning in his texts:

> "Soon will come a man, a white man," Erirola began, after the proper pause. "He is a missionary man, and he will come to-day. Ra Vatu is pleased to desire his boots. He wishes to present them to his good friend, Mongondro, and it is in his mind to send them with the feet along in them, for Mongondro is an old man and his teeth are not good. Be sure, O Buli, that the feet go along in the boots. As for the rest of him, it may stop here."

The tone of the passage is pure Jack London—filled with implications likely to turn the stomachs and offend the sensibilities of his contemporary readers. The precise reason that some critics regarded Jack London as "barbaric" is revealed in his treatment of these boots. For most of his white, Christian, middle-class, magazine-reading audience, the passage refuses to allow the expected stable interpretation, since it is exactly *not* an unwarrantable, savage attack on a messenger of God by a bestial, murderous, racial inferior. Instead, the boots read as a kind of synecdoche for (at least) four interpretations.

First, and most obviously, the request for Starhurst's boots represents the defeat of the (inevitable, generic) booted white man who has ventured into the shoeless integrity of established Fiji civilization. Note the way that London signals the importance of the image of feet: "In the early dawn John Starhurst was afoot, striding along the bush trail in his big leather boots, at his heels the faithful Narau, himself at the heels of a naked guide. . . ."

Second, the retrieval of the boots will necessarily effect at least a pause in the progress of a bothersome and (to the Fijians) weird Christianity, a religion that celebrates love but restricts the number of a man's wives, and that condemns cannibalism while it exalts the ingestion of bread that somehow means the same thing as the flesh of an incarnated God.

Third, the Buli's acceptance of the task of collecting the boots is an outward emblem of the political and religious unity on the island, significantly opposite to the universally negative response of Starhurst's "civilized" friends when they learn of his decision to convert the Fiji interior; thus, the code of honor practiced by the Fijians represents a kind of higher aesthetic, opposed by the rejected missionary's lonely and wrong-headed Pentecostalism—itself a fringe movement on the banks of the mainstream of Christianity.

Fourth, the intention of Ra Vatu, according to his interpreter Erirola, is apparently and perhaps genuinely based on a respectful wish to offer a toothsome gift to a toothless and disabled friend—a wish that reflects, sardonically and ironically, the highest of Christian impulses.

The last few minutes of Starhurst's life consist of an undignified wrestling match with an islander bent on exposing the white man's head to a large club. When he is shortly killed by the Buli of Gatoka, a thematic issue directly links the stories of Ah Cho and John Starhurst. In encouraging the Buli to undertake the assassination of Starhurst, Erirola says, "A little thing like a missionary does not matter." And the Buli agrees: "No, a little thing like a missionary does not matter," just as another group that happens to be in power might say, "It is only a Chinago."

In both "The Chinago" and "The Whale Tooth" power and not justice is the issue; reliance on text to provide meaning and its propensity to engender violence is the theme. And in both the inability of interacting cultural groups to understand/interpret each other's texts results in death.

London examines another issue connected to race relations in the comparatively well-known story "The Heathen." The idealized notion of friendship, about which Jack had written to Charmian, provides the emotional source material for the story. It is a complex vision—mythic, epic, romantic, even erotic.[5] It says as much about London's self-confidence as it does his insecurity that he could tell his lady-love of his long-term wish to find a male connection that would be great enough to cause him to lose himself in another. Though he could trace his idea of sublime masculine comradeship back to a "dream of [his] boyhood," his most thoughtful and poignant examinations of the complexities of male relationships appear in this series of stories, most of them written in the late summer and early fall of 1908 during the cruise of the *Snark*. Particularly significant is "The Whale Tooth," with its darkly comic story of a Pentecostal missionary who will accomplish a reenactment of Christian self-sacrifice, actually giving his life for the sake of others—though not quite in the way he had in mind. "The Heathen" examines more symbolically the idea of one individual being absorbed by another, again involving a character willing to sacrifice his life to save a friend. The third story in this group, composed in close sequence, "The Terrible Solomons" relates a cynical initiation comedy in which one individual is betrayed through a conspiracy that is a perversion of comradeship.

Though the surrounding fiction is liberally laced with London's typically dark humor, none at all appears in "The Heathen," and the apparently straightforward earnestness of its tone has been variously read during the sensibility shifts of the intervening decades. As Jeanne Campbell Reesman has succinctly observed, "Some readers have found this one of London's most moving portraits of interracial friendship, while others have objected to it as merely a 'loyal darky' fable emphasizing the unquestioning devotion of the black servant."[6]

In the highly politicized climate of today, several questions seem naturally to arise. Since London's originating idea for the story had specified only gender, not race, why did London introduce the racial difference between the friends in the first place? Can a person of color develop a genuine and authentic relationship with a white person without in every case selling out his racial or cultural integrity? Even though Charley keeps telling Otoo to stop calling him "master," is he necessarily tyrannizing his friend by the very fact that he is white? Why couldn't London have depicted a safer, non-politicized friendship and still have made his point?

The politics of such a story, by the way, were quite different from the tensions noted by present-day readers. In 1910, when Americans finally saw this tale, it would have offended most of the reading public by depicting a relationship that seemed morally improper and politically subversive. Particularly challenging to middle-class consciousness would have been the brilliant paintings of Anton Otto Fischer, which illustrated the story's appearance in *Everybody's*. (See story illustration.) Macmillan even used what would have been for London's audience the most disturbing of them as the frontispiece in the first edition of *South Sea Tales*. Fischer depicts a ragged, brutish, slumping white man walking at the side of a more admirably postured black man; at first glance, it actually seems they're walking hand-in-hand. Though the text identifies Otoo as a native of Bora Bora in Polynesia, Fischer has clearly decided to Africanize the character's features.

Perhaps one of the insights London gained as he realized his fantasy was "impossible" was that no white man could be expected to enter so fully and lovingly into so committed a comradeship. Was this merely another aspect of racism—this assumption that only a person of color could be so devoted to another, perhaps because of some imputed childlike naïveté? Charley, however, recognizes in Otoo a superiority of physical strength, of moral discipline, and of responsible maturity. None of these are traits of character associated with a racist's understanding of the Other. If there is one common ground to racist ideology, it must be the instinctive recoiling from the thought of "mixing blood" among the races. Yet this is symbolically the very thing Charley and Otoo decide to do as they perform the ritual of exchanging names. "In the South Seas," explains Charley, "such a ceremony binds two men closer together than blood-brothership."

Moreover, this dual identity, established by each having the other's name, suggests Jungian themes. Charley has been living the brainless, ambitionless, macho life of the typical white knockabout of the South Pacific, hanging around with white men who are described in animal images—"beast" and "gorilla." Like the narrator of London's *John Barleycorn,* Charley is drawn by peer pressure to masculine pastimes, such as drinking and gambling, which debilitate his finer nature. Jungians might see in him a persona developed out of social structures that ignore the anima. This aspect of human personality can only become fully developed through long association with women. Without it a man is only likely to develop the animus, or masculine side of his persona, gradually becoming more and more degenerate and brutish. London has Humphrey Van Weyden think such ideas about the crew of the *Ghost* in *The Sea-Wolf* (1904), long before the author gained an acquaintance with C. G. Jung's *The Psychology of the Unconscious* in 1916. Readers of the biographical literature on London will recall how profoundly the author reacted to the psychoanalyst's insights. They were so closely connected to London's own ideas about psychology that he experienced a shock, feeling himself to be "on the edge of a world so new, so wonderful, that I am almost afraid to look into it."[7] Seen in this light, Otoo convincingly functions as the repressed anima aspect of a single persona. Though Otoo proves his manhood to the infantile Charley by beating up another strong man, it is the example of his feminine sensitivity that awakens the repressed elements of Charley's persona.

Though Charley emphasizes their brotherly relationship, Otoo plays many roles in Charley's life. "He was brother and father and mother as well," admits Charley. Otoo serves as the white man's father as he helps Charley to reform his addictions and gain some sense of personal ambition to improve himself morally, physically, and financially; it is Otoo who instructs him in the ways of commercial advancement. "He made me," says Charley in acknowledging the importance of Otoo's advice, as well as implicitly suggesting a father's creation of a son. In the rearing of Charley's children Otoo assumes a surrogacy or perhaps takes on a grandfather's role.

But even the issue of gender, which London's fantasy specified as male, is far from unambiguous. London's language in characterizing Charley's frank rapture over Otoo makes it impossible to disagree with Jeanne Campbell Reesman when she notes, "Otoo is somewhat feminized, an interesting intersection of race and gender."[8] Several references occur to nursing and wet-nursing, and one to nursing Charley via coconut milk. In fact, this is Charley's first conscious experience upon waking after being washed up on shore, symbolically a reference to birth. As he comes to, he receives the metaphor of a proffered breast: "Otoo was pressing a drinking cocoanut to my lips." These references not only point up Otoo's feminine nurturing qualities, but it is also important to notice that Charley's appreciation of Otoo sometimes seems eroticized: "He was all sweetness and gentleness, a love-creature, though he stood nearly six feet tall and was muscled like a gladiator." "We have been mates together," is, of course, on the surface only a use of seafaring language, but given the relationship that develops, "mates" suggests marriage.

Their commitment to each other, however, is more binding than a marriage contract, which ends at death. Otoo's eyes become "luminous and soft with joy" when he hears Charley explain his devotion to his friend: "We have exchanged names. To you I am Otoo. To me you are Charley. And between you and me, forever and forever, you shall be Charley, and I shall be Otoo. It is the way of the custom. And when we die, if it does happen that we live again somewhere beyond the stars and the sky, still shall you be Charley to me, and I Otoo to you."

While "The Heathen" is a paean to the virtues of true comradeship, "The Terrible Solomons" subverts the concept at its most basic, racial level. Commenting on London's novel *Adventure*, composed at about the same time as "The Terrible Solomons," Lawrence Phillips argues that London's fiction contains material that suggests "the bankruptcy of the colonial ideal represented. . . . through an ideology of racial superiority and a mythology of adventure."[9] London further examines this bankruptcy in "The Terrible Solomons." Naive adventurer Bertie Arkwright, a tourist visiting this savage wilderness, thinks he should be able to count on the other whites. After all, they are experienced in dealing with the inherent dangers of the islands, and Bertie expects them to serve as guides and protectors. Instead of that expected comradely behavior, however, and ostensibly to teach Bertie a lesson, Captain Malu and his co-conspirators, by playing upon the inexperienced newcomer's racist fears of the natives, nearly frighten him to death.

An analysis of "Mauki" is likely to generate polarity in its readers. If a racially mixed character can play a messianic role, if a

Chinese laborer can be a victim of an inscrutable colonial process, if cannibal Fijians can be shown to harbor values as sincere as those of any Christian, and if a white man and a Polynesian can be the truest of friends, it is no surprise that London would depict Mauki as a hero. In the opening sentences we learn that Mauki's "hair was kinky and Negroid, and he was black. He was peculiarly black. He was neither blue-black nor purple-black, but plum-black." London's narrative tone is dry, reportorial, anthropological, and nonjudgmental here and in further discussions of Mauki's appearance. Similarly, the references in this and in other stories to the "inevitable white man" might be read as endorsements or celebrations of that inevitability, while other readers will think of a juggernaut of merciless, impersonal greed sweeping down on unprotected, exploitable innocents. On the surface Jack London tells his tale with apparent Naturalist objectivity, but it also seems to be true that, subtextually, London is not merely recording his hero's skin color—he is reveling in it, rubbing his magazine readers' noses in it, refusing to give them a main character they could imaginatively distort into the more comfortable cliché of the handsome (read "light-skinned") Noble Savage.

In contrast to the most-respected scientific writing of his contemporaries, London begins by choosing a unique and unlikely protagonist. Then, simply by recording the character's misadventures and by reporting without emotion or bias the character's thoughts, London manages to create a hero. The center part of the story is a record of escape and recapture as Mauki tries to return. In the final section of the narrative, Mauki's relentless drive for freedom meets an equally powerful urge to oppress and contain him.

Max Bunster, the exiled psychopathic overseer of the station, is a bully and a coward with a sadistic interest in pointless brutality. After research disappointingly proves that the skin of a shark is insufficiently lacerating, Bunster has had fashioned for himself a ray-skin glove that has the capability to remove a patch of skin with the merest touch.

This glove—which presumably only a psychopath could have conceived in the first place—plays a fascinating role in the last section of the story. It actually becomes the medium of exchange between the oppressor and the oppressed, the means through which Bunster communicates with Mauki. It mediates between the "civilized" and the "savage," between white and black, between masculine and feminine (as Bunster uses it on his wife), between the foreign, capitalistic intruder and the disenfranchised and enslaved. The mitten is used by the power holder to mock, torture, and destroy. Mauki, in managing to seize the device himself and using it to reverse the power role, turns the implement of torture into an emblem of triumph.

The ray-skin glove is also a typically dark naturalistic joke, as the underdog emerges victorious through the use of the very tool of his oppression. It serves also as a text with an ambiguous function: the brutal machismo of Bunster responds perversely to the effeminate Malaitan with a *tambo* that forbids the touch of women; instead, this is a masculine touch that will merely harm Mauki physically, not spiritually. Curiously, the mitten functions as their mutual tool of intercourse, the thing that physically bonds them with its painful "caress." It is also the tangible symbol of the domination and oppression, which when wrested from its owner cedes its power to the new possessor.

Finally, and perhaps most importantly, the mitten is a kind of deconstructive "MacGuffin." The difference between black and white was historically and literally the cause of the political and ethical relationship between the plantation owners and the black-birded laborers. Between the 1860s and the Australian order of parliament in the first decade of the twentieth century that formally discontinued the process of "recruitment," the islanders had been sought and caught precisely *because* of their presumed resilience to the tropical sun. Because its function is to rip off patches of skin with each "caress," the mitten therefore serves as an eraser of the difference between oppressor and oppressed. When Mauki removes the last of Bunster's whiteness, he has removed the only way to identify the Other, and without his skin, as a biological necessity Bunster's oppression stops. Mauki, we learn, preserves Bunster's head as a trophy, wrapped in "the finest of fibre lava-lavas," since it commemorates the successful overcoming of all of life's obstacles. For Mauki, an island king at the end of the story, it also serves as a text, since it provides a message that, in times of crisis, he may contemplate "long and solemnly." His subjects, too, know the meaning of the head, with its "sandy hair and a yellowish beard," for it "is esteemed the most powerful devil-devil on

Malaita, and to the possession of it is ascribed all of Mauki's greatness." Triumphant over the inevitable white man, Mauki emerges as the indomitable black man.

Not only was London refusing to participate in the popular and academic racism of his day, it seems to have been his intention to disappoint and shock his magazine readers with assaults on their complacent assumptions about race. Mainstream magazines of the period made frequent use of racial stereotypes, and of course missionary-and-cannibal jokes and cartoons flourished for at least half a century afterward. London turns his readers' expectations upside down through the examination of the psychology and sociology of a Solomon Islander. He then proceeds from that implicitly to indict the greed and sadism of the white oppressors. As a final irony, he concludes the story with Mauki as a respected and powerful hero. All this must have chafed the sensibilities of his readers.

Because the core of the plot of "Yah! Yah! Yah!" deals with the ruthless and monstrous revenge exacted by white colonialists on an island population, it is possible that, like "Mauki," several magazines rejected it because it failed to support the complacent and axiomatic racial and cultural assumptions of the middle-class, magazine-reading public.[10] More probably, the story assaulted them. London pursues the viciousness of colonialism in this undeniably outrageous story. To doubt this claim places a reader in an awkward position at the outset, and the discomfiture is never relieved.

In this light it might be helpful to discuss briefly the nature of contemporary responses to some of the features of London's fiction. Over the last several decades, readers have been alerted to forms of composition that achieve a conscious (or unconscious) colonialist goal of marginalizing, trivializing, or demonizing non-Western cultures by treating them as "exotic."

It would be impossible to deny that Jack London was motivated by the urge to see firsthand the remote and exotic places and people of the world. Furthermore, it would be difficult to argue that it was anything else than the "Otherness" of non-Western themes that in the first place attracted him to his voyage on the *Snark*.

A principal feature of travel literature is that a main character will face a crisis arising from interaction with unfamiliar cultures. But in "Yah! Yah! Yah!" what does the narrator learn about himself or the Other? The text is silent. Do the injustices and enormities reported result in any change in the power structure? Not at all. Indeed, the white colonialist project seems at least tacitly endorsed by the narrative. Further, London's depiction of atrocities in the coldly distant and uninvolved tone of voice that was often the goal of Naturalist writers seems to leave him vulnerable to the charge that he—the author himself—did not care about the brutal conditions he described. Without an outraged tone, the text might be read as an endorsement of the status quo on Oolong Atoll, and that the spindly, lightweight, drunken sadist McAllister quite rightly wields his enormous power over the islanders through the exercise of a fine Nietzschean will. Given the complexity of London's thinking in these stories, however, such a reading seems one-dimensional and simplistic.

Contemporary theorists on race sometimes argue that any representation of race undertaken by a member of the racial group that holds power inevitably produces a skewed picture. This is the mildest and least emotional characterization of the argument, and it seems impossible or at least incorrect to disagree with it. Certainly it is tempting to deconstruct a story that on its face seems racist while a second reading makes it seem not racist enough to be popular in its day and yet a third examination makes the text seem racist in spite of the author's intent. It is this tension that requires analysis. Still, even though white power is maintained in the end and despite the narrator's distantly lighthearted tone, "Yah! Yah! Yah!" is a story that exposes the colonialist project as an expression of massive, inhuman brutality.

Recent developments in postcolonial criticism suggest a nascent reactionary movement that rejects the pat simplicity of cultural binarism, urging that some texts that have been condemned as "orientalist" or "colonialist" may—even must—be read more ambivalently. If we choose to reject the claim that a text must be read as embodying a monolithic colonial project, new critical opportunities appear. This critical decision opens up the analysis and deconstructs the notion of a stable relationship between reader and writer. Such stability has been shown to be suspect and probably philosophically inconceivable, but, under the political pressures of modern liberalism, it has become fashionable to use literary criticism as a platform from which moral judgments about the author's character may be pronounced. Though one of the moving spirits of contemporary criticism celebrates destabilization, there is a point at which the action stops: interpretations that permit the critic to condemn texts for their stereotyping of gender, race, or culture are applauded as stable readings. Such influential critics as Edward Said and Homi Bhabha, however, are currently arguing that a simple binary "them/us" approach is inadequate for the analysis of complex colonialist texts. The reader of typical adventure and travel stories will find it helpful to pay attention to what happens to both the white explorer/hunter/sahib and the cultural Others with whom he interacts. The likelihood is that a trauma will be occasioned on both sides, and that the control of power and knowledge will not be so clearly limited to the possession of the racial overlord.

One way of marginalizing a people is to imply infantilism in descriptions of their behavior, and the heavy use of pidgin in some of these stories has sometimes seemed to support such a process. Though Naturalist fiction writers often made use of dialect in order to increase the verisimilitude of their characterization, read today such accuracy in the portrayal of the speech of nonwhites seems strained. It may even hint at parody or condescension. London's use of dialect in his characterization of the islanders at first makes today's readers uncomfortable, and several pages of "Yah! Yah! Yah!" consist almost exclusively of pidgin, or (as it was then called) bêche-de-mer English.

Some might defend London for his use of pidgin based on the fact that this language is still used throughout the islands as a means of communicating with those outside the social and linguistic designation of common speech called by the Solomoners "wontok," from the English "one talk."

Another critic, however, could still rightly point out that pidgin is an artificial and imposed language brought from outside the islands. Much of it is based on English shaped by Solomon grammatical conventions, and its obvious lilt and charm make it easy for readers to stereotype the islanders as quaint or childish, incapable of standard English.

London decided to employ pidgin very little after the publication of his 1911 novel, *Adventure*, but perhaps not because of any heightening of his political sensitivity. Realizing that pidgin presented difficulties for his foreign language translators, London may naturally have feared that it might affect international sales. Though pidgin is certainly here to stay and remains a central linguistic feature of the Pacific, and though London certainly played no part in pidgin's inculcation or development and was only reporting the situation as he found it, still the issue needs examination.

With its provocative title, "The Inevitable White Man" also seems at first to be a racist document celebrating the inevitable and natural control of whites over blacks. A closer look, however, reveals a much more layered text, informed by a perhaps surprisingly subtle irony. As the narrative voice records the statements of the characters without critical comment, a first reading might suggest the author's sympathies with the opinions of his characters. Apparently, the main reason for the characters' discussion is to present the white supremacist thesis that it is the white man's inevitable destiny to rule the black. Also, the central action of the story is the admiring description of an incident occurring twenty years before: a remarkably stupid white man with a preternatural gift of marksmanship manages to shoot down a boatload of kidnapped blacks who have temporarily escaped and are trying to return to their homes.

A more ambivalent reading, however, is suggested by the story's unusual narrative construction, suggesting multiple, bitterly satiric levels and implicit meanings within the characters' apparently unambiguous dialogue. London shows us here, as elsewhere, that critical allegations of monolithic colonialism and marginalization of the Other within the literature of travel and adventure need to be reexamined. Such stereotypes as the Great White Hunter of pulp fiction are deconstructed in London's fiction, subverted from the conventional, expected view of simple supremacy by their manifest weaknesses and moral degradation. Early in the story there are hints that readers ought to be alert for such ironic subtexts—parodies of popular fiction and anecdotes reminiscent of traditional tall tales, which satirically, rather than sympathetically, expatiate on the greed, stupidity, and insensitivity of the white interlopers as the cause of a chain of actions and reactions, inevitably leading to the casual destruction of island life and culture.

For example, in "The Inevitable White Man" Captain Woodward learns that a white man has been slain by the natives of New Ireland in retaliation for his execution of a petty thief. Woodward is shocked and bewildered by this unaccountable, mysterious urge of the islanders to take revenge on a white man who considered the theft of $3.50 worth of tobacco a capital offense! It is a less-than-subtle reading of this episode to see it as an endorsement of Woodward's racist insensitivity. Even if a reader is reluctant to admit the ironic nature of Woodward's outrage here, the main part of the narrative—Woodward's recounting of the precision-shooting slaughter of a boatload of Melanesians—can only be read as poker-faced, biting satire of white colonialist savagery.

Scenes like this have prompted Lawrence Phillips to make the mild observation that, while they might "encourage a certain wonder for the power of this one man holding so many in his sway, his ruthlessness and near sadistic pleasure as well as the distinct images of the methods and brutalities of slavery check any urge to unqualified admiration."[11] This brutal interior tale, interpreted in this way, provides a moral foundation from which to examine Woodward's character, and only thus can we see the full ugliness of his use of the Saxtorph episode to make a callous point about the impossibility of white people ever understanding blacks. Unlike the stupidity of the unimaginative Saxtorph, the swashbuckling Captain Woodward's complacent inhumanity marks him as one of London's darkest characters, one who, without knowing it, exposes his own unthinking cruelty and shallowness. Thus, in a bizarre way, the man who tells the story—Woodward himself—is in this sense worse than Saxtorph—the man who does the crime.

According to Roberts and Woodward, it is the white man's self-perception of "inevitability" that has called them to the Pacific and makes them behave toward the natives as they do. To them, it is inevitable that the white man must "farm the world" and in doing so "run" the black. This disingenuous attitude merely serves to disguise the inevitable truth—white man's greed, not some imagined racial superiority, is the underlying, rationalized excuse for their inhuman atrocities. In "The Inevitable White Man," London tells us a story shot through with irony. None of the characters—except probably the narrator (and this may well be why he chooses to tell us this story)—in the end gets the point of it all. Incapable of understanding "niggers," they are also incapable of interpreting the meaning of the very adventure they have related.

The last story in this collection gathers all these points together in an atmosphere of delusion, madness, and disgust. "The Red One" shows the horrors attendant on the clash of two utterly disparate ways of knowing truth. The main character, an Englishman named Bassett, sees the Melanesian world through the filter of fever, racism, sexism, and an intellectual rejection of ordinary humanism. "The Red One" is a story with epistemology as its theme and with both religious faith and scientific empiricism—the two primary human systems of gaining knowledge—as its ironically satirical targets. The work centers on the ways in which human interpretive systems are used to "read" an impenetrable text. The Guadalcanal depicted in this weird tale is a superheated madhouse in which no human being, white or black, appears in a positive light.

As London so ably demonstrates in the other Pacific tales, interpretation is a problematic issue. Reality is, first of all, seen through the characters' varying perceptual grids, a kind of mesh woven by nurture and nature that provides each perceiver with a uniquely personal way to select, sort, and organize his perceptions. For Bassett, the Bible, one of the interpretive tools he employs to sort his experiences, is used not as a religious text but as a collection of useful analogies; his central intellectual and emotional core is a coldly passionate drive to know what is real through reason and empiricism. In the earlier stories, London shows us a Pacific world thinly but profoundly populated by white intruders whose enormities can be attributed "inevitably" to their lack of intelligence coupled with an excess of greed. In "The Red One," he shows the bottomlessness of white perfidy, apparent even in a highly educated and ostensibly rational character.

The inappropriateness of the white man's presence in Melanesia is stressed by yet another of Bassett's limitations: he is sick with fever, his head damaged and only very slowly curing, a condition that powerfully alters his ability to understand his situation. His perceptions are twice referred to as "the sick man's fancy," so that imagination seems to be as reliable or unreliable as rational thought or objective information. Though it is true that malarial fever is a typical feature of real life on Guadalcanal, it may also be seen as symbolic of not only the white man's physical but also his moral alterity. The story drives home the irony of Bassett's complete dysfunction, perhaps most particularly painful for him because Bassett is a white European with a firm and still unshaken conviction of his own cultural, racial, and linguistic superiority. At one point,

> Bassett laughed aloud, almost with madness, at the thought of this wonderful messenger, winged with intelligence across space, to fall into a bushman stronghold and be worshiped by apelike, man-eating and headhunting savages. It was as if God's Word had fallen into the muck mire of the abyss underlying the bottom of hell; as if Jehovah's Commandments had been presented on carved stone to the monkeys of the monkey cage at the Zoo; as if the Sermon on the Mount had been preached in a roaring bedlam of lunatics.

Bassett is so immersed in his ethnocentric confidence that he fails to note the greater irony: Each of these great revelations *had* reached Europe by the time this story was being read, and, by 1916, Europe had benefited from its centuries-long awareness of the intimacy between God and man to the extent that it had hurled itself into the bloodiest war in its history. Indeed, Charmian London believed that "The Red One" grew out of the author's deep disillusionment with "the endless strife of humanity even unto the modern horrors of the Great War."[12]

Similarly limited by his confidence in "the pristine whiteness of his skin," Bassett never questions his axiomatic racism. The people he finds on the island are first "shadows" then "monkeys," often "apish," "kinky-headed," and finally "human beasts." Perhaps this aspect of Bassett's character is best seen at the moment when he realizes he can use Balatta's infatuation with him to advance the cause of knowledge—but the sexless lepidopterist must force himself to overcome his racist reservations about Balatta, who (though she is the most sympathetic character in the story) must be seen as the ultimate deconstruction of the pulp-fiction island princess.[13]

Earle Labor writes about London's Pacific world as a "symbolic wilderness" and notes that the writer used different South Seas locations to express different themes. Melanesia serves as "London's Inferno," a "source of further corruption—not of purification"[14] and certainly not a place where one can expect a positive resolution to the quest for knowledge. Filled with ambiguities, this infernal set of tales examines with irony, objectivity, humor, and bitter satire the underlying meanings of the interactions of the races during the colonial adventure in the Pacific islands.

Notes

1. For an informative examination of this idea worked out in turn-of-the-century literature, consult, for example, the fiction of Thomas W. Dixon—particularly *The Sins of the Father* (New York: Grosset & Dunlap, 1912) and the "science" of Harvard Ph.D. Lothrop Stoddard—particularly *Racial Realities in Europe* (New York: Scribners, 1925).
2. Labor, Earle, Robert C. Leitz III, and I. Milo Shepard, eds., *The Letters of Jack London* (Stanford: Stanford University Press, 1988), 3: 1534, 1545–47.
3. Clarice Stasz, *American Dreamers: Charmian and Jack London* (New York: St. Martin's, 1988), 159.
4. Labor et al., *Letters,* 3: 1219.
5. This letter is quoted extensively here in our introduction to "The Heathen." For the complete text of this interesting letter, see Labor et al., *Letters,* 1: 370–71.
6. Jeanne Campbell Reesman, *Jack London: A Study of the Short Fiction* (New York: Twayne, 1999), 131–32.
7. Charmian London, *The Book of Jack London,* vol. 2. (New York: Century, 1921), 323.
8. Reesman, *Jack London,* 131.
9. Lawrence Phillips, "The Indignity of Labor: Jack London's *Adventure* and Plantation Labor in the Solomon Islands," *Jack London Journal* 6 (1999): 197.
10. Labor et al., *Letters,* 2: 890. The claim that "magazine-editors [were] afraid to look at" "Yah! Yah! Yah!" seems to suggest that London had experienced rejection from editors even before they had read the story, having only the theme of the tale to consider.
11. Phillips, "The Indignity," 184.
12. Charmian London, *Book of Jack London,* 334.
13. Readers may imagine connections between "The Red One" and the monolith in Stanley Kubrick's *2001: A Space Odyssey* (1968). However, author Arthur C. Clarke told Earle Labor that he had never read London's story.
14. Earle Labor, "Jack London's Symbolic Wilderness: Four Versions," in *Jack London: Essays in Criticism,* ed. R. W. Ownbey (Santa Barbara, CA: Smith, 1978), 34–35.

Works Consulted or Cited

Barrow, Sir John. *The Mutiny of the Bounty*. Oxford: Oxford University Press, 1989. (First published in 1831.)

Basham, Horace A. "A Guide to Pitcairn." Auckland, New Zealand: Government of the Pitcairn Islands, 2000.

Baskett, Sam. "Jack London's Heart of Darkness." *American Quarterly* 10 (Spring 1958): 66–77.

Berkove, Lawrence I. "The Myth of Hope in Jack London's 'The Red One.' " In *Rereading Jack London*, edited by L. Cassuto and J. Reesman. Stanford, CA: Stanford University Press, 1996.

Bindon, James R. "Kuru: The Dynamics of a Prion Disease." http://www.as.ua.edu/ant/bindon/ant570/Papers/McGrath/ McGrath.htm

Bjerre, Jens. *The Last Cannibals*. New York: William Morrow, 1957.

———. *Savage New Guinea*. New York: Tower, 1964.

Boas, Franz. "Foreword." In *Coming of Age in Samoa*, by Margaret Mead. New York: Dell, 1961. (Reprint of 1928 edition.)

Boswell, James. *The Life of Samuel Johnson*, LL.D. Vol. 1. London: J. M. Dent, 1926.

Brown, Ellen. "A Perfect Sphere: Jack London's 'The Red One.'" *Jack London Newsletter* 11 (1978): 81–85.

Butterfield, Herbert. *The Whig Interpretation of History*. New York: Norton, 1965.

Cameron, Ian. *Lost Paradise: The Exploration of the Pacific*. Topsfield, MA: Salem House, 1987.

Campbell, Jeanne. "Falling Stars: Myth in 'The Red One.'" *Jack London Newsletter* 11 (1978): 86–96.

Cass, Philip. "The Infallible Engine: Indigenous Perceptions of Europeans in German New Guinea Through the Missionary Press." Paper presented to the Media History Conference, University of Westminster, London, July 1998. <http://cci.wmin.ac.uk/hist98/cass.html>

Cassuto, Leonard, and Jeanne Campbell Reesman, eds. *Rereading Jack London*. Stanford, CA: Stanford University Press, 1996.

Caton, Steven C. *Lawrence of Arabia: A Film's Anthropology*. Berkeley, CA: University of California Press, 1999.

Childs, Peter, and Patrick Williams. *An Introduction to Post-Colonial Theory*. London: Prentice Hall, 1997.

Clune, Frank. *Journey to Pitcairn*. Sydney: Angus and Robertson, 1966.

Collins, Billy G. "Jack London's 'The Red One': Journey to a Lost Heart." *Jack London Newsletter* 10 (1977): 1–6.
Davis, John. *Sun's True Bearing or Azimuth Tables.* London: J. D. Potter, 1900.
Day, A. Grove. *Jack London in the South Seas.* New York: Four Winds Press, 1971.
Dixon, Thomas. *The Sins of the Father: A Romance of the South.* New York: Grosset & Dunlap, 1912.
Docker, Edward Wybergh. *The Blackbirders.* Sydney: Angus and Robertson, 1970.
Douglas, Ngaire. *They Came for Savages: 100 Years of Tourism in Melanesia.* Lismore, New South Wales, Australia: Southern Cross University Press, 1996.
Engels, Frederick. "Letter to Minna Kautsky." In *Marx and Engels on Literature and Art.* Moscow: Progress Publishers, 1976.
Fischer, Katrina Sigsbee and Alex A. Hurst. *Anton Otto Fischer—Marine Artist.* Nantucket, MA: Mill Hill Press, 1984.
Ford, Herbert. *Pitcairn—Port of Call.* Angwin, CA: Hawser Titles, 1996.
Fowler, John. "Fiji: The Warrior Archipelago." http://www.tribalsite.com/articles/fiji.htm.
Goldman, Laurence R., ed. *The Anthropology of Cannibalism.* Westport, CT: Bergin & Garvey, 1999.
Grattan, C. Hartley. *The Southwest Pacific to 1900.* Ann Arbor: University of Michigan Press, 1963.
———. *The Southwest Pacific Since 1900.* Ann Arbor: University of Michigan Press, 1963.
Great Britain Hydrographic Office. *Pacific Islands, Volume I. Sailing Directions for the South East, North East and North Coasts of New Guinea, Also for the Louisade and Solomon Islands, the Bismark Archipelago, and the Caroline and Mariana Islands.* London: J. D. Potter, 1900.
Hall, James Norman. *The Tale of a Shipwreck.* Boston: Houghton Mifflin, 1934.
Hamilton, David Mike. *The Tools of My Trade: Annotated Books in Jack London's Library.* Seattle: University of Washington Press, 1986.
Harcombe, David. *Solomon Islands.* 1st ed. Singapore: Lonely Planet, 1988.
Hendricks, King. "Jack London: Master Craftsman of the Short Story." Thirty-third Faculty Honor Lecture. Logan: Utah State University, April, 1966.
Heyerdahl, Thor. *Fatu-Hiva.* New York: Doubleday, 1974.
Hogbin, Ian. *A Guadalcanal Society: The Kaoka Speakers.* New York: Holt, Rinehart and Winston, 1964.
Honan, Mark, and David Harcombe. *Solomon Islands.* 3rd ed. Hong Kong: Lonely Planet, 1997.
Imperato, Pascal James, and Eleanore M. Imperato. *They Married Adventure: The Wandering Lives of Martin and Osa Johnson.* New Brunswick, NJ: Rutgers University Press, 1992.
Johnson, Martin. *Cannibal-Land: Adventures with a Camera in the New Hebrides.* Boston: Houghton Mifflin, 1925.
———. *Through the South Seas with Jack London.* New York: Dodd, Mead, 1913.
Johnson, Osa. *Bride in the Solomons.* Boston: Houghton Mifflin, 1944.
———. *I Married Adventure: The Lives and Adventures of Martin and Osa Johnson.* Philadelphia: Lippincott, 1940.
Jorgenson, Jens Peter. "Jack London's 'The Red One': A Freudian Approach." *Jack London Newsletter* 8 (1975): 101–3.
Jung, Carl G. *The Psychology of the Unconscious.* London: Routledge, 1993.
Keesing, Felix M. *Native Peoples of the Pacific World.* Washington, D.C.: The Infantry Journal, 1945.
Keesing, Roger M. *Kwaio Religion: The Living and the Dead in a Solomon Island Society.* New York: Columbia University Press, 1982.

Keesing, Roger M., and Peter Corris. *Lightning Meets the West Wind: The Malaita Massacre*. Melbourne: Oxford University Press, 1980.
Kingman, Russ. *Jack London: A Definitive Chronology*. Middletown, CA: David Rejl, 1992.
———. *A Pictorial Life of Jack London*. New York: Crown, 1979.
Kirsch, James. "Jack London's Quest: 'The Red One.'" *Psychological Perspectives* 11 (1980): 137–54.
Labor, Earle. *Jack London*. New York: Twayne, 1974.
———. "Jack London's Pacific World." In *Critical Essays on Jack London*, edited by Jacqueline Tavernier-Courbin. Boston: Prentice Hall, 1983, 205–22.
———. "Jack London's Symbolic Wilderness: Four Versions." In *Jack London: Essays in Criticism*, edited by R. W. Ownbey. Santa Barbara, CA: Peregrine Smith, 1978, 31–42.
Labor, Earle, Robert C. Leitz III, and I. Milo Shepard, eds. *The Letters of Jack London*. 3 vols. Stanford, CA: Stanford University Press, 1988.
Labor, Earle, and Jeanne Campbell Reesman. *Jack London*. Revised edition. New York: Twayne, 1994.
Lal, Brij V., Doug Munro, and Edward D. Beechert, eds. *Plantation Workers: Resistance and Accommodation*. Honolulu: University of Hawaii Press, 1993.
Lange, Dorothea, et al. *The Thunderbird Remembered: Maynard Dixon, the Man and the Artist*. Seattle: University of Washington Press, 1994.
Leitch, Vincent B. *Deconstructive Criticism: An Advanced Introduction*. New York: Colombia University Press, 1983.
London, Charmian. *The Book of Jack London*. 2 vols. New York: Century, 1921.
———. *The Log of the Snark*. New York: Macmillan, 1915.
———. *Our Hawaii*. Honolulu: Patten Co., 1917.
London, Jack. *The Complete Short Stories of Jack London*. Edited by Earle Labor, Robert C. Leitz, III, and I. Milo Shepard. 3 vols. Stanford, CA: Stanford University Press, 1993.
———. *The Cruise of the Snark*. New York: Macmillan, 1911.
———. *The Letters of Jack London*, edited by Earle Labor, Robert C. Leitz III, and I. Milo Shepard. 3 vols. Stanford, CA: Stanford University Press, 1988.
———. *A Son of the Sun*. New York: Doubleday, 1911. See also *A Son of the Sun: The Adventures of Captain David Grief*, edited by Thomas R. Tietze and Gary Riedl. Norman: University of Oklahoma Press, 2001.
London, Joan. *Jack London and His Times*. Garden City, NY: Doubleday, 1939.
Maude, H. E. *Slavers in Paradise: The Peruvian Slave Trade in Polynesia, 1862–1864*. Stanford, CA: Stanford University Press, 1981.
McClintock, James I. *Jack London's Strong Truths: A Study of His Short Stories*. East Lansing: Michigan State University Press, 1997.
Meek, A. S. *A Naturalist in Cannibal Land*. London: Fisher Unwin, 1913.
Miller, Madeleine S., and J. Lane Miller. *Harper's Bible Dictionary*. New York: Harper & Row, 1961.
Mytinger, Caroline. *Headhunting in the Solomon Islands*. New York: Macmillan, 1942.
Oliver, Douglas L. *The Pacific Islands*. Cambridge, MA: Harvard University Press, 1958.
Ownbey, Ray Wilson, ed. *Jack London: Essays in Criticism*. Santa Barbara, CA: Peregrine Smith, 1978.
The Pacific Islands Experience. San Ramon, CA: International Video Network, 1990. Videotape.
Phillips, Lawrence. "The Indignity of Labor: Jack London's *Adventure* and Plantation Labor in the Solomon Islands." *Jack London Journal* 6 (1999): 175–205.

Pospisil, Leopold. *The Kapauku Papuans of West New Guinea.* New York: Holt, Rinehart and Winston, 1965.
Purdon, Charles J. *The Snider-Enfield Rifle.* Alexandria Bay, NY: Museum Restoration Service, 1990.
Ralston, Caroline. *Grass Huts and Warehouses: Pacific Beach Communities of the Nineteenth Century.* Honolulu: University Press of Hawaii, 1978.
Reesman, Jeanne Campbell. *Jack London: A Study of the Short Fiction.* New York: Twayne, 1999.
Reid, Alan. *Discovery and Exploration.* London: Gentry Books, 1980.
Riber, Jorgen. "Archetypal Patterns in 'The Red One.'" *Jack London Newsletter* 8 (1975): 104–6.
Riedl, Gary, and Thomas R. Tietze. "Fathers and Sons in Jack London's 'The House of Pride.'" In *Jack London: One Hundred Years a Writer,* edited by Sara S. Hodson and Jeanne C. Reesman. Los Angeles: Henry Huntington Library Press, 2003.
Robertson, H. A. *Erromanga: The Martyr Isle.* London: Hodder and Stoughton, 1902.
Shapiro, Harry L. *The Pitcairn Islanders.* New York: Simon and Schuster, 1968. Revised edition of *The Heritage of the Bounty,* 1936.
Sherry, Frank. *Pacific Passions: The European Struggle for Power in the Great Ocean in the Age of Exploration.* New York: William Morrow, 1994.
Shineberg, Dorothy. *They Came for Sandalwood: A Study of the Sandalwood Trade in the South-West Pacific, 1830–1865.* Carlton, Victoria, Australia: University of Melbourne Press, 1967. Cambridge: Cambridge University Press, 1967.
Spencer, Herbert. "Absolute Political Ethics." *The Nineteenth Century* (Jan. 1890): 119–30.
Stanley, David. *South Pacific Handbook.* Chico, CA: Moon Publications, 1996.
Stasz, Clarice. *American Dreamers: Charmian and Jack London.* New York: St. Martin's, 1988.
———. "Sarcasm, Irony, and Social Darwinism in Jack London's *Adventure." Thalia, Studies in Literary Humor* 12 (1992): 82–90.
Steevens, George W. *With Kitchener to Khartoum* (Edinburgh: Blackwood, 1898).
Stoddard, Lothrop. *Racial Realities in Europe.* New York: Scribners, 1925.
Tietze, Thomas R. and Gary Riedl. "Jack London and the South Seas." Jack London Collection, Sunsite Digital Library, University of California, Berkeley, CA: <Sunsite.Berkeley.EDU/London/essays/ southseas.html.> (accessed August 21, 1996).
———. "'Saints in Slime': The Ironic Use of Racism in Jack London's South Seas Tales." *Thalia, Studies in Literary Humor* 12 (1992): 59–66.
Usborne, Richard. *Clubland Heroes.* London: Barrie and Jenkins, 1953.
Wallis, Mary. *Life in Feejee: Five Years Among the Cannibals (by A Lady).* Suva: Fiji Museum, 1983. Reprint of Boston: William Heath, 1851.
Watson, Toby J. *Jack London's Snark: San Francisco.* Privately published, 1996.
Wheeler, Tony, and Jean-Bernard Carillet. *Tahiti and French Polynesia.* 4th ed. Hong Kong: Lonely Planet, 1997.
Williams, James. "The Composition of Jack London's Writings." *American Literary Realism* 23 (Winter 1991): 64–86.